The
Toyminator

ROBERT RANKIN

Copyright © Robert Rankin 2006
All rights reserved

The right of Robert Rankin to be identified as the author
of this work has been asserted by him in accordance
with the Copyright, Designs and Patents Act 1988.

First published in Great Britain in 2006 by
Gollancz
An imprint of the Orion Publishing Group
Orion House, 5 Upper St Martin's Lane,
London WC2H 9EA
An Hachette UK company

This edition published in Great Britain in 2009 by
Gollancz

1 3 5 7 9 10 8 6 4 2

A CIP catalogue record for this book
is available from the British Library

ISBN 978 0 575 08547 3

Typeset at The Spartan Press Ltd,
Lymington, Hants

Printed and bound in the UK by
CPI Mackays, Chatham ME5 8TD

The Orion Publishing Group's policy is to use papers that
are natural, renewable and recyclable products and made
from wood grown in sustainable forests. The logging and
manufacturing processes are expected to conform to the
environmental regulations of the country of origin.

FOR

JAMES CAMPBELL

FRIEND AND MENTOR.

Who inspired the writing of this book,
as with many others

And who put me back together
when I had all but fallen apart

No finer friend could any man have.

Thank you Jim.

1

The rain came down in great big buckets, emptied from the sky.

The city's population stayed indoors. Those of the clockwork persuasion greatly feared the rain, for rain brought on the terrible rust, the terrible corrosion. Those of fur dreaded sogginess, and those of wood, the stains. The rubber ducks were happy, though, but then they always are.

The city was Toy City, formerly Toy Town, and it stood there, somewhere over the rainbow, just off the Yellow Brick Road and beyond the mysterious Second Big O. And it stood there at this present time a-soaking in the rain.

The city's population blamed the rain upon the recently deposed mayor. In fact, the city's population now blamed almost everything upon the recently deposed mayor. And not without good cause for the most part, although blaming him for the inclement weather was, perhaps, pushing it a bit.

Not that the city's population were above pushing it a bit, for had they not risen up against the mayor and marched upon the mayoral mansion with flaming torches, pots of tar and many bags of feathers? And had they not dragged the city's mayor from his mayoral mansion, performed unspeakable acts upon his person and cast him beyond the city's gates, with the advice that he should never return, come wind or, indeed, come rain?

Indeed they had.

It had all been most unpleasant.

And if the tarring and feathering and the endurance of unspeakable acts and the casting forth from the city had been most unpleasant for the mayor, these things were as nought when compared to those things that were done to him by the kindly, lovable white-haired old

Toymaker, when the ejected mayor returned to the city under cover of darkness to seek sanctuary at his manse. Having cleaned up the ex-mayor, the kindly, lovable white-haired old Toymaker had demodified him. Which is to say that he removed all the modifications that he had made to the mayor in return for a great service that the mayor had performed for the city, in fact a great service for which he had been granted the office of mayor.

The kindly, lovable white-haired old Toymaker did not demodify the mayor in order to add insult to injury. He did not do it out of cruelty. Rather he did it out of compassion, blaming himself, he said, for making modifications that should never have been made – playing God, as he put it. He apologised profusely to the ex-mayor as he put him through the process of demodification. He told the ex-mayor that it was all for the ex-mayor's own good and that the ex-mayor would thank him for it one day, and then he had given the ex-mayor a nice cup of tea, patted him upon the head and sent him upon his way, offering his own words of advice, to whit, that the ex-mayor should in future keep within his remit and not aspire to a position above his natural station in life.

'Now go and be good,' said the Toymaker, slamming shut his front door behind the ex-mayor.

The door of Tinto's Bar hadn't opened all evening. What with the rain and everything, business had been slack. Business, in fact, was no business at all and Tinto's Bar was empty.

'I blame it on the ex-mayor,' said Tinto, to no one but himself, as he stood behind his bar, a dazzling glass in one dextrous hand, a bar-cloth in the other. 'I remember the good times, me. Well, I would if there'd ever been any.'

Tinto's Bar was long and low, all patterned in black and white chequerboard. A long and low counter it had, with a row of chromium barstools. There were tables and chairs that were shabby, but served. A dolly called Nellie, who worked the weekends. A pot man called Henry, who didn't.

Tinto the barman was something to behold. He was of the mechanical persuasion, powered by a clockwork motor, his body formed from pressed tin and glossily painted, though much of the gloss was now gone. His head was an oversized sphere, with a smiling face painted on the front. His body was a thing-a-me-oid (a cylinder with a hemisphere joined to each end of it), painted with a dicky bow and tuxedo. His arms were flat, though painted with sleeves and shirt cuffs, and the fingers of his hands were fully and wonderfully articulated.

Now, in the light of things that are shortly to occur, it might be well to mention that Tinto was a practising member of The Church of Mechanology, which was one of The Big Four religions in Toy City along with The Daughters of the Unseeable Upness, Big Box Fella, He Come and The Exclusive Brotherhood of the Midnight Growlers. Mechanologists held to the belief that the Universe was a vast clockwork mechanism, with the planets revolving about the sun by means of extendible rotary arms and the sun in turn connected to the galaxy by an ingenious crankshaft system, the entirety powered by an enormous clockwork motor, constantly maintained, oiled and kept wound by The Universal Engineer.

The Universal Engineer was pictured in religious icons as a large and jolly red-faced fellow in greasy overalls and cap. He held in one holy hand an oily rag, and in the other the Church's Sacred Writ, known as *The Manual*.

Followers of The Church of Mechanology considered themselves special and superior to all other varieties of toy, in that being clockwork they were *in tune* and *at one with* the Universe.

It could be argued that The Church of Mechanology was something of an End Times cult, subscribing as it did to the belief that, as individual clockwork toys enjoyed only a finite existence, due to the ravages of rust, corrosion, spring breakage and fluff in the works, so too did the Universe.

Elders of the church spoke of The Time of the Terrible Stillness, when the great mechanism that powered the Universe would grind to a halt, the planet would no longer turn upon its axis, the sun would no longer rise and even time itself would come to a standstill.

And at present, what with all the chaos caused by the ex-mayor when he was the then-mayor, there was much talk amongst the practising Mechanologists that The Time Of the Terrible Stillness was now rapidly approaching. In fact, the elders of each of The Big Four religions were presently preaching that The End Times were well and truly on their way, and everyone knew whose fault *that* was.

Tinto examined the dazzling glass and found it pleasing to behold. At least you knew where you were with a glass. If it was a beer glass, then you were probably in a bar. And as Tinto was in a bar, well, at least he knew where he was. Which was something.

'I think I'll close up early tonight,' said Tinto to himself, 'take a couple of bottles of five-year-old oil upstairs, watch the late-night movie, *Rusty the Rotten Dog*, drown my sorrows and pray for sunshine tomorrow. You have to make the effort, don't you? And laugh, too, or so I've been told, because you'll cry if you don't. And crying really rusts tin toys, as salt water's worse than rain.'

Tinto had recently taken to the reading of certain 'self-help' books. It was all very well being a practising member of The Church of Mechanology, or rather, in truth, it was *not*, it was just too damned depressing, and although Tinto could not actually remember any particularly good times, he was generally of a cheery disposition. Or he had been until recently.

Tinto was presently reading *Become A Merry Old Soul in Thirty Days*, penned by a certain O. K. Cole, a prominent Toy City Pre-adolescent Poetic Personality.* Tinto had even taken on The Fiddlers Three to play in the bar during Sunday lunchtimes. The Fiddlers Three had driven away his Sunday lunchtime clientele.

'It never rains, but it damned well buckets down,' said Tinto, 'yet a smile costs nothing and brightens any day.'

A noise of an unexpected nature drew Tinto's attention towards the door of his bar. For this noise came from its creaking hinges.

'Custom?' queried the clockwork barman. 'On such a night as this?'

The hinges creaked a little more; some rain blew into the bar.

'Who is there?' called Tinto. 'Welcome, friend.'

---

* The term preferred by Nursery Rhyme characters, to Nursery Rhyme characters. (As it were.)

The door, a smidgen open, opened a smidgen more. The brown button eye of a furry face peeped into Tinto's Bar.

'Howdy doody,' called the barman. 'Don't be shy, now. Hospitality awaits you here. That and beer and any seat that suits you.'

Smidgen, smidgen, smidgen went the door and then all-open-up.

And then . . . and then . . .

Tinto peered and had he been able Tinto would have gawped. And had his face been capable of any expression other than that which was painted upon it, there is just no telling exactly what this expression might have become. Tinto's voice, however, was capable of all manner of expression and the words that now issued through the grille in his chest did so in what can only be described as an awed whisper. And those words were . . .

'Eddie, Eddie Bear – is that really you?'

A sodden teddy stood in the doorway, a sodden and dejected-looking teddy. It put its paws to its plump tummy parts and gave them a squeeze, eliciting a dismal groan from its growler and dripping raindrops onto Tinto's floor.

'It *is* you,' said Tinto. 'It really *is.*'

Eddie Bear did shakings of himself. 'I couldn't borrow a bar-cloth, could I?' he asked.

Tinto's head revolved upon his tin-plate shoulders. 'You,' he said, and his voice rose in volume and in octave also. 'You! Here! In my bar! *You!*'

'Me,' said Eddie. 'Might I have a beer?'

'*You!*' Tinto's head now bobbed up and down, his arms rose and his dextrous fingers formed themselves into fists.

'I'll go,' said Eddie. 'I understand.'

'Yes, you . . . yes, you.'

Eddie turned to take his leave. Turned in such a sorrowful, forlorn and dejected manner, with such a drooping of the head and sinking of the shoulders, that Tinto, whose fists were now beating a rapid tattoo upon the highly polished bar counter, felt something come over him that was nothing less than pity.

'No,' said Tinto, his fists unfisting. 'No, Eddie, please don't go.'

Eddie turned and gazed at the barman through one brown button eye and one blue. 'I can stay?' he asked. 'Can I really?'

Tinto's head now bobbed from side to side. 'But you—'

'Were mayor,' said Eddie. 'Yes, I know and I'm sorry.'

'And you were—'

'Modified by the Toymaker. Hands with fingers and opposable thumbs, I know.' Eddie regarded his paws and sighed a heartfelt sigh.

'And—'

'Eyes,' said Eddie, mournfully, 'blue glass eyes with eyelids. All gone now. I'm just plain Eddie Bear.'

Tinto said nothing, but beckoned. Eddie crossed the floor towards the bar counter, leaving behind him little paw-shaped puddles.

'Sit down, then,' said Tinto. 'Have a beer and tell me all about it.'

'Could you make it something stronger than beer, please?' Eddie asked, climbing with difficulty onto what had once been his favourite barstool. 'I'm soaked all the way through and whatever I drink is going to get watered down.'

'I've got a bottle of Old Golly-Wobbler,' said Tinto. 'It's pretty strong stuff – even the gollies are afeared of it, and you know how those bad boys like to put it away.'

'Make it a treble then, please,' said Eddie.

Tinto, who had been reaching up for the bottle, which stood upon a glass shelf between the Old Kitty-Fiddler and the Donkey Punch (a great favourite with male ballet-dancing dolls), hesitated. Tinto's head revolved towards Eddie. 'You do have money?' he asked.

Eddie shook his sodden head and made the face of despair.

'Thought not,' said Tinto. 'Then you're only getting a quadruple measure.' For Tinto had trouble with maths.

'That will be fine, then.' And the corners of Eddie's mouth rose a little. But not any more than that.

Tinto decanted a measure of Old Golly-Wobbler, which might well have been a quadruple, into the dazzling glass that had so recently afforded him a small degree of pleasure because he knew where he was with it, and pushed the glass across the bar top towards the bedraggled bear. The bedraggled bear took it up between his trembling paws and tossed it away down his throat.

'Much thanks, Tinto,' said he. And Tinto poured another.

'It wasn't my fault,' said Eddie, when further Golly-Wobblers were gone and a rather warm feeling was growing in his tummy parts. 'I tried my best, I really did. I tried as hard as.'*

'And that's where you went wrong,' said Tinto, decanting a glass of five-year-old oil for himself and emptying it into his grille. 'No one wanted change, Eddie. Folk hate change and they came to hate you for trying to bring it about.'

'But things needed changing, *still* need changing.'

'No they don't,' said Tinto, and he shook his head vigorously. A nut or screw inside came loose and rattled all about. 'And now you've given me a headache,' said Tinto. 'When will all this madness end?'

'Pour me another drink,' said Eddie.

'And you'll pay me? *That* would make a change. And a pleasant one, too, I'm thinking.'

'Things do need changing,' Eddie said. 'Toy City is a wretched dystopia, Tinto, you know that.'

'I don't,' said Tinto. 'What does dystopia mean?'

Eddie told him.

'Well, I'll drink to that,' said Tinto.

'And so it needs changing.'

'Doesn't,' said Tinto. 'Certainly it's grim. Certainly toys don't get a fair deal. But if we didn't have something to complain about, then what would we have to complain about?'

Eddie Bear put his paws to his head. 'I saved this city,' said he, 'saved it from the Toymaker's evil twin. He would have wiped every one of us out if it hadn't been for me.'

'And your friend, Jack,' said Tinto.

'Yes, Jack,' said Eddie. And he made a wistful face. 'I wonder whatever became of Jack. He travelled into the world of men—'

'The world of men?' said Tinto. 'A world populated entirely by meatheads? There's no such world. That's a myth, Eddie. A fantasy.'

---

* As Eddie was unable to do corroborative nouns, Tinto would never know just how hard Eddie had tried, although given the sincerity of the bear's tone, the clockwork barman could only surmise that it had been very hard indeed.

'It isn't,' said Eddie, making imploring 'more-drink-please' gestures with his paws. 'There is a world beyond this one. Jack met a man who came from there. And that's where Jack went.'

'Didn't,' said Tinto, and he poured another drink for Eddie.

'Did too,' said Eddie.

'Didn't,' said Tinto. 'A little bird told me that he changed his mind, decided it was more fun to stay in the city with his girlfriend – that Jill from Madame Goose's bawdy house.' Tinto made the sacred sign of the spanner over the portion of his chest where his heart, had he possessed one, would have been, out of respect for the late Madame Goose who had come to an untimely end. 'That Jack hung around with that Jill for a while, but she soon spent all his money and he was reduced to working as a griddle chef in a Nadine's Diner.'

'He never was,' said Eddie.

'True as I'm standing here before you, large as life and twice as special. She left him, of course.'

'And a little bird told you this?'

'A robin. His name was Tom.'

'I don't believe a word of it.' Eddie downed his latest drink and began to fidget about on his barstool.

'Don't do it,' said Tinto.

'What?' said Eddie.

'What you're about to do.'

'And what am I about to do?'

'Try to balance on your head on that barstool.'

'I wasn't,' said Eddie.

'You were,' said Tinto. 'I know you well enough, Eddie. I know you're all filled up with sawdust and that when you drink, the drink soaks down to your legs and so you stand on your head so the drink goes there instead. And then you get drunk and silly and I have to throw you out.'

Eddie shrugged and sighed. 'My legs *are* now rather drunk,' he confessed. 'But Jack, still in Toy City? I can't believe it.'

'Not his fault,' said Tinto. 'He was in love. Females will do that kind of thing to you. Put you off what you're meaning to do. Confuse you, fiddle you out of your money, then run off with a wind-up action figure. I can't be having with females, me.'

'Have you ever had a girlfriend, Tinto?' Eddie asked.

'Loads,' said Tinto. 'And they all confused me, fiddled me out of my money and ran off with a wind-up action figure. Except for the big fat one.'

'She was nice, was she?'

'No, she ran off with a clockwork train. What was *that* all about? I ask you.'

Eddie shrugged. 'We all have a tale to tell,' he said, 'and most of those tales are sad.'

'And that's what bars are for,' said Tinto, 'so you can tell them into the sympathetic ear of a caring barman.'

'Quite so,' said Eddie, raising his empty glass between his paws. 'Cheers.'

'Cheers to you, too,' said Tinto. 'Now pay up or I'll kick you out, you bum.'

Eddie laughed. 'Most amusing,' he said.

'No, I mean it,' said Tinto. 'It's all your fault that it's raining.'

'It's not my fault at all.'

' 'Tis too,' said Tinto. 'Everything's your fault. Everybody knows that.'

'Doom and gloom,' said Eddie Bear.

'Still,' said Tinto, 'you have to look on the bright side, don't you? Or so I'm told. I'm reading this book, you see. It's going to make me merry in thirty days.'

'So how long have you been reading it for?'

'Oh, more than four days,' said Tinto. 'It's about forty-four, I think.'

'It's so good to be back here,' said Eddie.

'I thought I was throwing you out.'

'I have some money coming soon.' Eddie made encouraging motions with his glass.

'I fail to understand the motions you're making with that glass,' said Tinto, 'but what money would you have coming soon?'

'I've gone back to my old profession,' said Eddie.

'Walking round the garden?' said Tinto. 'I never really understood the point of that. A "teddy-bear thing", I suppose.'

'Not *that*, nor taking picnics in the wood. I mean my profession as a private eye. I'm setting myself up in Bill's office.'

'Bill Winkie?' Tinto made the sacred sign of the spanner again. 'Have you noticed, Eddie, that folk who come into contact with you seem to come to very sticky ends?'

'It wasn't my fault, what happened to Bill. We were as close as.' Eddie made a very sad face, for Eddie had loved Bill Winkie. Eddie had been Bill Winkie's bear. Eddie had avenged Bill's death, but Eddie still missed Bill. 'I won't be changing the name on his door,' said Eddie. 'It will still be "Bill Winkie Investigations".'

'Well, I doubt if you'd get too much business if you advertised yourself as "Ex-Mayor Eddie Investigations".'

Eddie made growling sounds. 'In Bill's memory,' he said. 'And I am confident that I shall soon have several wealthy clients on my books.'

'But you haven't yet?'

'Not as such.'

'Not as such?' said Tinto.

'Well, I haven't managed to get back into the office yet. It's padlocked up. And now I've only got these.' Eddie sadly regarded his paws.

Tinto made a sighing sound. 'That was a pity,' he said, 'the Toymaker taking those hands he'd fitted you with. Spiteful, that, I thought, although—'

'Although what?'

'Well,' said Tinto, 'it wasn't right, was it? A teddy bear with fingers and thumbs. That was all wrong. There was something really creepy about that. And I never liked those eyes he gave you, either. Teddies don't have blinking eyes. It's not natural. It's—'

'Stop it,' said Eddie. 'It's all right for you. Try living with only paws for just one week, see how you like it.'

'I'm sure I wouldn't like it, but that's not the point. We're all here for a purpose. I'm a clockwork barman. That was what I was made to be. Not a fireman, or a clown. Or a train! The city functions because the toys who live in it do what they were intended to do.'

'But the city *doesn't* function. The city is in a mess.'

'There you go again.' Tinto shook his head once more and once again it rattled. 'You can't go trying to change things, Eddie. Things might not be to your liking, but things are the way they are and we just have to get on with it. Although not for much longer, it appears.'

'Does it?' Eddie asked.

'It does, because The End Times are coming upon us. The Time of the Terrible Stillness draws near. Which, popular opinion agrees, is all your fault, by the way.'

'End Times,' said Eddie. 'That's as mad as. And it's *not* my fault.'

'I'm prepared to be reasonable.' Tinto poured himself another five-year-old, but hesitated to refresh Eddie's glass. 'I'm prepared to say that you are only *partially* to blame.'

'I'm not even *partially* to blame.'

'You're just in denial,' said Tinto. 'You need closure. It's all in the book I'm reading. I'll lend it to you as soon as I'm finished. Which should be in about fifty-three days, by my reckoning.'

Eddie fidgeted some more. 'If you won't give me any more drink I will be forced to stand upon my head,' he said.

'And I will be forced to throw you out.'

Eddie offered Tinto a bit of a smile. 'It's very good to see you again, Tinto,' he said. 'It's as good as, it really, truly is.'

Tinto poured Eddie another. 'It's good to see you, too,' he said. 'Even though you've brought The End Times upon us.'

Eddie Bear was more than just drunk when he left Tinto's Bar. He was rather full of bar snacks, too. Well, he had been rather hungry, and Tinto had become somewhat over-lubricated and somewhat generous in the process. As one will do if one is that kind of a drunk. He had also lent Eddie his copy of *Become A Merry Old Soul in Thirty Days*. Eddie was struggling to carry this, but at least it wasn't raining any more.

The streets were still deserted; street lamps reflected in puddles, gutters drip-drip-dripped. Eddie's footpads squelched horribly, but as his feet were drunk he didn't really notice.

Eddie had no destination. He'd been sleeping rough for weeks, trying in vain whenever the opportunity arose to enter Bill's office, slinking away at the approach of footsteps, hiding where he could.

Just how he thought he could set himself up as a detective and actually find any clients who didn't know and hate him was anybody's guess. But Eddie was a bear of substance and although he was presently down, more down in fact than he had ever been before, he was far from out.

Although, perhaps, not *that* far.

Eddie stumbled and squelched and hummed a little, too. It had been very nice of Tinto to offer him a welcome. He would definitely reward the clockwork barman for his kindness sometime. Possibly even financially. Well, anything *was* possible. Eddie hummed and stumbled and squelched. And Eddie felt optimistic, for the first time in what felt like an age. He'd pull through, he knew he would. Pull through, somehow. Make good. Make the population of Toy City proud of him. Make the Toymaker proud of him. He'd do *something*. He would, he really would.

And he would seek out Jack. Yes, he would definitely do that. Jack had been his bestest friend. They had been partners; together they had defeated the evil twin of the Toymaker. Together. He would seek out Jack and they would become partners once again. Do great things together. Jack could do things, great things. He could do things that Eddie could not, such as pick the padlock on Bill Winkie's office. For Jack was a meathead; Jack had hands with fingers and opposable thumbs.

'Jack and me,' said Eddie, as he stumbled and bumbled along, 'we were as close as. We were bestest friends. If Jack is still in the city I will find him. I will get on to that first thing in the morning. But for now I need somewhere cosy and dry to spend the night. An alleyway, perhaps.'

An alleyway presented itself, as they will when you are in your cups. Especially if you are in need of the toilet. Eddie was in need of the toilet as much as he was in need of somewhere cosy and dry, and so the alleyway that presented itself was a sort of dual-purpose alleyway. Or triple-purpose alleyway, if one were to be exact. Or quadruple, if you were Tinto.

The alleyway that presented itself to Eddie was of the type that was greatly favoured by 1950s American-genre private eyes. It had one of those fire escapes with a retractable bottom section, some dustbins and the rear door of a nightclub, from which drifted the suitably atmospheric tones of a mellow saxophone.

Eddie bumbled and stumbled into the alleyway and relieved himself to the accompaniment of much contented sighing. Even though sighing wasn't usually his thing. He lifted the lid off the nearest dustbin and then drew back in disgust. Bears have sensitive noses, after all. Another lid and then another, and then he found an empty dustbin and a new one, too. Eddie flung Tinto's book into this empty dustbin and, after something of a struggle, followed it.

'Hardly the most salubrious accommodation,' said Eddie, drawing the lid over himself and preparing to settle down for the night. 'I will probably laugh about this one day. But for all the life that's in me, I cannot imagine what day that might be. But,' and Eddie did further settlings, 'that day *will* come.'

And Eddie Bear, in darkness, settled down to sleep.

And slept.

And then awoke.

With more than just a start.

A terrible clamouring came to the ears of Eddie, a terrible rattling and jangling about. His dustbin bower was being shaken. Ferociously.

'Give a bear a break.' Eddie put his paws to his head. The din and the shaking grew fiercer.

Eddie rose and gingerly lifted the lid.

A great white light dazzled his vision. Sparks flew from somewhere and leapt all around and about.

Eddie's mismatched eyes took it all in. Whatever it was. There was a glowing orb of light, a sphere of whiteness. It grew, right there, in the middle of the alleyway, from nothing to something.

The shaking and rattling and the jangling too grew and grew. And then, just like that, because there was no other way to it, it ceased.

The shaking and the rattling and the jangling and the sparking and the light. It was gone, all gone.

But something else was there.

Eddie cowered and peeped through the gap between bin lid and bin. Something had materialised. Out of nowhere. Into somewhere. In this very alleyway.

It crouched. And then it rose. And as Eddie looked on, he could see just what this something was.

It was a bear.

A toy bear.

And this bear looked like Eddie.

Just like Eddie.

The bear rose, flexed its shoulders, glanced to either side.

And then made off at the hurry-up.

Eddie Bear sank down in his bin and gently lowered the lid.

'I think I may just give up drinking,' Eddie said.

2

The morning sun rose over Toy City. It was a big and jolly sun with a big smiley face and its name was believed to be Sam.

So the sun of Sam[*] shone down and the Toy City folk awoke.

The economy, for Toy City had such a thing, as everywhere seems to have such a thing these days, whatever the word might mean, was a little on the decline hereabouts. Wages were down and prices were up and the niceties of life seemed as ever the preserve of the well-to-dos, those who *had*, having more, and those who *had not*, less. The heads of the have-nots drooped on their shoulders as they trudged, or wheeled, or trundled to their places of work. Factory whistles blew, traffic lights faltered, trains were cancelled, dry-cleaning failed to arrive back upon the promised day and how come one is always in the wrong queue in the Post Office?

A rattling and jangling and shaking all about awakened Eddie Bear, from a sleep without dreams, because toy bears do not dream, to recollection, then horror.

'Oh my, oh dear. Whoa!' Sunlight rushed in upon the bear as his bin bower was raised and upended. And, 'No!' shrieked Eddie, affecting that high-pitched whine of alarm that one makes when taken with fear.

Up went the bin, and up and over and out came Eddie, down into the dustcart.

As will be well known to those who know these things well, these knowers being those who watch movies on a regular basis, movie garbage consists of cardboard boxes, shredded paper and indeterminate

---

[*] The sun's father's name was also Sam. As is often the case with suns.

soft stuff. When heroes fall, or are thrown, into such garbage they generally come up unsoiled and fighting.

Oh that life should as a movie be.

Eddie found himself engulfed in fish-heads, curry cartons, rotten fruit, stale veg and that rarest of all rare things, the dung of a wooden horse. Eddie shrieked and struggled and wallowed and sank and rose again and was presently rescued, lifted (at the length of an arm) and set down on the ground.

Garbageman Four looked down upon Eddie. 'What did you do that for?' he asked.

Eddie spat out something evil-tasting and peered up at Garbageman Four. Garbageman Four was part of a six-man matching clockwork garbageman crew, printed tin-plate turn-outs all. Garbageman Four considered himself to be a special garbageman, because only he had a number four printed on his back.

'What did I do *what* for?' Eddie managed to utter.

'Scream and shout and struggle about,' said Garbageman Four, rocking on the heels of his big tin work boots. 'Garbage is not supposed to do that. Garbage is supposed to know its place and behave the way it should.'

Eddie made growling sounds. 'I am *not* garbage,' he said. 'I'm an Anders Imperial. Cinnamon-coloured mohair plush, with woodwool stuffing throughout. Black felt paw pads, vertically stitched nose. An Anders Imperial. I have the special tag in my ear and everything.'

Garbageman Four leaned down and viewed Eddie's special tag. 'That's a beer cap, that is,' he said. 'And you're a grubby rubbish old bear. Now back into the truck with you and off to the incinerator.' But as Garbageman Four reached down towards Eddie, Eddie took off at the hurry-up.

His stumpy legs carried him beyond both garbageman and alleyway and out into a main thoroughfare. Clockwork motor cars whirred by, along with cycling monkeys, woodentop children going to school and a teddy or two who viewed him with disgust.

Eddie sat down on the kerb and buried his furry face in his paws. How had it come to this? How had he reached the rockiest of rock bottoms, sunk to the very depths of the pool? How, how, how had it happened?

His woe-begotten thoughts returned to his time as mayor. He had tried so hard to make things better for the denizens of Toy City. He really, truly had tried. But no matter how hard he'd tried or what actions he'd taken, he'd always somehow managed to make things worse. Every by-law, edict and new rule he'd put in place had somehow got twisted about. It had been as if someone or something had been out to sabotage everything he'd done with kindness in his heart-regions and the good of all in the foremost of his thoughts.

Eddie groaned. And now it had come to this. He was a down-and-out, a vagrant, a vagabond. Ill-smelling and disenfranchised. An outcast. The garbage truck rumbled by, its tin-plate wheels ploughing through a puddle that splashed over Eddie Bear.

Eddie added sighs to his groaning, then rose and squeezed disconsolately at himself. He was a mess and whatever optimism he might have felt the previous evening, optimism that had probably been buoyed up by the prodigious quantities of Old Golly-Wobbler he had imbibed, was now all gone and only pain remained.

Eddie did doglike shakings of himself, spraying puddle water onto a crinoline doll who tut-tut-tutted and strutted away, her haughty nose in the air.

'I need a drink,' said Eddie. And his tummy growled. 'I need breakfast,' said Eddie. And his tummy agreed.

As chance, or fate, or possibly both would have it, across the thoroughfare from Eddie stood a restaurant. It was a Nadine's Diner, one of a chain of such diners owned by Nadine Spratt, widow of the now-legendary Jack Spratt, Pre-adolescent Poetic Personality. Jack, as those who recall the nursery rhyme will recall, was the fellow who 'ate no fat', whilst his wife 'would eat no lean', and so, in the manner of the happy marriage they had once enjoyed, between the two of them they had 'licked the platter clean' and started two successful restaurant chains, his specialising in Lean Cuisine and hers in Big Fat Fry-Ups. Hers had been the more successful of the two businesses.

They had been going through a most colourful celebrity divorce at the time of Jack Spratt's demise, when he was plunged into a deep-fat fryer.[*]

Eddie gazed upon Nadine's Diner: a long, low building painted all in a hectic yellow, with a sign, wrought from neon, spelling out its name, as such signs are ever wont to do.

Eddie Bear sniffed, inhaling the smell of Big Fat Fry-Ups.

Eddie had no pockets to pat, so Eddie did not pat them. Because the thing, well, one of the things, about pockets is that sometimes they have small change in them. Small change that you have forgotten about, but small change that is just big enough to pay for a Big Fat Fry-Up. But Eddie didn't pat.

Eddie Bear made instead a face.

A face that had about it a multiplicity of expressions.

The chief amongst them being that of determination.

Eddie was determined that he should have breakfast.

And now was the time he should have it.

Being a bear well versed in the perils of stepping out onto a busy road without first looking one way and then the other, Eddie Bear did these lookings and when the way was clear of traffic crossed the road and wandered to Nadine's Diner.

Where he paused and pondered his lot.

It was not much of a lot to ponder. It was a rather rotten lot, as it happened. But it did require a degree of pondering. He could not, in his present soiled condition, simply swagger into the diner, order for himself the very biggest of Big Fat Fry-Ups, consume same with eagerness and, when done, run out without paying.

A subtler approach was required.

Slip around to the back, nip into the kitchen and steal? That was an

***

[*] See *The Hollow Chocolate Bunnies of the Apocalypse* for further details. In fact, buy a copy right *now* if you haven't already read it, read it all the way through, then go back to the first chapter of this book and start again. Because this is a sequel. And although a damn fine book in its own right, one in fact that should win any number of awards, but probably won't because there is no justice in this world, it might be best to read the first book first and the second book second. Only a suggestion.

option. Slip around to the back, knock on the door and then beg? That was another.

By the smiley sun called Sam! By the maker who'd made him! He'd once been the mayor of this city! Dined from plates of gold! Quaffed champagne with Old King Cole! Had his back massaged by a dolly with over-modified front parts! That he had sunk to *this*!

Eddie squared what shoulders he possessed. There had to be some other way.

Upon the door of Nadine's Diner hung a sign: HEP WANTED, it said.

' "Hep wanted"?' queried Eddie. 'That would be "help" wanted, I suppose. As in the offer of employment. Hmm.'

The dolly that leaned upon the countertop, a dolly with over-modified front parts similar to those of the masseuse who had once tended to Eddie, did not look up, or even down, at Eddie's approach. She was doing a crossword. The dolly was a most glamorous dolly, golden-haired of hair, curvaceous of curve, long-legged of leg and all around glamour of glamorousness. She was, as they say – and folk did when they saw her – absolutely gorgeous.

Now the question as to whether the absolutely gorgeous have very much in the way of brains is a question that in all truth does not get asked very often. Folk have a tendency to take other folk at face value. Well, at first, anyway. That thing about first impressions and all that. And that other question, 'If you are very beautiful, do you actually need to have very much in the way of brains?' is of course that other question. And in all truth, neither questions are questions that should be asked at all. To imply that because you are good-looking you are therefore stupid is an outrageous thing to imply. To think that you can gauge someone's intelligence by how good-looking they are, and if they are *very* good-looking then therefore they are stupid!

Outrageous.

Because, come on now, let's be honest here – if you are really good-looking, you don't need to be really intelligent.

And if that sounds outrageous, then how about this: there will always be a great many more ugly stupid folk in this world (or possibly any other) than there will be beautiful stupid folk.

Which might mean that things balance themselves out somewhere along the line. Or possibly do not. It's all a matter of opinion. Or intelligence. Or looks. Or . . .

'Four-letter word,' said the dolly in the prettiest of voices. 'Cow jumped over it, first letter *M*, fourth letter *N*.'

'Moon,' said Eddie, smiling upwards.

'What did you say?' The dolly turned her eyes from her crossword and over the counter and down towards Eddie.[*]

'Moon,' said Eddie, smiling angelically.

'Why, you dirty little sawdust bag!' The dolly glared pointy little daggers.

'I only said "moon",' said Eddie. 'Go on. Moon.'

The dolly's eyes narrowed. 'Just because I'm beautiful,' she snarled, 'just because I have blonde hair that you can make longer by turning a little thing-a-me-bob on my back – which makes me special, I'll add – you think I'm some stupid slutty bimbo who's prepared to moon for any scruffy . . .' she twitched her tiny nose '. . . *smelly* bear who comes in here and—'

'No,' said Eddie. 'You have me all wrong.'

'I don't think so, mister. I have you all right. Men are all the same – see a blonde head and a pair of big titties and they think they're on to an easy one.'

'No,' said Eddie. Well, yes, he thought. 'Well, *no*,' said Eddie, with emphasis. 'I meant the word in your crossword – the cow jumped over the moon.'

'What cow?' asked the dolly.

'The one in your crossword clue.'

'And did you see this cow?'

'I know of it,' said Eddie. 'It lives on Old MacDonald's farm.'

'Oh,' said the dolly.

'EIEIO,' said Eddie. 'As in "Old MacDonald had a farm".'

'Brilliant,' said the dolly.

'Excuse me?' said Eddie.

---

[*] Neat trick.

'That was another of the clues – "Where does Old MacDonald live?"'

'Glad to be of assistance,' said Eddie.

The dolly took to studying her crossword once more. Then she made a frowning face again and turned it back upon Eddie. 'Doesn't fit,' she said. 'Too many letters.'

'Eh?' said Eddie.

'Where Old MacDonald lives, "EIEIO" doesn't fit.'

'I've come about the job,' said Eddie. 'Help wanted.'

'It's *HEP* wanted,' said the dolly. 'Can't you read?'

Eddie sighed inwardly. 'Well, I've come to offer my HEP,' he said.

'You don't look very HEP,' said the dolly, giving Eddie the up-and-down once-over. 'In fact, you look very un-HEP and you smell like a drain with bad breath.'

'I had to dive into a cesspit to save a drowning dolly,' said Eddie. 'At no small risk to my own safety.'

'Can you play the saxophone?'

'I don't know,' said Eddie. 'I've never tried.'

'You're not tall enough anyway.'

'I grow larger when fed.'

'We were looking for a golly.'

'Typical,' said Eddie. 'Discrimination again. Because you're a teddy everyone thinks you're stupid. Only good for cuddling and picnicking in those damned woods.'

The dolly cocked her golden head upon one side. 'I know how it is,' she said. 'Folk just see the outer you, never the person who dwells within. Perhaps . . .'

'Yes?' said Eddie.

'No,' said the dolly. 'You're ugly and you smell. Get out.'

Eddie sighed outwardly and turned to take his leave.

'Eddie!'

Eddie ignored the voice.

'*Eddie!* Eddie, it's *you.*'

Eddie turned and Eddie stared and Eddie Bear said, 'Jack.'

Jack stood behind the counter next to the golden-haired dolly. He wore a chef's hat and jacket. And even to Eddie's first glance, he wore them uncomfortably.

'Eddie,' said Jack. 'It *is* you. It is.'

'It is,' said Eddie. 'And it's *you.*'

The kitchen of Nadine's Diner was grim. But then such kitchens are always grim. Such kitchens are places of heat and conflict, with shouting chefs and stress and panic and lots of washing-up. There was lots of washing-up to do in this particular kitchen.

Eddie sat upon a grimy worktop surrounded by many unwashed pots and pans. A rat nibbled on something in a corner; a cockroach crossed the floor. Jack stepped on the cockroach and shooed away the rat.

'That's Barry,' Jack told Eddie. 'He's sort of a pet.'

Eddie munched ruefully but gratefully on the burger Jack had fried for him.

Jack leaned on the crowded sink and wiped his hands on a quite unspeakable dishcloth. 'I thought you were dead,' he said.

Eddie looked up from his munchings and wiped ketchup from his face with a greasy paw. He was very, very pleased to see his friend Jack.

Jack smiled at Eddie and Eddie saw that Jack hadn't changed: he was still tall and spare and lithe of limb and young and pleasing to behold.

'I really thought you were dead. I heard what they did to you. I would have come to your rescue.'

'Would you?' Eddie asked.

'Well, no, actually,' said Jack. 'Not at that particular time.'

'What?' Eddie spat out some burger bun. Jack wiped it from his apron.

'You weren't exactly in my good books at that particular time,' said Jack. 'You're not exactly in them now.'

'Eh?' said Eddie.

'Edict Five,' said Jack, 'the one about abolishing the monarchy. *Your* Edict Five. And me an honorary prince. Did you forget that?'

'I thought you'd gone off to the other world. The world of men.

That's where you told me you were going. To sort out the clockwork President.'

'Well,' said Jack, and he made an embarrassed face, 'I *was* going to go, but the Toymaker *had* given me a castle to live in, and there *was* Jill . . .' Jack's voice trailed off.

'I heard about Jill,' said Eddie, packing further burger into his mouth. 'I'm sorry about that.'

'There's no trusting women,' said Jack. 'At least I've learned that whilst still young.'

'Don't be too cynical,' said Eddie. 'I know she hurt you, but that doesn't mean that all women are bad. You'll find the right one, and when you do she will make you happy every single day.'

'Yeah, right,' said Jack. 'But let's talk about you, Eddie. I *am* glad that you're alive, truly I am, but your—'

'Hands?' said Eddie. 'Eyes? The Toymaker took them away. He said that he blamed himself for what happened. That you shouldn't tamper with nature, which was pretty hypocritical coming from him, as he created me. He said I should go and do what I was created for.'

'And you're not keen?' Jack took up another cloth to wipe his hands upon, as the first cloth had made them ever dirtier.

'Was I ever?' Eddie asked. 'I am a bear of superior intellect. I am a special bear.'

'You are certainly that.'

'Jack,' said Eddie, 'how would you feel about teaming up again? The old team, you and me, back in business together.'

'The old team?' Jack laughed and his laughter was not pleasing to Eddie's ears, especially to the one with the special tag in it. 'The old team? How many times did I come close to being killed?'

Eddie shrugged.

'Nine times,' said Jack. 'I counted.'

'You enjoyed the adventure. And we saved the city.'

'Yes, and I'd still be living grandly if it hadn't been for you fouling it up with your Edict Five.'

'I was just trying to make things right.'

'You're a very well-intentioned little bear.'

'Don't patronise me, Jack. Never patronise me.'

Jack shook his head. 'You're unbelievable,' he said. 'Look at the state of you. Sniff the smell of you. Go back into business together? What business?'

'If we build it, they will come,' said Eddie. 'We have Bill's office. Well, we will as soon as you have picked the lock and we can get inside. Then we'll set up. We can call ourselves "Jack Investigations" if you want.'

Jack shook his head. 'And what will we investigate?'

'Crimes,' said Eddie.

'I thought the police investigated crimes. Those jolly red-faced laughing policemen. And Chief Inspector Bellis.'

'As if they care about what happens to the likes of us.'

'The likes of *us*?' Jack raised an eyebrow. 'I don't think it's *us*, Eddie. You are a toy and I am a—'

'Meathead,' said Eddie. 'I know.'

'Man,' said Jack.

'And so you are one of the privileged.' Eddie had finished his burger. But as he was still hungry, he made the face of one who was.

'I'll fry you up another,' said Jack. 'But, no offence, you know what I mean.'

'And you know that that was what I was trying to change. The injustice of the system. The way toys are treated as if they are nothing at all.'

'They are treated as if they are toys,' said Jack, applying himself once more to that Hellish piece of equipment known as a griddle. 'No offence meant once more.'

'Toys have feelings, too,' said Eddie.

Jack turned from the griddle and gazed upon Eddie. The two of them had been through a great deal together. They had indeed had adventures. They had indeed had a relationship that was based upon trust and deep friendship. A lad and a toy bear. Absurd? Maybe. But then, what isn't?

'Eddie,' said Jack, 'it really is truly good to see you once more.'

'Thanks,' said Eddie. 'The same goes for me.'

'Eddie?' said Jack.

'Jack?' said Eddie.

'Would you mind very much if I were to give you a hug?'

'I would bite you right in the balls if you ever tried.'

'Thank goodness for that,' said Jack, 'because you smell like shit.'

Jack really didn't need *that much* persuading. He put up a spirited, if insincere, struggle, of course, citing the possibilities of promotion in the field of customer services and the pension plan and putting forward some unsupportable hypothesis that young women found griddle chefs sexy. But he really didn't take *that much* persuading and, come ten of the morning clock, with Sam shining down encouragingly, Jack took what wages he felt he was owed from the cash register, plus a small bonus that he considered he deserved, and with it his leave of Nadine's Diner.

'It's spoon,' he told the crossword-solving dolly as he made his departure. 'What the dish ran away with.'

'Does this mean you're running away from me?' asked the dolly.

'Not a bit of it,' said Jack. 'I'll pick you up at eight. Take you to the pictures.'

Outside in the encouraging sunlight, Eddie said, 'Jack, are you *doing it* with that dolly?'

'Well . . .' said Jack.

'Disgusting,' said Eddie. 'You should be ashamed.'

'I am,' said Jack, 'but I'm trying to work through it.'

'And succeeding by the look of it.'

Jack tried to make a guilty face.

'You're a very bad boy,' said Eddie.

The building hadn't changed at all, but then why should it have changed? It was a sturdy edifice, built in the vernacular style, Alphabet brick, with a tendency towards the occasional fiddly piece, which gave it that extra bit of character. Bill Winkie's office was on the first floor above the garage, which might or might not still house his splendid automobile. Eddie did ploddings up the stairway. Jack did long-legged stridings.

'It feels a bit odd,' said Jack as he followed Eddie, who with difficulty had overtaken him, along the corridor that led past various offices towards the door that led to Bill's, 'being back here again.'

'We did have some adventures, though.'

'All of them life-endangering.'

'But we came through, Jack, and—'

'Look at us now?' Jack asked.

'We'll get back on top. Somehow.'

'I'll give it a week,' said Jack.

'You'll what?' And Eddie turned.

'I've a week's money in my pocket. I'll give it a week with you. That's fair.'

'It's *not* fair,' said Eddie. 'Give a month at least.'

'Well, we'll see how it goes. So where's this padlock that needs picking?'

'It's here,' said Eddie. But much to his surprise it was not. 'It *was* here,' said Eddie, 'only yesterday, but now it seems to have vanished.'

'Perhaps someone else has moved in.' Jack viewed the door of Bill Winkie's office, *BILL WINKIE INVESTIGATIONS* etched into the glass. There were some holes in the woodwork where the hasp of a padlock had been. The door was slightly open. Jack did not feel encouraged by this turn of events.

'The door's open,' said Eddie. 'That's as encouraging as.'

'No it's not,' said Jack. 'it's suspicious.'

'Depends on how you look at it,' said Eddie. 'It's like the glass of water that is either half-full or half-empty, depending on how you look at it.'

'I'm sure there's wisdom in your words.'

'I'm sure there isn't,' said Eddie. 'You'd best go first, I'm thinking.'

'And why would you be thinking that?'

'Well,' said Eddie, 'you're bigger than me and have about you an air of authority. And should there be anyone in that office who shouldn't be there, you can shoo them away, as it were.'

'I see,' said Jack. 'And that would be your considered opinion, would it?'

'Well, actually, no,' said Eddie. 'I hardly gave it any consideration at all.'

Jack shook his head and pushed open the door. It squeaked a little on its hinges, but it was a different squeak from the door hinges of Tinto's Bar. An octave higher, perhaps.

Jack and Eddie peeped into the office.

The office hadn't changed at all.

Light drifted through the half-opened blinds, falling in slanted rays upon the filing cabinet, which contained little other than empty beer bottles; the desk that Jack had broken and inadequately repaired; the carpet that dared not speak its name; the water cooler that cooled no water; and all of the other sparse and sundry bits and bobs that made a private detective's office a private detective's office.

'Ah,' sighed Eddie, 'home again,' and he sniffed. 'And don't it just smell good?'

Jack took a sniff and said, 'Rank.'

'Rank,' agreed Eddie. 'But it's a good rank, don't you think?'

'I do.'

'And it's great to be back.'

'It is.'

'And we will have great times, Jack, exciting times.'

'Will we?' said Jack. 'Well, yes, perhaps.'

'We will,' said Eddie. 'We will.'

Jack looked at Eddie.

And Eddie looked at Jack.

'There's just one thing,' said Jack.

'One thing?' said Eddie.

'One thing,' said Jack.

'And what would that one thing be?'

'That one thing,' and Jack now glared at Eddie, 'that one thing would be that thing *there*. That one thing that you are so studiously ignoring. That one thing *right there*, lying on the carpet that dares not speak its name. Are you following me, Eddie? I'm pointing now, pointing to that one thing – do you see it?'

Eddie followed the pointing finger. And, 'Ah,' said Eddie. 'You would be referring, I suppose, to the dead body that is lying there upon the floor.'

Jack nodded slowly and surely. 'That would be it,' he said.

3

'It's a monkey,' said Eddie.

'It's a *dead* monkey,' said Jack.

'It might only be sleeping,' said Eddie.

'It is *dead*,' said Jack.

'Or run down,' said Eddie, approaching the monkey on the floor. 'Its clockwork might just have run down – and run down is a small death, you know, amongst clockwork folk.'

'Look at its eyes,' Jack approached Eddie, who was approaching the monkey. 'Those eyes are dead and staring.'

'They're glass eyes,' Eddie said. 'They always stare like that.'

The monkey lay upon the carpet that dared not speak its name. It was one of those monkeys that clap little brass cymbals whilst bouncing up and down. That is all they do, really, but children, and indeed adults, seem to find them very, very entertaining. Indeed, they can never get enough of those monkeys that clap their cymbals together and bounce up and down. Very popular, those monkeys are.

Although this one, it appeared, was dead.

Eddie looked sadly upon the monkey. It lay there, on its side, frozen in mid-clap. This was clearly a monkey that would clap and bounce no more.

'Wakey-wakey, Mister Monkey,' said Eddie. 'You can't sleep here, you know.'

'It's dead, Eddie – look at it.'

'Perhaps if I were to give its key a little turn?'

'Good idea, Eddie,' said Jack. 'You give its key a little turn.'

'You think I should?'

'No, I *don't*.'

'Stay put, Jack,' said Eddie, and he plodded slowly about the fallen monkey. Eddie leaned over the monkey and sniffed, then stepped back from the monkey and viewed it, his chin upon his paw. He dropped to his knees and examined the non-speaking carpet, then glanced at the ceiling and grunted.

Jack looked on and watched him. He'd seen Eddie go through this performance before and he'd seen Eddie draw conclusions from such a performance. Significant conclusions.

Eddie climbed to his paw-footed feet and looked up at Jack. 'There's been dirty business here,' he said. 'This monkey is certainly as dead as.'

'Murdered?' Jack asked.

'Something more than that.'

'Something *more*?'

'This monkey is something more than just as dead as.'

'I don't know what you mean,' Jack said.

'Nor do I,' said Eddie. 'Stand back a little further, Jack, if you will.' And Jack stood back accordingly.

Eddie reached out a paw and lightly touched the monkey.

There was a sound, as of a gentle sigh. And with it the monkey crumbled. Crumbled away to the accompaniment of the whispery sigh. Crumbled away to dust.

Jack looked at Eddie.

And Eddie looked at Jack.

'Now *that* isn't right,' said Eddie.

They swept up the dust of the monkey. Well, not so much *they* as Jack. Well, Jack had hands with opposable thumbs after all. Eddie did hold the dustpan.

'Pour what you can of him into this beer bottle,' said Eddie, fishing one with difficulty from the filing cabinet. 'There might be something significant to be learned from the dust.'

'Did you know this monkey?' Jack asked as he tried to do what Eddie wanted.

'Hard to say,' said the bear. 'Your cymbal-playing monkey is a classic toy, of course, an all-time favourite, but telling one from the other . . . I don't know. There was one called Monkey who was with the circus. He used to drink in Tinto's, but Tinto threw him out because he was too noisy. I knew another one called Monkey, who was also with the circus, did this act where he played the cymbals and bounced up and down. And—'

'So they all look the same, do the same thing, are all with the circus and are all called Monkey?'

'That's about the strength of it.' Eddie struggled to cork the beer bottle, then set it down on Bill's desk.

'I've got a lot of Monkey left over,' said Jack.

'Put it in the bin,' said Eddie.

'Shouldn't we cast it to the four winds, or something?'

Eddie grinned at Jack. 'See what a nice fellow you are,' said he. 'How caring. What was it you said about toys only being toys?'

'That wasn't what I said. Or I hope it wasn't.'

'There's been dirty work here,' said Eddie. 'Strange, dirty work. It would seem that we are already on a case.'

'Oh no.' Jack shook his head. 'That's not how it works and you know it. Someone has to offer us a case. And pay us to take it on. Pay us, Eddie, you know what I'm saying?'

Eddie nodded thoughtfully. 'So what you're saying,' he said, 'is that we should ignore the fact that a dead monkey crumbled into dust on the carpet of this office and wait until we get some meathead client to offer us money for finding their lost dog or something?'

'Well, I'm not saying *that*, exactly.'

'So what are you saying, then?'

Jack gave some thought to an appropriate answer. 'I'm saying,' said Jack, 'that perhaps we should give this some thought. Perhaps over a drink.'

'At Tinto's?' said Eddie.

'At Tinto's,' said Jack.

Eddie took a shower, because Bill's office owned to a bathroom. And Jack squeezed Eddie dry, which Eddie didn't enjoy too much, although it made Jack laugh. And Eddie unearthed his old trenchcoat and fedora, and so too did Jack, and so they both now looked like private detectives. And they took themselves down to the garage and, much to their joy, found Bill's splendid automobile just waiting to take them away.

And so they took themselves away in it, with Jack driving.

As ever, too fast.

It was early yet at Tinto's, so trade was still slack. Some construction-worker figures with detachable yellow hardhats and gripping hands gripped beer glasses and engaged in anato-philosophical discussions on the good-looks/intelligence dialectic. Eddie had no trouble getting served.

'Howdy doody,' said Tinto. 'Eddie Bear, come to pay off his tab, by Golliwog. Joy and gladness are mine, to be sure, all praise The Great Engineer.'

'The beers are on Jack,' said Eddie.

'And howdy doody, Jack,' said Tinto.

'Nine beers, please,' said Jack, lowering himself onto a barstool and speaking from between his now raised knees.

'Nine, eh?' said Eddie. 'This should be good.'

Tinto poured a number of beers. Eddie disputed this number and Tinto poured more. Then Jack and Eddie got into the thirteen beers.

'Just like the good old days,' said Jack, raising his glass and emptying it down his throat.

'What days were those?' asked Tinto. 'I must have missed them.'

'Eddie and I have *temporarily* renewed our partnership,' said Jack. 'And there *were* great days and will be again.'

'Bravo,' said Eddie, raising his glass carefully between his paws and emptying a fair percentage of the beer into his mouth.

'Enjoy your great days while you can,' said Tinto, taking up Jack's empty glass and giving it a polish. 'The End Times are upon us and *they* won't prove to be so great.'

'End Times?' said Jack.

'Don't get him going on that,' said Eddie.

'Doubter,' said Tinto to Eddie. 'If you were of the faith you'd understand.'

'I have my own faith,' said Eddie, struggling with another glass. 'I am a member of The Exclusive Brotherhood of the Midnight Growlers.'

'A most exclusive brotherhood,' said Tinto, 'as you are the only member.'

'We don't proselytise,' said Eddie. 'You're either a Growler, or you aren't.'

'You should join The Church of Mechanology before it's too late.' Tinto made the sign of the sacred spanner. 'Already the prophecies are being fulfilled. Did you see today's paper?'

Eddie shook his head.

'The faithful are being carried off to glory.' Tinto's voice rose slightly. 'They are being taken up by the big horseshoe magnet in the sky.'

'And that's in the paper?' Eddie asked.

'S.T.C.' said Tinto.

'Ecstasy?' said Eddie.

'S.T.C.' said Tinto. 'Spontaneous Toy Combustion.'

Eddie looked at Jack.

And Jack looked at Eddie.

'Go on,' said Eddie.

'The monkeys,' said Tinto. 'The clockwork monkeys. All over the city. Last night. They combusted.'

'All of them?' Eddie looked aghast. He *was* aghast.

'Puff of smoke,' said Tinto. 'All of them gone. All of them. Not that there were that many of them, only about half a dozen. The papers says it was S.T.C., but that's not the truth of it. Carried off to glory, they were. Transcended their physical bodies.'

Eddie and Jack did mutual lookings at each other once more.

'I may be next,' said Tinto, 'so you'd better pay up for these drinks. I want my cash register to balance if I'm going.'

'Now, just hold on, Tinto,' said Eddie. 'Are you telling me that all the monkeys – and I am assuming that you mean the cymbal-playing monkeys that bounce up and down?'

Tinto nodded.

'That all of these monkeys combusted last night – is that what you're saying?'

'I think it was *you* who just said that,' said Tinto, 'but correct me if I'm wrong.'

'But what happened?'

'It's what the papers say. Or rather what they don't.'

'This *is* a case,' said Eddie to Jack. 'This is a serious case.'

'*All* the cymbal-playing monkeys?' said Jack to Tinto.

'Thirty-three. Or was it eighty-seven?'

'You said about half a dozen.'

'Well, I'll say anything, me,' said Tinto, 'as long as it makes me popular.'

'Show me this paper,' said Eddie Bear.

And Tinto showed him the paper.

It was the *Toy City Mercury* and the spontaneously combusting monkeys had not made the front-page headlines. Eddie located a small article on page thirteen, sandwiched between advertisements for kapok stuffing and dolly hair-styling.

Eddie read the article. 'Eleven monkeys,' he whispered.

'Twelve counting the one in the beer bottle,' said Jack.

'The one in the beer bottle?' said Tinto.

'Nothing,' said Eddie. 'But this is all rot. Who is this Professor Potty who has come up with the S.T.C. theory, anyway?'

'Eminent scientist.' Tinto gathered up further empties and took to the polishing of them. 'He does that thing where he pours one flask of liquid into another flask and then back again.'

'And?' said Eddie.

'That's about as far as it goes, I think,' said Tinto. 'Not much of an act. But better than playing the cymbals and bouncing up and down. Each to his own, I say. It takes all sorts to make a world.'

'At least he didn't blame it on me,' said Eddie.

'Yes he did,' said Tinto, 'on the next page.'

Eddie had Jack turn the page.

Eddie read, aloud this time: ' "Although there is no direct evidence to link the monkeys' demise to the ex-mayor," Professor Potty said, "I can see no reason not to." '

Jack did foolish titterings.

'This is *so* not funny,' said Eddie.

'Will you be giving yourself up, then?' Tinto asked. 'I wonder if there's a reward. If there is, would you mind if I turned you in?'

'Stop it,' said Eddie. 'It isn't funny.'

'No, it's not,' said Jack, struggling to regain sobriety. 'But it's all very odd, Eddie. Do you have any thoughts?'

'I think I'd like to meet this Professor Potty and—'

'Other than those kinds of thoughts.'

'No,' said Eddie. 'Not as yet. I wonder whether Chief Inspector Wellington Bellis and his jolly red-faced laughing policemen will be investigating?'

'What's to investigate?' Tinto asked. 'The monkeys were taken up to the great toy box in the sky. What could be simpler than that?'

'Maybe so,' said Eddie, 'but I suspect that there's a great deal more to their manner of departure than meets the eye. Bring the rest of the drinks to the corner table over there, Jack. We shall speak of these things in private.'

'What?' went Tinto. 'The cheek of you! If you and Jack are on a case, then I should be part of it. I seem to recall helping you out considerably the last time.'

'You certainly did, Tinto,' Eddie said. 'But see, you have more customers,' and Eddie indicated same who were entering the bar. 'We will not presume upon your time, but we'll let you know how we're getting on and ask your advice when we need it.'

Tinto made disgruntled sounds, but trundled off to serve his new clientele. Jack loaded what drinks remained onto a convenient tray and joined Eddie at a secluded corner table.

'Why all the secrecy?' he asked, when he had comfortably seated himself.

'I don't want to alarm Tinto,' whispered Eddie. 'These monkeys were murdered, I'm sure of it.'

'You can't be sure of it,' said Jack.

'From the evidence left behind in Bill's office, I can,' Eddie said. 'The padlock had been torn from the door – our cymbal-clapping corpse-to-be couldn't have done that. Whoever killed the monkey removed the padlock and waited in Bill's office, knowing that the monkey would come there, is my guess. He sat in Bill's chair and smoked a cigar – *this cigar*.' Eddie produced a cigar butt from the pocket of his trenchcoat with a dramatic flourish and displayed it to

Jack. 'There was evidence of a struggle and a round burned patch on the ceiling. The monkey was murdered, but as I said, he was more than just murdered. The worst of it is that I think the monkey must have known that someone was trying to kill him and he came to Bill's office for help, probably thinking that some new detective had taken up residence there. And had I been able to get into that office earlier, perhaps I could have helped him.'

'Or perhaps you would have been murdered, too?'

'Perhaps,' said Eddie, taking up another beer.

'So where do we go from here?'

'We have several options. We might visit Professor Potty and see whether he has anything useful to impart. We might visit Chief Inspector Bellis, perhaps get his blessing, as it were, to work the case.'

'And perhaps get yourself arrested?'

'Perhaps,' said Eddie once again. 'But I have another idea. What we have to consider here, Jack, is motive. Why would someone want to murder every cymbal-playing monkey in Toy City?'

Jack looked at Eddie.

'Apart from the fact that they are a damned nuisance,' said Eddie. 'This seems to have been a very well-planned mass-murder. All in a single night? All the work of a single killer? I wonder.'

'So what do you have in mind?'

'This,' said Eddie, and he pushed the cigar butt in Jack's direction, 'this is the only piece of solid evidence we have. It's an expensive cigar. I wonder how many cigar stores in Toy City stock them? I wonder if they might recall a recent client?'

'Seems logical,' said Jack. 'So how many cigar stores *are* there in Toy City?'

'Just the one,' said Eddie.

It had to be said that Jack was very pleased to be back behind the wheel of the late Bill Winkie's splendid automobile. It was an Anders Faircloud, made from pressed tin the metallic blue of a butterfly's wing. It was long and low and highly finned at the tail. It had pressed-tin wheels with breezy wide hubs and big rubber tyres.

Jack, who hadn't driven for a while and who could in all honesty never have been described as a competent driver, nevertheless felt confident behind the wheel. Perhaps just a little overconfident. And as it happens, Jack was also now a little drunk. He and Eddie left Tinto's Bar and Jack followed Eddie's directions to Toy City's only cigar store.

'Slow down!' shrieked Eddie, cowering back in his seat.

'I am slowed down,' said Jack. 'Don't make such a fuss.'

'Slow down, it's right here. No, I didn't say turn left!'

The car, now turned left upon two of its wheels, bumped up onto the pavement. Shoppers scattered and those with fists shook them. Jack did backings up.

'We'll walk in future,' Eddie cowered. 'I'd quite forgotten all this.'

'I know what I'm doing,' said Jack, reversing further into oncoming traffic.

'We're all gonna die,' said Eddie.

Toy City's only cigar store, Smokey Joe's Cigar Bar, was a suitably swank affair, with lots of polished wood and a window full of smoking ephemera – all those things that look so interesting that they really make you want to take up smoking.

Jack ground the polished wheel-hubs of Bill's splendid automobile along the kerb before Smokey Joe's Cigar Bar and came to a juddering halt.

Eddie, who had seriously been considering converting to Mechanology and preparing to make his personal apologies to whom it might concern for not joining earlier, climbed down from the car, waddled around to Jack's side and, as Jack climbed out, head-butted him in the nuts.

Jack doubled up in considerable pain.

'When I say "slower", I mean it, you gormster!' said Eddie. 'Now act like a professional.'

Jack crossed his legs and wiped tears from his eyes. 'If you ever do that to me again,' he said, 'I will tear off your head and empty you out.'

'Jack, you wouldn't!'

'Right now I feel that I would.'

'Then I'm sorry,' said Eddie. 'So if you are up to it, do you think that you could see your way to limping into Smokey Joe's Cigar Bar, doing your toff act and finding out who bought the cigar?'

'I'll try,' said Jack. 'Sometimes I really hate you.'

'Do you?' said Eddie.

'Not really,' said Jack.

Jack did a bit of trenchcoat adjustment and fedora tilting, pushed open the door and entered Smokey Joe's Cigar Bar. The door gave a merry *ting, ting* as he did so.

'You shouldn't do that,' the bell told the door. 'That's my job.'

Jack stood in the doorway and breathed in Smokey Joe's Cigar Bar. And for those of you who have never been in a cigar store, that is just what you do: you breathe it in, is what you do.

There is a magic to cigars, a magic never found in cigarettes. Cigars are special; there are complicated procedures involved in the manufacture of them. There is certain paraphernalia necessary for the proper smoking of them, such as special end-cutters, and certain matches for the lighting thereof. And who amongst us does not know that the very best of all cigars are rolled upon the thigh of a dusky maiden? A cigar is more than just a smoke, as champagne is more than just a fizzy drink, or urolagnia is more than just something your girlfriend might not indulge you in, no matter how much money you've recently spent buying her that frock she so desperately wanted. And so on and so forth and suchlike.

Jack breathed in Smokey Joe's Cigar Bar.

'It really smells in here,' he said.

Eddie Bear made growling sounds.

'A fine smell, though,' said Jack.

Mahogany-framed glass cases displayed a multiplicity of wonderful cigars, cigars of all shapes and sizes and colours, too. There were pink cigars and blue ones and some in stripes and checks. And of their shapes, what could be said?

'These ones look like little pigs,' said Jack, and he pointed to them.

Eddie cocked his head on one side. 'Do you see what *those ones* look like?'

'And how might I serve you, sir?'

Jack tipped up the brim of his fedora and sought out the owner of the voice: the proprietor of Smokey Joe's Cigar Bar, Smokey Joe himself.

'Ah,' said Jack as he viewed Smokey Joe.

The proprietor smiled him a welcome.

> Smokey Joe was a sight to behold
> A sight to behold was he.
> His head was a ball,
> And his belly a barrel,
> His ears were a thing of beaut-ee.
>
> He was built out of brass,
> And if questions were asked
> Regarding the cut of his jib,
> He'd reply with a laugh
> And a free autograph,
> Signed by a pen with a nib.
>
> And he chugged a cigar
> In his own cigar bar,
> For bellows were built in his chest.
> And he blew out smoke-rings
> And numerous things,
> Which had all his clients impressed.

'What exactly *was* that?' asked Eddie.

Jack shrugged. 'Poetry?' he said.

'Odd,' said Eddie. 'Now go for it, Jack.'

And so Jack went for it.

'My good fellow,' said Jack, 'are you the proprietor of this here establishment?'

'That I am, your lordship,' said the proprietor, sucking upon his cigar and blowing out a puff of smoke in the shape of a sheep. 'Smokey Joe's my name and I am the purveyor of the finest cigars in Toy City.'

'Well, be that as it may,' said Jack.

'It may well be because it is, your lordship.'

'Right,' said Jack. 'Well, now we've established that, I require your assistance concerning a cigar.'

'Then you have certainly come to the right place, your lordship. If there is anything that needs knowing about cigars and isn't known to myself, then I'll be blessed as a nodding spaniel dog and out of the window with me and into the duck pond.'

'Quite so,' said Jack.

'And you can use my head for a tinker's teapot and boil my boots in lard.'

'Most laudable,' said Jack.

'I'll go further than that,' said Smokey Joe. 'You can take my wedding tackle and—'

'I think you've made your point,' said Jack. 'You know about cigars.'

'And pipes,' said Smokey Joe. 'Although that's only a hobby of mine. But every man should have a hobby.'

'Well, if they can't get a girlfriend,' said Jack.

'You are the very personification of wisdom.'

'Well . . .'

Eddie gave Jack's left knee a sound head-butting. 'Get on with it,' he whispered.

'Cigars,' said Jack, to Smokey Joe. 'Well, one cigar in particular.'

'Would it be the Golden Sunrise Corona?' asked Smokey Joe. 'The veritable king of cigars, made from tobacco watered by unicorn's wee-wee and rolled upon the thigh scales[*] of golden-haired mermaids?'

'No,' said Jack. 'But you sell such cigars?'

'No,' said Smokey Joe, 'but a proprietor must have his dreams. And speaking of dreams, last night I dreamed that I was a chicken.'

'A chicken?' said Jack.

'They worry me,' said Smokey Joe.

---

[*] The debate regarding whether mermaids can be described as having thighs continues. And remains unresolved.

'They do?' said Jack. Eddie head-butted his left knee once more. 'Well, I'm sure that's very interesting,' said Jack, 'but I have urgent business that will not wait. I need a straightforward answer to a simple question. Do you think you could furnish me with same?'

Smokey Joe nodded, puffed out a question-mark-shaped smoke cloud and said, 'I'd be prepared to give it a try, but things are rarely as simple as they seem. Take those chickens, for example—'

'I am in a hurry,' said Jack. 'I merely wish to know about a cigar.'

Smokey Joe let free a sigh of relief, which billowed considerable smoke. 'Not chickens, then?' said he.

'No,' said Jack. 'What is your problem with chickens?'

'The scale of them,' said Smokey Joe.

'Chickens don't have scales,' said Jack. 'Chickens have feathers.'

Smokey Joe fixed Jack with a troubling eye. 'Beware the chickens,' said he. 'If not now, then later. And somewhere else. I am Smokey Joe, the only cigar store proprietor in Toy City. I am one of a kind. I am special.'

Jack sighed somewhat at the word, but Smokey Joe continued.

'I have the special eye and I see trouble lying in wait ahead of you. Trouble that comes in the shape of a chicken.' Smokey Joe blew out a plume of cigar smoke, which momentarily took the shape of a chicken before fading into the air of what had now become a cigar store somewhat overladen with 'atmosphere'.

Eddie Bear shuddered. 'Just ask him, Jack,' he whispered, and fumbled the cigar butt from his trenchcoat pocket. Jack took the cigar butt and placed it before Smokey Joe on his glass countertop.

'This cigar,' said Jack, 'did it come from this establishment?'

Smokey Joe leaned forward, brass cogs whirring, cigar smoke engulfing his head. He viewed the cigar butt and nodded. 'One of mine,' he said. 'A Turquoise Torpedo.'

'But it's brown,' said Jack.

'But what's in a name?' said Smokey Joe. 'Or what's not? It may be brown, but it tastes like turquoise.'

'And it is one of yours?'

'It is.'

'Then my question is this: do you recall selling any of these cigars recently?'

Smokey Joe nodded. 'Of course I do. I recall the selling of every cigar, because in truth I don't sell many.'

'And you sold one of these cigars recently?'

'I sold one hundred of these cigars yesterday evening.'

'One hundred,' said Jack. 'That is an incredible number.'

'Really?' said Smokey Joe. 'I always thought that the most incredible number must be two, because it is one more than just one, yet one less than any other number, no matter how great that number might be. And there must be an infinite number of numbers, mustn't there be?'

'I'm sure there must,' said Jack. 'But please tell me this: would it be possible for you to describe to me the individual who purchased those one hundred cigars from you yesterday?'

'Your lordship is surely mocking me,' said Smokey Joe, adding more smoke to his words.

'No, I'm not,' said Jack. 'I'm well and truly not.'

'But your lordship surely knows who purchased those cigars.'

'No,' said Jack. 'I well and truly don't.'

'Of course you do,' said Smokey Joe.

'Of course I don't,' said Jack.

'Do,' said Joe.

And, 'Don't,' said Jack.

And, 'Do,' said Joe once more.

'Now listen,' said Jack, 'I am not asking you a difficult question. Please will you tell me who purchased those cigars?'

'I will,' said Smokey Joe.

'Then do so,' said Jack.

'Then I will,' said Smokey Joe. And he did. 'That bear with you,' he said.

4

'It wasn't *me*.' And Eddie fell back in alarm. 'It wasn't me – I'm as innocent as.'

'It *was* you, you scoundrel.' And Smokey Joe huffed as he puffed. 'I'd know the looks of you as I'd know the colour of moonlight, those mismatched eyes and your scruffy old paws.'

'It's cinnamon plush,' Eddie protested. 'I am an Anders Imperial.'

'Oh yes? Oh yes?' Smokey Joe did rockings and smoke came out of his ear holes. 'You weren't wearing that fedora when you came into this here establishment, but I'll wager that under it there's a bottle cap in your left ear.'

'That's my special tag.' Eddie now cowered behind Jack's legs. This was all a little much.

'Scoundrel and trickster,' puffed Smokey Joe, pointing an accusing cigar at this scoundrel and trickster.

'Now just stop this,' Jack said. 'I feel certain that you have made some mistake.'

'Mistake?' said Smokey Joe and rolled his eyes, which seemed to smoke a little, too. 'He took one hundred of my finest Turquoise Torpedoes and I demand proper payment.'

'I am confused,' said Jack. 'You said that my associate here purchased these cigars from you.'

'With tomfoolery coin of the realm.'

'Still not fully understanding.' Jack gave his shoulders a shrug.

'Bogus coin, he paid me with. A high-denomination money note, in fact. I placed it into my cash register and moments after he left it went poof.'

'Poof?' said Jack, miming a kind of poof, as one might in such circumstances.

'Poof,' went Smokey Joe. 'And never take up mime as a profession. The money note went poof in a poof of smoke and vanished away.'

'A poof of smoke?' said Jack, not troubling to mime such a thing.

'And of no smoke that I have ever seen and I've seen all but every kind.'

'I am most confused,' said Jack.

'And me also,' said Eddie. 'And wrongly accused. Let's be going now.'

'Oh no you don't,' said Smokey Joe, and with the kind of ease that lent Jack the conviction that it was hardly the first time he had done such a thing, Smokey Joe drew out a pistol from beneath his counter and waggled it somewhat about.

'Now hold on,' said Jack. 'There's no need for that.'

'There's every need,' said Smokey Joe. 'You were thinking to depart.'

'Well, yes, we were.'

'And you cannot. We shall wait here together.'

'For what?' Jack enquired.

'The arrival of the constables, of course.'

'Ah,' said Jack. 'And you expect their arrival imminently?'

'I do,' said Smokey Joe. 'I pressed the secret button beneath my counter when you entered my store. It connects by a piece of knotted string to the alarm board at the police station.'

'Most unsporting,' said Eddie.

'Which is why I engaged you in a lot of time-wasting toot,' said Smokey Joe, 'to give the police time to appear.'

'Then all that business about chickens?' Jack asked.

'That *wasn't* toot. You should fear those chickens. I know whereof I speak.'

'You failed to mention that I should similarly fear the arrival of the constables.'

'I kept that to myself. Now just you stand still, or I will be forced to take the law into my own hands and shoot you myself.'

'For stealing one hundred cigars?' Jack threw up his hands. Smokey Joe cocked the pistol.

'Easy, please,' said Jack, his hands miming 'easy' motions and miming them rather well. 'I will pay you for the cigars. There's no need to go involving the police.'

'But I never bought the cigars,' said Eddie. 'It wasn't me, Jack, honest.'

'I know it wasn't, Eddie.'

'It was too,' said Smokey Joe. 'And his soggy feet made puddles on my floor. I had to employ the services of a mop and bucket. And they don't come cheap of an evening, I can tell you. They charged me double.'

'I'll pay you whatever you want,' said Jack.

'With *what*?' whispered Eddie.

'I'll write you an IOU,' Jack told Smokey Joe. 'I'm a prince, you know.'

'Then why aren't you wearing a crown?'

'Actually, I am,' said Jack. 'It's under my fedora.'

'It never is,' said Smokey Joe.

'It never is, is it?' said Eddie.

'In fact,' said Jack, 'you can have the crown and all the jewels on it. Will that be payment enough?'

'It must be a very small crown to fit under that hat,' said Smokey Joe, cocking his head in suspicion.

'Would you mind doing that again?' asked Eddie.

'Why?' said Smokey Joe.

'Well, you did it rather well, and it's not the sort of thing you see every day.'

Smokey Joe obligingly did it again.

'Even better the second time,' said Jack.

'Thanks,' said Smokey Joe.

'So, would you like to see the crown?'

'More than anything else I can presently imagine.'

'Right, then,' said Jack, and he swept off his hat with a flourish. It was a considerably flourish. A considerably hard and sweeping flourish. As flourishes went, this one was an award-winner. So hard and sweeping was this award-winning flourish that it knocked the pistol right out of Smokey Joe's hand and sent it skidding across the store floor.

'Run!' shouted Jack to Eddie. And both of them ran.

Although they didn't run far.

They ran to the door and through the doorway and then they ran no further. They would have dearly liked to, of course. They would dearly have loved to have run to Bill's car and then driven away in it at speed. But they did not. They came to a standstill on the pavement and there they halted and there they raised their hands.

Because there to greet them outside the store were very many policemen. Some stood and some knelt. All of them pointed guns. They pointed guns as they stood or knelt and they laughed and grinned as they did so. For these were Toy City's laughing policemen, though this was no laughing matter.

A very large and rotund policeman, a chief of policemen in fact, leaned upon the bonnet of Bill's splendid automobile. He was all perished rubber and he was smoking a large cigar. It wasn't a Turquoise Torpedo, of course, but an inferior brand, but he puffed upon it nonetheless and seemed to enjoy this puffing. Presently he tapped away ash and shortly after he spoke.

'Well, well, well,' said Chief Inspector Wellington Bellis, for it was none but himself. 'Surely it is Eddie and Jack. Now what a surprise this is.'

The 'shaking down' and the 'cuffing up' were uncomfortable enough. The 'flinging into the police van' lacked also for comfort, and the unnecessary 'necessary restraint', which involved numerous officers of the law either sitting or standing upon Jack and Eddie during the journey to the police station, lacked for absolutely any comfort whatsoever. In fact, the unnecessary 'necessary restraint' was nothing less than painful. The 'dragging out of the police van', the 'kicking towards the police cell' and the 'final chucking into the cell' were actually a bit of a doddle compared to the unnecessary 'necessary restraint'. But not a lot of fun.

'I can't believe it,' Eddie said, at least now uncuffed and brushing police boot marks from his trenchcoat. 'Wrongly accused and arrested. And this only our first day on the case.'

'My first and indeed my last,' said Jack.

'Now don't you start, please.'

'Look at me,' said Jack. 'They trod on me, they sat on me. That Officer Chortle even farted on me. And I could never abide the smell of burning rubber.'

'We'll soon be out of here,' said Eddie. 'As soon as my solicitor arrives.'

'*You* have a *solicitor*?'

'I'm entitled to have one. I know the law.'

'But do you actually *have* one?'

'Not as such,' said Eddie. 'It's always details, details with you.'

'And it's always trouble with you.'

'You love it really.'

'I don't.'

The face of the laughing policeman whose name was Officer Chortle, a name that made him special because it was printed across his back, grinned in through the little door grille.

'Comfortable, ladies?' he said.

'I'm innocent,' said Eddie. 'Wrongly accused. And Jack's innocent, too. He's an innocent bystander.'

'Looks like a hardened crim' to me,' chuckled Officer Chortle. 'And a gormster.'

'How dare you,' said Jack. 'I'm a prince.'

'Aren't no princes,' laughed Officer Chortle. 'That mad mayor we had did away with princes.'

Jack cast Eddie a 'certain' look.

'And,' said Office Chortle, 'who can forget Edict Number Four?'

'I can,' said Eddie. 'What was it?'

'The one about curtailing police violence against suspects.'

'Ah, that one,' said Eddie. 'How's that going, by the way?'

Officer Chortle chuckled. Menacingly. 'And when it comes to it,' he continued, 'you look a lot like that mad mayor.'

'No I don't,' said Eddie. 'Not at all.'

Officer Chortle squinted at Eddie. 'No, perhaps not.' He sniggered. 'The mad mayor had matching eyes and those really creepy hands.'

'They *were not* creepy,' said Eddie. 'And neither was the mayor mad.'

'Not mad?' Officer Chortle fairly cracked himself up over this. 'Not mad? Well, he wasn't exactly cheerful when the mob tarred and feathered him.'

Eddie shuddered at the recollection. 'Has my solicitor arrived?' he asked.

'I'll have to ask you to stop,' said Officer Chortle. 'Solicitor, indeed! If you keep making me laugh like this I'll wet myself.'

'We are innocent,' said Eddie. 'Let us out please.'

'The chief inspector will interview you shortly. You can make your confessions to him then if you wish. Although if you choose not to, I must caution you that me and my fellow officers will be calling in later to beat a confession out of you. And as we do have a number of "unsolveds" hanging about, you will find yourselves confessing to them also, simply to ease the pain.'

And with that Officer Chortle left, laughing as he did so.

'Perfect,' said Jack. 'So it's prison for us, is it?'

'It might be for you,' said Eddie, 'if it's anything more than a summary beating. You're the meathead, after all. You have some status. It will be the incinerator for me. I'm as dead as.'

'We have to escape,' said Jack.

'I seem to recall,' said Eddie, 'that you do have some skills with locks. Perhaps you'd be so good as to pick this one on the door and we will, with caution, go upon our way.'

'Ah, yes indeed,' and Jack sought something suitable.

And he would probably have found it also had not a key turned in the lock, the door opened and several burly though jolly and laughing policemen entered the cell and hauled him and Eddie from it.

Chief Inspector Wellington Bellis's office was definitely 'of the genre'. It had much of the look of Bill Winkie's office about it, but being below ground level it lacked for windows. It didn't lack for a desk, though, a big and crowded desk, with one of those big desk lamps that they shine into suspects' eyes.

The walls were lavishly decorated with mug shots, press cuttings and photographs of crime scenes and horribly mutilated corpses. Eddie recognised the victims pictured in several of these gory photographs: the P.P.P.s who had been savagely done to death by the kindly, lovable white-haired old Toymaker's evil twin during the exciting adventure that he and Jack had had but months before.*

Upon the floor was a carpet, which like unto Bill's dared not to speak its name. And it was onto this carpet that Jack and Eddie were flung.

'This treatment is outrageous,' Jack protested. 'I protest,' he also protested. 'I demand to speak to my solicitor.'

'All in good time,' said Bellis, settling himself into the chair behind his desk and gesturing to the two that stood before it. 'Seat yourselves. Would you care for a cup of tea?'

'A cup of tea?' Jack got to his knees and then his feet.

'Or coffee?' said the chief inspector.

'I'd like a beer,' said Eddie.

Chief Inspector Bellis frowned upon him.

'Or perhaps just a glass of water.' Eddie arose and did further dustings down of himself.

'You'll have to pardon the officers,' said Bellis, leaning back in his chair and further gesturing to Jack and Eddie. 'Sit yourselves down, if you will. The police officers do get a little carried away. They are so enthusiastic about maintaining law and order. They do have the public's interests at heart.'

'They don't have one heart between the lot of them,' said Eddie, struggling onto a chair. 'They're all as brutal as.'

'They overcompensate,' said Chief Inspector Bellis. 'I expect it's just the overexuberance of youth, which should really be channelled into sporting activities. That's what it says in this book I've been reading – *Learn to Leap Over Candlesticks In Just Thirty Days*, by J. B. Nimble and J. B. Quick. Perhaps you've read it?'

'I'll purchase a copy as soon as I leave here,' said Eddie. 'Do you suppose that will be sooner rather than later, as it were?'

'Well, we'll have to see about that. There are most serious charges.'

'*Charges?*' said Eddie. 'There is more than one charge?'

'You can never have too many charges.' Chief Inspector Bellis

---

* Which is to be found chronicled in that damn fine book (and *SFX* award-winner) *The Hollow Chocolate Bunnies of the Apocalypse*. Available from all good booksellers.

grinned from ear to ear, then back again. 'It's like having too many chickens. You can never have too many chickens, can you?'

'Chickens *again*?' said Jack.

'I like chicken again,' said Bellis. 'Again and again. I can't get enough of chicken.'

Jack shook his head. 'I am assuming that you are talking about *eating* chicken?' he said.

'Obviously. But it's such a dilemma, isn't it?'

Eddie shook his head and wondered where all *this* was leading to.

'You see,' said the chief inspector, 'my wife makes me sandwiches for my lunch.'

'Chicken sandwiches?' Jack asked, not out of politeness, but possibly more as a diversionary tactic, in the hope that perhaps Chief Inspector Bellis would just like to chat about sandwiches for a while, before sending him and Eddie on their way.

'That's the thing,' said Bellis. 'I like chicken sandwiches. But I also like egg sandwiches. But you'll notice that although you mix and match the contents of sandwiches – cheese and onion, egg and cress, chicken and bacon – no one ever eats a chicken and egg sandwich.'

Eddie looked at Jack. And Jack looked at Eddie.

'He's right,' said Jack.

'He is,' said Eddie. 'So why is that, do you think?'

'Because of the eternal question,' said Bellis.

'Ah,' said Eddie.

'Ah,' said Jack.

'What eternal question?' said Eddie.

'Oh, come on,' said Bellis. 'What came first, the chicken or the egg? I mean, how could you eat the sandwich? You wouldn't know which bit to eat first. You'd go mad trying. And believe me, I have tried. And I have gone mad.'

'Most encouraging,' whispered Eddie to Jack. 'I can see this being a long and difficult evening.'

'Is it evening already?' asked Jack.

'Let's just assume that it is.'

'There's no solution to it,' said Chief Inspector Bellis. 'It's one of those things that's best left alone. Forgotten about, in fact. In fact, let us never mention the subject again.'

'I'm up for that,' said Eddie, offering the chief inspector an encouraging smile. 'So, is it all right if Jack and I go now?'

Chief Inspector Bellis shook his head. 'Not as such,' he said. 'In fact, not at all. There are these charges to be considered. Things do not look altogether good for you.'

'But I am innocent,' said Eddie.

'That, I'm afraid, is what they all say.'

'But Eddie *is* innocent,' said Jack. 'And I can prove it.'

'Can you?' Eddie asked.

'Of course I can,' said Jack. 'The proprietor of the cigar store said that Eddie purchased those cigars yesterday evening, did he not?'

'I heard him say that,' said Eddie.

Chief Inspector Bellis perused notes upon his desk. 'That *is* what he said,' he said. 'Shortly before eight, last evening, just before he closed up.'

'That's right,' said Jack. 'He said something about the rain and Eddie leaving puddles on his floor.'

Chief Inspector Bellis did further perusings and nodded.

'Then it can't have been Eddie,' said Jack.

'No, it can't,' said Eddie. 'I have an alibi. I was in Tinto's Bar at that time, and that's right across the city.'

Chief Inspector Bellis made a thoughtful face. It was a very good thoughtful face and both Jack and Eddie were tempted to ask him to make it once more. But only tempted. They showed laudable restraint. 'Well, an alibi is an alibi,' said the chief inspector. 'But I can see no reason why we should let that stand in the way of letting the law take its course and justice getting done.'

'Eh?' said Eddie.

'What?' said Jack.

'Well,' said Bellis, 'as I won't be following up on the alibi, it hardly matters, does it?'

'Eh?' said Eddie again.

And Jack did another '*What?*' Although louder than the first.

'Crime and punishment share a certain empathy,' Chief Inspector

Bellis explained, 'in that both are dispassionate. The criminal goes about his work in a dispassionate manner. He cares not whom he hurts or harms. He doesn't care about the feelings of others. And so the law behaves towards the criminal in a similar manner. The law cares not for the criminal, it simply seeks to lock him away so that he may perform no further crime.'

'But I'm innocent,' said Eddie.

'And if I were not dispassionate, I would care for your woes,' said Bellis. 'But that would be unprofessional. I must never get personally involved. There's no telling what might happen if I did so, is there?'

'You might free the innocent and convict only the guilty,' was Eddie's suggestion.

'The distinction between guilt and innocence is a subtle one.'

'No, it's not,' said Eddie. 'You're either guilty or you're not.'

'I'll thank you not to confuse the issue. Charges have been made and you have been arrested. End of story, really.'

'This is outrageous,' said Jack. 'I demand to speak to your superior.'

'I don't think that will be necessary.'

'Oh yes it will,' said Jack. 'I will see justice done. I really will.'

'You tell him, Jack,' said Eddie.

'You'll tell me nothing,' said Chief Inspector Bellis, 'because I am dropping all the charges.'

'You are?' said Eddie.

'I am,' said Bellis, 'because I *know* you are innocent.'

'You *do*?' said Eddie.

'I *do*,' said Bellis. 'And upon this occasion I am prepared to let the fact that you *are* innocent stand in the way of letting justice be done.'

'You *are*?' said Eddie. 'Why?' said Eddie.

'Because in return for this, *you* are going to do something for me. Something that I surmise you are already doing and something I wish you to continue doing.'

'I am now *very* confused,' said Eddie.

'I believe I am correct in assuming that you have returned to your old profession,' said Bellis, 'that of detective.'

Eddie nodded.

'You see, I *know* that it was not you who purchased those cigars with the mysterious combustible currency.'

'You do?' said Eddie once more.

'I do,' said Bellis once more. 'You see, I have these.' And he drew from his desk a number of plasticised packets and flung them onto his desk.

Eddie took one up between his paws and examined it. 'Cigar butt,' he said.

'Eleven cigar butts,' said Bellis, 'one found at each of the cymbal-playing monkeys' resting places. All over the city. Eleven cigar butts. The twelfth you showed to Smokey Joe. You went there to enquire whether he recalled who he sold it to, didn't you?'

'I did,' said Eddie.

'And the twelfth monkey?'

'Dead in Bill's office,' said Eddie.

'Intriguing, isn't it?' said Bellis. 'And they all died within minutes of each other. And I do not believe that you ran all over the city on your stumpy little legs wiping each and every one of them out – did you?'

Eddie shook his head.

'And now you are investigating these crimes?'

'Yes,' said Eddie. 'I am. *We* are.'

'And I would like you to continue doing so.'

'Really?' said Eddie. 'You would?'

'Twelve monkeys,' said Bellis. '*All* the cymbal-playing monkeys. Annoying blighters they were, I agree, but they were our kind. They were toys. The murderer must be brought to justice.'

'I don't understand,' said Eddie.

'About justice?'

'Well, I understand about that. Or at least your concept of it. Which is as just as.'

'Did you read the paper?' asked Bellis. 'The crimes made page thirteen. I requested of my "superior" that I be allowed to put a special task force on the monkeys' case. The memo I received in reply stated that it was a low priority.'

'Typical,' said Eddie. 'Disgusting, in fact.'

'I do so agree,' said Bellis. 'I blame it on that mad mayor we had.'

'Now just hold on,' said Eddie.

'Yes?' said Bellis.

'Nothing,' said Eddie. 'Go on, please.'

'You,' said Bellis, 'you and Mr Jack here are going to act on my behalf. You are going to be my special task force. You will report directly to me on whatever progress you are making. Do you understand me?'

Jack nodded. 'Up to a point,' said he. 'So we will report directly to you to receive our wages, will we?'

Chief Inspector Bellis made a certain face towards Jack. One that Jack did not wish to be repeated.

'Would there be any chance of a reward, then,' Jack asked, 'if we could present you with a suitable culprit?'

Eddie now gave Jack a certain look.

'Sorry,' said Jack. 'The *real* culprit, then? The *real* murderer?'

'Exactly,' said Bellis. 'And in return for this public-spirited action I will forget about all the trumped-up charges that we have piled up against the bear.'

'But I'm innocent,' said Eddie.

'I think we've been through that,' said Bellis. 'you and Jack will be my secret task force. You *will* find the murderer.'

'We'll certainly *try*,' said Eddie.

'Oh, you'll do more than that. You will succeed.'

'Thanks for the vote of confidence.'

'Or you'll feed the boiler.'

'Ah,' said Eddie.

'Ah indeed,' said Bellis.

'Hm,' went Eddie. 'Well, we'll certainly do our very, very best to succeed. You can be assured of that.'

'Nice,' said Bellis.

'But the trouble is,' said Eddie, 'that the only clue we had was the cigar butt. And that just led to a case of mistaken identity. So I have no idea what to do next.'

'I'm sure you'll think of something,' said Bellis.

'I'm not *too* sure,' said Eddie.

'Brrrr,' said Bellis. 'Is it cold in here, or is it just me?'

'Ah,' said Eddie.

'Ah indeed,' said Chief Inspector Bellis.

5

'That Bellis is a monster,' said Eddie. 'I'm fuel for his boiler for certain.'

'Look on the bright side, Eddie,' said Jack. 'At least we have our freedom.'

They'd had to walk all the way from the police station to the cigar shop to pick up Bill's car, but now they were back in Tinto's Bar and Tinto was pouring them a number of beers.

'I'm doomed,' said Eddie.

'You're not,' said Jack. 'He wants the case solved. And he knows that if anyone can solve it, then you are that someone.'

'Thanks for that,' said Eddie.

'Well, you can,' said Jack.

'Not for that,' said Eddie. 'For calling me some*one* rather than some*thing*.'

'I'd never call you some*thing*,' said Jack. 'You're Eddie. You're my bestest friend.'

'So we're definitely back in business together? You haven't let this first day out put you off? You're not going to quit on me?'

'As if I would. But it is a mystery, isn't it? Twelve monkeys dead, seemingly within minutes. And the cigar butts. And the cigar man thinking you'd bought the cigars from him. What do you make of it all?'

'Dunno,' said Eddie. 'Something very odd happened last night. I thought I saw something in the alleyway where I was dossing down in a dustbin, but the timing is all wrong. I do have to say, Jack, that I have no idea at all what is going on. But whatever it is, I don't like it very much.'

'How are those beers coming, Tinto?' Jack asked.

'Slowly,' said the clockwork barman. 'Could you see your way clear to giving my key a couple of turns – I think I'm running down here.'

Jack leaned across the bar and did the business with Tinto's key.

'Thank you,' said Tinto.

'You're welcome,' said Jack.

'Let's drink the beers,' said Eddie. 'It has been a long and trying day.'

'Ah, yes,' said Jack. 'And it's definitely evening now.'

'So we should drink beers and get drunk. That is my considered opinion.'

'And the case?'

'I don't know,' said Eddie, taking up a beer between his paws and moving it towards that portion of his face where many beers had gone before. And, 'Ah,' said Eddie, when he had done with his beer. 'That does hit the spot.'

'You drink too much,' said Jack.

'Too much for *what*?' said Eddie.

Jack shrugged and said, 'I dunno.'

'Then don't presume to,' said Eddie. 'Just drink.'

'You don't think that you should be applying yourself to the case in hand?'

'Not right now,' said Eddie. 'And nor should you. I seem to recall that you were supposed to be meeting up with a certain dolly from Nadine's Diner tonight.'

'Oh dear,' said Jack. 'I'd quite forgotten about her.'

'Bad boy,' said Eddie. 'Very bad boy.'

Jack perused his wristlet watch. The time was eight of the evening clock. Jack held the watch against his ear: it was ticking away like a good'n and he had no cause to doubt its accuracy. Mind you, Jack had taken that watch to pieces a couple of times to see just what made it run, as Jack knew all about clockwork. Inside that watch there was nothing to be found except for a couple of cogs that connected the winder to the hands. There was no evidence whatsoever of a conventional mechanism.

But then *that* in a watchcase was Toy City. It still made little sense to Jack. Watches without mechanisms that kept perfect time.

Telephone receivers connected by pieces of string. Wooden folk and folk like Eddie, a bear all filled with sawdust, yet a bear that walked and talked and thought and felt. And Jack felt for that bear.

'You've gone somewhat glassy-eyed,' said Eddie. 'Are you drunk already?'

'No,' said Jack. 'No, I'm not. I was only thinking.'

'About the dolly?' Eddie raised his glass and would have winked had he been able.

'About a lot of things,' said Jack.

'Well, don't let me keep you from the dolly.'

'No,' said Jack. 'The dolly can wait. We have a case to solve.'

'Case-solving is done for the day,' Eddie said. 'We will start again upon the morrow, as refreshed as and as ready as.'

Jack sank two more glasses of beer.

'Go on, Jack,' said Eddie. 'I'll be fine here. Go and have a good evening out. I'll see you here later if you want, or if you have a big night of it, then at Bill's office at nine o'clock sharp tomorrow.'

'Okay,' said Jack, and he rose from his stool, being careful not to crack his head upon the ceiling. 'If it's okay, then I'll see you tomorrow. Is it all right if I—'

'Take Bill's car? Of course.'

'Nice,' said Jack. 'Then I'll be off. And don't drink *too* much, will you?'

Eddie slid Jack's share of the remaining beers in his direction and said, 'Goodbye, Jack.'

And Jack left Tinto's Bar.

Jack drove slowly through the evening streets of Toy City. He could have driven at his normal breakneck pace, of course, but he only really did that to put the wind up Eddie. So Jack drove in a leisurely manner, even though he was late to meet the dolly.

Jack did do some thinking as he drove along, about Toy City and about Eddie, and Chief Inspector Bellis and the mysterious deaths of the cymbal-playing monkeys, and at length, when he arrived at Nadine's Diner, he was none the wiser than when he'd set forth.

The dolly, Amelie, stood outside the now-lit-up diner, her shift done and her temper all-but. As Jack approached her in Bill's car, he wondered a lot about her. She was, well, how could he put it? So *lifelike*. Just like a *real* girlfriend. Whatever a *real* girlfriend was. One of flesh and blood like himself, he supposed. Did that make his relationship with Amelie somewhat . . . *indecent*? Jack asked himself. *Perverted? Wrong? Twisted?*

'Easy now,' Jack told himself.

Amelie noticed Bill's car before she recognised the driver. She made a very winsome face towards the shiny automobile and hitched up her short skirt a little to show a bit more leg.

'Strumpet,' said Jack to himself.

Bill's car whispered to a standstill and Jack cranked down the window. 'Care for a ride?' said he.

'You?' and Amelie lowered her skirt. 'It's *you*. You're late, you know.'

'Blame the garage,' said Jack. 'I have just taken possession of this automobile.'

'It's *yours*?' The dolly now fluttered her eyelids.

'All mine,' said Jack. 'I have taken a new job. One with considerable cachet. Would you care for a ride?'

'I *would*.' And Amelie tottered around to the passenger door and entered Bill's automobile.

'It smells of manky old bear in here,' she said as she twitched her pretty nose.

'Mechanics,' said Jack. 'Highly skilled, but rarely bathed. You know how it is with the lower ranks.'

'Oh, indeed I do.' And the dolly crossed her legs. Such long legs they were, so shapely and slender. They were almost like re—

'Where to?' Jack asked. 'A romantic drive in the moonlight?'

'A show,' said Amelie, adjusting her over-tight top, which looked to be under considerable strain from her enhanced front parts.

'A show?' Jack said, and his wonderings turned to his wallet. He wondered just how much money he had in it. Not a lot, he concluded, not a lot.

'A lovely night for a drive,' he said.

'Then drive me to a show.'

'A puppet show?' Jack asked. 'A Punch and Judy show?'

'A proper show at a proper club. Let's go to Old King Cole's.'

'Ah,' said Jack, as Eddie had done whilst speaking to Chief Inspector Bellis.

'You're not ashamed to be seen with me, are you?' asked Amelie.

'No,' said Jack. 'Not at all. Anything but. If it's Old King Cole's you want, then Old King Cole's you shall have.'

'You are such a sweetie.' Amelie leaned over and kissed Jack on the cheek. A delicate kiss, a sensuous kiss. Just like a re—

'Old King Cole's it is,' said Jack.

Now Old King Cole was indeed a merry old soul and when he wasn't writing self-help manuals, which was all of the time nowadays as he'd only written the one, he could mostly be found at his jazz club, a rather swank affair on Old King Cole Boulevard, a place where one came to be seen.

Old King Cole had long ago sacked his fiddlers three in favour of a more up-beat ensemble: a clockwork trio, comprised of a saxophonist, drummer and piano player. There had been a brief period when he had toyed with a twelve-piece cymbal-playing monkey ensemble, but in the end had considered it rather too avant-garde, preferring a more traditional sound. The sound of jazz.

Now jazz is jazz. You either love jazz or you hate it. There is no middle ground with jazz and it's no good saying you like *some* jazz. Liking *some* jazz is not *loving* jazz. All right, neither is it *hating* jazz, but that is not the point. To truly love jazz you have to have a passion for it. You have to be able to get right inside it, to feel it, to . . . blah blah blah blah and so on and so forth and suchlike.

Old King Cole loved jazz. Before the passing of the infamous Edict Five, which had dispensed with royalty in Toy City, he had been King of Toy City and with him jazz had reigned supreme. After the ousting of the now infamous mad mayor, he was royalty once more and although jazz had never truly reigned supreme (in anyone's opinion other than his own) it was back at the top with him, as far as he was concerned, and if you are King you can believe whatever you want because few will dare to contradict you.

Old King Cole's jazz club was grand. It was stylish. It was magnificent. This was no gaudy piece of flash, this was old money spent well, the work of master builders.

It had been constructed to resemble a vast grand piano, atop it a gigantic candelabra, its candles spouting mighty flames. A liveried doorman, in a plush swaddle-shouldered snaff jacket with cross-stitched underpinnings and fluted snuff trumbles, stood to attention before double doors that twinkled with carbustions of cremmily, jaspur and filigold, made proud with Pultroon finials and crab-handle 'Jerry' turrets, after the style of Gondolese, but without the kerfundles.

On his feet the liveried doorman wore crab-toed Wainscotter boots in the trumped end-loungers style and[*]

On his head he wore a bowler hat.

Jack cruised up in Bill's automobile, leaned out from his open window and bid the liveried doorman a good evening.

The liveried doorman viewed Jack down the length of his nose. A nose that had been considerably lengthened by the addition of an ivorine nasal Kirby-todger.[†]

Above his moustache.

'Good evening to you, sir,' said he, raising a richly ornamented glove, richly ornamented with . . .[‡] ornaments. 'The valet will park your car for you, your lordship. Kindly leave the keys with me.'

'Splendid,' said Jack, and he climbed from the car.

Amelie the dolly did likewise.

The liveried doorman stiffened slightly, in the manner of one who is suddenly taken aback. One who has seen something troubling.

Jack turned towards Amelie, who was struggling to pull down the hem of her minuscule skirt, which appeared rather keen to remain where it nestled.

'Something bothering you?' Jack asked the liveried doorman, affecting, as he did so, a most haughty tone.

[*] Stop it *now*! Ed.
[†] Last warning! Ed.
[‡] Careful now. Ed.

'Of course not, your lordship,' said the liveried one, straightening a sleeve that was richly embellished with . . . rich embellishments.

As further liveried individuals swung wide the double-doors, with their, er, pretty bits and bobs on them, Jack, with Amelie now on his arm, entered Old King Cole's.

And Jack became all too suddenly aware that he was hardly dressed for the occasion. And he became suddenly aware of much more than that. Heads were turning, whispers were being whispered behind hands and there were tut-tut-tuttings in the air.

And then it dawned upon Jack that Amelie's choice of Old King Cole's for an evening out had hardly been arbitrary. She simply could not have gained entrance here alone, nor in the company of a non-human companion. She would never have got past the liveried doorman.

Another liveried personage now approached Jack. 'Excuse me, your lordship,' said he.

'You are excused,' said Jack. 'Trouble me no more.'

'But I regret that I must,' said the fellow. 'Are you a member here?'

'Naturally,' said Jack.

'If I might just see your membership card?'

'Well, if you must.' Jack fished into a trenchcoat pocket, drew out his wallet and from this extracted his membership card.

The liveried personage took this, examined it at length, held it up to the light and examined it some more. Presently he returned it to Jack. 'My apologies, your lordship,' said he.

'And I should think so, too,' said Jack. 'Now guide us to a favourable table and leave us there whilst you fetch champagne.'

'Champagne?' Amelie did girlish gigglings. The liveried personage led them to a table. It was a rather far-flung table some way away from the stage and in a somewhat darkened corner.

'Is this the best table you have?' Jack asked.

'The *very* best, your lordship. The most exclusive. The most private.'

'Then I suppose it will have to do. The champagne now, and make it your best.'

'Our best?'

'Your best,' said Jack.

And Jack held out Amelie's chair for her and the dolly settled into it. Jack sat himself down and rubbed his hands together.

'You're really a member here?' asked Amelie.

'Of course,' said Jack. 'A while back, Eddie and I performed a great service for Old King Cole – that of saving his life from the kindly, lovable white-haired old Toymaker's evil twin. He made Eddie and me honorary life members of his club. Although now that I come to think of it, Eddie never received *his* membership card. It got lost in the post, or something.'

'Is Eddie that manky bear who turned up at the diner today looking for work?'

'Eddie is my bestest friend,' said Jack. 'In fact, he is my partner in my new business enterprise.'

'*You* are in partnership with a teddy?' Amelie raised pretty painted eyebrows and pursed her pretty pink lips.

'This surprises you?' Jack asked.

'Teddies are so common,' said Amelie.

Jack laughed. And the champagne arrived. The liveried personage immediately presented Jack with the bill.

Jack waved this away with the words, 'I have an account here.'

'You do?' asked the dolly when she and Jack were alone once more.

'Let's not fuss with details,' said Jack, pouring champagne. 'Let's just try to enjoy the evening.'

'Dolly Dumpling is on,' said Amelie. 'I've always wanted to see her perform live. And I've always wanted to come here. It's so big, isn't it? And so lush.'

'It's certainly that.' Jack tasted the champagne and found that it met with his taste. 'But personally I hate it.'

Bubbles of champagne went up the dolly's nose. 'You hate it?' she said. 'You can't hate this.'

'I'm not blind,' said Jack. 'And neither are you. We both saw them whispering and pointing.'

'Yes,' said Amelie. 'I know. I know that my kind aren't welcome here.'

Jack shook his head. 'Eddie was right,' he said, 'when he tried to change things, make them better. But it was your kind, as you call them, that rose up against him.'

'I don't understand,' said Amelie. Further champagne bubbles did further ticklings.

'That manky bear was once mayor,' said Jack. 'The mayor who tried to change things here.'

'The mad mayor?' Amelie sneezed out champagne. 'That manky bear? But the mayor had blue glass eyes and those creepy hands.'

'He cared,' said Jack, 'and still does. He would have changed things for the better.'

'Things can't be changed,' said Amelie. 'Change is wrong, everyone knows that. Things are supposed to be as things are. And toys are supposed to do what they were created for. That's Holy Writ, everyone knows that. And no one could trust that mayor, not with those eyes and those creepy hands.'

Jack sighed and shrugged. 'Drink your champagne. Do you like it, by the way?'

'I love it,' said Amelie. 'And Jack?'

'Yes?' said Jack.

'I love you, too.'

Now *this* caught Jack by surprise. And caused him confusion and shock. He had not reckoned on that. Had *never* reckoned on *that*. He'd worked with Amelie for four or five months at that diner. And yes they had become friendly. And *yes* they had become lovers. But that was only to say that they had 'made love', which is to say that they had 'had sex'. Make love sounds nicer, but making love is really, truly, just *having sex* when it comes right down to it. And Amelie and Jack had come right down to it on quite a few occasions, and Jack had really been hoping that they would be coming-right-down-to-it once more, later, in the back of Bill's car. Because location and circumstance are both big factors in making coming-right-down-to-it the very great fun that it should be. And it had not slipped by Jack that coming-right-down-to-it with Amelie had been pretty indistinguishable from coming-right-down-to-it with a re—

'Don't tell me you're drunk already,' said Jack, smiling as he did so.

'No,' said Amelie. 'Not at all.' And she blew Jack a kiss and thrust out her augmented front parts.

Jack blew her a kiss in return. 'I think you're lovely,' he said.

'But do *you*—'

'Oh, look,' said Jack, 'there's someone going up on the stage.'

That someone was Old King Cole.

He'd put on a bit of weight since the last time Jack had seen him. Put on a bit of age, too, as it happened.

'He looks ill,' said Jack.

And the old King did.

He had to be helped onto the stage by minions. It must be one of the best things about being a king, having minions. Minions and underlings. And if you are a wicked king, evil cat's-paws, too. There's a lot of joy to be had in being royalty. There did not, however, seem to be much in the way of joy to be found in Old King Cole's present condition. Even though he *did* have the minions.

And everything.

His minions struggled to manoeuvre his considerable bulk. They pushed and pulled. And two of them, who seemed to chuckle as they did so, went, 'To me,' 'To you,' 'To me,' 'To you,' which won some appreciation from those who were into that kind of thing.[*]

The to-me-ing and to-you-ing minions positioned Old King Cole before the microphone. The old King one-two'd into it.

'Good evening, my people,' he said, once satisfied with his one-two-ings, 'and welcome to Saturday night at Old King Cole's.'

'It's Wednesday,' said Amelie.

Jack just shrugged.

'Welcome one, welcome all and welcome to an evening of jazz.'

'Nice,' said someone, for nowadays someone always does.

'Tonight we have a very special treat. A lady who is big in jazz. And when I *say* big, I *mean* big. Tonight, we are honoured by a very big presence, a very big talent. It is my pleasure to introduce to you

[*] And let's be honest here, who isn't? Because when it comes to royalty amongst the ranks of British entertainers, the Chuckle Brothers reign supreme. No? Well, please yourselves, then.

someone who needs no introduction. I give you the one, the only, *the* Dolly Dumpling.'

There was a bit of a drum roll from somewhere and the crowd at its tables set down its champagne and put its hands together.

Further to-me-to-you-ings took place and Old King Cole was shuttled from the stage. Darkness fell, then lights came up. A curtain rose to reveal musicians. Clockwork musicians, all shiny and well polished, with pressed-tin instruments, printed-on tuxedos and matching moustaches. Matching *what*? you might ask. And well might you ask it. There was a sax player, a pianist and a drummer, too, and then behind them a further curtain rose and as it did so a spotlight fell.

And a gasp went up from the assembled crowd.

A gasp that was joined to by Jack.

> She was *simply* enormous,
> Her frock was a circus tent,
> Her chins numbered more
> Than a fine cricket score,
> And her weight would an anvil have bent.

> Her breasts were so large, and I'll tell you how large,
> For if larger there were, none there found them,
> Her breasts were so large, and I'll tell you how large,
> They had little breasts orbiting round them.

'What was *that*?' asked Jack.

'What was *what*?' asked Amelie.

'Must have been poetry, or something,' said Jack. 'But *that* is one big woman.'

And she was. They sort of cranked Dolly Dumpling forward. There was some winching gear involved, which in itself involved certain pulleys and blocks and some behind-the-scenes unwilling help from minions (who did at least say, 'To me, to you,') and liveried personages (who considered themselves above that sort of thing).

Ropes groaned and blocks and winches strained and Dolly Dumpling moved forward.

The musicians cowered before her prodigious approach, and thanked whatever Gods they favoured when the approaching was done.

A microphone did lowerings on a wire and Dolly Dumpling breathed into it.

It was a deep, lustrous, sumptuous breath, a breath that had about it a fearsome sexuality. A deeply erotic breath was this, and its effect upon the crowd was manifest.

Toffs in dinner suits loosened their ties; ladies in crinolines fluttered their fans. Jack felt a shiver go through him.

Dolly Dumpling rippled as she breathed. It was a gentle rippling, but it, too, had its effect. That such a creature, of such an exaggerated size, could achieve such sensuality with a single breath and a bit of body rippling, seemed to Jack beyond all comprehension, but it *was* something, something extraordinary. Yet it was *nothing*, nothing at all, when set against the effect her voice had when that fat lady sang.

There are voices. And then there are VOICES and then there is SOMETHING MORE. It doesn't happen often, but when it does, well, when it does, IT DOES.

Jack's champagne glass was almost at his lips. And that is where it stayed, unmoving, throughout Dolly Dumpling's first song. And it never reached Jack's lips at all even after that, because at the conclusion of the song Jack set it down to use his hands for clapping. And this went on, again and again and again.

How she reached the notes she did and how she held them there were matters beyond discussion and indeed comprehension. How she achieved what she achieved may indeed never be known. And when she breathed, 'Please do all get up and dance,' then all got up and danced.

The dancefloor wasn't large but now it filled and as Dolly Dumpling's voice soared and swooped and brought notes beyond notes and sensations with them that were *beyond*, the crowd swayed and shimmied, trembled and danced. How they danced!

Jack took Amelie in his arms and although having no skills at all as a dancer, shimmied and swayed with the rest. And waltzed, too. And then did that jazz-dance sort of thing that can't really be described and which you either *can* do, or *can't*. And Jack couldn't. Dinner suits and crinoline. Slicked-back hair and coiffured coils. Menfolk and womenfolk. Jack and a dolly. Around and around and around.

Love and magic in the air, enchantment and wonderment and joy, joy, happy joy.

And.

'I say, chap, careful where you're treading.'

'Sorry,' said Jack to his fellow dancer. Then he did a bit of a dip and a flourish and then had a little kiss with Amelie. 'Isn't this wonderful?' said Jack as he twirled the dolly round. And Amelie shook her preposterous front parts and blew some kisses to Jack.

And Dolly Dumpling's voice rose and fell and the band was pretty good, too.

And 'Careful, chap, what you're doing there,' said that fellow again.

'It's crowded,' Jack called to the fellow that he had just stepped upon for a second time. 'Sorry, just enjoy.'

'Lout,' said the fellow's partner. Loud enough to be heard for a fair circle round. 'Disgusting, coming in here with that thing.'

Jack stiffened in mid-second dip and approaching kiss and said, 'What did you say?'

'She said, "Disgusting",' said the fellow, 'lowering the tone of this establishment.'

'*What?*' went Jack.

'Leave it,' said Amelie.

'No, I won't leave it.' Jack turned to confront the fellow. A very dapper fellow, he was, probably some son or close relative of a prominent P.P.P. 'What is your problem?' asked Jack, in the manner of one who didn't know.

'You know well enough,' said the fellow. 'Bringing that thing in here and flaunting it about.'

'That *thing*,' said Jack, 'is my girlfriend.' The words 'is my girlfriend', however, were not heard by the fellow Jack had spoken to, because, at the conclusion of the word 'thing', Jack had thrown a punch at the fellow, which had caught him smartly upon the jaw and sent him floorwards in an unconscious state. Most rapidly.

'*Monster!*' screamed the fellow's partner, and screaming so set upon Jack.

Most violently.

6

At least in a bar brawl you know where you are.

There are so many moments in life when you really don't know where you are. Where you stand, how you're fixed, what you're up against and so on and so forth and suchlike. Life can be tricky like that. It builds you up and it knocks you down. The build-up is generally slow, but it leads to overconfidence. The knocking down is swift and it comes out of nowhere. And it hurts.

But at least in a bar brawl you know where you are.

You generally have a choice of three places. Right in the thick of it, getting hammered or doing the hammering. Just on the periphery, where a stray fist or flying bottle is likely to strike you. Or right on the edge, at the back of the crowd, which is the best place to be. You can always climb up on a chair and enjoy the action without too much danger of taking personal punishment.

Back of the crowd is definitely the best place to be in a bar brawl.

In life, well, that's another matter, but in a bar brawl, it's the back. You know where you are at the back.

Jack was *not* at the back. For Jack was indeed the epicentre. And when it came right down to it, Jack was *not* a fighter. He was rarely one to swing the first fist and why he had done this now troubled him. But not so much as the other thing troubled him. This other thing being the handbag that was repeatedly striking his head. The partner of the fellow Jack had floored was going at Jack as one possessed. And possessed of a strong right arm.

Jack sheltered his head with his hands and yelled, 'Stop!' But the violence ceased to do so. And Jack's shout of, 'Stop!' echoed hollowly through the air, for the music had ceased and the dancing had ceased and all conversation likewise had ceased and all eyes were upon Jack.

And then Amelie swung a handbag of her own and floored Jack's attacker.

Which somehow increased the sudden silence, made it more intense.

Jack uncovered his head and glanced all around and about himself. Stern faces stared and glared at him, eyebrows and mouth-corners well drawn down. Fingers were a-forming fists, shoulders were a-broadening. Jack now glanced down at the two prone figures on the dancefloor. A little voice in Jack's head said, 'This isn't good.'

'Right,' said Jack, now squaring his narrow shoulders. 'We're leaving now. No one try to stop us.'

The sounds of growlings came to Jack's ears, and not the growlings of dogs. The crowd was forming a tight ring now, a very tight ring with no exit.

Jack stuck his right hand into his trenchcoat pocket. 'I've a gun here,' he cried, 'and I'm not afraid to use it. In fact I'll be happy to use it, because I'm quite mad, me. Who'll be the first then? Who?'

The ring now widened and many exits appeared. Jack's non-pocketed hand reached out to Amelie, who took it in the one that wasn't wielding her handbag. 'Come on,' said Jack. 'Let's go.'

And so, with Jack's pocket-hand doing all-around gun-poking motions, he and Amelie headed to the door. And well might they have made it, too, had not something altogether untoward occurred. It occurred upon the stage and it began with a scream. As screams went this was a loud one and coming as it did from the mouth of Dolly Dumpling it was a magnificent scream. Exactly what key this scream was in was anyone's guess, but those who understand acoustics and know exactly which pitch, note, key or whatever is necessary to shatter glass would have recognised it immediately. For it was that very one.

Behind the bar counter, bottles, optics, glasses, vases, cocktail stirrers and the left eye of the barman shattered. Champagne flutes on tables blew to shards and next came the windows.

Jack turned and Jack saw and what Jack saw Jack didn't like at all.

The stage was engulfed in a blinding light. Dolly Dumpling was lost in this light, as were the clockwork musicians.

Dolly's scream went on and on, if anything rising in pitch. A terrible vibration of the gut-rumbling persuasion hit the now-cowering crowd and signalled that mad rush that comes at such moments. That mad rush that's made for the door.

Screams and panic, horror and bright white light.

Jack should have run, too, for such was the obvious thing to do. He should have taken to his heels and fled the scene, dragging Amelie with him. But Jack found, much to his horror, that his feet wouldn't budge. The expression 'rooted to the spot' had now some definite meaning to him, so instead he gathered Amelie to himself and as the crowd rushed past did his bestest to remain upright and in a single piece.

The crowd burst through the doors of Old King Cole's, tumbling over one another. Unshattered glass erupted from these doors. It was a cacophony of chaos, a madness of mayhem, a veritable discord of disorder. A pandemic of pandemonium.

And worse was yet to come.

'And worse was yet to come,' said Tinto to Eddie Bear, in Tinto's Bar, some way away from the pandemic of pandemonium and even indeed the tuneless tornadic timpani of turbulence.

'Worse than what?' asked Eddie, who hadn't been listening, but *had* been getting drunk.

'The mother-in-law's pancake-cleaning facility burned to the ground,' said Tinto, 'so we had to release all the penguins and Keith couldn't ride his bike for a week.'

'You *what?*' Eddie asked.

'I knew you weren't listening,' said Tinto. 'Nobody ever listens to me.'

'They listen when you call time,' said Eddie. 'Though mostly they ignore it. But they *do* listen, and *that* is what matters.'

'That's some consolation,' said Tinto. 'But not much.'

'Take what you can get,' said Eddie. 'That's what I always say.'

'I've never heard you say it before.' Tinto took up a glass to clean and cleaned it.

'Perhaps you weren't listening,' Eddie suggested. 'It happens sometimes.'

'Well,' said Tinto, 'if I see one of those spacemen, I'll tell them that's what I think of them.'

'You do that,' said Eddie. 'And you can tell them what I think of them, too. Whatever that might be.'

'Should I wait until you think something up?'

'That would probably be for the best.' Eddie took his beer glass carefully between his paws and poured its contents without care into his mouth. 'And by the by,' he said, once he had done with this, replaced his glass upon the counter top and wiped a paw across his mouth, 'which spacemen would these be?'

'I knew you weren't listening,' said Tinto.

'You know so much,' said Eddie, 'which is why I admire you so much.'

'You do?' Tinto asked.

Eddie smiled upon the clockwork barman. 'What do *you* think?' he asked in return.

'I think you're winding me up,' said Tinto. 'But not in the nice way. I hope they get *you* next, that will serve you right.'

'Right,' said Eddie. 'What *are* you talking about?'

'The spacemen with the death rays,' Tinto said.

'Ah,' said Eddie, indicating that he would like further beers. '*Those* spacemen. I was thinking about the *other* spacemen, which is why I got confused.'

'Are you drunk?' asked Tinto.

'My feet are,' said Eddie. 'You might well have to carry me to the toilet.'

'Now *that*,' said Tinto, 'is *not* going to happen.'

'I rather thought not, but do tell me about the spacemen.'

'You're not just trying to engage me in conversation in order that I might forget to charge you for all of those beers?'

Eddie made the kind of face that said, 'As if I would,' without actually putting it into words.

'Good face,' said Tinto. 'What does it mean?'

'It means *what* spacemen?' said Eddie.

'*The* spacemen,' said Tinto, 'who blasted the clockwork monkeys with their death rays.'

'Now this is new,' said Eddie.

'Not to *those* spacemen.' Tinto took up another glass to polish, without replacing the first. Eddie looked on with envy at those dextrous fingers. 'I'll bet *those* spacemen blast clockwork monkeys all the time.'

Eddie Bear did shakings of his head, which made him slightly giddy, which meant at least that the beer was creeping up.

'Tinto,' said Eddie, 'please explain to me, in a simple and easy-to-understand fashion, *exactly* what you are talking about.'

'The clockwork monkeys,' said Tinto, 'the ones that got blasted. They got blasted by spacemen.'

Eddie sighed. 'And who told you *that*?' he asked.

'A spaceman,' said Tinto.

'A spaceman,' said Eddie. '*What* spaceman?'

'*That* spaceman.' Tinto pointed, glasses still in his hand and everything. 'That spaceman over there.'

Eddie turned his head to view this spaceman.

And Eddie Bear fell off his stool.

'Drunk!' cried Tinto. 'Out of my bar.'

'I'm *not* drunk.' Eddie did further strugglings and managed at least to get to his knee regions. 'It's your responsibility. Where is this spaceman?'

'You *are* drunk,' said Tinto. 'You drunkard. Over there,' and Tinto pointed once again.

'Ah,' said Eddie, rising with considerable difficulty and swaying with no apparent difficulty whatsoever.

Across the bar floor at a dim corner table sat a spaceman. He was a rather splendid-looking spaceman, as it happened. Very shiny was he, very silvery and well polished. He was all-over tin plate but for a tinted see-through plastic weather dome, which was presently half-raised to permit the passage of alcohol.

Eddie tottered and swayed in the spaceman's direction. The spaceman looked up from his drink and wondered at Eddie's approach.

Before the spaceman's table Eddie paused, but still swayed somewhat. 'Ahoy there, shipmate,' said Eddie Bear.

'Ahoy there *what*?' The spaceman's voice came as if from the earpiece of a telephone receiver, but in fact came from a grille in his chest similar to Tinto's. The spaceman raised a rubber hand and waggled its fingers at Eddie.

'Might I sit down?' asked the bear.

'Your capabilities are unknown to me,' said the spaceman. 'Was that a rhetorical question?'

Eddie drew out a chair and slumped himself down onto it. He grinned lopsidedly at the spaceman and said, 'So, how's it going, then?'

'I come in peace,' said the spaceman. 'Take me to your leader.'

'Excuse me?' said Eddie.

'Sorry,' said the spaceman. 'That one always comes out if I don't control myself. As does, "So die, puny Earthling," and, curiously, "I've done a wee-wee, please change my nappy." Although personally I believe that one was programmed into me by mistake. Probably Friday afternoon on the production line – you know what it's like.'

'I certainly do,' said Eddie, 'or would, if it weren't for the fact that I am an Anders Imperial, pieced together by none other than the kindly, lovable white-haired old Toymaker himself.'

'I come from a distant star,' said the spaceman.

'I thought you said production line.' Eddie Bear did paw-scratchings of the head.

'Perhaps on a distant star,' the spaceman suggested.

'Perhaps,' said Eddie, 'but then again—'

'Let's not think about it.' The spaceman took up his glass, put it to his face, but sadly found it empty. 'I was about to say, let's just drink,' he said, 'but I find to my utter despair that my glass is empty. Would you care to buy me a drink?'

'Not particularly,' said Eddie. 'But thanks for asking.'

'In return I will spare your planet.'

Eddie shrugged what shoulders he possessed. 'I would appear to be getting the better part of that particular deal,' he said. 'If I possessed the necessary funds I think I'd buy you a drink.'

'Perhaps you could ask the barman for credit?'

'Perhaps you could menace him with your death ray and get the drinks in all round.'

'Perhaps,' said the spaceman.

'Perhaps indeed,' said Eddie.

The spaceman sighed and so did Eddie.

'I wish I were a clockwork train,' said the spaceman.

'What?' Eddie said.

'Well,' said the spaceman, 'you know where you are when you're a train, don't you? It's a bit like being in a bar brawl.'

'No, it's not,' said Eddie.

'No, I suppose it's not. But you do know where you are. Which line you're on. Which station you'll be coming to next. It's not like that for we spacemen.'

'Really?' said Eddie, who was losing interest.

'Oh no,' said the spaceman, ruefully regarding his empty glass. 'Not a bit of it. We could be anywhere in the universe, lost in space, or on a five-year mission, or something. Drives you mad, it does, makes you want to scream. And in space no one can hear you scream, of course.'

'Tell me about the monkeys,' said Eddie, 'the clockwork cymbal-clapping monkeys. Tinto tells me that you know who blasted them.'

'I do,' said the spaceman.

'I'd really like to know,' said Eddie.

'And I'd really like to tell you,' said the spaceman, 'but my throat is so dry that I doubt whether I'd get halfway through the telling before I lost my voice.'

'Hm,' went Eddie.

'   ,' went the spaceman.

'Two more drinks over here,' called Eddie to Tinto.

'Dream on,' the barman replied.

'Two then for the spaceman and in return he promises not to reduce Toy City to arid ruination with his death ray.'

'Coming right up, then,' said Tinto.

'I need a gimmick like that,' said Eddie, but mostly to himself.

'Who did you say was paying for these?' asked Tinto as he delivered the spaceman's drinks to his table.

'You said they were on you,' said Eddie Bear, 'because it's the spaceman's birthday.'

'Typical of me,' said Tinto. 'Too generous for my own good. But you have to be cruel to be kind, I always say. Or something similar. It's all in this book I've been reading, although I seem to have lost it now. I think I lent it to someone.' Tinto placed two beers before Eddie and Eddie shook his head and thanked Tinto for them.

'So,' Eddie said, when Tinto had wheeled away and the spaceman had moistened his throat, 'the clockwork monkeys.'

'What a racket they make,' said spaceman. 'Or, rather, *made*. Tin on tin. If I had teeth, that noise would put them on edge. I don't approve of willy-nilly blasting with death rays, but I feel that in this case it was justified.'

'I suppose that's a matter of opinion,' said Eddie, tasting beer. 'I'm not so sure that the monkeys would agree with you.'

'Each to his own,' said the spaceman. 'It takes all sorts to make a Universe.'

'So it was *you* who blasted the monkeys?'

The spaceman shook his helmeted head. The visor of his weather dome snapped down and he snapped it up again. 'Not me *personally*,' said he. 'I come in peace for all mankind. Or in this case all toykind. It would be the vanguard of the alien strikeforce who did for those monkeys. And I know what I'm talking about when I tell you these things. Trust me, I'm a spaceman.'

Eddie sighed once more. He really couldn't be doing with sighing, really. Sighing was *not* Eddie's thing.

'Do you know where this vanguard of the alien strikeforce might be found at present?' Eddie asked.

The spaceman made a thoughtful face, although some of it was lost on Eddie, being hidden by the shadow of his visor.

'Was that a yes or a no?' Eddie asked.

'It was a thoughtful face,' the spaceman explained, 'but you couldn't see much of it because it was mostly lost in the shadow of my visor.'

'Well, that explains everything.'

'Does it?' asked the spaceman.

'No,' said Eddie, 'it doesn't. Do you know where they are, or do you not?'

'They could be anywhere.' The spaceman made expansive gestures. 'Out there, Beyond The Second Big O. The Universe is a very large place.'

Eddie sighed once more. Loudly.

'Or they could still be right here. They said they fancied going to a nightclub, to hear some jazz, I think.'

There was no jazz playing at Old King Cole's, only that terrible scream and that piercing white light. And then there was a silence and a stillness and even some darkness, too.

Jack, who was now on his knees holding Amelie to him and shielding them both as best he could, looked up.

A great many of the light bulbs in Old King Cole's had blown and the club was now lit mostly by tabletop candles. Which gave it a somewhat romantic ambience, although this was, for the present, lost upon Jack.

'What happened?' asked Amelie, gaining her feet and patting down her skirt. 'That screaming, that light – what happened?'

'Something bad,' said Jack. 'Be careful, now, there's broken glass all about.'

Amelie opened her handbag, pulled out certain girly things and took to fixing her hair and touching up her make-up.

'Nice,' said Jack, and then he peered all around. They appeared to be alone now, although Jack couldn't be altogether certain, what with the uncertain light and his lack of certainty and everything.

The stage was now in darkness; beyond the broken footlights lay a black, forbidding void.

'Dolly?' called Jack.

'Yes, darling,' said Amelie.

'No,' said Jack. 'Dolly Dumpling. Dolly, are you there?'

No voice returned to Jack. There was silence, there was blackness, there was nothing more.

'I don't like it here now,' said Amelie, tucking away her girly things and closing her handbag. 'In fact, I didn't like it here at all before, either. They were horrid, Jack. I'm glad you hit that horrid man.'

'I'm glad you hit his horrid partner,' said Jack. 'Perhaps they are still lying on the dancefloor.' Jack made tentative steps across broken glass, reached the dancefloor and squinted around in the ambient gloom. 'I think they upped and ran,' he said.

'Let's go too, then,' said Amelie. 'I know much nicer places than this. We could go to Springfellows, where all the clockworkers hang out. Or the Hippodrome, where all the hippos hang out. Or Barbie's, where dollies' bosoms often hang out.'

'No, not yet.' Jack was squinting hard now into the blackened void beyond the darkened footlights. 'Do you think you could bring me over one of those candles from the tables, maybe two?'

'Well, I could, but I don't really want to.'

'Please,' said Jack.

'Well, as you ask me so nicely. And as I love you so much.'

Jack did uneasy scuffings with his feet. Amelie crunched through broken glass and brought him a candelabra. Jack held it up before him.

'This *is* rather romantic,' said Amelie, as she nuzzled close to Jack. 'And there's no one here but us. We could—'

'We could *what*?' Jack asked.

'You know what.'

'What, here?'

'We could,' said Amelie. 'And I might let you do that thing that you've always been wanting to do, but I haven't let you do yet because you haven't told me you love me.'

'Ah,' said Jack. '*That* thing.'

Amelie blew Jack kisses.

'Tempting though that is,' said Jack, 'and believe me, it's *very* tempting, I don't think it would be a very good idea right at this moment.'

'Huh,' huffed Amelie. 'Perhaps you can't do it anyway.'

Jack put a finger to his lips. 'Just a moment,' he said, in the tone known as hushed. 'I think something very bad has happened here. I want to look on the stage.'

'Shall I wait here and take off all my clothes while you have a look?'

'Just wait here.' Jack kissed Amelie's upturned face. It was such a beautiful face. It was just like a re—

Amelie grasped Jack by the arm. 'Is there going to be danger?' she asked.

'I hope not,' said Jack.

'Shame,' said Amelie. 'I really love danger.'

'Just wait here. And if I shout "run", just run – will you do that for me?'

'I will, my love.'

Jack gave a sigh that would have done credit to Eddie[*] and haltingly approached the blacked-out stage. Certain sounds now came to Jack, but not from the stage before him. These sounds were of distant bells. The bells that topped police cars. These sounds were growing louder.

Jack climbed up onto the stage, holding the candelabra before him. Its wan light shone upon more broken glass and then upon the piano. And as Jack moved gingerly forward, more there was to be seen, and to this more that was to be seen Jack took no liking whatsoever.

Candlelight fell upon the face of the clockwork pianist. It was a face incapable of expression, and yet as Jack peered, he could see it, see it in the eyes, eyes now lifeless, eyes now dead – that look of absolute fear.

Jack held out the candelabra and moved forward once more.

The saxophonist lay on his side. The drummer did likewise. The pianist was flat on his back.

Jack knelt and touched the pianist's tin-plate chest. And watched in horror as it sank beneath his touch, dissolved and crumbled into dust.

Jack stood and Jack trembled. What had done this? He'd been aware of nothing but a blinding light. Seen no one. No *thing*.

Now trembling somewhat and wary that whoever or whatever had

[*] Even though sighing really wasn't Eddie's thing. As it were.

done this might not yet have departed the scene of the crime, Jack took a step or two further.

And then took no more and gasped.

By the light of the candelabra he saw her. Her head lolled at an unnatural angle, the neck with its many chins broken, the show clearly over. The fat lady would sing no more.

And . . .

'Hold it right there and put up your hands.'

Torchlights shone through the now not so ambiently candlelit Old King Cole's. Many torchlights held by many policemen. Laughing policemen, all of them, with names such as Chortle and Chuckles.

'Hands you, up villain,' came shouts, and Jack raised his hands.

And then they were on him and Jack went down beneath the force of truncheons.

'The force,' said the spaceman to Eddie, 'it's either with you, or it's not.'

'And it's with you, is it?' Eddie asked.

'Oh yes,' said the spaceman. 'I was thinking of going over to the Dark Side just for the thrill of it, you know. We all have a dark side, don't we?'

'Only if I sit down in a dirty puddle,' said Eddie. 'Whose round is it?'

'Yours,' said the spaceman. And he waggled his rubber hands at Eddie. 'It's your round, so go and get the drinks.'

'It's not my round,' said Eddie.

'Damn,' said the spaceman. 'That never works. I should have gone over to the Dark Side. They have better uniforms and everything.'

'Well,' said Eddie, 'I'd like to say that it's been fascinating talking to you.'

The spaceman raised a thumb.

'I'd *like* to,' said Eddie, 'but—'

'Eddie,' called Tinto, 'there's a telephone call for you.'

'A call for me?' called Eddie. 'I wonder who that might be?'

'Chief Inspector Bellis,' called Tinto in reply. 'Jack's just been . . . Now, what would that be?'

'I give up,' called Eddie. 'What would it be?'

'It's a five,' called Tinto. 'Like two is a double and three is a treble and four is a quadriplegic.'

'Four is quadruple,' called Eddie.

'Well, it's whatever five is,' called Tinto.

'Quintuple,' said Eddie.

'That's it,' called Tinto. 'He's just been arrested for quintuple murder.'

7

Night-time is the right time, when it comes to crime.

Obviously it's the right time for criminals, because they can skulk about in shadows and perform their heinous acts under the cover of darkness. But it is also the right time for policemen, because the flashing lights atop their squad cars look so much more impressive at night, and it is to be noticed that once they have reached a crime scene and blocked off the surrounding roads with that special tape that we'd all like to own a roll of,* they never switch off those flashing lights, even though they must be running the cars' batteries down, because those flashing lights just look *so good*. They give the crime scene that extra something. They are a must. They are.

'Switch off those damn lights,' shouted Chief Inspector Bellis, stepping from his special police car – the one with the double set of flashing lights and four big bells on the top – and striking the nearest laughing policeman about the helmet. 'They give me a headache.'

'Aw, Chief,' went several laughing ones, though these were out of striking distance.

'Just do it,' roared Bellis, 'and do it now.' And he crunched over broken glass and approached the ruination that had so recently been Old King Cole's.

Jack stood in the doorway, flanked by two burly constables. Jack was in handcuffs.

'And take *those* off!' bawled Bellis.

'Aw,' went one of the burly officers of the law. 'But Chief—'

'But me no buts. And where's that bear?'

---

* Well, just think of the fun you could have, sticking it over a friend's front door while they're out and seeing their expression when they come home.

Bellis had actually picked Eddie up from Tinto's. Which had come as quite a surprise to the bear. Eddie was now asleep in Bellis's car. The driver, a special constable with the name 'Yuk-Yuk' printed on his back, leaned over the back of his seat and poked the sleeper with the business end of his truncheon.

Eddie awoke in some confusion, tried to rise, but failed dismally. He had been sleeping on his left side, with the result that his left arm and leg were now drunk, whilst the rest of him was sober.

'Out!' urged the driver, prodding Eddie once more.

Eddie tumbled from the car, fought his way into the vertical plane and then shambled in a most curious manner towards the fractured front doors of Old King Cole's.

'Hurry up,' urged Bellis, 'or I will be forced to arrest you on trumped-up charges and bang you away for an indefinite period.'

'I'm doing my best,' Eddie said.

And, 'It wasn't me,' said Jack. 'Hi, Eddie.'

'Hello, Jack.' Eddie's left leg gave way beneath him and Eddie sank down on his bum.

'I'm not impressed,' said Bellis. 'Not impressed at all.'

'It wasn't me,' Jack said once more, 'in case you didn't hear me the first time.'

Bellis did glarings at Jack and then dragged Eddie to his feet. 'How many of you officers have been inside this building corrupting the crime scene?' he asked.

Numerous officers – all of the officers, in fact – made guilty faces. But one of them said, 'We *all* had to go in, Chief – this mass-murderer put up quite a struggle.'

'Oh no I didn't,' said Jack.

'Oh yes you did,' said officers all, laughing as they did so.

'Well, stay out now. Come on, you two.' Bellis dragged Eddie and prodded Jack.

'But sir,' said one of the burly policemen who had been guarding Jack, 'this meathead is a mad'n, sir. He'll do for you soon as give you a look.

'Stand aside, you gormster.'

*

Now, it had to be said that at least the policemen had set up some lights, and the interior of Old King Cole's was now well lit throughout.

And what with the devastation and the flashing of the police car warning lights, none of which had actually been switched off, it was a pretty impressive crime scene.

Eddie leaned his drunken parts against a fluted column and surveyed the wreckage. 'The last time I was here,' he said, 'was on the night I was elected mayor. Remember that, Jack? What a night that was, eh?'

'Silence,' said Bellis.

'Sorry,' said Eddie.

'I didn't do it,' said Jack.

'Shut up,' said Bellis, and Jack shut up.

Chief Inspector Wellington Bellis puffed up his chest and then blew out a mighty breath. 'Right,' said he, 'we are all alone now. Examine the crime scene. Do whatever it is that you do. Find me clues. Go on, now.'

'Then I'm not under arrest for quadruple murder?[*]' said Jack.

'Did you do it?' asked Bellis.

'No,' said Jack.

'Then get to work.'

'Oh,' said Jack. 'Eddie?'

Eddie shrugged. 'Let's go to work,' said he.

'Right,' said Jack, rubbing his palms together. 'Well, already I deduce—'

'Jack,' said Eddie.

'Eddie?' said Jack.

'Jack, *I* am the detective. You're my sidekick, remember?'

'I thought we were partners,' said Jack.

'Oh, we are,' Eddie said, 'and in partnership you do what you do best and I do what I do best.'

'So what do *I* do best?' Jack asked.

---

[*] Clearly Tinto's reference to quintuple murder at the end of the previous chapter must have something to do with his problem with numbers. Clearly!

'Well,' said Eddie, 'you might start by trying to find three unbroken glasses and an unbroken bottle of something nice.'

'I never drink on duty,' said Bellis.

'Naturally not,' said Eddie. 'The three glasses are for me – it's thirsty work, this detective game.'

Bellis made a certain face. Eddie got to work.

Jack sought bottle and glasses. Bellis watched Eddie work. He watched as the little bear climbed carefully onto the stage, dropped carefully to his belly and did peerings all about. Did risings up and chin-cuppings with paws. Did standings back with head cocked on one side. Did pickings up of somethings and sniffings of same. Did careful steppings amidst broken footlight glass. Did clamberings up onto Dolly Dumpling and peepings here and there.

Presently Bellis tired of all this.

'What do you think?' he called to Eddie. 'What do you think happened here?'

'Same as the monkeys,' said Eddie. 'Their inside workings are gone. Nothing left but shells.'

'And Dolly Dumpling?' Bellis asked.

'Neck broken,' said Eddie. 'One big twist. And that's one big neck to twist.'

'Come on,' said Bellis. 'I've freed your chum here. I picked you up in my car. I can put you in the frame for the cigar heist any time I wish. Give me something I can use. This is serious now.'

'Oh yes,' said Eddie. 'It's serious now that a meathead's been murdered. Was it not serious before then?'

'*I* put you on the case,' said Bellis. 'You know that *I* thought it was serious.'

'Quite so,' said Eddie. 'Well, I'll tell you what I have, although it isn't much and it doesn't make a lot of sense.'

Bellis said, 'Go on.' And Eddie did so.

'Firstly,' said Eddie, 'I have to ask Jack a question.'

Jack's head popped up from behind the bar counter where he had been searching for glasses.

'You were here when this happened?' Eddie asked.

Jack nodded.

'Then how come you didn't see it happen? I can tell by the way the broken footlight glass lies that the band members fell before the footlights blew. Surely everyone in this room saw the murders occur.'

Jack shook his head. 'There was a really bright light,' he said. 'It swallowed up the stage and Dolly screamed and her scream shattered all the glass.'

'Can you describe this bright light to me?'

'Yes,' said Jack. 'It was a light and it was bright.'

'Would you like me to strike him about the head a bit?' Bellis asked Eddie.

'That won't be necessary. I'll do it myself later.'

'Oi!' said Jack.

Eddie grinned and said, 'I'll tell you what this crime scene tells me. Someone or something appeared upon this stage. It didn't come up either of the side steps, nor did it come from backstage, nor did it spring up out of a trap door, because there is none. It simply *appeared*.'

'Things can't simply appear,' said Bellis. 'That defies all the rules of everything. Perhaps whatever it was came down from above.'

'It didn't,' said Eddie. 'It appeared, and with the aid of some kind of hideous weaponry it literally sucked out the inner workings of the band, their very substance.'

'But not those of Dolly Dumpling,' said Jack.

'It wasn't after her,' said Eddie, 'but she was close enough to see what happened, so she had to be silenced.'

'Things don't just appear out of nowhere,' said Bellis.

'This did,' said Eddie. 'I can see all the evidence. After the slaughter, when the lights were out, Jack came up onto this stage alone, holding a candelabra.'

'I did,' said Jack.

'And two burly constables came up afterwards, roughed Jack up a bit and pulled him from the stage.'

'They did,' said Jack.

'Sadly destroying vital evidence,' said Eddie.

Chief Inspector Wellington Bellis shook his head. 'This is madness,' he said.

'If you have a better explanation,' Eddie said.

'Any explanation would be better than yours, which is no explanation at all.'

'Something has come amongst us,' said Eddie, 'something evil, something different, the likes of which Toy City has never experienced before. Whatever did this is not of this world.'

'Right, that's it,' said Bellis. 'I'm just going to arrest the two of you and have done with it.'

'On what grounds?' Eddie protested. 'You know we're not responsible for any of this.'

'On the grounds,' said Bellis, 'that if this were to get out, we'd have panic in the city.'

'No one will hear it from me,' said Eddie.

'Nor me,' said Jack. 'Will they hear it from *you*, Chief Inspector?'

'No, they certainly *will not.*'

'Then let Jack and me go about our business,' Eddie said. 'I already have certain leads to follow up. I will keep you informed of our progress – discreetly of course.'

Chief Inspector Wellington Bellis looked perplexed. Indeed, he *was* perplexed.

Jack drove away in Bill Winkie's splendid automobile. Eddie sat in the back, next to Amelie.

'I suppose we won't be going on to that other club now,' she said.

'I'll drop you home,' said Jack. 'I'm sorry the evening didn't go better.'

'We can make up for *that*,' said Amelie.

Eddie wished that he possessed eyebrows, because if he had he could have raised one now.

'I'll see you tomorrow,' said Jack. 'Eddie and I have business to attend to.'

The sulky Amelie was dropped at her door, kissed by Jack and waved goodbye to. Jack and Eddie continued on their way.

'Fine-looking dolly,' said Eddie. 'Fine long legs and big—'

'Stop,' said Jack. 'And tell me.'

'Tell you what?'

'Whatever it was you were holding back from Bellis. You know more than you're telling.'

'Of course I do,' said Eddie, 'but I wanted to put the wind up Bellis.'

'You put the wind up me, too. Monsters from outer space, is that what you're saying?'

'Perhaps,' said Eddie. 'Perhaps.'

'So go on, tell me.'

'I don't know if I should.'

'We're partners, Eddie. You can trust me, you know you can.'

Eddie shrugged and sighed. 'I know,' he said, 'but this is bad and it really doesn't make sense.'

'Just tell me, Eddie, perhaps I can help.' Jack swerved violently around a corner, dislodging Eddie from his seat.

'Slow *down*!' cried Eddie. 'Slow *down*!'

Jack slowed down. 'Where are we going anyway?' he asked.

'Back to Tinto's,' said Eddie.

'Of course,' said Jack. 'Where else?'

Eddie sat and tried to fold his arms. As ever, he did so without success.

'Out with it,' said Jack.

'All right,' said Eddie. 'There *was* other evidence that I didn't mention to Bellis. I can tell you the height of the murderer. I can tell you his weight. I can tell you his race and his covering.'

'Go on then,' said Jack.

'My height,' said Eddie, 'my weight, my race and my plush covering.'

'A teddy?' said Jack. 'A teddy is the murderer?'

'Not just any teddy. An Anders Imperial.'

'Just like you.'

'Not just like me – more than that.'

'I don't understand,' said Jack, taking yet another corner without much slowing down.

'Paw prints,' said Eddie. 'Paw prints are as individual as a meathead's fingerprints. Even with mass-produced toys, they're all slightly different. They're all individual.'

'So you could identify the killer from those paw prints?'

'I already have,' said Eddie.

'So you know who the murderer is? Eddie, you are a genius.'

Eddie shook his head. Sadly so, as it happened. 'I know who the murderer is,' said he, 'but I also know that he can't be the murderer.'

'You're not making sense.'

'Jack,' said Eddie, 'I recognised your footprints on that stage.'

'It wasn't me,' said Jack, and he took another corner at speed, just for good measure.

'I know it wasn't *you*. But I could recognise your footprints anywhere, as well as I could recognise my own. And that's the problem.'

Jack shook his head. 'You're really making a meal of this,' said he. 'If you recognised the paw prints, *who* is the murderer?'

'I recognised the paw prints of the murderer,' said Eddie, 'because they are *my* paw prints. But I'm *not* the murderer!'

Presently, Jack screeched to a halt before Tinto's Bar and the two alighted from the car.

'I hope he's still here,' said Eddie.

'Tinto rarely recognises licensing hours,' said Jack.

'Not Tinto, the spaceman.'

'What spaceman? There's a spaceman in Tinto's Bar?'

'I spoke with him earlier. He told me that it was a member of the vanguard of the alien strikeforce who had blasted the monkeys.'

'Ah,' said Jack. 'You had been drinking at the time, hadn't you?'

'I'd had one or two,' said Eddie, 'but I know what he told me. And he told me that these aliens fancied a visit to a jazz club.'

'Old King Cole's,' said Jack.

'Precisely,' said Eddie.

'But an alien teddy bear, who is *your* doppelgänger?'

'Stranger things have happened,' said Eddie.

'Name one,' said Jack.

'Let's go in,' said Eddie.

Tinto's Bar was rather crowded now. In fact, it was rather crowded with a lot of swells that Jack recognised as former patrons of Old King Cole's.

Jack swore beneath his breath.

Eddie, whose hearing was acute, chuckled.

'We don't want their type in here,' said Jack.

'And *whose* type would that be?' Eddie asked.

'You know what I mean.' Jack elbowed his way towards the bar and Eddie followed on in Jack's wake.

Tinto was serving drinks every which way. Jack located an empty barstool and hoisted Eddie onto it. 'Drinks over here, Tinto,' he called.

'You'll have to wait your turn,' called Tinto. 'I have posh clientele to serve here.'

Jack ground his teeth.

Eddie said, 'The spaceman was over there in the far corner, Jack – can you see if he's still there?'

Jack did head-swerves and peepings. 'I can't see any spaceman,' he said. 'A couple of gollies playing dominoes, but no spaceman.'

'Tinto,' called Eddie to the barman, 'if you can tear yourself away from your new best friends . . .'

Tinto trundled up the bar. 'Did you hear what happened at Old King Cole's?' he asked.

'Yes,' said Eddie. 'But tell me this – where did the spaceman go?'

'Is that a trick question?' Tinto asked.

'No,' said Eddie.

'Shame,' said Tinto.

'So, *do* you know where the spaceman went?'

Tinto scratched at the top of his head. 'Space?' he suggested. 'Is that the right answer? Do I get a prize?'

'You do,' said Eddie. 'You win the chance to pour Jack and me fourteen beers.'

'Fourteen?' said Tinto, and he whistled. 'Was that the star prize?'

Tinto wheeled off to do the business.

Jack said, 'Eddie, did you *really* meet a real spaceman?'

'It all depends what you mean by "real".'

'No it doesn't,' said Jack, elbowing a swell who really didn't need elbowing.

'He was a clockwork spaceman,' said Eddie. 'But who is to say whether all spacemen are clockwork?'

'He was a *toy* spaceman?'

'And who is to say that *all* spacemen aren't toy spacemen?'

'I'd be prepared to say it, but as I don't believe in spacemen, it hardly matters whether I say it or not.'

'So you don't believe in the concept that there might be other worlds like ours out there somewhere and that there might be life on them?'

Jack shrugged. 'Back in the town where I was brought up, there was a lot of talk about that sort of thing. Alien abductions, they were called. People would be driving their cars at night, down some deserted country road, then there'd be a really bright light and then they'd be driving their cars again, but a couple of hours would have passed and they'd have no memory of what had happened. Then this fellow started hypnotising these people and all sorts of strange stories came out about what had happened during the missing hours. That they'd been taken up into space by space aliens and experimented upon, had things poked up their bums.'

'Up their bums?'

'Apparently the space aliens do a lot of that kind of thing.'

'Why?' Eddie asked.

'I don't know,' said Jack. 'Perhaps they have a really weird sense of humour, or they are a bit pervy – who can tell with spacemen?'

'And these people were telling the truth?'

Jack shrugged. 'Who can say? In my humble opinion they were all mentals.'

'So you're not a believer?'

'No,' said Jack, 'I'm not. I know what I believe in and I know what I don't. And I don't believe in spacemen.'

'I seem to recall,' said Eddie, 'when I first met you on the first night that you arrived in Toy City, that you didn't believe toys could walk and talk and think and live.'

'I still find *that* hard to believe,' said Jack.

Eddie made exasperated noises. Tinto arrived with the drinks on a tray. There were many drinks. Many more than fourteen.

'We're three drinks short here,' said Jack.

Tinto trundled away to make up the shortfall.

Eddie chuckled once more. 'You fit in quite nicely here now though, don't you, Jack?' he said.

'I still find it hard to believe. But I know it's true.'

'Then maybe we'll have you believing in spacemen before it's too late.'

'Too late?' said Jack. 'Too late for what?'

'Too late to stop them,' said Eddie. 'Too late for us all.'

'You're serious about this, aren't you?'

'As I said to Bellis, "If you have a better explanation."'

Jack tucked into his share of the beers. 'Spacemen,' he said and he shook his head.

'There's no telling what's out there,' said Eddie, 'Beyond The Second Big O.'

'I've heard that expression used before,' said Jack. 'What exactly does it mean?'

Eddie shrugged. 'It's just an expression, I suppose. I don't know where I heard it first. It means beyond, beyond what we know, someplace other that's different. Really different.'

'But why The Second Big O? Why not The First Big O? Why an O at all?'

'I don't know,' said Eddie, tasting beer. 'I know most things, but I don't know *that*.'

'Perhaps the Toymaker would know.'

'Perhaps, but I have no inclination to ask him.' Eddie regarded his paws. 'Taking my hands away. That was really mean.'

'They were rather creepy,' said Jack.

'They were *not* creepy! They were wonderful, Jack. I loved those hands.'

'Perhaps if you save Toy City from the alien invasion he'll fit you with another pair.'

'Do you really think so?'

'Anything's possible.'

'You believe that, do you?'

'Absolutely,' said Jack, raising his glass to Eddie.

'Then let's drink to the fact that anything's possible,' said Eddie, raising his glass between his paws. 'Let's have a toast to that anything.'

'Let's have,' said Jack, raising his glass, too.

'To spacemen,' said Eddie. 'As possible as.'

'Did I hear someone say "spacemen"?' said Tinto.

'Jack's a big believer,' said Eddie.

'There was one in here earlier,' said Tinto.

'Really?' said Eddie. 'How interesting.'

'Well, he wasn't *that* interesting. He spent most of his time cadging drinks. But he did leave something for you.'

Eddie shook his head sadly. 'You didn't think to mention this before?' he said. 'It might be important.'

'You said it was,' said Tinto.

'I just said it might be,' said Eddie.

'No,' said Tinto, 'you said it might be important. And then you said it was and then you left with it.'

'Curiously,' said Eddie, 'you aren't making any sense at all.'

'When I gave it to you,' said Tinto, 'you thanked me for it and you tipped me for giving it to you.'

Eddie shook his head once more. 'And when did I do this?' he said.

'A few minutes ago, when you came in here before.'

'What?' said Eddie.

And Jack looked at Eddie. 'A few minutes ago?' said Jack, now looking at Tinto.

'Yes,' said Tinto, now looking at Eddie. 'You took the message he left for you, then you left. Then you came back in again, and here you are.'

'Message?' said Jack. 'The spaceman gave Eddie a message?'

'No, he left it with me and *I* gave it to Eddie. Do try to pay attention.'

'What did this message say?' Eddie asked.

'Well, you read it,' said Tinto. 'You must know what it said.'

'*I* did *not* read it,' said Eddie, 'because *I* was *not* in here a few minutes ago.'

'It *was* you,' said Tinto. 'I'd know a scruffbag like you anywhere.'

'Tinto,' said Jack, 'Tinto, this is *very* important. What did this message say?'

Tinto fluttered his fingers about. 'As if I would look at the contents of a secret message,' he said.

'*Secret* message?' said Eddie.

'That's what it said,' said Tinto. 'Top-secret message for your mismatched eyes only.'

'What did it say?' asked Jack.

'I have customers to serve,' said Tinto. 'Posh customers. I have no time to shilly-shally with hobbledehoys like you.'

'What did it say, Tinto? This is *very*, *very* important.'

'It didn't say much,' said Tinto. 'Just the location, that's all.'

Eddie threw up his paws and shouted, 'What location, Tinto?'

'No need to shout,' said the barman. 'Just the location of where the spaceship had landed, that's all.'

8

'Toy Town?' said Jack as he drove along with Eddie at his side.

Eddie cowered in the passenger seat. 'Please slow down,' he said.

Jack slowed down, but said, 'Toy Town,' once more. 'The supposed location of the supposedly landed spaceship. Supposedly. But I thought that Toy City *is* Toy Town, just grown bigger.'

'What a lovely way you have with words,' Eddie said. 'Toy City *is* Toy Town grown bigger. But not quite in the same location. From what I've heard of the original Toy Town, it was an idyllic, paradisical sort of place, nestling against a sunny hillside – always sunny, of course, I don't think it ever rained there.'

'I'm sure it must have,' said Jack, taking another corner in a dangerous fashion and sending Eddie sprawling.

'Seat belts,' Eddie said as he climbed once more onto his seat and glared a glare at Jack.

'What would those be?' Jack asked.

'Something I've just invented, for strapping yourself into your seat in a car.'

'Sounds dangerous,' said Jack. 'You might get trapped or something, say if the car were to go over a cliff and into a river, or something. Am I going the right way? And tell me more about Toy Town.'

'It's a bit of a way yet, and you are going the right way and the car will need a few more windings-up before we get there. But, as I say, it was the original town built for toys and P.P.P.s, from the original kit, if you believe what the followers of the Big Box Fella, He Come, Jack-in-the-box cult do. Toys lived there in harmony and happiness. Then there were more toys and suburbs were built and then places for the toys to work in were built beyond these, and then homes for the rich who made money out of these enterprises beyond this. And so on and so forth and eventually up grew Toy City, of evil reputation. Folk sort of moved away from Toy Town – it fell out of favour, reminded them of their humble beginnings. The desire for progress and evolution forced them out of their simple paradise to search for a more sophisticated lifestyle, so they came to live and work in Toy City.'

'I don't quite follow the logic of all that.' Jack drummed his fingers on the steering wheel. 'But it's still there, is it? The original Toy Town? Who lives there now?'

'I think it's a bit of a ghost town now.' And Eddie shivered. 'You hear stories about odd folk who live there. Outcasts. I thought of going there myself after I lost my job as mayor. They make movies there, I believe.'

'Movies?' said Jack, and he grinned towards Eddie. 'I've always wanted to be in a movie.'

'Since when?' Eddie raised an imaginary eyebrow. 'This is the first I've heard of such a thing.'

'You mean you've never wanted to be in a movie?'

'Have you ever seen a Toy City movie, Jack?'

Jack shook his head. 'I haven't,' he said, 'but I'll bet they're much the same as the movies I watched in the town where I grew up. Action and adventure.'

Eddie laughed. Loudly. 'Action and Adventure?' he managed to say. 'Not a bit of it – they are as dull as. Biopics, they're called. Always about prominent P.P.P.s, with constant remakes. If I watch that Jack and Jill go up that damned hill one more time, I'll puke.'

'He does fall down and break his crown – that must be quite exciting.'

Eddie sighed and he was so sick of sighing. 'Trust me, Jack,' he said, 'they're dull. Dull, dull, dull.'

'So why does anyone go to see them?'

'It's complicated,' said Eddie. 'I'll explain it to you sometime, but not now. And see, just up ahead, where the street lamps end – we're almost there.'

The street lamps ended at the top of a hill. Jack drew the car to a rather unnecessarily sharp halt and he and Eddie climbed from it.

Jack peered out and down at a moonlit landscape. 'Oh,' was all he could find to say for the moment.

Jack stood beside Eddie, who peered in a likewise fashion, and a little shiver came to Eddie, which wasn't caused by the chill of the night.

There was something about Toy Town that haunted Eddie. It haunted all toys in Toy City to a greater or lesser extent. Toy Town represented something, something that had been but no longer was: paradise, before the fall. In truth, few toy folk ever ventured there. Toy Town was almost a sacred place. A place perhaps for pilgrimage, but somehow, too, for reasons that, like going to see P.P.P. biopics, were too complicated to explain, a place to be feared. An *other* place. A place not spoken of.

It *was* complicated.

'Looks pretty dilapidated,' said Jack, 'but in a romantic kind of a way. The way that ancient ruins sometimes do.'

'Hm,' said Eddie, and he shivered a little bit more.

'What's that up there?' asked Jack, and he pointed.

'Ah,' said Eddie. 'The sign.'

The sign rose above the hilltop. Great white letters, standing crookedly. Great white letters spelling out 'TO TO LA.'

' "To to la"?' said Jack. 'What does that mean?'

'It originally spelled "TOYTOWNLAND",' said Eddie. 'That was the name of the original development. Seems as if some of the letters have fallen down. It's a very long time since I've been here. And I think I've now been here long enough again. Let's come back in the morning, Jack. Or perhaps you might come back on your own.'

'*On my own?*' Jack looked at Eddie. 'What's the problem?' he asked. 'Eddie, are you scared of something?'

'Me?' said Eddie, straightening what shoulders he had. 'I'm not scared of anything. We bears are brave, you should know that. We're as bold as.'

'Right,' said Jack. 'But you do seem to be trembling somewhat.'

'It's cold,' said Eddie.

Jack, having eyebrows, raised them.

'Yeah, well,' said Eddie, 'there's something about this place. Something I'm not comfortable with.'

'Well, I'm not altogether comfortable myself. I'm not too keen on getting blasted by a space alien death ray, you know.'

'I thought you didn't believe in the concept of space aliens.'

'I don't,' said Jack, 'but something zapped the monkeys and the clockwork musicians. And whatever it is, I don't want it to zap me as well. Nor you, as it happens.'

'We shall proceed with caution, then. I'll lead the way, you go first.'

Jack said, 'Eh?' But Jack led the way. 'Where am I leading this way to?' he whispered to Eddie as he led it. Down and down a hillside, through gorse and briars and unromantic stuff like that.

Eddie battered his way through nettles. 'Keep a low profile,' he counselled. 'And keep an eye out for anything that looks like a landed spaceship.'

'As opposed to something that actually *is* a landed spaceship?'

'You know exactly what I mean.'

Jack, keeping the lowest of low profiles despite the heightness of his height, did furtive glancings all around and continued in the downwards direction. At length, and one too long for Jack, who was now somewhat briar-scratched about in the trenchcoat regions, and who now had Eddie riding upon his shoulders due to Eddie being briar-scratched about in more personal regions, the intrepid detectives reached a bit of a road, a bit of which led into the romantic ruination of Toy Town.

'They're pretty little houses,' Jack whispered, 'but they've got holes in their roofs and everything. Do you really think anyone lives here any more?'

'We bears have almost mystical senses,' Eddie whispered back. 'We can sense things. And I sense that we are being watched.'

'By spacemen, do you think?'

'There's a tone in your voice,' said Eddie. 'Put me down, please.'

And Jack put Eddie down.

Jack said, 'I don't see any landed spaceships. But then perhaps landed spaceships have some kind of advanced camouflage and can look like ruined houses. In which case, I can see lots of spaceships. Which one do—'

'Stop it,' said Eddie. 'We *are* being watched. And I don't like it here.'

'I'll protect you,' said Jack. 'I have my gun.' Jack patted his pockets. 'Oh no,' he said. 'I don't have my gun – one of the laughing policemen confiscated it.'

'We're doomed,' said Eddie. 'Do you still have your watch?'

'I do,' said Jack, holding his wrist up to the moonlight. 'It's nearly two-thirty. Time travels fast when you're having a good time, doesn't it?'

'Turn it in,' said Eddie. 'You're as scared of this place as I am.'

'I'm afraid of no man,' said Jack.

'There's something out there,' said Eddie. 'And it ain't no man.'

Which rang a distant bell, somewhere.*

'Which way do you want to go?' asked Jack.

'Home,' said Eddie.

'That's not what I meant, and you know it.'

'It's what I mean,' said Eddie. 'I used to live here. I'd like to see my old home.'

'Oh,' said Jack. 'Right. Lead on, then.'

And Eddie led the way.

He led the way to Toy Town Square. There were ruined shops all around and about: a butcher's, a baker's, a candlestick maker's, a cheese shop and a dolls' hospital.

Jack peered through the grime-stained window of a tailor's. 'This really is a proper ghost town,' he said. 'There's still a display in this window and suits of clothing hanging up.' Jack moved on through the square. 'Same in the cheese shop,' he said. 'It's full of old cheese. How come when the traders moved away they left their stock behind?'

'They moved away fast,' said Eddie. 'In a single day. All at once.'

'But I thought you said—'

---

* Yes, of course you know where!

99

'I know what I said. I didn't say how fast they all moved to Toy City.'

'What happened here, Eddie? Something bad, was it?'

'I don't want to talk about it now.'

Jack shook his head. 'Are we still being watched? What do your special senses tell you?'

Eddie nodded. 'We're still being watched. Come on, this way.'

And so they moved on, across the moonlit square, into a side alley that wasn't really lit very well at all, into worrying darkness, then out into some small light.

'Ah,' said Jack. 'I see.'

Before them stood a little house. A pretty little house. It was a man-sized pretty little house. A flaky painted sign upon the aged front door spelled out the name 'WINKIE' in archaic lettering.

'Bill Winkie's house,' said Jack. 'The house of Wee Willy Winkie. And you were his bear.'

'I was Bill's bear,' said Eddie. And he produced a key from his trenchcoat pocket. 'Would you care to let us in, Jack?'

Jack took the key from Eddie. 'You have the key with you,' he said, 'but you didn't know we were coming here. I mean—'

'I've always carried it, one way or another, and the another way wasn't very comfortable,' Eddie said. 'I carry it as a kind of good-luck charm, or something.'

'Oh.' Jack said no more, but tried the key in the lock. After some struggling, he turned it. 'Are you sure about this?' he asked Eddie. 'Sure that you want to go in? It might be painful for you. I know how much you loved Bill.'

'It will be painful,' said Eddie, 'but I have to. There's something I have to know.'

'All right.' Jack drew the key from the lock, returned it to Eddie, then pressed his hands to the door, which opened, silently.

'There should be a candle box on the wall to your left,' said Eddie. Jack felt around to his left, found the candle box, located candles within it and a tinderbox, fumbled about with the tinderbox, drew sparks, then fire from it, lit a candle. Jack held up this candle.

'What do you see?' Eddie asked.

'Just a room,' said Jack. 'Quite tastefully furnished. Are you coming in, then?'

Eddie followed Jack.

Jack spied candles set in wall sconces, others upon a table. Jack lit these candles with his. Soft light filled the room.

Eddie gazed around and about it. 'Just as I feared,' he said.

'Feared?' Jack asked. 'What did you fear?'

'The hinges on the front door have been oiled and there's no dust,' said Eddie. Look at the tables and the chairs and the floor – no dust. Someone's living here.'

'Upstairs, do you think? Asleep?'

'Possibly. Jack, give me a hand, if you will.'

'What's this, then?'

Eddie was tugging at a rug. 'Help me with this.'

Jack did tuggings, too. They tugged the rug aside.

'Ring in the floorboards,' said Eddie. 'Secret compartment. Lift the trap door, Jack.'

'Oh,' said Jack. 'Exciting. What's down there?'

'You'll see.'

Jack pulled upon the ring and the trap door lifted. He held up his candle. 'Golly,' he said.

'Golly? Where?'

'Term of surprise,' said Jack, 'not golly as in golliwog.' And then Jack did awed whistlings. 'This is what you'd call an arms cache,' said he, once done with these whistlings.

'Well, Bill *was* a private eye.'

'And part-time arms dealer?' Jack beheld the stash that lay beneath, steely parts glinting in the candlelight. There were many guns there, big, impressive guns, toy guns all, although toy guns got the business done in these parts.

'Just haul up some weaponry.'

'Okey-dokey,' said Jack, 'will do.' And he lowered himself into the secret hideaway beneath and handed weapons up to Eddie. And as he did so, Jack did thinkings. What exactly was all this about? went one of these thinkings. What exactly happened here in Toy Town that drove its population away at the hurry-up, without their possessions?

Why would Bill Winkie really have needed so much high-powered weaponry? And there would have been more thinkings along these lines had not Eddie hurried Jack up and broken the chain of these thinkings.

'It's too much to carry anyway,' said Jack.

'And those grenades,' said Eddie.

'This is ridiculous,' said Jack.

'You'll thank me for it later.'

'What was *that*?'

'What?' said Eddie.

'I thought you bears had special senses,' whispered Jack. 'I heard something.'

'Come on, then, hurry up – gather up guns and let's be off.'

The sound of voices now came to the ears of both Eddie and Jack.

'On second thoughts,' whispered Eddie, now tossing weaponry back down to Jack, 'it might be more propitious for us to hide.'

'But we're all tooled-up.'

'These guns are *very* old.'

'Sling the rest of them down here and follow on, then.'

Eddie did so. Jack climbed from the secret hideaway, extinguished candles, did complicated in-the-dark back-tuggings of the rug and lowerings of the trap door over him and Eddie.

Voices, slightly muffled now but growing louder nonetheless, were to be heard above.

'And *I* say that I locked the door behind us,' said one voice.

'And *I* say that you forgot,' said another. 'And as I'm in charge, that's final.'

'Oh yes, so who put you in charge?'

'You know perfectly well. This operation has to be carried out with military precision. I'm in charge, you are merely my comedy sidekick.'

'I'm *not* a comedy sidekick, I'm a professional.'

'Light the candles, then.'

There came now the sound of a slight scuffle, followed by a heavy thump. Right on top of the trap door.

Eddie flinched, as did Jack, though neither saw the other do it.

'Good comedy falling,' said one of the voices. 'See, you excel at that kind of thing. Stick to what you know. I'll be in charge, you do the comedy falling about.'

'I didn't do it on purpose. Someone scuffed up this rug. Someone's been here.'

'Well, they're not here now.'

'They might be upstairs, asleep.'

'There's no one here. Just you and me and our little cargo, of course. You didn't damage the cargo with your comedy falling, did you?'

'Of course I didn't. I'll put it here on the table – do you want to see it?'

'Best see it, I suppose. Not that I really want to.'

'No, nor me – they give me the creeps, they way they move about in their little jars. They're really horrid.'

Eddie looked at Jack in the darkness beneath.

Jack looked at a spider. He thought he was looking at Eddie.

'One little peep, then,' said one of the voices above.

'One is quite enough. I'll be glad when this job is done. If it ever is done. I can see this job going on for ever. Or at least until everyone in Toy City is jarred-up. They are valuable commodities back home. The boss will have us jar-up the entire city, you see if I'm wrong.'

'It's not right, you know.'

'Right doesn't enter into it. It's business, pure and simple. Gather them up, take them back, that's what we're paid for.'

'But they're living beings.'

'They're toys.'

'Yes, but *living* toys.'

'Well, of course they are. There wouldn't be much point in going to all this trouble if they weren't living, would there?'

'But it's murder when it comes right down to it.'

'Murder of *toys*?'

'Oh, look at that one in the jar at the end. It's really agitated.'

'The bandleader. He's frisky all right, just like those monkeys. Shut the case up, I don't like looking at them.'

Eddie and Jack heard muffled clickings.

Then they heard a voice say, 'Get your stuff from upstairs and we'll be off. We have to deliver tonight's cargo by dawn.'

And then they heard departing footsteps.

Then returning footsteps.

Then departing footsteps again and the slamming of the front door.

'Do you think they're gone?' Jack whispered.

'Hold on a bit longer,' said Eddie. 'Just to be sure.'

Time passed.

'They've gone,' whispered Eddie.

Jack pushed up the trap door, rug and all, emerged from the hideaway, blundered around in the darkness and eventually brought light once more to the late Bill Winkie's parlour.

'Well, what do you make of all *that*?' Jack asked.

'Nothing good,' said Eddie.

'Shouldn't we be following them?' Jack asked.

'No,' said Eddie, 'we shouldn't.'

'Why not?'

'Because we're not ready to deal with this yet, Jack. We don't know what's going on – we have to know more.'

'Then we should follow them now.'

'They said they were delivering tonight's cargo. They'll be coming back tomorrow, I would guess. Let's make certain we're ready and waiting for them then.'

'Sound enough,' said Jack. 'But what were they talking about? What did they have in their jars?'

'Souls, perhaps,' said Eddie. 'The souls of the clockwork band.'

'Their souls, Eddie? What are you saying?'

'You heard what I heard, Jack. Draw your own conclusions.'

'I heard what you heard, Eddie, but did you hear *what* I heard? *What* we heard?'

'I don't know what you mean,' said Eddie.

'Oh, I think you do. The voices, Eddie. You heard the voices.'

'Of course I heard them. Now stop talking, let me think.'

'No,' said Jack. 'You heard them as I did. You heard those voices.'

'I heard them,' said Eddie. 'Now stop.'

'Not until you've said it.'

'Said what?'

'You know exactly what. Now say it.'

'I don't know what you're talking about.'

'Yes you *do*, Eddie. Say it.'

'All right!' Eddie glared at Jack. 'I know what you want me to say that I heard. And all right, I *did* hear it, same as you heard it. Their voices. All right, I heard them.'

'Say it,' said Jack.

'They were *our* voices,' said Eddie. 'Yours and mine. Our voices. All right, I've said it – are you happy?'

'No,' said Jack. 'I am *not*. They *were* our voices. What does this mean?'

'It means,' said Eddie, 'that not only is there a doppelgänger of me doing these murders, but there's one of you, too.'

Jack did shudderings. 'I was really hoping that you might have been able to come up with a comfier explanation than that,' he said.

'Comfier?' said Eddie.

'This is really scary stuff,' said Jack. 'Doppelgängers of you and me? I don't know about the soul-stealing business, but murdering doppelgängers is scary enough for me. Were they space aliens, do you suppose?'

Eddie shrugged as best as he was able. 'I suppose so,' he said.

'But space aliens don't go stealing souls,' said Jack.

'Oh, you know all about the habits of space aliens now, do you?'

'I know what I know,' said Jack. 'There's a blinding light and the space aliens abduct you, stick instruments up your bottom and then return you hours later with your memories erased. That's what space aliens do.'

'You do talk twaddle, Jack.'

'Listen,' said Jack, 'that's what space aliens do, if there are space aliens. But as I don't believe in space aliens, I don't care whether you believe me or not.'

Eddie was now thumping his head with his paws.

'I hate it when you do that,' said Jack.

'It helps to jiggle my brainy bits about,' said Eddie. 'Aids cogitation. We have all the clues, Jack, I'm sure we do. We can figure this thing out. *I* can figure this thing out.'

'Let's tell Bellis what we heard here,' said Jack. 'Let him and his laughing policemen lay in wait for these—'

'Doppelgängers of us?' said Eddie.

'Whatever they are.'

Eddie gave his head some further thumpings. 'Something is coming,' he said.

'An idea?' asked Jack. 'An answer? What?'

'Something,' said Eddie. 'Something.'

'Something,' said Jack. And then he said, 'Eddie?'

'What, Jack, what?'

'Eddie, something.'

And then something came upon them. It came upon them in a blinding light, which rushed at them through the windows and up through the cracks between the floorboards and around the trap door and in through the keyhole and down the chimney and even up the plughole in the sink in the kitchen. And this light was white and this light was pure and this light was fearsome.

And Eddie clung to the legs of Jack and Jack held Eddie's head in one hand and shielded his eyes with the other. And Eddie screamed. And Jack screamed. They screamed together. Together as one. And the bright white light engulfed them, surrounded them and swallowed them up.

And was gone.

'Careful,' said Eddie. 'Look where you're driving.'

Jack swung the wheel; the car all but struck a fence. Nearly went over a cliff and into a river. Jack jammed his foot upon the brake.

'That was close,' he said.

'You dozed off,' said Eddie. 'Fell asleep at the wheel.'

'I'm sorry,' said Jack. 'It's been a long night. I'm tired.'

'You were asleep.'

'I'm sorry, I said. Where are we?'

'Nearly home, I think.'

'Nearly home?'

'Nearly home.'

'But—' said Jack.

'But what?'

'But we weren't driving home. We were—'

'We were what?'

'We were somewhere, weren't we?'

'We were at Tinto's Bar and now we're driving home.'

'No,' said Jack. 'We were somewhere else after Tinto's Bar – we went somewhere else.'

'No we didn't,' said Eddie. 'We had a beer, several, in fact. Many, in fact.'

'I didn't,' said Jack. 'I'm confused.'

'See, you did have beers.'

'Did you have beer?'

'Do my kind defecate in the woodland regions?'

'Then you're drunk.'

Eddie felt at his legs. 'I'm not,' said he. 'My legs are not.'

'Something happened, Eddie, something weird.'

'Jack, you're not making sense.'

'There was a light,' said Jack. 'A very bright light.'

'You *are* drunk.'

'I'm not,' said Jack. He looked at his watch. 'Five a.m. in the morning,' he said. 'The sun's coming up.'

'Five in the morning?' said Eddie. 'That's odd. I thought it was about two.'

'There was a bright light,' said Jack. 'I remember a light. And there's something more.'

'Something more?'

'My bottom's sore,' said Jack.

'Oh,' said Eddie. 'That's funny.'

'It's not,' said Jack. 'It hurts.'

'No, I didn't mean that it's funny like that. I mean it's funny because my bum is sore, too.'

Jack looked at Eddie.

And Eddie looked at Jack.

'Aaaaaaagh!' they both agreed.

9

'No,' said Eddie. 'No, no, no.'

'Yes,' said Jack. 'I think so, yes.'

It was nine of the morning clock now and they hadn't slept, or at least they thought they hadn't slept. They were back in Bill Winkie's office. Eddie sat on Bill Winkie's desk in a bowl of iced water. Jack sat in Bill's chair upon several cushions.

And, 'No,' said Eddie once again. 'It can't have happened, no.'

'I don't get you at all,' said Jack, rootling around in desk drawers in search of a bottle of something. 'You were the one saying that it was space aliens and now we've been abducted by space aliens and returned with our memories erased and you're saying no, it can't have happened. Why are you saying this, Eddie?'

'Because,' said Eddie, shifting uncomfortably upon his sore bottom. 'Just because, that's all.'

'Just because they're *my* kind of space aliens.' Jack shifted uncomfortably in Bill's chair. 'That's it, isn't it? You wanted clockwork space aliens with tin-plate ray guns and now you're jealous—'

'Jealous?' said Eddie.

'No,' said Jack, 'jealous is not the word I mean. You're miffed.'

'That's nothing like jealous at all.'

'But you are miffed, because it was *my* space aliens. Because I was right and you were wrong.'

'Then pat yourself on the back for being right.' Eddie made a huffy face. 'But pat yourself on the shoulders to avoid your punctured bum.'

'Stop. Don't even think about that. What do you think they did to us?'

'If I don't even think about it, then I don't know.'

'We were abducted.' Jack now made a different face from the one he had previously been making, the one that would have turned the milk sour if there'd been any milk around, but there wasn't any, because he and Eddie hadn't got around to buying any, as they spent most of what money they had upon alcohol. The different face that Jack made was of that variety that one sees in those big paintings of the saints whilst they are being horribly martyred in some unspeakable fashion (which often tends to involve certain pointy things being thrust up certain tender places). It is the face of the beatified. There's no mistaking it.

'What does *that* face mean?' asked Eddie.

'It means that we have become two amongst the chosen.' Jack linked his fingers, as in prayer. 'It means we're special, Eddie.'

'I was special anyway.' Eddie splashed iced water about himself. 'I have a special tag in my ear to prove it and everything.'

'We were taken up,' said Jack, in the voice of one evangelising. 'We were taken up into the light.'

'By sexual perverts,' said Eddie. 'Don't forget that part.'

'They might have implanted us,' said Jack, in no less evangelising a tone. Well, perhaps just a little less. Perhaps with a hint of a tone of troubledness to it.

'You mean they've made us pregnant?' Eddie all but fell out of his bowl.

'No,' said Jack. 'They stick implants up your nose.'

'Up your bum, up your nose? What is the matter with these people?'

'We can't be expected to understand them,' said Jack. 'Their thinking patterns are totally different from ours. It would be like you trying to communicate with a beetle.'

'Some of my best friends are beetles,' said Eddie. 'But this doesn't make any sense, the way you're talking. I seem to recall that you *do not believe in space aliens.*'

'I've been converted,' said Jack. 'I've seen the light.'

'Just like that? There could be all manner of other explanations. You shouldn't go jumping to conclusions.'

'The bright light. The missing time. The erased memories. The . . .'

Jack indicated the area of his anatomy that rested gingerly upon the cushions. 'It all fits together. There's no point in denying it.'

'All right,' said Eddie. 'All right. Something happened to us. Something worrying.'

'We were taken up into the light.'

'Stop saying that or I'll bite you somewhere that will take your mind off your sore bottom. Although not by many inches.'

Jack crossed his legs, said, 'Ouch,' and uncrossed them again.

'Something happened to us,' Eddie continued. 'I don't know what and you don't know what, either. Somehow we will have to find out what. It all has to be part of the case. A big part. Think hard, Jack. Do you remember anything at all?'

'Leaving Tinto's,' said Jack. 'Driving. Then a really bright light, then waking up in the car, which was nearly going over a cliff and into a river.'

'And nothing else?'

'Nothing.'

Eddie dusted at his trenchcoat; its hem was sodden in the water bowl. 'We went somewhere after we left Tinto's. Hold out your hands, Jack.'

Jack gave a doubtful look. 'Why?' he asked. 'You're not going to bite me, are you?'

'I just want to look at your hands. Stick 'em out.'

Jack stuck 'em out.

Eddie examined Jack's hands. 'Interesting,' he said. 'Turn them over.'

Jack turned them over.

'*Very* interesting,' said Eddie. 'Now stand up, turn slowly around and show me the soles of your shoes.'

'Are you having a laugh, Eddie?'

'Please just humour me.'

Jack rose carefully, pushed back the chair carefully, did a slow twirl, with equal care, then lifted one foot and then the other towards Eddie. With insufficient care, Jack fell down in a heap.

'Always the comedy sidekick,' said Eddie. 'What would I do without you?'

'I'm not a comedy sidekick,' said Jack, rising *very* carefully and lowering himself with considerable care back onto the cushions.

'Well, you had an interesting night out,' said Eddie, 'by the evidence upon your person.'

'Did I?' said Jack. 'Go on.'

'You took a walk in the countryside,' said Eddie, 'through gorse and briar, then along a yellow-bricked road. You lit a candle from a tinderbox and you handled several antique weapons.'

'I did all *that*? How can you tell?'

'I could leave you in awe of my special senses,' said Eddie, splashing water at Jack, 'but the evidence is all over you, on your coat, the soles of your shoes, your fingers and fingernails. And lean over here a little.'

Jack did so and Eddie sniffed at him.

'What?' said Jack.

'You need a shower,' said Eddie. 'Your personal hygiene is a disgrace. Typical of teenage boys, that is.'

'Thanks a lot,' said Jack.

'Only kidding. There's a smell about you, Jack.' Eddie sniffed at himself. 'And about me also. A different smell. One I've never smelled before.'

'The smell of space aliens?' Jack took to sniffing himself.

'Very probably so. We have to find out what happened to us.'

'I could hypnotise you,' said Jack. 'Hypnotic regression, it's called. Take you back to the moment when we saw the bright light. That's how it's done.'

'Jack,' said Eddie, 'do you *really* know how to hypnotise someone?'

'I do in theory.'

'But you've never actually done it.'

'I've never had sex with a chicken, but I know how to do it, in theory.'

Eddie looked very hard at Jack.

'Sorry,' said Jack. 'I don't know why I said that. But you know what I mean.'

'I certainly do *not*.'

'No. But you know what I mean.'

'Forget it,' said Eddie. 'Teddies cannot be hypnotised.'

'You don't know that. Don't knock it 'til you've tried it, I always say.'

'And thus the chickens walk in fear.'

'What did you say?'

'Nothing. But teddies cannot be hypnotised. I tried it once and it didn't work on me.'

Jack looked hard at Eddie. 'Why did you try?' he asked.

'I had this theory,' said Eddie, 'that if hypnotists can hypnotise folk into doing anything they want them to do—'

'I'm not sure that's true,' said Jack.

'It is around here,' said Eddie. 'Believe me. Well, my theory was simple: I'd get the hypnotist to hypnotise me into being Toy City's greatest hypnotist, then I'd be able to place anyone I wanted under my control.'

'That's outrageous,' said Jack.

'Naturally, I would only have used my powers for good.'

'Well, naturally.' Jack now made a *very* doubtful face.

'But it didn't work,' said Eddie. 'The hypnotist said that he'd really tried his hardest. I had to go for ten sessions. It was very expensive.'

'Hm,' went Jack. 'Did it ever cross your mind—'

'What?' Eddie asked.

'Nothing,' said Jack. 'So teddies can't be hypnotised. But I'll bet I could be. Shall we visit this hypnotist and see if he can do it?'

'Ah,' said Eddie. 'I don't think he's practising any more.'

'Oh,' said Jack. 'Why not?'

'Well, he gave up when he got out of hospital.'

'Why was he in hospital?' Jack asked.

'He took a rather severe biting,' said Eddie.

'Right,' said Jack, and he recrossed his legs and kept them recrossed, though it hurt. 'So,' said Jack, 'hypnotists are not a happening thing, then.'

'Oh, they are,' said Eddie. 'Though not that one. I know another one. I think we'll pay him a visit.'

'Right,' said Jack once more. 'There's just one thing.'

'What's that?'

'First I think I'll take a shower and then we'll take some breakfast.'

They took their breakfast at Nadine's Diner. They travelled there in Bill's car, via the nearest pawnbrokers, where they pawned Bill's water cooler. Well, money *was* short, and they *were* on an important case. And they *were* very hungry indeed.

And on the way into the diner, Jack purchased the morning's edition of the *Toy City Mercury*.

They took a table by the window, ordered a Big Boy's Blow-Out Breakfast a-piece, with double hash browns, muffins, dumplings, pancakes, cheesecakes, fishcakes, fairy cakes and Fanny Lapalulu's Fudgecake Surprise. Jack spread the paper before him and perused the front page news. 'DOLLY DUMPLING DEAD' ran the headline, which told it as it was. And beneath it ran text that didn't.

'Freak accident?' said Jack. 'Struck by lightning?'

'Well, what did you expect?' Eddie asked.

'The truth,' said Jack.

'In a newspaper?'

Jack shrugged. 'Well, not *all* of the truth, perhaps.'

'And what is the truth? No one saw anything except a really bright light. It could have been lightning.'

'It wasn't lightning, you know that.'

'I know that, you know that. Oh, damn, *he* knows that, too.'

'He?' Jack looked up. 'Oh dear,' he said.

Chief Inspector Wellington Bellis smiled his perished smile upon them. 'Good morning, gentlemen,' he said. 'Might I sit down and join you?'

'Oh yes, please do,' said Eddie. 'How wonderful to see you again so soon.'

'I thought I might find you here, filling your faces.' Wellington Bellis took a seat. 'You've seen the paper, I see.'

'For what it's worth.' Jack tossed the thing aside.

'It's worth a great deal,' said Bellis. 'We don't want panic in the streets, now do we? We want to get this thing tied up all neat and nice, as quickly as possible, don't we?'

'Of course we do,' said Eddie. 'Jack and I were just planning our next move when you arrived. Such a pity you've derailed our train of thought.'

'Such a pity,' said Bellis, and he reached out and squeezed Eddie's left paw.

'That hurts rather,' said Eddie. 'Would you mind not doing that?'

'I want results,' said Bellis, 'and I want them fast. I need the culprit banged up at the hurry-up. And if I do not have the real culprit, I will have to make do with the next best thing. Do I make myself clear?'

'Very clear,' said Jack. 'Please stop doing that to Eddie.'

'Always the little bear's protector.'

'Eddie is my friend. Please let go of his paw.'

Bellis let go of Eddie's paw. Eddie gave it rubbings with his other one.

'You wouldn't want any harm to come to this dear little chap, would you, Jack?' asked Bellis, smiling horribly. 'Such a pity that would be.'

'There's no need for this.' Jack glared daggers at the chief inspector. 'We are doing all that we can. We want to sort this out as much as you do. Especially after what happened to us.'

'What?' said Bellis. 'What is this of which you speak?'

'Jack's talking about Old King Cole's,' said Eddie. 'That's what you were talking about, wasn't it, Jack?' Eddie made a frowning face at Jack.

'Ah,' said Jack. 'Ah, yes. That's exactly what I was talking about. Very upsetting for me, that was. I didn't sleep a wink last night.'

'Yes,' said Bellis. 'You certainly look like shi—'

'Two Big Boy's Blow-Out Breakfasts,' said a waitress. A long dolly waitress, with long dolly legs that went right up. 'Excuse me, sir, if you would.'

Bellis rose from his chair and gazed down upon the two detectives. 'Results,' said he. 'And fast. Or else.' And he drew a rubber finger across his rubber throat. 'Enjoy your breakfasts.'

And Bellis departed.

'What a bastard,' said Jack.

'Language,' said Eddie. 'There's a lady present.'

'Oh, that's all right,' said the waitress. 'I'm not much of a lady. A couple of drinks and I'm anyone's, really.'

'Really?' said Jack. 'What time do you finish your shift?'

'Jack,' said Eddie.

'Sorry,' said Jack.

'Six o'clock,' said the waitress.

'Jack,' said Eddie.

'Might we have a pot of coffee, please?' said Jack.

The waitress departed and Jack watched her do so.

'Please keep your mind on the case,' said Eddie. 'You're as randy as.'

'I think she fancies me,' said Jack.

'Of course she fancies you,' said Eddie.

'I have a definite way with the ladies,' said Jack, preening at his trenchcoat lapels.

'You don't,' said Eddie, tucking into his breakfast.

'I do,' said Jack, now tucking into his. 'Amelie says that she loves me.'

'Well, of course she would.' Eddie thrust breakfast into his mouth, which made his words difficult to interpret.

'Because I'm so handsome and nice,' said Jack, although there was much of the, 'Beccmmnth mmn sm hndsmn and nnnce,' about the way he said it.

'No, Jack,' said Eddie. 'That's not why and you know it.'

'It is why,' said Jack. 'Sort of.'

'Not,' said Eddie. 'It's because you're a meathead, Jack. Amelie could aspire to nothing better than marrying a meathead. *Any* meathead.'

'That's rubbish,' said Jack, spitting muffin as he said it. 'She loves me for me, not for what I am.'

'Don't kid yourself,' said Eddie, spitting pancake back at Jack. 'You have meathead status. Why do you think she wanted you to take her to Old King Cole's? What was that fight you got into about?'

'I never mentioned to you that I'd got into a fight.'

'Evidence,' said Eddie, making a breezy paw gesture towards his partner against crime. 'You punched someone. And someone else – a lady, I presume – struck you several times with a sequinned handbag.'

'You really are a *very* good detective,' said Jack.

'I'm a *special* detective,' said Eddie. 'But believe me, Jack, cruel as it sounds, she loves you for your status.'

'Well, all thanks for *that*,' said Jack.

'*All* thanks? I thought you'd be devastated.'

'Well, I'm not, you cruel little sod.'

'Less of the little.'

'I'm not ready to get involved in another relationship,' said Jack. 'I'm still smarting from the last one. I'll settle for the deeply satisfying shallow sex and have done with it for now.'

'You're a very bad boy,' said Eddie.

'I'm a teenage boy,' said Jack. 'What do you expect from me, sincerity?'

'Stop now,' said Eddie. 'It's too early in the day for such honesty. Tuck into your breakfast, then we'll get this hypnotism thing done. Then—'

'Then?' said Jack.

'I really don't have a clue,' said Eddie.

Their breakfasting done and their bellies distended, the two detectives dabbed at their mouths with napkins and grinned at one another.

'It's not a bad old life,' said Jack.

'It has its moments,' said Eddie.

Jack went up and paid the bill.

And took the waitress's telephone number.

Jack wound up Bill's car and he and Eddie entered it.

'So, where to?' Jack asked.

'The circus,' said Eddie, 'that's where.'

'I don't like the circus,' said Jack. 'I've never been one for clowns.'

'Odd that, isn't it?' said Eddie. 'Clowns are such a popular thing at the circus, but you'll never find anyone who actually likes them. Odd that, isn't it?'

Jack shrugged and said, 'I suppose so. So where is this circus?'

'I'll guide you,' said Eddie. 'But please drive slowly or I'll throw up in your lap.'

Jack drove slowly, with considerable care. He followed Eddie's guidings and eventually drew up the car before a rather colourful funfair affair in a part of the city that he'd never been to before.

Jack looked up at the colourful banner that hung between colourful posts. 'Count Otto Black's Circus Fantastique,' he read. Aloud.

'You'll like the count,' said Eddie. 'Or at least I hope you will.'

'You do?'

'Yes,' said Eddie, 'because then it will sort of balance things out.'

'It will?'

'It will,' said Eddie, 'because I can't stand the sight of him.'

The sight of him was something to behold. At Eddie's urging, Jack knocked upon the colourful door of a colourful gypsyesque caravan. This door opened and Jack beheld Count Otto Black.

Count Otto Black was tall. He was beyond tall, if such a thing is possible. Beyond tall and well gaunt with it was the count. High above on his facial regions were wonderful cheekbones, just beneath deeply set eyes of the deepest of sets. And just above a great black beard that nearly fell to his waist, the count's nose was a slender arc; the count's hair, long and black. Count Otto Black wore wonderful robes of rich purple velvet and plush. Mystical rings adorned his long and slender fingers.

'Count Otto,' called Eddie. 'Hello up there.'

Count Otto Black gazed down upon his visitors.

'I must be off now,' said Jack.

'No you mustn't,' said Eddie.

'Oh yes, I really must.'

'So,' said Count Otto Black. And it was a long and deep 'So'. 'So, Eddie Bear, you have returned.'

'Like the old bad penny,' said Eddie. 'You look well.'

Jack looked down upon Eddie Bear. Eddie looked far from at ease.

'Let's go,' whispered Jack. 'I don't like this fellow at all.'

Count Otto Black took a step back and the colourful door began closing.

'No, please, your countship,' called Eddie, 'this is very important. We're sorry to bother you, but it *is* important. You are the only one who can help us.'

The colourful door reopened a tad.

'We need you to use your special powers.'

'Ah,' said the voice of the count. 'You are hoping once more to become Toy City's greatest hypnotist.'

'No,' said Eddie. 'Not that.'

'I still bear the scars on my ankles,' said the voice of the count.

Jack looked at Eddie. 'I thought you said—'

'I did apologise for that,' said Eddie, ignoring Jack.

'Only after I kicked you over the big top,' said the voice of the count.

'I think we're on a loser here,' said Jack. 'And I hate to say this, Eddie, but have you ever considered anger-management counselling?'

The colourful door of the count's caravan slammed shut.

'Let's get out of here,' said Jack.

'No,' said Eddie. 'We have to know what happened. The count is the only man who can help us.'

'*Man?*' said Jack. 'Not *meathead*?'

'He's a bit special, the count.'

Jack raised eyebrows. Two of them. Both at the same time. And both high.

'Stop doing that,' said Eddie. 'You're only doing it because I can't.'

'I'm impressed,' said Jack, 'you showing respect for a meathead.'

'I'm not prejudiced,' said Eddie.

'Well, we're stuffed here,' said Jack. 'Let's get back in the car.'

'No,' said Eddie. 'We must do this. *You* must do this. Leave this to me.'

Jack dusted imaginary dirt from his trenchcoat shoulders. 'Go on, then,' he said.

Eddie called out to Count Otto Black. 'Count Otto,' called Eddie, 'this is very important. You are the one man who can help us.'

The colourful door of the colourful caravan remained colourfully shut.

'The fate of Toy City depends on you,' called Eddie.

The door, colourful as it was, did not at all colourfully budge.

'It's about your monkeys,' called Eddie.

A moment passed and then the door opened a smidgen.

'Your clockwork cymbal-playing monkeys,' called Eddie. 'Jack and I are on the case. Jack is a special investigator. I'm . . .' Eddie paused.

The door didn't move.

Eddie took a deep breath. 'I'm his comedy sidekick,' called Eddie.

The door opened wide.

'Say that again,' said Count Otto Black.

'Jack is a special investigator,' said Eddie, 'investigating the monkey case. He needs your help.'

'No,' said Count Otto. 'Say the last bit again.'

'I'm . . .' said Eddie.

'Again,' said the count. 'And loudly.'

'I'm his comedy sidekick,' said Eddie.

The colourful interior of Count Otto Black's colourful carnival caravan was very much the way that such interiors are in movies. Although not those of the Toy City P.P.P.s persuasion. Those circus movies, with handsome juvenile leads who are trapeze artistes and up-and-coming starlets who ride white horses side-saddle around the circus ring, but seem to do little else. And there are elephants, of course, and a bloke who gets shot out of a cannon. And those clowns that no one actually really likes. And a fat lady and a stilt-walker, and high-wire walkers and even fire-walkers sometimes. And a head without a body that was dug from the bowels of the Earth. But none of these are particularly relevant to the appearance of the interior of the count's colourful carnival caravan. The relevant point about the interior that gave verisimilitude to those featured in movies was that it was so much bigger on the inside than it was on the outside.

Phew.

'Why are they bigger on the inside than the outside?' Jack asked Eddie.

'That's obvious,' said Eddie. 'So you can get a camera crew in, of course.'

'Be seated,' said Count Otto Black, taking to a big old colourful chair of his own and indicating a lesser. Jack sat down on this lesser chair. Eddie sat down on the floor.

'I feel that you could have seated yourself in a somewhat more comical manner than *that*,' said Count Otto Black.

Eddie sighed. Rose. Toppled backwards. Lay with his legs in the air.

Jack winced and chewed upon his bottom lip.

'Funny enough for you?' Eddie asked.

'I'd like to see it again,' said the count.

Eddie obliged. 'Are you satisfied now?'

'Very much so,' said Count Otto Black. And he extended a long hand to Jack. 'So you are a special investigator,' he said.

Jack took the count's hand and shook it. It was a very cold hand indeed. Very cold and clammy.

The count took back his hand and Jack said, 'Yes, I am a special investigator and I believe that you can help me in my investigations.'

'Into the death of my monkeys.'

'They were all *your* monkeys?'

'Each and every one worked for me. There are not too many openings for cymbal-playing monkeys nowadays.'

'No,' said Jack, 'I suppose not. I never really thought about it.'

'They are a great loss to my circus.'

'I suppose they would be.'

'In what way?' asked the count.

'Eh?' said Jack.

'Shouldn't that be "pardon"?' asked the count.

'Pardon?' said Jack.

'In what way do you suppose they would be a great loss to my circus?'

Jack glanced at Eddie. It was a 'hopeless' glance. Sometimes a single glance can say so very much. Without actually saying anything at all. So to speak.

'Please don't do it to him, Count,' said Eddie, making a rather pathetic face towards Count Otto Black. 'Jack, my . . . employer, *is* a very special investigator, very good at his job, but he's not up to matching wits with you.'

'I'm up to matching wits with anyone,' said Jack. 'Show me a wit and I'll match it.'

'Time *is* of the essence,' said Eddie. 'Please, Count.'

'Quite so,' said Count Otto Black. 'So I suppose you have come here to examine the murder scene. Five of my monkeys gone to dust in their dressing room.'

'Well, not exactly,' said Jack. 'I assume that the laughing policemen have already visited the crime scene.'

'And stomped it into oblivion. What, then?'

'Well,' said Jack, 'it's like this.'

And Jack explained to Count Otto Black exactly what it was like. He spoke at length and in detail.

The count listened and then the count nodded. And then the count finally said, 'And so you wish me to hypnotise you, regress you to the point when you were engulfed by the very bright light and draw out your repressed memory of what happened next.'

'Exactly,' said Jack.

Count Otto Black nodded thoughtfully.

'No, I won't do it,' he said.

10

'No?' said Jack. 'No?'

'No,' said Count Otto Black. And he said it firmly. Definitely. Without reservation or regret.

'No?' said Jack once more.

'Absolutely no.' The count stretched out his great long arms, brushing his fingertips against the opposite walls of the caravan. 'And I will tell you for why: because it would be dangerous, very dangerous, to you, to your mental health. You have to understand this. Your memory was not artificially erased by some piece of advanced space-alien technology. You did it yourself. Your own brain did it.' And Count Otto stretched out a hand to Jack and tapped him lightly on the forehead. 'Whatever happened to you was so appalling, so utterly terrifying, that it was too much for you to take in and retain. Your mind rejected it, spat it out, closed itself to these horrors. The door within closed. It would be folly to reopen it.'

'No,' said Jack, and he shook his head. 'I don't believe that. I've seen horrors enough. Nothing could be *that* bad.'

'Really?' said the count. 'And yet I feel that I could whisper words into your ear that you would wish until the end of your days that you had never heard me utter.'

'That I consider most unlikely,' said Jack.

'Really?' said the count, and he leaned in Jack's direction.

'Don't let him do it, Jack,' cried Eddie, leaping up. 'I saw him do it once to a clown. It wiped the smile right off his face.'

'Big deal,' said Jack.

'A smile painted on a tin-plate head,' said Eddie. 'Wiped it right off. The smile fell to the ground and a crow swooped down and carried it off to his nest.'

'Eh?' said Jack.

'Trust me,' said Eddie. 'Don't let him do it.'

'All right, all right, but we have to know what happened, Eddie, and if hypnosis is the only way, then hypnosis it has to be.'

'I won't be persuaded,' said Count Otto Black.

'We'll give you money,' said Eddie.

'How much money?' asked the count.

And now a period of negotiation began, of bargaining and bartering and wrangling. It was a protracted period and resting times were taken at intervals, whilst negotiators sat and smoked cigarettes, or paced up and down, or worked out calculations on small bits of paper.

It was coming on towards teatime before all was said and done.

'And that's my final offer,' said Eddie.

'I'll take it,' said the count. Palms were spat upon, or in Eddie's case, a paw, then spitty palm and spitty paw were clapped together.

'Now just hold on,' said Jack. 'I want to get this straight. Count Otto will hypnotically regress me—'

'Taking no responsibility for the potential damage to your mental health,' said the count.

'Yes, I understand that. But you will regress me in exchange for *what*, exactly?'

Eddie read out the list of the count's demands.

'Bill's car,' he read, and Jack groaned.

'And your trenchcoat.' Further groanings.

'And your hat and your watch.' Eddie paused. Jack groaned doubly.

'Fifty per cent of the reward money.'

'*What* reward money?' Jack asked.

'Oh, there *will* be reward money,' said Count Otto Black. 'When all else fails.'

'That doesn't make sense,' said Jack. 'That means when Eddie and I fail.'

'You're right,' said the count. 'I want sixty per cent.'

Eddie sighed. 'We agreed on fifty. And forty on the film rights.'

'Film rights?' said Jack.

'There's a movie in this.' The count mimed camera crankings. 'I would want to play myself, of course, although perhaps it might be better if I were to play the juvenile lead.'

Eddie shook his head and sighed once more.

'I'll have my solicitor go into all the details of the subsidiary rights, marketing offshoots, merchandising deals and suchlike.'

'How long will *that* take?' asked Jack, whose patience had worn beyond thin.

'No time at all,' said Count Otto. 'I keep him in that box over there.'

'He does,' came a muffled voice from that box.

'Fine,' said Jack. 'Fine – take everything we've got. The car, my coat, my watch. Do you want my shoes, too?'

The count made so-so noddings with his head.

Jack threw up his hands and said, 'Ludicrous.'

'I think the count has been very reasonable,' said Eddie.

'Yes, well, *you* would. He doesn't want your hat, your coat and your watch.'

'I can't wear a watch,' said Eddie. 'Watches fall off my paws – I don't have wrists.' And Eddie made a sorrowful face that almost had Jack sympathising.

'Oh no you *don't*,' said Jack. 'It's not fair. It's not.'

'It is most fair,' said Count Otto Black, 'because I am taking nothing from you that you will want.'

'Oh, I think you are,' said Jack. 'The car. The coat. The watch.'

'No.' Count Otto shook his head. 'You will have no need of these things after I have put you through the period of hypnotic regression. All you will have need of is heavy sedation and the immediate use of a straitjacket.'

'Hm,' went Jack, as 'Hm' usually served him adequately at such times.

'So let us begin.' Count Otto Black linked his fingers together and did that sickening knuckle-cracking thing that some folk take delight in doing to the distress of those who have to watch them doing it. 'To work, to work. And let me ask you this.'

Jack tried to do the knuckle-cracking thing with his own fingers, but failed dismally. 'Ouch,' said Jack. 'It hurts.'

'I have to ask you,' said the count, wiggling his fingers and, unseen, his toes, 'what is the last thing you remember *before* the big white light?'

'Leaving Tinto's Bar,' said Jack.

'Although we know that we did more,' said Eddie. 'Went through a briar patch and along a yellow-brick road.'

Count Otto Black made a thoughtful face, but as most of it was lost beneath his beard, the degree of its thoughtfulness was lost upon Jack and Eddie.

'We will take Tinto's Bar as a starting point,' said he. 'Why did you leave Tinto's Bar?'

'Because Tinto had given a note from a spaceman to what he thought was Eddie, but wasn't,' said Jack.

'And what did that note say?'

'It said that the location of a landed spaceship was Toy Town,' said Jack, 'so we went to Toy Town in the car.'

'Hold on,' said Eddie. 'I don't remember any of *that*. How come you didn't mention that you remembered *that* earlier?'

'He couldn't,' said Count Otto Black.

'Why not?' asked Eddie.

'Because he didn't remember it.'

'So how come he remembers it now?'

'Because I just hypnotised him.'

'What?' said Eddie. 'I never saw you do *that*.'

'You did,' said Count Otto, 'but I hypnotised *you* so you won't remember how I did it.'

'You didn't,' said Eddie.

'Crow like a rooster,' said Count Otto Black. 'You *are* a rooster.'

'Cock-a-doodle-do!' went Eddie.

'And rest,' said the count. And Eddie rested.

'So you left Tinto's Bar and travelled to Toy Town,' said the count to Jack. 'What happened next?'

'We went to Bill Winkie's house,' said Jack. 'Eddie still had the key and we let ourselves in. And Eddie showed me all these weapons hidden beneath the floor. And then we heard someone coming and we hid beneath the trap door.'

'Tell me what you heard then,' said the count.

And Jack spoke of the conversation that he and Eddie had overheard, regarding things in jars and suchlike. And he told the count that the voices they had heard had been their own voices. And then how they'd climbed out of the hideaway and how there had then been a very bright light.

'And what happened *next*?' asked Count Otto Black.

Jack sat in his chair and stared into space. His eyes grew wide and his hands gripped the arms of his chair. His knuckles whitened, as did his face. Eddie looked on and Eddie looked on with a sense of growing fear.

'The light,' went Jack. 'The terrible light.'

'Go on,' said the count. 'The light can't hurt you now.'

'Oh,' went Jack. 'They're coming for us. Out of the light, they're coming.'

'Gently now,' said Count Otto Black. 'You're quite safe here, they can't hurt you here. Who is coming out of the light?'

'Not *who*,' said Jack, and cold sweat formed upon his brow and trickled down his cheeks. 'It's *what*, not who. They are not men.'

'Are they toys?' asked the count.

'Not toys. Oh, now, they're taking us. Up into the light. They have us. In that place, that bright place. They're putting things up our— Ouch! Stop! Ouch!'

'We'll take a little break there, I think,' said the count.

'No, we can't,' said Eddie. 'Painful as this is, we have to finish.'

'It's too painful for me,' said the count.

'Too painful for *you*?'

'Indeed,' said Count Otto. 'I need to take a wee-wee. I should have taken one earlier. I can't hold on any longer.'

Count Otto Black went off to the toilet. Presently, he returned.

'All better now,' he said. 'I took a poo as well, just to be on the safe side.'

'Too much information,' said Eddie. 'And you've quite spoiled the mood.'

'Well, it's neither here nor there,' said the count, settling himself down into his chair and wiggling his fingers at Jack. 'He'll be nothing more than a vegetable when all this is done.'

'No, I won't,' said Jack. 'I'll be fine.'

'See how brave he is?' said Eddie. 'He's as noble as.'

'Please yourselves,' said Count Otto. 'Pray continue, Jack. Tell us all about the rectal probings.'

Over in the big top, high-wire walkers paused in their practisings, struck by the screams from Count Otto's caravan. Pigeons fled their airy perches. Dogs howled in the distance.

'Much too much information,' said Eddie, rubbing at his own bum and feeling rather queasy.

'All right,' said the count, 'they did all that to you.'

'They did more,' said Jack. 'They did . . .'

Count Otto Black leaned close as Jack whispered.

'They never did?' he said. The count's eyes started from their sockets. The count rushed outside and was sick.

'Nice going,' said Eddie to Jack, whilst the count was outside up-chucking. 'Nice to see the count getting a bit of his own medicine. Because, after all, he is an *evil* hypnotist.'

'And worse is yet to come,' said Jack.

'Oh good,' said Eddie. 'I'll just keep my paws over my ears, then.'

'Best to,' said Jack.

Count Otto returned and Jack continued with his tale.

And eventually he was done.

Count Otto Black sat staring at Jack and Jack sat staring at him.

'Are you all right, Jack?' Eddie asked.

Jack said, 'Yes, I'm fine.'

'No feelings of empathy towards members of the vegetable kingdom?'

'Fine,' said Jack. 'Now I've got it all out of my system, I'm fine.'

'Well, thanks very much, Count Otto,' said Eddie. 'Count Otto? Can you hear me? Are you all right?'

*

Jack drove away from Count Otto Black's Circus Fantastique. He drove away in Bill's Anders Faircloud. Jack was wearing his trench-coat and his fedora and his watch.

'Well, I wasn't expecting *that*,' said Eddie, who sat once more in the passenger seat. 'Who'd have thought it, eh? Your revelations driving Count Otto Black into a vegetative state? Who'd have seen that coming, eh?'

'Anyone with more than sawdust for brains,' said Jack. 'It was what is called a telegraphed gag. One that you could *really* see coming.'

'So we really *were* abducted by spacemen.' Eddie whistled and kicked his legs about.

'No, we weren't,' said Jack.

'We *weren't*?' said Eddie. 'But we were taken up into the light and terrible bottom experiments were performed on us.'

'True,' said Jack. 'There's no denying that.'

'But you're saying that it *wasn't* spacemen?'

Jack shook his head.

'Then what?'

'Chickens?' said Tinto. 'You were abducted by chickens?'

It was early evening now and they were in Tinto's Bar.

'He's winding you up,' said Eddie. 'And before you say it, *not* in the nice way.'

'I'm not,' said Jack, counting the drinks that he had ordered and trying to reconcile them with the number that Tinto had delivered. 'We were abducted by chickens. Big ones in spacesuits. Horrible, they were, with nasty beaks and evil little eyes.'

'And *you* remember this?' asked Tinto of Eddie.

'No,' said Eddie, tasting beer. 'I do not. The count only hypnotised me to prevent me from remembering how he hypnotised Jack.'

'Oh, slow down there,' said Tinto. 'Too much information.'

'We're done with that line now,' said Eddie. 'It wasn't relevant anyway.'

'I just fancied using it,' said Tinto. 'I'm a barman. I *do* have rights, you know.'

'You have the right to remain silent,' said Eddie. 'Why not use it now?'

'Because I want to hear about the chickens. Could you give me a bit of a wind, please, Jack, I'm running down.'

Jack leaned over the bar counter and turned the key in Tinto's back.

'Howdy doody,' said Tinto to Jack. 'Can I help you, sir?'

'We were talking about the chickens,' said Jack. 'The ones that abducted Eddie and me.'

'Well, yes,' said Tinto. 'You told me that. But I'm rather confused. These space chickens, was it them that blasted the cymbal-playing monkeys with the deaths rays?'

Jack looked at Eddie.

And Eddie looked at Jack.

'Nice mutual lookings,' said Tinto, plucking spent glasses from the bar and giving them a polish, 'but hardly an answer to my question.'

Jack now took to tasting beer. 'I'm rather confused myself,' he said. 'We *were* abducted by chickens, for reasons unknown.'

'They'd have their reasons,' said Tinto. 'They probably stuck implants up your bum.'

'They stick those up your nose,' said Jack.

'Nose, bum, it's all the same to me. Bits of body never do what they're supposed to anyway. Take that sailor doll over there.' Tinto pointed and Jack did lookings across. 'Obviously built upside down,' said Tinto.

'He looks the right way up to me,' said Jack.

'Then how come his nose runs and his feet smell?'

'We should have seen *that* one coming,' said Eddie.

'But it wasn't the chickens, was it?' said Jack to Eddie. 'We heard who did the murderings – it was those doppelgängers of us.'

'Probably in league with the chickens,' said Tinto, and he tittered.

'Did you just titter?' asked Eddie.

'There's a screw loose in my voice box,' said Tinto. 'Are you going to pay for these drinks or engage me in further conversation in the hope that I'll forget to ask you for the money?'

'It's always served me well in the past,' said Eddie.

'Well, not tonight,' said Tinto. 'Pay up. Twenty-five beers and that's . . .' And Tinto named the sum in question and that sum in question was correct.

'How did you work *that* out?' asked Eddie.

'Aha!' went Tinto, and he touched his printed nose. 'Because I have a pocket calculator.'

'So where do you keep it? You don't have any pockets.'

'Who said that?' asked Tinto.

'I did,' said Eddie.

'Well, that just shows you how smart *you* are,' said Tinto. 'I don't need a pocket to own a pocket calculator, because a pocket calculator is a calculator in the shape of a pocket. I thought everyone knew that.'

'Actually, *I* didn't,' said Jack. 'Might we have a look at this calculating pocket?'

'Certainly,' said Tinto, and he rootled beneath the bar counter and brought out something that resembled a bag made out of shiny fabric. 'Wallah,' went Tinto.

'Wallah?' went Eddie.

'Wallah,' went Tinto. 'That's the calculating pocket's name.'

'Wallah?' went Jack.

'Yes?' said Wallah. 'How can I help you?'

Jack looked at Eddie.

And Eddie once more looked upon Jack.

'And there was me thinking that I'd seen everything,' said Jack, 'what with the space chickens and all. Where did you get this calculating pocket, Tinto?'

'I do have a name,' said the calculating pocket.

'Excuse me,' said Jack.

'Won her in a competition,' said Tinto. 'You have to work out the number of gobstoppers in a big jar.'

'And *you* got that right?' asked Eddie.

'Well, I had a little help,' said Tinto. 'I asked to meet the prize first, before I bought a ticket to enter the competition, and I asked her to work it out.'

'That's called cheating,' said Eddie.

'And your point is?' Tinto asked.

'No point at all,' said Eddie. 'But it was dishonest.'

'Possibly so,' said Tinto, 'but then so is engaging a barman in conversation in the hope that he will forget to charge you for your drinks.'

'You can put a "Hm" in about now if you wish, Jack,' said Eddie.

'Hm,' Jack put in.

'So pay up, or you're barred,' said Tinto.

Eddie sighed, pawed his way into a trenchcoat pocket, wormed out a wallet and set it down upon the bar top. 'Help yourself,' he said.

Jack viewed the wallet and Jack viewed Eddie.

Tinto helped himself to money and wheeled himself off to the till.

'Where did that come from?' Jack asked.

'Count Otto's pocket,' said Eddie.

'You stole his wallet?'

'Well, he won't be needing it now, will he? He'll be needing heavy sedation and a straitjacket.'

'I'm sure there's some kind of justice or moral in that,' said Jack, 'but for the life of me I can't think what it might be.'

'I'm sure there must be somewhere,' said Eddie, 'if you think very hard about it. Same again?'

'I haven't finished these yet.'

'Then drink up, it's Count Otto's round once more.'

'I'll have a short, if I might,' said Wallah the calculating pocket.

Jack reached forward and picked up Wallah.

'Put me down,' said the pocket.

Jack shook the pocket about.

'And don't do that, it makes me feel sick.'

'How do you think it works?' Eddie asked. 'It's probably empty – have a look inside.'

'Don't you dare,' said Wallah. 'We hardly know each other.'

'Just a little peep,' said Jack.

'Certainly not,' said Wallah. 'Not until you've bought me a drink, at least. What kind of a pocket do you think I am?'

'A female one for certain,' said Jack.

'Don't start,' said Eddie. 'I know where that line of thinking is going.'

Jack returned Wallah to the counter top. 'This is all very entertaining,' he said.

'Not *that* entertaining,' said Eddie.

'Well, maybe a *bit*,' said Jack, 'but it's not helping *us*, is it? That other you and me will probably be coming back tonight to perform more evil deeds. Suck the life out of more innocent citizens of Toy City. They have to be stopped, Eddie, and we have to stop them.'

'I know,' said Eddie. 'But I don't quite know how.'

'We go back to Toy Town,' said Jack, 'get our hands on those weapons at Bill Winkie's. Lie in wait, then blow the blighters away.'

'Blow the blighters away?'

'Bang, bang, bang,' went Jack, and he mimed blowings away. 'Case closed and we collect the reward.'

'Case closed, perhaps, but there's no reward.'

'Then we'll settle for case closed.'

'No,' said Eddie, taking further beer. 'It's not enough. That other me and you, they are evil cat's-paws for some big boss somewhere, who wants whatever is in those jars. The soul-stuff of the murder victims, or whatever it is. It's the big boss we're looking for.'

'Fair enough,' said Jack. 'I'll hold the cat's-paws at gunpoint and you can bite the details out of them.'

'That does have a certain brutal charm.'

'I hate to interrupt you,' said Wallah, 'but you really are going about this all the wrong way.'

'Excuse me, please,' said Eddie, 'but Jack and I are professionals. We are private detectives. We know our own business.'

'Oh, get you,' said Wallah. 'Too proud to take some kindly offered advice.'

'I didn't say *that*,' said Eddie.

'You did, in so many words,' said Jack.

'Please yourself, then,' said Wallah. 'Don't listen to me. I don't care.'

'We'd like to listen,' said Jack. 'What would you like to tell us?'

'*He* doesn't want to listen,' said Wallah.

Eddie shrugged.

'Yes, he does,' said Jack.

'He doesn't, and he's not even funny. You should get yourself a better comedy sidekick than him.'

'Cheek,' said Eddie, raising a paw.

'Don't hit me,' cried Wallah.

'He's not hitting anyone.' Jack moved Wallah beyond Eddie's hitting range. 'Talk to *me*,' he said. 'You'd like to talk to *me*, wouldn't you?'

'Actually, I would.' Wallah's voice was *definitely* female. Jack gave Wallah a little stroke.

'What a lovely soft hand you have,' said the calculating pocket.

Eddie turned his face away. 'I'm going to the toilet,' he said.

Tinto returned with Eddie's change, but finding no Eddie returned this change to his till.

'I could help you,' said Wallah to Jack. 'I could help you to solve this case.'

'That's very kind of you,' said Jack, and he gave unto Wallah another little stroke.

Wallah the pocket gave a little shiver.

'How *exactly* could you help us?' Jack asked.

'There is an expression,' crooned Wallah, and it was a crooning little voice, 'in crime-solving circles, when seeking a culprit of a crime involving theft. That expression is "follow the money".'

'I don't follow you,' said Jack.

'I haven't finished yet,' said Wallah. 'These present crimes – the murdered monkeys and the clockwork band – your comedy sidekick is right in that you must follow the money, as it were, to the big boss. But doing so will require a degree of calculation that you and your sidekick, and no offence intended here, are not sufficiently skilled in making. And that's where I come in.'

'I still don't *exactly* follow you,' said Jack, but he gave Wallah another stroke. And Wallah sighed. Erotically.

Jack withdrew his hand.

'Please don't stop,' whispered Wallah.

Jack stared down at the calculating pocket. There was something not altogether wholesome about this.

'Further crimes will be committed,' Wallah crooned further. 'And in order to get ahead of the game and succeed, it will be necessary to calculate where these crimes will take place and what they will be. And that is where I come in. Let me help you. I really *can* help you. I *really can*.'

'How, *exactly*?' said Jack once more.

'Lean over a bit and let me whisper.'

Jack leaned over and Wallah whispered.

Eddie returned from the toilet.

'Why exactly,' said Eddie, climbing up onto his barstool, 'do blokes feel it necessary to pull all the toilet rolls out and throw them all over the floor? And will someone please explain to me the purpose of flavoured condoms?'

'Stop, *please*!' said Jack. 'That's quite enough of *that*.'

'Do *you* use flavoured condoms?' asked Eddie. 'And if so, *what* flavour? I'd have thought chocolate was out of the question.'

'*STOP!*' shouted Jack. 'I don't know what comes over you at times.'

'Just idle speculation,' said Eddie.

'Well, be that as it may, drink up your drinks – we're leaving.'

'*We?*' said Eddie.

'We,' said Jack.

'Now that surprises me,' said Eddie, 'because I recall you taking the telephone number of that dolly in Nadine's Diner this morning and asking her what time she got off. I bought you some flavoured condoms, by the way.'

'That dolly will have to wait,' said Jack, although there was a note of regret in his voice. 'Something has come up regarding the case. We have to go.'

'What?' said Eddie. 'And why?'

'Another crime is about to be committed. Another murder. Several murders, in fact.'

'And how did you work this out?'

'It's a *calculated* guess,' said Jack.

*

They drank up their beers and they left Tinto's Bar.

Tinto waved them goodbye, took their empty glasses and polished them clean.

'It was a real joy to get money out of that Eddie Bear,' he said to the pocket that lay on the counter top. 'And I stiffed him for his change and everything. That's the last time he ever gets one over on me.'

The pocket on the counter top had nothing to say in reply to this.

But then again, trenchcoat pockets rarely do.

11

'No,' said Eddie. '*Not* the ballet.'

He sat in the passenger seat of the Anders Faircloud once more. Jack was once more at the wheel. But for once the Anders Faircloud was not performing high-speed death-defying automotive man-oeuvres. It was sort of poodling along and clunking sounds were issuing from the bonnet regions.

'You've overwound this car,' said Eddie to Jack. 'And you've trashed the engine with all your high-speed death-defying automotive manoeuvres.'

'I'll fix it when I have time,' said Jack, ramming his foot floorwards but eliciting little response. 'I know clockwork. And I'll soup-up the engine, spraunch the springs, caflute the cogs, galvate the gears and other things of a workshop nature generally. You wait until you see how fast it will go then.'

'The poodling's fine by me,' said Eddie, 'but as I was saying, oh no, *not* the ballet.'

'The ballet it has to be.' Jack poodled through a red light, causing concern amongst righteous motorists. 'That is where the next murders will occur. We can be ahead of the game this time, Eddie.'

Eddie yawned and shuddered slightly. 'As I am sure you know,' he said, between further yawns, which set Jack off, 'we bears are known for our remarkable stamina, and can go for many days without sleep.'

'Bears hibernate all winter,' said Jack, informatively.

'Yes, but that's because they stay up all summer clubbing 'til dawn.'

'And your point is?' Jack asked.

'I'm knackered,' said Eddie. 'Done in, banjoed, wrecked and smitten. I don't think I can take the ballet.'

'The ballet is soothing,' said Jack. 'You can take a little nap.'

'I'll take a *big* nap, believe me. And that is not professional for a crime fighter. Five minutes of ballet and I'll be gone from this world.'

'You'll be fine.' Jack smiled and drove; the car lurched and hiccuped.

Eddie yawned once more, this time behind his paw, did little lip-smacking sounds and promptly fell asleep.

'We're here,' said Jack, and he woke Eddie up.

There was no real question as to whether when they built the Toy City Opera House, which also housed the ballet, that they had built it for the patronage of toys. They hadn't. This was a man-sized affair, as was Old King Cole's, built for the elite of Toy City. The elite that was man.

Jack had to cruise around for a bit looking for a place to park, but once parked-up, in a rather seedy alleyway, he and Eddie plodded on foot to the glorious, grand establishment.

'It's beautiful, isn't it?' said Jack.

'Frankly, I hate it,' said Eddie. 'It sends out all the wrong messages.'

'Right,' said Jack. 'Well, I don't really recall exactly what the protocol is here. The last time we came was when you were first made mayor, remember? We had some times then, didn't we? We were fêted everywhere.'

Eddie *did* remember. 'Wasn't I sick in the royal box?' he said.

'Yes,' said Jack. 'Just a little. So I think I'd better carry you in under my coat, or something.'

'You *what?*'

'We don't want any unpleasantness, do we?'

'I could wait in the car, I don't mind.'

'Eddie, a crime is going to be committed here. A murderous crime. A multiple murderous crime.'

'You have yet to tell me how you know this to be.'

'I have my sources,' said Jack, and he stuck a hand into his pocket. A tiny sighing sound coming from within went unheard by Eddie.

Because Eddie was now nearly being stomped upon.

The fashionable set, Toy City swells, the fêted glitterati, were hustling and bustling around the two detectives. Exclusive fragrances perfumed the air, diamonds dazzled and shimmered amongst fur stoles, gowns and gorgeousness.

'Do you have tickets?' Eddie called up to Jack.

'No,' said Jack, and he grinned.

'Phew,' said Eddie. 'Then at least we won't get in.'

'We'll get in – I have my special lifetime membership card.'

'You hung on to that?'

'I have a walletful,' said Jack, 'for all those posh places that wanted the bear and his partner who had saved Toy City to patronise their premises.'

'Scumbags all,' said Eddie. 'Scumbags and treacherous turncoats. And my lifetime membership was lost in the post, as I recall.'

'You'll be back on top, Eddie,' said Jack, lifting Eddie from his paw pads and tucking him under his arm. 'Once we've saved the city once more.'

Eddie made a growly groan. 'Just listen to yourself,' he said.

'I'm confident,' said Jack, elbowing his way into the crowd with his free elbow. 'We have the edge, we'll succeed.'

'The edge?' and Eddie shook his head.

The Toy City Opera House owned to a doorman whose livery put that of Old King Cole's severely to shame. This man was magnificent. So much so that thankfully he was beyond description.

He held up his gloved hand against Jack's slovenly approach.

'No tradesmen,' said this personage.

'How dare you,' said Jack, making the face of outrage and adopting once more the haughty tone. 'I am a lifetime honorary member of this here establishment, and can therefore attend any opera or ballet, free of charge, in the very bestest seats that you have, as it happens. Would you care to see my gilt-edged membership card?'

'Dearly,' said the doorman. 'Few things would give me greater joy.'

'That's a smirk on your face,' said Jack, lowering Eddie to the marble flooring and rootling out his wallet. 'We shall see who's smirking soon.' Jack flicked through a number of cards that offered him lifetime privileges, some at certain establishments that really suited Jack.

'There,' said he, presenting the doorman with a grand-looking one.

The doorman perused this grand-looking card. He held it close to his smirking face, inspected it carefully, raised it up to the light. Marvelled at the watermark and the special metallic strip. Checked the ID photo and everything. 'Wow,' he went, and he whistled. 'You weren't pulling my plonker-piece, were you, your princeship.'

'No, I wasn't,' said Jack. 'Now hand it back and stand aside and be grateful that I do not report you for your insolence.'

The doorman whistled once more and returned Jack's card to him. Then he leaned forward, still smirking, and informed Jack in a curt and brusque manner exactly what Jack could do with himself.

'What?' went Jack. 'How dare you!'

'I dare,' said the doorman, 'because your card has no currency here. Shove off.'

'What?' went Jack. 'What?'

'Do you ever read the newspapers?' the doorman asked Jack.

'Actually, I do,' Jack said.

'Well, not too long ago,' said the doorman, 'Toy City was plagued by a mad mayor. A hideous freak, he was, with glass dolly eyes and these really creepy hands—'

Eddie flinched and took shelter at the rear of Jack.

'Well, this abhorrence put into place certain edicts,' the doorman continued. 'He appeared to have it in for his betters, you see. Inferiority complex, inverted snobbery or have it as you will. I've been reading all about that kind of business in this self-help manual I bought. Anyway, this mad mayor did away with all the privileges of the monarchy. Edict Five, as I recall.'

Jack said, 'What?' and Jack looked down at Eddie. Around and behind himself and then again down at Eddie.

Eddie made a foolish face and shrugged.

'Ah,' said Jack. 'Ah, but—'

'Ah, but what?' asked the doorman.

'Ah, but the mad mayor was kicked out. Tarred and feathered.'

'Yes.' The doorman smiled. 'But not all his edicts were rescinded. Actually, the management of the Opera House quite liked Edict Five – they were fed up with the monarchy always poncing free tickets for all the best bashes.'

'Oh,' said Jack.

'So on your way,' said the doorman. 'Scruffy trenchcoated oik that you are.'

'You will answer for this,' said Jack.

'Word has it,' said the doorman, 'that The End Times are upon us, and that all of us will answer soon for something or other.'

'You must let us in,' Jack protested.

'Us?' said the doorman. 'I wouldn't have let you take that tatty bear in with you anyway.'

'But,' said Jack, 'we are detectives. We're here on a case. We have the authority of Chief Inspector Wellington Bellis.'

'Yes, of course you have, sir. Now move along please, we have posh people trying to get in.'

'Let us in!' Jack demanded.

'Please don't make me use force,' said the doorman. 'As enjoyable as it would be for me, I regret to say that it would probably leave you with permanent damage.'

Jack made fists and squared up to the doorman.

The doorman made bigger fists and squared himself down to Jack.

'You haven't heard the last of this,' said Jack.

'I can assure you that I have,' said the doorman, 'because I am no longer listening.'

Posh folk pushed past Jack on either side. Jack retreated down the marble steps with Eddie following on.

'You and your bloody edicts,' Jack said to Eddie.

'Actually, I feel rather justified in imposing that one,' said the bear. 'Can we go home now, please?'

'We have to prevent a crime.'

'I'm still not really convinced.'

'Eddie, evil will be done here and only we can stop it.'

'You could call your associate, Chief Inspector Wellington Bellis.'

'He might not have faith in my source,' said Jack.

'About your source—' said Eddie.

'Damn,' said Jack, and he sat down on the kerb. 'Damn, damn, damn.'

Eddie sat down beside his friend. 'Tell me about this source of yours,' he said.

'Can't,' said Jack. 'I am sworn to secrecy.'

'What?' said Eddie. 'Why? We don't have secrets. We're partners.'

'Look, Eddie, I don't want to go into it now. We have to get inside the Opera House and that's all there is to it.'

'Well,' said Eddie, 'if your mind is made up, and that *is* all there is to it, then you'd best follow me.'

'Where to?'

'Just follow.'

Jack rose and followed Eddie. The little bear led him around the corner and down an alleyway and to the stage door. Several Stage Door Johnnies surrounded the stage door.

'Disgusting,' said Eddie, stepping over one of them. 'You're supposed to flush those things away.'

Jack made an appalled face. 'Was that a condom gag?' he asked.

'Take it as you will,' said Eddie. 'Knock at the door, please, Jack.'

Jack knocked at the door.

The backstage doorman opened it. He was a clockwork fellow, somewhat rusty and worn.

'Ralph,' said Eddie.

'Eddie?' said Ralph.

'Ralph, how good to see you after all this time.'

'All this time?' said Ralph, and he scratched at his tin-plate topknot, raising sparks.

'We're here on a bit of business,' said Eddie. 'Would you mind letting us in?'

'Again?' said Ralph.

'Why is he saying "again"?' Jack asked Eddie.

'I don't know,' said Eddie. 'Why are you saying "again", Ralph?'

'Because I've already let you in once,' said Ralph. 'And your comedy sidekick there.'

'What?' said Jack.

And, 'What?' said Eddie. And, 'Oh dear,' said Eddie. 'This is bad.'

'How did you get past me?' Ralph asked. 'I never saw you go out again.'

'We didn't,' said Eddie. 'That wasn't us.'

'Oh yes it was,' said Ralph. 'I'd recognise those crummy mis-matched button eyes, and the tatty old raincoat and the—'

'Have to stop you there, Ralph,' said Eddie. 'Those were two impersonators. Two very bad and evil beings.'

'Uncanny,' said Ralph.

'What?' said Eddie once more.

'That's what you said to me earlier, when I let you in. You said that two impersonators might turn up and try to get in, but that I was to refuse them entry because they were very bad and evil beings.'

And Ralph slammed the stage door shut upon Jack and Eddie.

And Jack and Eddie stood in the alley.

And Jack said, 'Damn,' once more.

Eddie Bear looked up at Jack. 'It seems,' said Eddie, 'that I was wrong and you were right. We *have* to get into the Opera House.'

'We *should* phone Bellis,' said Jack, 'get him to bring a task force, the Army, whatever is necessary. Everything. What do you think?'

Eddie gave his head a couple of thumpings. 'I think not,' said he. 'And before you ask why, I'll tell you for why. These murderers, or soul stealers, or whatever Hellish things from beyond or above they are, are disguised as *us*. And it does not require the gift of precog-nition to predict the inevitable consequences, as in when a bunch of overexcited police snipers gun us down by mistake.'

'Ah,' said Jack. 'You think that might happen?'

'I'd give you a very good odds on it,' said Eddie. 'We will have to deal with this on our own. Just you and me.'

'So how do we get in there?'

'Well,' said Eddie, and he cupped what he had of a chin in a paw, 'it will have to be the sewers.'

Jack made a sour face and Jack said, 'The sewers?'

'It's an Opera House,' said Eddie. 'Ergo it has a phantom.'

'A *what*?' said Jack.

'A phantom,' said Eddie.

'No,' said Jack. 'I mean, what's an *ergo*?'

'Most amusing,' said Eddie. 'But every Opera House has a phantom. Everyone knows that. It's a tradition, or an old charter, or something. And the phantom always lives in the bowels of the Opera House and rows a boat through the sewers.'

'And he does this for a living?'

'He's a phantom,' said Eddie. 'Who can say?'

'I don't like the sound of him very much.'

'We really *are* wasting time,' said Eddie. 'Let's find some conveniently placed sewer-hole cover to lift and get down to business.'

'Aren't sewers filled with business?' Jack asked.

'Yes, and Stage Door Johnnies, and crocodiles, too, I'm told.'

'Perhaps if I bribed that doorman . . .'

A sewer-hole cover was conveniently located not many paces before them. Jack looked up and down the alleyway and then took to tugging, then struggling, then finally prying open.

'Here it comes,' he panted. And here the cover came, up and over and onto Jack's foot.

'Ow!' howled Jack. And his 'Ow' echoed down along the sewer beneath them.

'Keep it quiet,' said Eddie. 'And get down the hole.'

'I'll get business on my trenchcoat,' said Jack.

'Time is wasting,' said Eddie. 'You brought us here to save lives, didn't you?'

Jack lowered himself into the unpleasantness beneath, then called up to Eddie and Eddie jumped down. Jack caught Eddie, reached up and pulled the sewer-hole cover back into place.

Eddie and Jack stood in darkness. And in smelliness also.

'Whoa!' went Jack, holding his nose and fanning his face. 'This is revolting – I'm up to my ankles in business here.'

'I'm nearly up to my bottom,' said Eddie. 'But it's quite a pleasant smell. Once you've acclimatised yourself.'

'So, which way do we go?'

'That way,' said Eddie.

Jack sighed deeply. 'I can't see a thing in the darkness. Which way do you mean?'

'*That* way,' said Eddie.

'Oh, *that* way,' said Jack. 'I see.'

But of course he did not. But he did follow Eddie by holding his ear. And Eddie strode forward with confidence, because, as he informed Jack, bears are noted for their remarkable night vision and natural sense of direction.

Presently they reached the inevitable dead end.

'Brilliant,' said Jack.

'Up the ladder,' said Eddie. 'Put your hands out – there's rungs in the wall.'

Jack put his hands out. 'Ah,' he said.

There were strugglings and pantings and it's hard to climb a ladder in the darkness with one hand holding your nose. But at length the two now somewhat ill-smelling detectives emerged into a kind of underground chamber, bricked all around with big stone slabs and lit by flaming *torchères* in wall sconces. There was an old organ in one corner of this chamber and at this sat an old organist, playing an old organ tune.

Jack dusted down his trenchcoat, but demurred at wringing out its sodden hem. Eddie squeezed at his soggy legs and dripped fetid water.

The old organist suddenly burst into song.

> The gulls that circle overhead
> Cry out for crumbs and bits of bread.
> The gulls that circle underfoot
> Are very rarely seen.

'What a wonderful song,' said Jack.

'I hated it,' said Eddie.

'Who said *that*?' asked the old organist. And he turned. And Jack and Eddie beheld . . . the Phantom of the Opera.

'Oh my goodness,' said Jack, and he fell back in considerable disarray.

The Phantom wasn't the prettiest sight, but he wasn't the ugliest, either. He was somewhere in between, but at a certain level in between that made him, or perhaps it was a her, or indeed an it, utterly, utterly . . .

'What is the word I'm looking for?' Jack did whispering to Eddie.

'Search me,' said the bear in reply. 'Average, bland, standard, run-of-the-mill, insipid, dull, middling, trite, mediocre, commonplace.'

'That's enough,' said Jack. 'But that's what it is.'

'Aaagh,' went the Phantom. 'Do not gaze upon my ubiquitousness.'

'And that's a good'n,' said Eddie. 'Possibly the best'n. He's as ubiquitous as.'

'What are you doing here?' The Phantom raised his voice, but it didn't really seem to raise. It droned somewhat. Which was odd as his, or her, or its, singing had been sweet. Although Eddie had hated it. 'Have you come to mock me for my generality? Come to laugh at the cursed one? The one too dull and everyday to be noticed?'

'We noticed you at once,' said Jack. 'And I really loved the singing.'

'You did?' said the Phantom. 'You *really did*?'

'It was a beautiful song. But we're lost. We need to get up into the Opera House. Would you help us, please?'

'I rarely venture above,' said the Phantom. 'My appearance is too lacking in extremity even to draw notice. Folk don't even know I'm there.'

'Who said that?' said Eddie.

'Stop it,' said Jack. 'It's not funny.'

'Oh, it is,' said the Phantom, wringing hands of abundant nonentity. 'They all laugh. It's all the Toymaker's fault.'

'The kindly, lovable white-haired old Toymaker?' said Jack.

'Unless you know of another.'

Jack shook his head.

'He wanted to create a toy that would be loved by all, that would appeal to all. So he took a bit of this and a bit of that and a bit of the other and he blended them all together. But did he create something that would universally be loved by all?'

Jack shook his head slowly. 'No?' he suggested.

'Correct,' said the Phantom. 'I am everything. And by being everything, I am nothing. I am a Phantom.'

'That's very sad,' said Jack.

'But we are in a hurry,' said Eddie.

'That *is* true,' said Jack. 'Do you think, Mister Phantom, that you could be kind enough to show us the way up into the Opera House. It is *Mister* Phantom, is it, or is it *Miss* or *Missis*?'

'If only I knew,' said the Phantom. 'Then, if I *did* know, I'd know whether some of the urges I feel at times are natural rather than perverse.'

'Difficult,' said Jack.

'Time,' said Eddie, pawing at an imaginary wristwatch.

'That bear's no master of mime,' said the Phantom. 'And what is *he*, anyway?'

'I'm an Anders Imperial,' said Eddie. 'Cinnamon plush—'

'That's a beer-bottle top in your ear hole.'

'That's my special button tag.'

'Oh no it's not.'

'Oh yes it is.'

'Time,' said Jack, and he pointed to his wristwatch.

'I'll take you up,' said the Phantom, 'but I'll caution you to take care.'

'Oh yes?' said Jack.

'Something is amongst us,' said the Phantom. 'I can sense it. Something that pretends to be us, but is not. Something other. Something apart. Something from Beyond The Second Big O.'

'We are aware of this,' said Jack, 'and it is our job to stop it.'

'Really?' the Phantom voiced surprise, but in a manner too dull and too monotone to express the emotion. 'Really, I *am* surprised. But you *must* beware. This something, and there is more than one of these somethings – there are two, in fact – these somethings will destroy us all, they will suck the very life force out of Toy City, leaving it an empty shell.'

Jack looked at Eddie.

And Eddie looked at Jack.

'Please lead us up,' said Jack.

The Phantom led the way. He, she or it, or all of the aforementioned, had a certain height to whatever he, she or it was. But it was an indeterminate height that was difficult to quantify. It was neither one thing nor the other; it lay somewhere in between, but beyond.

'If they ever make a movie of *this*,' Eddie whispered up to Jack, 'they'll have a real problem casting this, er, being.'

'They'll probably get Gary Oldman,' said Jack. 'He can play anyone.'

'Who is Gary Oldman?'

'Search me,' said Jack. 'I think my mind's wandering again. It was poetry yesterday. I probably *do* need some sleep.'

'This way,' said the Phantom, leading onward.

And onward the Phantom led and eventually his leading was done with the opening of a secret panel, as is so often the case with Phantoms. 'This is the royal box,' he, she or it said. 'You'll have a good view of the show from here – no one uses it any more. Something to do with Edict Five. Did you ever hear of it?'

'Never,' said Eddie. 'Thank you for helping us, Mister, er, well, Phantom.'

'I do have a name,' said the Phantom.

'Oh,' said Jack. 'What is it?'

'Ergo,' said the Phantom. 'I'll be leaving you now.'

'Nice fellow,' said Jack, once the Phantom had departed. 'Or woman, or whoever, or whatever.'

Eddie shrugged and climbed into a most comfortable-looking queenly kind of a chair. 'All right, I suppose, if you like that kind of a thing.'

Jack dropped down into the chair next to Eddie's, a most sumptuous kingly kind of a chair. Jack gazed all about the royal box. It was all gold twirly bits and gilt wallpaper.

And then Jack looked out from the box and into the Opera House proper. He had been there before, had Jack, as too had Eddie, and this *was* the royal box that Eddie had been sick in. Although it didn't smell of sick now, or possibly it did, a bit. It smelled a bit like sawdust. And Jack marvelled anew at the wonders of the Opera House.

'It really *is* an incredible place,' said Jack.

'Gaudy,' said Eddie. 'Gaudy.'

Jack looked out over the audience.

And then Jack whispered to Eddie, 'They're out there somewhere, our lookalikes, about to strike.'

'Did your, er, *secret* source tell you just *who* they are intending to strike at?' Eddie asked.

'The orchestra,' Jack whispered in return.

Eddie stood up on his chair and peered down into the orchestra pit. And Eddie counted on his paws, which meant counting two at a time. And when Eddie had finished his counting, Eddie turned to Jack.

'The orchestra?' said Eddie. 'The *entire* orchestra?'

'According to my source,' said Jack, 'who calculated the odds. There were twelve monkeys and then there was the jazz trio. Three times twelve is thirty-six and there are thirty-six orchestra members here. The murders are growing in a mathematical progression.'

'Jack, the *entire* orchestra? All of them?'

'That's what my source suggests.'

'Jack,' said Eddie, 'look down at the orchestra, if you will.'

Jack looked down upon the orchestra.

'Jack, count the number of members of the orchestra, if you will.'

Jack counted.

'Jack, tell me the number you have arrived at, if you will.'

Jack said, 'Yep, that's thirty-six, including the conductor, I'm afraid.'

'Jack, so many folk. This will be a massacre. What are we going to do?'

'Well,' said Jack, 'I *have* thought about this, and the way I see it is—'

But then Jack's words were swallowed away, for the orchestra struck up.

12

Now Jack felt that he could understand a clockwork orchestra. In a way. Which is to say that he understood the principles involved. A clockwork orchestra was an orchestra of automata – clockwork figures programmed, as it were, to perform a series of pre-planned tasks, to pluck certain strings, to touch certain keys, to finger certain notes. In fact Jack, with his knowledge of clockwork, apprenticed as he had been in a factory that produced clockwork figures, felt confident that he had the ability to personally create a reasonably efficient and melodic clockwork orchestra. It was only down to knowing how clockwork functioned and what it was capable of.

But the trouble was.

The trouble was, as the trouble had been ever since Jack had first arrived in Toy City, in what now felt to him like a distant past, the trouble was that the clockwork orchestra playing beneath him was actually playing. These were not simple (or indeed complex) automata going through their mechanical motions. No, not a bit of it. These were clockwork musicians, but they were *real* musicians. They actually played, and some of them sometimes hit the wrong notes.

They *really* played. They thought. They used their skills.

But clockwork brains? It was a mystery to Jack. It had always been a mystery and it remained a mystery still.

Jack glanced at Eddie. The little bear looked out anxiously over the audience, down upon the clockwork orchestra. That bear, as Jack knew, had nothing in his head but sawdust. Yet he thought, saw, heard, felt. Loved.

It was above and beyond a mystery. And although Jack felt certain that his own senses – those of a living, breathing man – did not deceive him, that he really *was* here in Toy City, a city where toys lived and moved of their own accord, it was beyond his comprehension as to how. And Jack knew that he cared for these ersatz creatures, these living toys. He wished no harm to come to them. In fact, like Eddie, he wished that something could be done to ease their lot, which was for the most part a pretty rotten one.

Jack looked out once more towards the orchestra: they were hammering into the overture. Going at it with gusto. These thinking, feeling clockwork musicians knew nothing of the threat that was presently hanging over them, that at any moment the terrible light might strike and their very essences would be torn from their bodies.

'Eddie!' bawled Jack. 'We have to get down there. To the stage.'

'You *do* have a plan?' Eddie bawled back.

'I need the toilet,' bawled Jack.

'You need *what*?'

Jack and Eddie left the royal box. There was no one in the corridor. Jack located the nearest gentlemen's toilet.

'Bottle job, is it?' Eddie asked.

'Just give me a minute, please. Wait here.'

Jack slipped into the gentlemen's toilet, closing the door behind him. He locked himself into the nearest stall and withdrew from his trenchcoat Wallah the calculating pocket.

'You've a lovely soft hand,' crooned Wallah.

'Yes,' said Jack, 'I'm sure I have. Now, you must help us, please. You were absolutely right about the orchestra being the next target and I'm still not certain how you arrived at your calculations.'

'That's because I haven't explained it to you,' said Wallah, in a husky tone. 'And it's not really necessary that I do, is it?'

'No,' said Jack, 'not at the moment. But please, tell me, what should Eddie and I do next? The murderers are already in the building and they could strike at any moment. Eddie and I have to stop them.'

'Well then, my dearest—' said Wallah.

'Dearest?' said Jack.

'Well, you're such a dear boy.'

'Please tell me,' said Jack. 'I don't know what to do.'

Wallah did snugglings into the palm of Jack's hand. 'You'll need a plan,' she whispered.

'Yes,' said Jack, 'and very fast indeed.'

'Then hold me up to your ear and let me whisper.'

Jack emerged from the gentlemen's toilet.

'All right now?' Eddie asked. 'I hope you didn't forget to wash your hands.'

'I have a plan,' said Jack.

'Now, that's a coincidence,' Eddie said, 'for I have a plan as well.'

'Nice,' said Jack. 'But my plan is this—'

'You'll want to hear mine first,' said Eddie.

'No I won't,' said Jack.

'Oh, I think you will – mine is a real blinder. It's as brilliant as.'

'Mine is calculated to achieve optimum success,' said Jack.

'Ooh,' went Eddie. 'Optimum success.'

'Time,' went Jack, doing wristwatch tappings, 'time is surely running out.'

'Then we'll run backstage and on the way I will explain to you my plan.'

'And if it doesn't conflict with mine, we'll put it into operation.'

'Jack, there's something you're not telling me.'

'You know there is.'

'Then tell me, please.'

'I won't.'

And the two took to jogging down the corridor.

It's really quite easy to move about unseen, as it were, in a big Opera House when a production is underway. After all, the audience are in their seats, the front-of-house staff, who are not required again until the half-time rush for the bar, are outside having a fag and discussing what rubbish they think the production is and how much better they could do it themselves. The technical staff are deeply engaged in their technical stuff, gaffers are gaffing and best boys, who don't really have a role to play in the running of a successful ballet, and who would be better off getting back to whatever movies they should be being the bestest of boys on, are generally to be found in the stars' dressing rooms, sniffing the roses and drinking champagne out of glass slippers. But some folk have all the luck and best boys have most of it.

And so it *really is* quite easy to move about unseen, behind the scenes, as it were, in a big Opera House when a production is under way.

'Up this way,' said Eddie.

'Might I ask why?' Jack asked.

'It's part of my plan. Any objection?'

'Actually, no,' said Jack. 'It's part of my plan also.'

Jack and Eddie were backstage now, that wonderful place where all the flats are weighted down and there are big ropes everywhere and curiously it smells a bit like a stable.* Unlike the front of the stage. Which smells quite unlike a stage.

As a matter of interest for those who have never attended a ballet, or those who have attended a ballet but sat either up in the circle or further back in the stalls, it is to be noted that if you are ever offered front-row stall seats to the ballet, *do not* accept them. If you do attend the ballet, take a look at the front row of stalls seats. Notice how few folk are sitting there, and how uncomfortable these folk look.

Why? you might well ask. What is all this about? you also might ask. Well, the answer is this: what you can smell when you sit in the front row of the ballet is a certain smell. And it is a smell quite unlike stables. What you can smell when you sit in the front row of the ballet is . . .

Ballet dancers' feet.

Why ballet dancers' feet smell quite so bad is anybody's guess. Probably because ballet dancers work so hard that they don't have time to wash their feet as often they should, would be anybody's *reasonable* guess.

But there it is.

---

* It really does.

Never accept front-row seats for the ballet.

Never.

Understood?[*]

'Why does this backstage smell of stables?' Jack asked Eddie.

'Because of the hay bales that are used as "running chuffs".'

'Ah,' said Jack. 'But what are—'

'This way,' said Eddie.

'That was the way I was going,' said Jack. 'But what are—'

'Let's hurry,' said Eddie. 'I have a *very* bad feeling coming upon me, and as you know, we bears are noted for our sense of—'

'Let's just hurry,' said Jack.

And so they hurried and presently they found themselves, and indeed each other, upon a high gantry, which held the above-stage lighting rigs. There were lots of ropes all about and wires and cables, too.

'We're here,' said Eddie.

'Yes we are,' said Jack. 'About this plan of yours.'

'Let me ask you just one thing,' said Eddie. 'Does your plan involve a chandelier?'

'Actually, it does,' said Jack.

'Mine, too,' said Eddie.

'Well, what a coincidence that is.'

'Really?' Eddie raised his imaginary eyebrows. 'And yet this is an Opera House, and we did meet the Phantom of the Opera. And the one thing everyone remembers about the Phantom of the Opera, and indeed associates with operas, is the big chandelier that hangs above the centre of the stage. Which gets dropped upon someone.'

'Well, I wouldn't know about *that*,' said Jack.

'Nor me,' said Eddie. 'I just made that bit up to pass some time.'

'Oh,' said Jack. 'Why?'

'Because *that*,' said Eddie, and he pointed with a paw, 'is a *very* big

---

[*] And I'm not joking here. When I worked in a prop house, I regularly received free tickets from one of the staff who was dating a Covent Garden ballet dancer. The tickets were always front-row tickets. I used to breathe through my mouth.

chandelier and I'm not exactly certain how we'll be able to drop a thing that size on anyone.'

'Aha,' said Jack. 'Gotcha.'

'Gotcha?' said Eddie. 'What means this odd word?'

'It means that my calculated plan extends a little further than your own. I know exactly how to drop that chandelier upon the evildoers.'

'Assuming of course they stand directly beneath it when we do the dropping,' Eddie said.

'Eddie,' said Jack, 'let's face it: it's a pretty preposterous idea. But this *is* a pretty preposterous situation. All of this is utterly ludicrous.'

'When you put it like that, how can we fail?'

'Well said. Now bung your furry ear hole in my direction and let me whisper into it.'

And so Jack whispered. And when his whispering was done, which, it has to be said, was quite loud whispering as it had to make itself heard above the spirited strains of the orchestra beneath, Jack straightened and Eddie looked up at him.

And then Eddie said, 'No way.'

'No way?' said Jack.

'Absolutely no way,' said Eddie. 'What do you take me for? You'll get me killed.'

'It will work,' said Jack. 'You'll be fine. It's a calculated risk.'

'I won't be fine, I'll die. You do it.'

'I can't do it. It has to be you.'

'And what do I do it with?'

'You do it with a spanner. This spanner.'

'And where did you find that?'

'Backstage, next to the "thunder sheet".'

'And what's a—'

'Don't start with me. I know you made up "running chuffs".'

'But I've only got paws, Jack. No hands with fingers and opposable thumbs.'

'It'll only take a few turns – you'll manage.'

'Oh, look,' said Eddie. 'The ballet has begun.'

*

Now ballets and operas have several things in common. Swanky costumes they have in common, and too much stage make-up. And music, of course – they are both traditionally very musical affairs. But the most notable thing that they share is the storyline. The one thing that you can always be assured of if you go to the opera or the ballet is, in the case of the opera, lots of really good loud singing, and in the case of the ballet, lots of really wonderful dancing, and *in the case of both, really rubbish* storylines.

They *are* rubbish. They always are. You always know what's coming next. Who the baddy is and who the goody. The jokes, such as they are, are telegraphed a mile off. Rubbish, they all are. Rubbish.

Eddie watched the dancers a-dancing beneath. Very pretty dancing dolls they were, of the variety that pop out of musical boxes, only bigger.

'What is this ballet all about?' he asked Jack.

'Boy sees girl, villain sees girl, boy meets girl, villain sees boy meet girl, boy gets parted from girl due to villain's villainy, boy remeets girl and boy gets girl in the end.'

'And *that's* the story?' Eddie asked.

'Yes,' said Jack. 'Clever, isn't it?'

'That would be irony, would it?'

Jack said, 'We should be doing our stuff!'

Eddie said, 'I don't want to!'

Beneath them, dolly ballerinas twirled. The hero, a wooden dolly who given the bulge in his tights apparently had wood on, did pluckings up on the heroine and twistings of her round in the air and the doing of something that is called a pas de deux. And also a full-tilt whirly-tronce, a double chuff-muffin rundle and a three-point turn with the appropriate hand signals and other marvellous things of a quite balletic nature.

The villain of the piece, imaginatively costumed in black, lurked in the limelight at stage left, posturing in a menacing fashion and glowering 'neath overlarge painted eyebrows.

Eddie said, 'Don't do this to me, Jack.'

Jack said, 'It has to be done.'

And then Jack did it, but did it with care. He lifted Eddie from his paw pads, raised him to shoulder height and then hurled him. Eddie, wearing the face of terror, soared out over the dancers beneath. Jack buried his face in his hands and prayed for a God to believe in and wished Eddie well. And Eddie landed safely in the topmost crystal nestings of the mighty Opera House chandelier.

Unseen by dancers, orchestra or audience.

Jack peeped out through his fingers and breathed a mighty sigh. Eddie clung to the chandelier and growled in a bitter fashion. Jack waved heartily to Eddie.

Eddie raised a paw to wave back and all but fell to his death. Jack rootled the spanner from a nameless pocket and waggled it at Eddie.

Eddie steadied himself in his crystal nest and prepared to do catchings.

And it could have been tricky. In fact, it could have been disastrous. That spanner could have fallen, down and down onto dancers beneath. But it didn't, for it was a calculated throw.

And Eddie caught that spanner between his paws and offered a thumbless thumbs-up back to Jack.

And Eddie peeped down from his lofty crystal eyrie. Through twinkling crystals, which presented the world beneath as one magical, he viewed the dancers, the orchestra and even the backstage, smelling of stables, which lurked behind the flats. It was a pretty all-encompassing overview, and one that brought no little sense of awe to Eddie Bear.

And of course bears *are* noted for their tree-climbing abilities and fearlessness of heights.

Eddie clung to the chandelier, and if he had had knuckles, these would at this time have been white. As would his face. From fear.

Jack grinned over at Eddie. 'Bears are noted for their tree-climbing abilities and fearlessness of heights,' he said to himself, 'so Eddie will be fine.'

Beneath, the villain enticed the heroine. Well, menaced was better the word. But as he did this via the medium of skilful dance, a degree of menace was lost.

And Jack looked down from on high, as did Eddie, and then Jack saw what Eddie saw, although from a different perspective.

Along the backstage the two of them crept, one Jack and the other one Eddie. The Jack carried two large suitcases. The Jack upon high's eyes widened, though the Eddie upon high's could not. Jack now did blinkings and rubbings at his eyes. That *was* him below. It really was. Though of course it really wasn't. But it looked like him and walked like him, or at least Jack thought that it did.

Although it didn't look altogether right. Jack screwed up his eyes and did long-distance squintings. What was wrong with this picture?

'He's the wrong way round,' whispered Jack. 'Oh no, he's not – it's just that I've never seen myself like that. I've only seen myself in a mirror.' And Jack did frantic wavings of the hands towards Eddie. Frantic mimings of a spanner being turned.

But Eddie wasn't looking at Jack. Eddie was looking down upon his other self. 'Damn fine-looking bear,' said Eddie to his own self. 'Anders Imperial. Cinnamon plush coat . . .'

Down below, backstage, the other Eddie and the other Jack were unpacking the contents of the suitcases and assembling some rather snazzy-looking hi-tech equipment.

Above, Jack's motions to Eddie became ever more frantic. Jack sought things to throw at the bear.

Eddie gawped at his other self. It was a damn fine-looking bear, but *what* was it? Spaceman? Space *chicken*? What? Where had it come from? Why did it look like him? Why was it doing whatever it was it was doing? And whatever *was* it doing?

Eddie now glanced in Jack's direction. Jack seemed to be doing a foolish dance.

'Spanner!' mouthed Jack. 'Release the chandelier,' he mouthed also.

'Ah,' went Eddie. 'Oh, yes.'

Beneath the two detectives, their other selves, the other Eddie and the other Jack, appeared to have concluded the setting up of their hi-tech and Hellish apparatus. The Jack was now adjusting settings, twiddling dials, making final preparations.

Eddie on high laboured with the spanner – not easy between teddy paws – at the great nut and bolt that secured the chandelier to the ceiling above.

Ballet dancers twisted and twirled. The villain, who wouldn't get around to stabbing the hero until at least the third act, did more posturing and glowering with his eyebrows. The orchestra did the slow bit that involved violins.

The other Jack did straightenings up and rubbings of his hands.

Eddie struggled with the spanner. It was a tricky nut.

Jack glanced here and there and everywhere, down at the dancers, up at Eddie, down at their other selves, out towards the orchestra. Jack felt helpless. He *was* helpless.

Eddie continued his struggling, but the tricky nut wouldn't budge.

'What do I do? What do I do?' Jack took to flapping his hands and doing a kind of tap dance.

Something tweaked him hard in the groin. Jack ceased his kind of tap dance.

'Ow,' went Jack. 'Who did that to me?'

His groin got tweaked once again.

'Stop it! Oh, it's you.' And Jack drew Wallah from his trenchcoat and held her to his ear.

'My calculations regarding the nut-turning potential of the bear would appear to be incorrect by a factor of one-point-five,' said Wallah. 'It will be necessary for you to jump from the gantry onto the chandelier and turn the nut yourself. Do take care to cling onto something safe when the chandelier falls.'

'What?' went Jack.

'It's a calculated risk,' said Wallah. 'And as I will be with you and I care about you, believe me, it is the product of most careful and meticulous calculation.'

'I can't do that,' said Jack. 'I can't.'

Eddie struggled hopelessly to turn the nut.

Lights began to pulse on the hi-tech apparatus far below.

'No,' said Jack. 'I can't. I can't.'

A big white light began to grow backstage.

'No,' said Jack. And he climbed onto the handrail of the gantry. 'No, I can't. I can't. I can't. I . . . ooooooh.'

And Jack leapt into the wide blue yonder, as it's sometimes known. And he soared, as in slow motion, and struck the mighty crystal chandelier. And did scrabblings. And did clawings. And did grippings. And did holdings on.

And did sighings.

And.

'Hello there, Jack,' said Eddie. 'I wasn't expecting you.'

'They're . . .' Jack huffed and puffed and clung on also and climbed a bit, too, until he was level with Eddie. 'They're going to blast the orchestra. We have to drop the chandelier upon them.'

'Such was my plan,' said Eddie, 'but I cannot shift the nut.'

'Let me.' And Jack took the spanner.

And down below the other Jack's fingers hovered above a big red button. And the other Jack looked down towards the other Eddie. And the other Jack smiled and the other Eddie smiled back. And those smiles were evil smiles. And the other Jack's finger pressed down upon the blood-red button.

And above, Jack fought with the tricky nut. 'It's a tricky nut,' said he.

'Get twisting,' howled Eddie, looking fearfully below. 'Oh no – something terrible's happening.'

The white and awful light spread out from the hi-tech whatnot. It penetrated the rear of the stage flat, emerged through the painted backdrop and spread out onto the stage. The ballet dancers shielded their eyes, ceased their pirouetting and fled in confusion. The clockwork orchestra engaged in orchestration played on regardless, regardless.

'Twist the blighter,' Eddie further howled.

The awful light flooded the stage.

Other howls went up now, these from the audience. The explosion of light blinded their eyes and folk rose from their seats in confusion.

Jack got a purchase upon that nut. 'I think it's giving!' he said.

The other Jack adjusted controls, did twistings of his own of buttons rather than nuts. The terrible light swept out from the stage and dipped down into the orchestra pit.

It fell upon the orchestra. Musicians rose to take flight, to escape from a terrible something. Dread. Panic. Confusion.

'Hurry, Jack, hurry!' cried Eddie.

'I'm hurrying.' Jack put his back to his work. The chandelier swung beneath him. Crystals shook. Jack forced at the nut, and the nut began slowly to turn.

But now terrible cries and screams came from the orchestra.

Terrible cracklings and poppings and sounds of hideous horribleness.

'Swing it,' cried Eddie. 'As you turn that nut, swing the chandelier – we have to drop it right on top of these monsters. Quick please, Jack, the musicians are dying. They're killing them, Jack.'

'I'm trying. I'm trying. Oh!'

Off came the nut, away from the bolt.

And . . .

'Nothing's happening!' Jack shouted.

'You'll have to kick the bolt out,' Eddie shouted back.

'How will I do that?'

'Use this!'

The voice came in a shouted form from the lighting gantry. Upon this now stood the Phantom of the Opera. He held a hammer in his hand.

'Catch it and knock out the bolt.' The Phantom threw the hammer. Jack caught the hammer. Jack used the hammer. Jack knocked out the bolt.

Then things happened in sort of slow motion. In the way that they would if this were a movie (instead of real life, as it obviously was!).

Jack knocked out the bolt.

The bolt spiralled away into space.

The chandelier fell (in slow motion, of course).

The light beneath penetrated the orchestra, bored its way into their very beings, sucked away at their very soul-stuff.

The chandelier fell.

With it fell Eddie and Jack.

Down went that chandelier. Down and down upon the other Jack and the other Eddie, who at its coming down looked up to see it doing that very thing.

Down too went Eddie and Jack.

The orchestra, writhing and dying in the terrible light.

The chandelier falling.

Now the Phantom, gripping a dangling rope. Swinging down from the gantry.

The chandelier falling.

The other Jack and the other Eddie looking up.

The orchestra dying.

The Phantom swinging (normal action now, not slow motion).

He gathers up Jack and Eddie as they fall, sweeps onward, lands them and himself all safely upon another gantry, just lower down on the other side of the stage.

Nice work.

The chandelier smashes down (normal action).

And explodes.

Into a million crystal fragments.

Spiralling crystals fly in all directions, which you can do really well with CGI nowadays.

The awful light dies.

Things go very dark.

Very still.

Cut!

That's a take!

Well done, everyone.

13

'Oh my goodness,' croaked Eddie. 'Are we still alive?'

'You are alive,' said the Phantom, lowering Eddie to the floor of the lower gantry, 'and so is your companion.'

'That is *not* what I mean.' And Eddie craned what neck he had to peer down at the shattered chandelier. It had probably been a most expensive chandelier, but there wasn't much of it left now. 'I mean the *other* we, the other me and Jack – are *they* still alive?'

Jack took to peering, clinging to the gantry handrail, his knees now wobbling somewhat.

'Can you see?' Eddie asked. 'Did we smash those blighters good?'

'I can't see,' said Jack. 'But I can see . . . Oh dear, Eddie.'

'What is it? What can you see?'

'The orchestra,' said Jack, and he said it in a strangled whisper. 'It's the orchestra, Eddie. All the musicians are dead.'

Eddie buried his face in his paws. 'This is as bad as,' he said.

'Oh Eddie, I'm so sorry.' Jack leaned down and patted his friend. 'I'm so very sorry. It's all my fault.'

'All *your* fault?' Eddie looked up with a bitter face. 'It's not *your* fault, Jack. You did everything you could. You were as brave as. It was my fault. The fault of these stupid paws. I couldn't turn the spanner. If only I'd had my hands—'

'You did *your* best,' said the Phantom in his or her (or its) toneless manner. 'And you couldn't be expected to have hands. Hands, indeed? You'd look like that creepy mayor. In fact—'

'It *was* my fault.' Eddie regarded with bitterness his fingerless, thumbless paws. 'Everything has been my fault.'

'Stop it, Eddie,' said Jack. 'You did what you could. I should have leapt over to the chandelier in the first place.'

'You were both very brave,' said the Phantom, 'and you had no care for your own safety.'

'And you saved us both,' said Jack. 'We owe you our lives.'

'Oh, it was nothing. The least I could do.'

'I won't forget this,' Jack said.

Eddie sighed, and he so hated sighing. 'We'd better go down,' he said. 'There is nothing we can do for the orchestra, but if the other me and the other you are still alive down there, I'm going to see to it that they don't remain so much longer.'

'Steady, Eddie,' said Jack.

'I'll lead the way,' said the Phantom. 'It's a bit complicated, but it does involve another secret panel.'

'We could just go down these steps,' said Jack.

'What, and miss the secret panel?'

'It's probably for the best,' Jack said.

And Jack led the way down the staircase to backstage. Much of the backdrop had collapsed beneath the fallen chandelier and Jack was able to look out across the empty stage, over the silent orchestra pit and the deserted auditorium.

Eddie Bear raised an ear. 'I hear police sirens in the distance,' he said.

'Let's make haste, then,' said Jack, and he began to sift amongst the ruination that had been the chandelier.

'Anything?' Eddie asked.

'You might help,' said Jack.

'No, I might not,' said Eddie. 'That's a lot of broken glass – I could cut myself and lose my stuffing.'

Jack did further siftings and added some rootlings to these. 'There's something,' he said.

'Bodies?' Eddie asked. Hopefully.

'No,' said Jack. 'Their machine is here, all broken in pieces. Which is something, though not very much.'

'But no bodies?'

'No,' said Jack. 'Ah, I see.'

'You see bodies?'

'I don't see bodies. But what I do see is the trap door.'

'And it's open, I suppose.' Eddie made low growling sounds. 'They've escaped.'

Jack was dragging ruined chandelier to this side and the other. 'Then we'll go after them,' he said.

'What? When they seem capable of vanishing away in a puff of smoke? Like my one did at Old King Cole's?'

'I don't think they'll find it quite so easy this time,' Jack said. 'Their machine is busted, after all.'

'Their killing machine? What has that to do with them making their escape?'

'It has to double as a means of transportation, surely?'

'That doesn't *really* follow,' said the Phantom, who hadn't said much lately and had done absolutely no rootling or sifting either. 'You are making a supposition there that is not based on any empirical evidence.'

'Please keep out of this,' said Jack. 'You saved our lives and for that we are extremely grateful, but Eddie and I must now pursue these monsters. Pursue them to their lair.'

'And destroy them,' said Eddie.

'Well, apprehend them, at least.'

'Destroy them,' said Eddie. 'At least.'

'Well, we'll see how things take shape when we catch up with them.'

'And how will we do *that*?' Eddie asked.

Jack now made a certain face. 'Now, excuse me,' he said, 'but don't I recall you telling me at some time or another – yesterday, in fact – how bears are noted for their tracking abilities?'

'Ah, yes,' said Eddie. And he sniffed. 'And I have the scent of the other me in my nostril parts right now.'

'Then sniff on please, Mister Bear,' said Jack.

'Mister Bear,' said Eddie. 'I like that, Mister Bear.'

'Then sniff on, if you will.'

'I will.'

Jack thanked the Phantom once more and promised that he would return as soon as matters were sorted and take he, she or it out for a beer, or a cocktail, or a measure of motor oil. Or something. Eddie

Bear too said his thanks and then he and Jack descended into the void that lay, uninvitingly, beneath the open trap door.

And not before time, as it happened, for now laughing policemen swarmed into the auditorium. And rushed in the direction of the stage. But there they found nothing, for the trap door was closed and the Phantom had melted away.

'Which way?' Jack asked.' I can't see a thing.'

'Follow Mister Bear,' said Eddie. 'And I'm here – stick out your hand.'

And Jack followed Eddie and Eddie Bear sniffed the way ahead. Which just went to show how subtle a bear's smelling sense can be, considering the stink of all that business down there.

'They might be hiding down here,' Jack whispered, 'waiting to get us.'

'They're not,' said Eddie. 'My nose tells me that. But if they're still upon our world, then Mister Bear will find them.'

Jack was about to voice words to the effect that he might soon grow tired of Eddie calling himself Mister Bear, but then he considered that he probably wouldn't. Mister Bear sounded good; it lent Eddie dignity.

'After you, Mister Bear,' said Jack.

And Mister Bear led on. And soon he and Jack were no longer in the Opera House; they were outside in the car park. Police car roof lights flashed around this car park, and Eddie and Jack moved with stealth.

'Actually, why are *we* moving with stealth?' Jack asked.

'Because,' said Eddie, 'this would be the moment when the misidentification scenario kicks in and we both get arrested.'

'I'll bet I can move with more stealth than you,' Jack said.

'And I'll bet you cannot.'

Eddie did further sniffings at the evening air. 'To use one of your favourite words,' he said, 'damn.'

'They took a car, didn't they?' Jack asked.

'That is what they did, but I can still track them. We'll just have to get the Anders Faircloud and skirt around the police cordon until I can pick up the scent again.'

'Right,' said Jack, and he plucked up Eddie. 'Then let's do this fast.' And with that Jack took to his heels in a stealthy kind of a way.

There followed then far more skirting around the police cordon than either Eddie or Jack might have hoped for. Jack drove with his head down, but Eddie had to stick his out of the window.

They were outside Tinto's Bar when Eddie picked up the scent once more.

'That's typical,' said Eddie. 'How dearly I'd like a beer.'

'Beers later, justice first,' said Jack.

'Nice phrase,' said Eddie. 'We could put that on the door of the office. And on our business cards. Put your foot down, Jack, that way.'

Jack now put his foot down, but the car just poodled along.

'I'll paint it on the door of the car, too,' said Jack. 'After I've given it a service.'

And so they moved off, in *cold* pursuit. Which indeed was a shame, because there's nothing like a good car chase to spice things up. A good car chase always has the edge, even over falling chandeliers.

Eddie kept on sniffing and Jack kept on driving.

And sometime later Eddie said, 'We're getting close now, Jack.'

And Jack looked out through the windscreen and said, 'We're approaching Toy Town again.'

'Damn,' said Eddie once more, and he smote his head with a paw. 'It was obvious they'd return here. We should have reasoned it out. We've wasted too much time.'

'We might still have the element of surprise on our side.' Jack switched off the headlights and the car did poodlings to a halt. 'Down the hillside once more,' said Jack, 'and this time we'll keep a careful lookout. Any big bright lights and we run like bitches.'

'Like *what*?' Eddie asked.

'Lady dogs,' said Jack. 'What did you think I meant?'

And down the hillside they went, through those briars and that gorse and even those nettles and stuff. And Jack held Eddie above them all, and troubled not about his trenchcoat.[*]

'To Bill's house, is it?' whispered Jack.

'That's what my nose tells me,' said Eddie.

Across the yellow-bricked road they went, across the town square and through that darkened alley. Finally, Jack set Eddie down.

'You could have walked the last bit,' he said.

'I was conserving my energy.'

'Still have the key?'

'Of course.'

But Jack didn't need it. The door to Bill Winkie's was open.

'Stay here,' said Jack. 'I'll go inside and see what's what.'

'What's what?' Eddie asked.

'This is neither the time nor the place,' Jack said, and he slipped into the house.

And presently returned.

'They're not in there,' Jack told Eddie.

'No,' said Eddie. 'But all those guns are.'

And so the two detectives went inside and availed themselves of weapons. Jack did mighty cockings of a mightier firepiece.

'The old M134 7.62mmm General Clockwork Mini-gun,' said Jack. 'My all-time favourite.'

'Everyone's all-time favourite,' said Eddie, 'but somewhat heavy for me and tricky to fire without fingers.' And Eddie selected weaponry that was built with the bear in mind.

'And now?' Jack asked as he slipped bandoliers of bullets over his shoulders and tucked grenades in his pockets.

'Payback time,' said Eddie.

That full moon was in the sky once more, silver-plating rooftops, and a chill was in the air. Jack turned up his collar and Eddie sniffed the chillified air.

'Follow me,' said Eddie Bear, and with that said led the way.

They threaded their way through alleyways, and up front paths and

[*] Well, it *was* all soiled with the sewage.

out of back gardens and finally Eddie said, 'Stop a minute, Jack. That's where they went. Up there.'

Jack looked up, up the hill he looked, the hill that rose up behind the conurbation that was Toy Town. The hill upon which those great letters stood. Those letters that had once spelt out TOYTOWNLAND.

'Up there?' Jack said. 'But what's up there, anyway?'

Eddie shook his head.

'And on the other side of the hill, what?'

Eddie shook his head once more. 'I've never been to the other side of that hill,' he said. 'In fact . . .' and he paused.

So Jack asked, 'What?'

'Oh, it's a crazy thing,' said Eddie. 'A silly thing. It's just what some toys believe.'

'Well, go on then and tell me.'

'No,' said Eddie. 'You'll laugh.'

'I'm really not in a laughing mood right now.'

'It's a silly thing, it's nothing at all.'

'Just tell me, Eddie.'

'Did you say "Just tell me, Mister Bear"?'

'I did.'

And so Eddie told him. 'It's just a belief, a myth, probably, but it's what we were brought up to believe. I was told by Bill when I was his bear never to wander up that hill, because if I did, I'd be lost.'

'That's fair enough,' said Jack. 'Bill cared about you. You were his bear. He loved you, he didn't want you to get lost.'

'Not *get* lost, Jack. *Be* lost.'

'*Get* lost, *be* lost, what's the difference, Edd— Mister Bear?'

'The difference is,' said Mr Eddie Bear, 'that I would *be* lost. The theory was that that hill marks the end of Toy Town – the end of everything, in fact. Beyond that hill is nothing. If you went over that hill you'd fall off the edge of the world and be gone for ever.'

'Well, that *is* silly,' said Jack.

'There,' said Eddie. 'I knew you'd say that. I wish I hadn't told you now.'

'Hang on there,' said Jack. 'Hold on, if you will.'

Eddie didn't know what to hold on to, so he stood his ground.

'Beyond that hill lies the end of this world – that's what you were told?'

Eddie nodded and continued standing his ground.

'Eddie,' said Jack, 'look up there – what do you see?'

'A dark and threatening hillside,' said Eddie. 'Well, threatening to me.'

'Yes, I can see that, but what else?'

'The Toy Town letters, that's all.'

'Eddie, look at those letters and tell me what you see.'

'Not much – most of them are gone. I see "TO TO LA".'

'And beyond that lies the end of this world?'

'Look, it's just what I was told. You believe these things when you're young.'

'Wake up, Eddie,' said Jack. 'Look at the letters. What do they say? What do they tell you about the *beyond*?'

'About the beyond?' And Eddie scratched at his head.

'You're not going to get it, are you?' Jack said. 'Even though it's there, staring you in the face?'

Eddie Bear looked up at Jack. 'I don't know what you mean,' he said.

'Wake up, Eddie,' said Jack once more. 'You've used the phrase yourself enough times. Something about "Beyond The—"'

'Second Big O,' said the suddenly enlightened Eddie. 'Beyond The Second Big O.'

'Exactly,' said Jack. 'And there it is, The Second Big O in what once spelt TOYTOWNLAND. That's where these invaders have come from. They come from Beyond The Second Big O – and *that* is The Second Big O.'

Eddie Bear looked up at Jack. 'You genius,' he said.

'Well, thank you, Mister Bear,' said Jack, 'but I just reasoned it out. That's what we detectives do, reason it out.'

'Or calculate,' said Eddie, 'As in the Opera House business. Do you feel up to confiding in me about that yet?'

'Later,' said Jack. 'For now we have to get after the murderers. What does your nose tell you, Eddie?'

'It tells me,' said Eddie, dismally, 'that that is the way they went. Beyond The Second Big O.' Eddie sniffed. '*Through* The Second Big O.'

'Then that's where *we're* going. Come.' And Jack set off. And then Jack turned. 'Come on, then,' he said.

But Eddie once more stood his ground. Most firmly so, in fact.

'Well, come on then, Eddie,' said Jack. 'Let's go, come on now.'

'Ah,' said Eddie and Eddie stood firm.

'Come on now,' said Jack.

'I can't,' said Eddie. 'I just can't come.'

'What do you mean?'

'I mean that I can't go through there,' Eddie said. 'We must call Bellis, get him to employ troops, send an armed task force through, if he will. If he dares.'

'Dare?' said Jack. 'What's to dare? We've got weapons, Eddie. Stop this foolishness, come on.'

'I can't come on, Jack. I can't. It's the end of my world up there. I don't know what will happen if I leave my world.'

'There's only the two of them. We're a match for them.'

'There isn't just two, Jack. If there's another world beyond that O, then there could be a whole worldful, another whole worldful and not yours or mine.'

'You don't know what's there and you won't know until we've gone through and found out. Those monsters that are impersonating us have killed *your* kind, Eddie, many now of *your* kind. They'll return and kill more if we don't stop them.'

'We'll lie in wait, then,' said Eddie.

'You can walk,' said Jack, 'of your own accord, or else I'll carry you.'

'You wouldn't!' Eddie drew back in alarm. 'You wouldn't treat me like *that*.'

'All right, I wouldn't, but I'm pleading with you, Eddie. Let's go after them now, before the scent goes cold. We'll be careful and I'm damn sure that they won't be expecting us.'

'You don't understand,' said Eddie. 'You didn't grow up here.'

Jack looked down at Eddie Bear. The bear was clearly shivering.

'You *are* afraid,' said Jack. 'You really are.'

'Yes I am, Jack. I *really* am.'

Jack cocked his head from one side to the other. 'You knew,' said he. 'You've known all along.'

'Know what?' said Eddie. 'What did I know?'

'You knew what the phrase meant. Beyond The Second O. If you grew up here and you were told you'd be lost if you went over that hill, you *had* to know what the phrase meant.'

'Well, perhaps I did. But it doesn't matter now, does it?'

'Look,' said Jack, 'whatever is out there, I'll protect you. I'll protect you with my life.'

'I know you will, Jack – you've done it before.'

'Then come with me.'

'I can't.'

'Then I will go alone.' And Jack turned to do so.

'No,' cried Eddie. 'Jack, please don't go up there alone.'

'Then come with me, Eddie. Come with me, *Mister* Bear.'

Eddie dithered and dithering wasn't his style. 'Let's go tomorrow,' he said. 'In the daylight.'

Jack hefted his mighty Mini-gun. 'I'm going *now*,' he said, 'and if you won't come, if you *can't* come, then I understand. You're brave, Eddie. I know you're brave. But if this is too much for you, then so be it. Wait here and I'll be back as soon as I can.'

'Jack, please don't go.'

'I must.'

And with that Jack turned away, looked up the hill, up at the letters TO TO LA, and then Jack set off up the lonely hillside, and Eddie Bear watched him go.

And Eddie Bear made faces and scuffed his paw pads in the moonlit dirt. He couldn't let Jack go up there on his own, he couldn't. There was no telling what kind of trouble he'd get himself into. Eddie would have to go, too. No matter how great his fear.

And Eddie took a step or two forward.

And then a step or two back.

'This is ridiculous,' said Eddie. 'I *can* do it. I *must* do it. I *can* and I *must* and I *will*.'

But he couldn't.

The figure of Jack was diminishing, as is often the case with perspective. Eddie watched as Jack climbed higher, bound for that Second Big O.

'Come on, Eddie,' the bear told himself. 'Jack is your bestest friend. You would never forgive yourself if he came to harm and you could have protected him from it.'

'I know,' Eddie now told himself, 'but I've been hoping against all hope that there was another solution. That the murderers *were* simply spacemen, or something. Something not of this world, but *not* something from Beyond The Second Big O. Because beyond there lies a terrible, dreadful something. That's what I was taught and that is what I believe.'

'And you're letting your bestest friend wander into that something alone,' Eddie further told himself. 'What kind of bear are you?'

'A terrified one,' Eddie further, further, further told himself.

'Oh, what do I do? Tell me, what do I do?' And Eddie, although no devout bear, prayed to the God of All Bears. 'I don't know what to do,' Eddie prayed. 'Please won't you send me a sign?'

And perhaps it was the God of All Bears, or perhaps it was not, but a sign was made manifest to Eddie. Manifest in the Heavens, it was, as such signs often are.

And Eddie looked up and Eddie beheld. And he beheld it on high.

The moonlit sky was studded with stars, but one was brighter than all the rest. Eddie Bear peeped through his button eyes. 'There's a new star in Heaven tonight,' he said.

And the new star, the bright new star, grew brighter still.

'Is that you, Mister God?' asked Eddie.

And brighter and closer grew this star until it was all over big.

And Eddie looked up at this very big star.

And Eddie Bear said, 'Oh no!'

For this star, it now seemed, was no star at all. This star now grew even bigger and hovered now overhead. For this star, it seemed, was no star at all. It was a spaceship instead.

A proper flying saucer of a spaceship, all aglow with twinkling lights and a polished underbelly.

And the saucer now hovered low above Eddie and Eddie could make out rivets and tin plate and a sort of logo embossed into the underside of the brightly glowing craft. And this logo resembled a kind of stylised, in-profile sort of a head. And this was the head of a chicken.

And a bright light swept down upon Eddie.

And Eddie Bear took to his paw pads.

And onward scampered Eddie with the spaceship keeping pace, and the light, a sort of death-ray one, he supposed, a-burning up the grass and gorse and briars and nettles and stuff.

'Wah!' cried Eddie as he scampered. 'Wah! Oh, Jack. Help me!'

Jack, a goodly way up the hill, turned and looked over his shoulder. And Jack saw the spaceship and Jack saw Eddie.

And Jack was frankly afeared.

And when Jack had managed to summon a voice, this voice cried, 'Eddie, hurry!'

'I *am* hurrying.' And Eddie was, his little legs pounding beneath him. And Jack now hefted his great big gun and flipped off the safety catch.

The spaceship, keeping pace with Eddie, burned up the hillside behind him. The gorse and briars and nettles and stuff took all to blazing away. A goodly fire was spreading now, fanning out to Eddie's rear.

'Hurry!' cried Jack. And then he let rip. Let rip with the Mini-gun. The clockwork motion hurled projectiles through six revolving barrels. Barrels spat flame and bullets, bullets that tore tracer-like into the moonlit sky.

And the craft moved onward, bullets bouncing from its hull. And the light swept onward, raising fire in Eddie's wake.

And the bear rushed onward, bound for his bestest friend.

'You're a really bad spacecraft,' cried Jack, and he flung the Mini-gun aside and brought forth a grenade from his trenchcoat pocket. 'Come on, Eddie, faster now,' and Jack pulled the pin and wondered how many seconds 'til *Boom!*

'Ow!' went Eddie. 'Ouch!' And his heels took fire.

'One,' said Jack. 'Two. How many? Ten, I suppose, so three, no, that would be four now, or maybe six, or seven, or . . . damn.'

And Jack hurled the grenade.

And it was a good hurl, but it fell short.

And a big chunk of hillside exploded.

And some of that hillside rained down upon Eddie.

'Don't do that, Jack!' cried the bear.

Jack pulled out another grenade and once more pulled the pin.

'One, two, three, four,' Jack counted. 'Hurry, Eddie, hurry, eight, nine, oh!' And Jack did another hurling and ducked his head as he did so. For the spacecraft was very near now, as indeed was Eddie.

'Quickly, Eddie.' And Jack snatched up the bear and ran very fast indeed.

And next there came an explosion, an explosion on high. And the spaceship swung about in the sky, flames roaring from its upper dome area. And then it began its plunging down, in Jack and Eddie's direction.

'Oh no!' shouted Jack, and he ran and he leapt, a-clutching Eddie tight. And as the spaceship smashed down to the hillside with a mighty explosion, which far exceeded that of the falling chandelier and probably had the edge over even a car chase when it came to exciting spectacle, Jack leapt for his life, leapt with Eddie, up and through and beyond.

Jack leapt through The Second Big O.

And through and out and into nothing.

And down and down and down.

And Jack tumbled down.

And Eddie, too.

And down and down and down.

And, 'Oooh!' cried Eddie.

And, 'Ouch!' cried Jack.

And, 'Ooooh!' and, 'Ouch!' and, 'Ow!'

And then all finally became still and silent and Jack lay upon grass, and so did Eddie, and moonlight fell down on them both.

'Are we still alive?' Eddie asked. 'And this time I *do* mean us.'

'So it would seem.' Jack patted at his limbs. None, it appeared, were broken.

Eddie did flexings at his seams, and none, it seemed, were torn.

'And *where* are we?' And Eddie looked all about himself.

'We went through The Second Big O.'

'Oh no!'

'But we're still alive, don't knock it.'

'And we are . . .' Eddie felt at the ground. 'We're on grass, on a hillside.'

'Because we're on the other side of the hill,' said Jack. 'Which means that you had nothing to fear. I'd like to say, "I told you so," but as I didn't it wouldn't help much.'

'On grass,' said Eddie. 'On grass.'

'On grass,' Jack said. 'Just on the other side of the hill.'

'Well,' said Eddie, and Eddie rose, 'I don't know what you were making all the fuss about.'

'*Me?*' said Jack. '*I* was making all that fuss? Sorry?'

'I forgive you,' said Eddie.

'What?' said Jack.

'It doesn't matter, forget it.'

Jack now climbed to his feet. He dusted down his trenchcoat, sniffed at his fingers and said, 'Yuk!'

'You'll want to get that trenchcoat cleaned,' said Eddie. 'I know a good dry-cleaners. Although I've never understood how dry-cleaning works – do you know how it does?'

'Don't change the subject, Eddie.'

'What subject would that be?'

Jack smiled down upon Eddie. 'It doesn't matter, *Mister* Bear. We're both safe and that's all that matters.'

'You certainly taught those space chickens something,' said Eddie. 'Don't mess with my bestest friend Jack. That's what you taught them. Well done you.'

'It *was* a big explosion,' said Jack. 'Actually, I'm quite surprised that a lot of flaming spaceship didn't rain down upon us. Pretty lucky, eh?'

'Pretty *damn* lucky,' said Eddie. And looked all around and about.

'And so this is it?' he said. '*This* is what I spent my whole life dreading? The land Beyond The Second Big O. And all it is is another hillside – not much of a big deal, eh, Jack?'

Jack didn't answer Eddie. Jack was gazing back up the hillside. Up in the direction from which he and Eddie had tumbled down and down.

'Not much, eh, Jack?' said Eddie once again. 'Eh, Jack?'

But Jack didn't answer.

'Jack, are you listening to me?' asked Eddie.

And Jack stirred from his staring. 'Eddie,' said Jack, 'tell me this.'

'Tell you what?'

'Well, we plunged through The Second Big O, didn't we?'

'We did.'

'The Second Big O in the remaining few letters of what once spelled out "TOYTOWNLAND" and now just spell "TO TO LA".'

'That we did,' said the bear.

'So, looking back,' said Jack, 'at those big letters, we should see the reverse of "TO TO LA". "AJ OT OT", in fact.'

'Indeed,' said Eddie, 'but I don't know how you were able to pronounce that.'

'But that's not what I'm seeing,' said Jack. 'Those big letters on the hillside, they're not spelling out "AJ OT OT".'

'They're not?' said Eddie.

'They're not.'

'So what *are* they spelling?'

And Jack pointed upwards and Eddie looked up upwards and then Eddie said, 'What does *that* mean?'

And Jack said slowly, 'I don't know what it means, but those letters spell out "HOLLYWOOD".'

14

'Hollywood?' said Eddie Bear. 'What does *Hollywood* mean?'

'Place name, I suppose,' said Jack, a-dusting at his trenchcoat. 'This coat is going to need some serious cleaning.'

'Forget the coat!' And Eddie raised his paws. 'We *are* in another world, Jack. This isn't just the other side of the hill.'

'Seems so.' Jack stretched his shoulders and Jack also yawned, tiredness catching up with him. 'But it looks pretty much like the world we just came from – there's nothing scary here.'

Eddie Bear shuddered and shook his head. 'There is something scary, I know it.'

'You *don't* know it, Eddie. You're just disorientated.' Jack sniffed at the air and Jack took off his trenchcoat. 'It's warmer here at least, which is nice.'

Eddie now also sniffed the air and with these sniffs he stiffened. 'No, Jack,' he said. 'Not nice, not nice at all.'

'You've picked up the scent again?'

'Not the scent, Jack. Not the scent.'

'Then what?'

Eddie gave the air another sniffing. 'Meatheads, Jack,' he said, and there was fear in his growly voice.

'Men?' said Jack. 'Nearby? Where?'

'Everywhere,' said Eddie Bear. 'We're in the world of the meatheads.'

Jack looked back at the Hollywood sign. 'The world of the meatheads,' he said.

*

Now, for those who have an interest in such things as these, it is to be noted that . . .*

For those who do *not* have an interest in such things, it probably doesn't matter.

'So what do you think we should do now?' Jack asked.

'Go back,' said Eddie. 'Climb through The Second Big O up there and hope it leads back to our own world.'

'Perhaps I put it poorly,' said Jack. 'What I meant to say was, now that we *are here*, *to stay*, until the job is done, what should we do next?'

Eddie yawned mightily. 'Don't think I haven't noticed,' he said, 'that there is a vast city down the hill, all lit up in the night. How about us finding somewhere safe and taking a bit of a sleep?'

Jack did further yawnings, too. 'Good plan, Mister Bear,' said he.

As going forward was fearsome for Eddie, they tramped back to the Hollywood sign. And from there Jack looked out at the lights of the big city that lay below. And it was (and is) an impressive sight. And Jack was suitably impressed. And behind the sign they located the little hut where the bulb-man who had tended to the lights way back in the nineteen-thirties had spent his illuminating existence.

The door was padlocked, but Jack soon had the padlock picked.

---

* The Hollywood sign is probably the most famous sign in all of the world. It was erected in 1923 to advertise the housing development beneath it. The original letters, fifty feet high and thirty feet wide, spelled out 'Hollywoodland' and were lit up nightly by more than four thousand bulbs. With a chap living in a little hut behind the sign, whose job was to change them when they needed changing. Nice work if you can get it. In 1932 an aspiring young starlet named Peg Entwhistle threw herself off the H. Others followed her example, but to avoid the bad publicity their names went unpublished in the Los Angeles press. In 1939, the light-bulb chap was sacked, the sign fell into disrepair and all its light bulbs were stolen. But then in 1949, the Hollywood Chamber of Commerce restored the sign, knocking down the 'land' bit at the end. By 1978 it was all knackered again, so the Chamber of Commerce got a fund-raising campaign going, raised enough cash to completely restore the sign and have kept it looking smart ever since. With the aid of sponsorship from Hollywood stars. Apparently Alice Cooper sponsors The Second Big O.

The two exhausted detectives crept into the little hut, pulled shut the door and settled down in the darkness upon ancient light-bulb boxes. And in less time than it takes to interpret a Forgotheum conundrum, using as your baseline the Magwich/Holliston Principle, they were both quite fast asleep.

A big smiley sun rose over the Hollywood Hills. It didn't have a big smiley face like the one that rose over Toy City, but it got the job done and its rays slipped in through the dusty panes of the little old hut and touched upon sleeping faces.

Jack awoke with a yawn and a shudder, blinked and sniffed and clicked his jaw. Hopes that the doings of the previous night had been naught but dreamstuff ebbed all away as Jack surveyed his surroundings.

Man-sized shed with a man-sized door. Man-sized tools hanging on a rack. A pile of what looked to be newspapers tied up with string. 'A world of men,' said Jack to himself. 'Hardly a nightmare scenario. I grew up in a town inhabited by men and women; Toy City has to be the only city inhabited by toys. Probably everywhere else, no matter on which world, is inhabited by men.' Jack paused for a moment then, before adding, 'Except those inhabited by an advanced race of chickens, that would be.' A further pause. 'But looking on the bright side, Eddie didn't smell chickens last night, only men.'

'Talking to yourself again?' asked Eddie, awakening.

'Only time I ever have an intelligent conversation,' said Jack.

'Most amusing.' Eddie now looked all about himself. 'Shame,' said he. 'As you know, we bears never dream, but I really hoped that I might have dreamed this last night.'

'I'm sure there's nothing to get alarmed about, Eddie. As I was just saying to myself, I come from a town exclusively inhabited by men.'

'Nice place, was it?' Eddie asked.

'Well,' said Jack.

'Well,' said Eddie, 'I seem to recall that you hated it so much that you ran away from it.'

'Which doesn't mean to say that this Hollywood place won't be nice. Chin up, Eddie, let's look on the bright side, eh?'

Eddie's tummy rumbled. 'Breakfast would be nice,' he said. 'Perhaps there's a farm nearby where we could steal some eggs, or something.'

'Steal some eggs? Have you decided to give up detective work and pursue a life of crime?'

'You possess local currency, then?'

'Well.'

Eddie was up now and peeping through the door crack. 'Much as I hate to do it, then,' he said, 'let's wander carefully into this world of meatheads and see what there is to be seen.'

'Trust me,' said Jack. 'Everything will be fine.'

And so down Mount Lee they went,[*] with Jack whistling brightly in order to disguise his nervousness and Eddie quoting and requoting Jack in his head. 'Everything will be fine,' he requoted. 'What a load of old toot.'

Eventually they reached a fence, climbed over it and found a road.

'See,' said Jack, 'nothing to be worried about.'

'I've never had a particular terror of roads,' said Eddie. 'You gormster.'

'There are houses here, nice houses,' said Jack. 'Should I knock and ask for a glass of milk or something?'

'Let's head on down,' said Eddie. 'We saw all the lights last night – this must be a very big city. Big cities have alleyways, many of them behind restaurants. We'll just rifle through some bins.'

'I'm not doing *that*!'

'Well, you make your own arrangements, then. I'm as hungry as.'

It's a long walk down to LA proper. But you do pass some very nice houses on the way. Homes of the Hollywood stars, they are, although Jack and Eddie weren't to know this yet.

'These are really swish houses here,' said Jack.

'Probably the homes of the local P.P.P.s.' Eddie peered in through

---

[*] For it is indeed upon Mount Lee that the Hollywood sign is to be found.

magnificent gates, curlicues of bronze and steel, intricate and delicate, held fast by padlock and chain.

'*Ra! Ra! Ra! Ra! Ra!*' It was a most excruciating sound, loud and raw and fierce. Something huge slammed against the gate, causing Eddie to fall back in alarm. A monstrous hound yelled further *Ras!* and snarled with hideous teeth.

'Down, boy,' called Jack. 'Nice doggy, down.'

'Run for your life,' howled Eddie.

'It's all right, it can't get through the gates.'

'I hate it here, Jack, I hate it.'

They walked along the centre of the road. To either side of them now, growly dogs appeared at padlocked gateways and bid them anything but a warm welcome.

'You don't think,' said Jack, 'that you might have got it all wrong, Eddie? We're not in Dog World, are we?'

'Gormster.'

And then they had to get off the road and off the road with haste.

'*Ba! Ba! Ba! Ba! Ba!*' went this scary something.

And then something wonderful rushed by.

Jack looked on and he did so in awe. 'An automobile,' he said.

And such an automobile was this. An electric-blue Cadillac Eldorado, circa 1955. Big fins, fabulous tail-lights, all the trimmings. Nice.

'Wow,' went Jack as the Cadillac sped on. 'Did you ever see anything quite like that?'

Eddie shook his shaken head. 'Did you see the *size* of it?' he said. 'I've seen swimming pools smaller than that. And . . .' And Eddie rubbed at his nose and coughed a little, too. 'That wasn't clockwork, was it, Jack? It had smoke coming out of the back.'

Jack shrugged and Jack said, 'Let's keep moving.'

'I'm hungry.'

'So am I.'

And so they wandered on. But for the *Ra*-ing dogs and the *Ba*-ing car they saw no more signs of life.

'Where is everybody?' Eddie asked.

'Sun's just up,' said Jack. 'I suppose it's early yet.'

'What time do you have on your wristwatch?'

Jack checked his watch, shook it, put it to his ear. 'It's stopped,' he said. 'That's odd, it's never stopped before, although—'

'Although what?'

'Well, I never understood how it worked anyway – it doesn't have any insides, just a winder connected to the hands.'

'I thought that was all a watch needed,' said Eddie.

'No,' said Jack, and they wandered on.

And at last reached Hollywood Boulevard.

Eddie looked up and Eddie was afeared. 'Jack,' whispered Eddie, 'Jack, oh Jack, those are very large buildings.'

'A world of men,' said Jack. 'Look – there's a hotel, what does it say? The Roosevelt.'*

Jack looked up with considerable awe. 'I love *that*,' he said.

'I hate it,' said Eddie. 'But there is one thing I do know about hotels: they always have a lot of dustbins round the back.'

Now it is a fact well known to those who know it well, and those who know it well do not necessarily harbour a particular interest in the foibles of architects, that the rears of hotels are always rubbish. Which is to say that whilst the front façades display all the architectural splendours that those who commissioned their construction could afford, the rears of the buildings are a proper disgrace. They're all waste pipes and rusty fire escapes and dustbins, lots of dustbins.

Jack stood in the alleyway to the rear of the Roosevelt, looking up at the waste-pipe outlets and rusty fire escapes; Eddie sniffed his way along the dustbins.

'This one,' said Eddie. 'Lid off please, Jack.'

'This is disgusting, Eddie.'

'Look,' said Eddie, 'I'm not proud of this sort of thing, but it's a

---

* The Roosevelt Hotel is a magnificent Spanish-colonial-style affair, built in 1927 and thoroughly unspoilt, and it is to be noted that not only were the very first Academy Awards presented there, but Marilyn Monroe did her first ever professional photoshoot beside the pool.

bear thing, okay? We bears might be noted and admired for our exquisite table manners, but we do like a good old rummage around in a dustbin now and then. *You* do things that *I* find abhorrent, okay?'

Jack lifted the dustbin lid. 'What things do I do that you find abhorrent?' he asked.

Eddie shinned into the dustbin. 'You shag dollies,' he said.

'I . . . em . . .' Jack sniffed in Eddie's direction. There was a rather enticing smell issuing from the dustbin.

'They must have had a big do on last night,' said Eddie. 'Look at all this lot.' And he passed Jack an unnibbled cake and a piece of cheese.

'It might smell nice, but I could catch something horrible.'

'Wipe it clean on your trenchcoat . . . No, on second thoughts . . .'

There was a remarkably large amount of edible food to be found in that dustbin, and it appeared to have been gift-wrapped in paper napkins and needed next to no wiping off.

Jack had a rumbling stomach, but dined without any joy.

His repast complete, Eddie sat with his back against the dustbin and his paws doing pattings at his swollen belly. 'Now that was what I call breakfast,' he said. 'I couldn't eat another thing.'

'Not even this wafer-thin mint?' asked Jack, which rang a bell somewhere.

Jack sat down beside Eddie. 'Well, on the bright side,' he said, 'and we must always look on the bright side, much as I loathe the idea of dining from dustbins, it looks like we'll never starve in Hollywood.'

'What the Hell, fella? What d'ya think you're at?'

Jack looked up in startlement. A ragged man looked down.

If Jack had known anything of the Bible, Jack might have described this man as biblically ragged. He was wild of eye and wild of beard, of which he had more than his share. What face of him was to be seen above the beard and around the eyes was tanned by grime and sunlight. His clothes hung in ribbons; his gnarled hands had horrid yellow nails.

'My Goddamn trashcan!' roared this biblical figure.

'Excuse me?' said Jack, with exaggerated politeness.

'My Goddamn breakfast, you—'

'Sorry,' said Jack, and he rose with some haste to his feet. 'We're new to these parts, we had no idea.'

The biblical figure pushed past him and rootled around in the open bin. 'You ate my cake! She said there'd be cake.'

'It was very nice cake,' said Eddie. 'I'm not sure what flavour, but very nice nonetheless.'

The biblical figure turned his wild eyes back to Jack. 'So,' said he, 'a wise guy, is it, making growly voices?'

'No,' said Jack, 'I didn't – that was Eddie.'

'Eddie?' The wild eyes looked wildly about.

'Hello there,' said Eddie. 'Pleased to meet you.'

The wild eyes looked down.

The wild eyes widened.

'There is some cake left,' said Eddie. 'I tried to eat it all, but I'm ashamed to say that I failed.'

'For the love of God!' The biblical figure fell back against the bin and floundered about like a mad thing. Jack offered what help he could and eased him once more into the vertical plane.

'Get your Goddamn hands off me!'

'Only trying to help,' said Jack.

'Make it do it again, go on.'

'Sorry?' said Jack.

'That little furry thing, make it talk again.'

'I'm not a *thing*,' said Eddie. 'I'm an Anders Imperial, cinnamon plush coat—'

'Holy Baby Jesus!' went the biblical figure, which was suitably biblical but somewhat blasphemous, because you are not supposed to use the name of Jesus in that fashion. 'How does it do that? Is it on strings?'

'*On strings?*' said Eddie. 'How dare you.'

'You're working it somehow.' The wild eyes turned once more upon Jack. 'It's a Goddamn puppet of some kind, ain't it?'

'Ah,' said Jack, most thoughtfully. 'Yes, you're right, of course.'

'Eh?' said Eddie.

'Knew it.' The biblical figure did a little dance. 'Darnedest thing I ever saw. How much do you want for it?'

'He's not for sale,' said Jack. 'He has, er, sentimental value.'

'Eh?' said Eddie, once again.

'Shush,' said Jack to Eddie.

The ragged man knelt down before Eddie. 'Cute little critter, ain't he?' he said. 'Though real ragged and he don't smell too good.'

'That's good, coming from *you*,' said Eddie, shielding his nostrils.

'Darnedest thing.' And the ragged fellow rose and did another dance.

'Well, nice as it was to meet you,' said Jack, 'and sorry as we are about eating your breakfast, being unaccustomed to, er, trashcan protocol in this vicinity—'

'Eh?' now went the ragged man.

'We must be moving along,' said Jack. 'We're—'

'Carny folk,' said the ragged man. 'Don't tell me, let me guess from your accent. English, is it? Carny man from England, I'll bet.'

'English carny man?' said Jack slowly.

'Here with the circus. I'll bet this is one big midway attraction.'

'That's right,' said Jack. 'And we, er, *I'm* an English carny man and I should be on my way.'

'Can't let you do that, buddy.'

'Sorry,' said Jack, 'but I must.'

'Nope. I can't let you do that.' And from a ragged pocket the ragged fellow pulled a knife. And it was a big one and it looked sharp.

'Now see here,' said Jack, which is what folk always say first under such circumstances.

'You ate my breakfast – you owe me, buddy. I'll take your furry thing here in payment.'

'No,' Jack said. 'You will not.'

The knife was suddenly very near Jack. What sunlight the alleyway gathered fell on its polished blade.

'You don't really want to do that,' Jack said, which is another thing folk say in such circumstances – the brave, tough ones, anyway.

'Don't I really?' The gnarled hand flicked the blade before Jack's eyes.

'No,' said Jack, 'you don't. Because if you do not put that knife away at once, I will have no option other than to blow your balls off.'

'Jack, really,' said Eddie.

The ragged man did wild-eyed glancings downwards.

Jack held a pistol, aimed at the ragged man's groin.

'Now what the Hell do you call *that*?'

'It's a gun,' said Jack. 'Perhaps you've not seen one before.'

'I've seen plenty o' guns, fella, but that ain't a real one – that one's a toy.'

'It will cause you considerable damage at this close range,' said Jack.

'Oh yeah? What's it gonna do, hit me with a little flag with "BANG" written on it?'

'It does *this*,' said Jack, and he aimed the gun into the air and pulled the trigger.

And nothing happened.

Jack squeezed the trigger once more and then once again. Nothing else happened either.

'That's odd,' said Jack, examining the pistol.

'Ain't it just!' And the knife's blade flashed once more before Jack's face. 'Hand me the puppet or I'll cut ya deep.'

'But you don't understand—'

'I understand *this*.' And the knife went up. And the knife went down. And the knife fell into the alleyway. And the wild eyes of the biblical figure crossed and then they closed and the figure fell to the ground.

Eddie Bear stood on the dustbin, holding between his paws the dustbin lid.

'Nice shot,' said Jack. 'Right on the back of his head.'

'His conversation tired me,' said Eddie. 'What a most unpleasant man.'

Jack took the lid and helped Eddie down. Eddie went over and bit the ragged man on the nose.

Jack said, 'Don't do that.'

'I think we had best be on our way,' said Eddie. 'I'll just bet they have policemen in this city too and I don't think I want to meet them.'

Jack shook his pistol about. 'This is really odd,' he said. 'First the wristwatch, now this pistol. I wonder.' Jack pulled a grenade from his pocket and removed the pin.

'No, not *here*,' said Eddie.

'I just want to test a proposition.' Jack hurled the grenade and ducked. And Jack counted, too, up to twenty.

'Doesn't work,' said Jack. And he pulled out his remaining weaponry from his pockets and tested it, too. And none of that worked either.

'This I find worrying,' Jack said, and Eddie agreed.

Eddie tested the gun that he had, and as this didn't work either he tossed it away. 'We'll be in trouble when we finally track down our other selves,' he said. Miserably.

'Well,' said Jack, 'looking on the bright side once again, given that amazing automobile we saw, I'll just bet they have some really amazing weapons here.'

'Well, that we already know,' said Eddie. 'Don't we? The death rays and everything.'

'If they come from here,' said Jack. 'Perhaps they came from Chicken World.'

The ragged man made moaning sounds.

'Time to go,' said Eddie.

They reached the end of the alleyway and looked out at the world beyond, the world of men. And men were moving now, out and about on Hollywood Boulevard. Well-dressed men and women, too. The men wore fedoras and double-breasted wide-shouldered suits. The women wore colourful dresses; they looked most appealing to Jack.

'Now, Eddie,' said Jack to the bear, 'I don't want you to take offence at this, but I think it would be better if I carried you. It would appear that in these parts talking bears are the exception rather than the rule.'

'I'd gathered that,' said Eddie. 'I'm not stupid, you know. I'm as intelligent as.'

'Then if you'll pardon me,' said Jack, 'I'll carry you, Mister Bear.'

And so Jack carried Eddie along the boulevard.

And what Jack saw he marvelled at. And not without good cause. The bright storefronts displayed wondrous things, things all new to Jack, although not perhaps new – different, maybe.

There were electrical stores, their windows filled with radio sets and televisions and record players and washing machines, but all of a style unknown to Jack, as were the garments in the clothes stores. Jack lingered long before a trenchcoat shop. Eddie urged him on.

'Low profile,' whispered Jack. 'Please behave yourself.'

And soon Jack stood before Mann's.[*]

Jack looked up in awe beyond awe.

Then Jack looked down at the pavement.

'Handprints,' he said to Eddie, and he set the bear down and he gazed upon them. 'Clark Gable,' whispered Jack. 'Shirley Temple, the Marx Brothers – I wonder what this is all about.'

'They're movie stars, of course.' The voice was the sweetest of voices, and it issued from the sweetest of lips.

Jack looked up at the speaker. A pretty girl looked down.

She wore a colourful dress that reached to her knees, beneath which rather shapely legs reached down to elegant shoes.

Jack's eyes lingered on these legs before moving up, with some deliberation, to view the pretty face of the speaker. It was that of a flame-haired beauty with stunning green eyes. A girl who was roughly Jack's age.

'Movie stars?' said Jack.

'Of course. What did you think they were?'

---

[*] Now, again for those who harbour an interest in such things, it is to be stated that Mann's Chinese Theatre can truly be described as the jewel in Hollywood's crown. Created in the late nineteen-twenties by Sid Grauman, this oriental-style folly, with its sixty-nine-foot-high exotic bronze roof and its wealth of architectural detail, dazzles the eye and is the palace for the 'royalty' of Hollywood.

Jack rose slowly to his feet. He did not possess the nose of Eddie, but this girl smelled beautiful and Jack drew in her fragrance.

'You're sniffing me,' said the pretty girl. 'I don't think that's very nice.'

'I'm so sorry,' said Jack. 'If I was rude, will you please forgive me?'

'It doesn't matter, you're funny.'

'Am I . . . I . . .'

'My name is Dorothy,' said Dorothy. 'I'm from Kansas. Where are you from?'

'England?' Jack suggested.

'I knew it,' said Dorothy. 'I recognised your accent at once. England is so romantic. Do you know the Queen?'

'Oh yes,' said Jack. 'Very well.'

'And do you wear a bowler hat and take your tea at three?'

'Every day,' said Jack. 'With the Queen, naturally.'

Eddie made a growling noise.

Dorothy looked down. 'What a sweet little bear,' she said. 'Is it yours?'

'Mine,' said Jack. 'His name is Eddie.'

'Eddie Bear, how cute. Might I pick him up and give him a cuddle?'

'I wouldn't advise it,' said Jack. 'He's a bit smelly.'

'You're a bit smelly, too,' said Dorothy. 'You smell of poo.'

'An unfortunate incident,' said Jack, 'but in the line of business. My name is Jack, by the way, and I'm a detective.'

'A detective, how exciting.' And Dorothy put out her hand and Jack most gently shook it.

'I'm an actress,' said Dorothy. 'Or will be, as soon as I'm discovered.'

'Discovered?' Jack asked.

'By an agent. I've got my publicity shots, and I've been around to lots of agents, but they're not very nice. They want you to do . . . *things*.' Dorothy cast down her eyes.

Jack felt he could imagine what things. 'And so these are the handprints of famous movie stars?' he said.

'Yes,' said Dorothy. 'And mine will be here one day. Once I'm discovered.'

'You're a very beautiful girl,' said Jack. 'I'm sure someone will discover you soon.'

'I hope so. I don't like what I'm doing now.'

'What, talking to me?'

'No, I have to work as a kitchen maid in the hotel just up the road. The Roosevelt.'

'Ah,' said Jack.

'It's very hard work, but at least it allows me to do a bit of good.'

'In the kitchen?'

'Well, not really in the kitchen. I package up all the leftover food that the rich people don't eat and leave it in the trashcan outside for the homeless. There's a poor old man who lives in the alley – the scraps I leave are his only food.'

'Ah,' said Jack once again.

'But I *will* be discovered. And when I am, and when I'm wealthy, I'll feed as many of those poor souls as I can.'

'That's a very wonderful thing to say,' said Jack. 'You are a beautiful person.'

'But tell me about you,' said Dorothy. 'You're a detective. That must be very exciting. Do you catch a lot of criminals? Did they send you over from England on a special case? Are you working for the Queen, or is it the President?'

'Well,' said Jack.

And Eddie growled again.

'It's been lovely to meet you,' said Jack, 'but we, that is, *I* have to be going.'

'Won't you stay for just a little longer, have a cup of coffee?'

'I'm embarrassed to say that I don't have any money.'

'It's only a cup of coffee, I'll pay.'

'No, I couldn't, really.'

'Oh please, it will be my treat and you can tell me all about England.'

'Well,' said Jack.

And Dorothy smiled upon him.

'Just one cup,' said Jack, and he gathered up Eddie.

*

And then Jack strolled along Hollywood Boulevard. And he felt rather good, did Jack. Rather 'Top of the world, Ma', as it happened. The sun shone down and here was he, with a beautiful girl on his arm. And as Jack walked on, smelly as he was, he caught the occasional envious glance from a young male passer-by.

'Now this *is* the life,' thought Jack to himself. 'I could make a home in this place. Perhaps I could set myself up as a private detective, and take a wife, perhaps a wife who was a movie star. Yes, this *is* the life. I really love this place.'

'We're here,' said Dorothy. 'This is it.'

And Jack looked up and said, 'Ah.'

They stood before the Golden Chicken Diner. It was a symphony of chrome and neon. A neon chicken on high flashed on and off, in profile, pecking up and down.

'It's one of a growing chain,' said Dorothy. 'They're springing up everywhere. The chicken burgers are very popular and the coffee is good, but cheap.'

'Right,' said Jack. 'It looks wonderful. Let's go inside.'

And then Jack stopped. And then Jack stared. And then Jack said, 'Oh no!'

And Dorothy looked at Jack, who now stared wide-eyed. And she watched as Jack took Eddie from under his arm and held him up before his chest.

And Eddie stared and saw what Jack saw, and Eddie Bear mouthed, 'No!'

In the front window of the Golden Chicken Diner there was a garish sign. It was a big garish sign and it advertised the fare on sale.

But not only did it advertise this, it also advertised something else. It advertised special offers and what came free with these.

COLLECT 'EM ALL (said this garish sign)
FREE WITH EVERY FAMILY SPECIAL
A CLOCKWORK CLAPPING MONKEY or
A CLOCKWORK BAND MEMBER or
A CLOCKWORK ORCHESTRA MUSICIAN
AND COMING SOON

LAUGHING POLICEMEN
AN ENTIRE SET OF TOY TOWN FIGURES
INCLUDING
TINTO THE CLOCKWORK BARMAN
AND
EDDIE THE CUDDLY BEAR

15

When Jack could find his voice he whispered, 'What does it mean, Eddie, what?'

Eddie just stared and Dorothy said, 'What is the matter, Jack?'

'It's this . . . this sign.'

'Free toy figures.' Dorothy smiled. 'Don't they have free offers in England? These are incredibly popular. They only started a day or so ago, with the clockwork monkey. Everybody's collecting the figures now, not just kids, but grown-ups. There's something about them, something—'

'Special?' said Jack. 'Something special?'

'Yes, that's the word. They're not like ordinary toys.'

Eddie wriggled gently in the arms of Jack.

Jack said, 'This needs thought, much thought.'

'Thought about what?' Dorothy was steering Jack into the Golden Chicken Diner.

Jack held back. 'Let's go somewhere else,' he said. 'In fact, perhaps it would be better if I were to see you later on, this evening or something. I think I should be pressing on with my case.'

'I'm not letting you go that easily.' Dorothy clung to his arm. 'At least let a girl buy you a cup of coffee. And I want to hear all about this case of yours.'

'No,' said Jack. 'I don't . . .'

But Dorothy tugged at Jack's arm and Jack let himself be drawn into the Golden Chicken Diner.

It was within, as without, swathed in chrome and neon. A long chrome counter, behind which at measured intervals were mounted splendid chromium cash resisters, behind which stood personable young women wearing skimpy gold costumes. They sported golden caps and these in turn sported corporate logos: profiled pecking chickens. One of the girls said, 'How might I serve you, please?'

'Two coffees, please,' said Dorothy.

'And a large glass of beer,' said Eddie.

Dorothy looked up at Jack. 'How did you do that?' she asked, and she smiled as she asked it.

'Just a trick,' said Jack, but in a distracted voice, as he was viewing large posters that hung upon the walls to the rear of the serving counter. These were adorned with dozens of pictures of the special-offer free Toy Town figures. Jack instantly recognised Chief Inspector Bellis, and the cigar shop proprietor, monkeys and musicians, several of the laughing policemen that he had recently fallen foul of, Tinto the clockwork barman and . . .

'Amelie,' whispered Eddie.

'Sorry?' said Dorothy. 'What did you say?'

'Amelie,' Jack pointed. 'I know her, she's my—'

'She's your what?'

'It doesn't matter,' said Jack. 'Or rather it *does*, very much.'

Eddie set free a dismal growl. For Eddie could see, as indeed could Jack, Eddie's own picture up there.

'I don't understand it,' said Jack. 'I don't.'

'You are a very strange boy. Ah, here are our coffees.'

'And where's my beer?'

Dorothy laughed. 'That really *is* very clever.'

'Get him a beer, please,' said Jack. 'He needs it and I need one, too.'

'I can't get beer – I'm underage and so are you. Don't be so silly.'

'Bad bad meathead world,' grumbled Eddie.

'Stop it now.' Dorothy paid for the coffees and carried them to a vacant table. 'Come on, Jack,' she called.

With difficulty Jack tore his eyes away from the colourful posters and carried Eddie to the table. He pulled out a chair and seated the bear upon it.

'Horrible world,' grumbled Eddie.

Dorothy looked nervously at Jack. 'You weren't touching him when he said that,' she said.

'Just a trick,' said Jack.

'I'm not so sure.' Dorothy gave Eddie a close looking-at. 'There's something about this stuffed toy of yours. Something—'

'Special?' Jack suggested.

'Different,' said Dorothy. 'Odd, perhaps.'

Jack stared into his coffee cup. He recalled his conversation with the cigar proprietor who had told him, 'I have the special eye and I see trouble lying in wait ahead for you. Trouble that comes in the shape of a chicken,' and also his conversation with Eddie when they first went to Toy Town and had talked about souls being stolen and all of Toy City being under threat.

'Stealing their souls,' said Jack. 'Taking their very essence. And for *this*?'

'Please tell me what you're talking about.' Dorothy looked over at Jack. 'You're frightening me.'

'I'm sorry.' Jack shook his head. 'I'd like to tell you, but I can't. And even if I could, you wouldn't believe me. You'd think I was mad.'

'This is California,' said Dorothy. 'Everyone's mad here. There was an Englishman like you, well, he was a Scotsman, but I think that's the same thing. His name was Charles Rennie Mackintosh, and he said that if you turn America on its side, everything that is not screwed down rolls to California.'

'I'm sure that's very profound,' said Jack, 'but it means nothing to me. Is this California? I thought it was Hollywood.'

'It is Hollywood, but Hollywood is part of LA, which is in California. California is a state in America. But why am I telling you this? You know where you are, surely.'

Jack shook his head. 'Hold on,' he said. 'You said LA.'

'LA,' said Dorothy. 'Los Angeles.'

'LA,' said Jack. 'TO TO LA. To LA. It was a signpost.'

'I'm more confused than ever.'

'And so am I,' said Jack.

'You're coffee's getting cold.'

Jack sipped at it.

'Do you like it?' Dorothy asked.

'It's fine, thank you.'

'Beer would be better,' Eddie said. 'This is a nine-pint problem.'

'You didn't do that,' said Dorothy to Jack. 'You were sipping your coffee when it spoke.'

'I'm not an *it*,' said Eddie. 'I am an Anders Imperial. Cinnamon plush coat—'

'Not now,' said Jack.

'He speaks by himself.' And Dorothy's green eyes grew wide.

'It's just a trick.'

'It *isn't* a trick.'

'All right. It's a small child in a costume.'

'Oh no it isn't.'

'Let's go to a bar,' said Eddie. 'There's bound to be one somewhere that will serve us.'

'It's speaking by itself, it really is.'

'And I'm not an *it*! Get rid of her, Jack. We have to press on now, find our other selves, stop them doing what they're doing and fast.'

'I agree,' said Jack. 'This is bad, very bad.'

'It's alive, Jack! Make it stop!' And tears sprang into Dorothy's eyes.

'Listen,' said Jack, 'please be calm. I'm sorry.'

'But it's alive.'

'Will you please stop calling me an it?'

'Make it stop, it's frightening me.'

'Eddie, please be quiet.'

Eddie made growling sounds.

Dorothy rose to flee.

'No,' said Jack. 'Please don't go.'

'Let her go, Jack.'

'No. Please stay.' Jack rose, took Dorothy gently by the shoulders and sat her back down. 'I'll tell you,' he said. 'I'll tell you everything. But before I do, you must promise me that you will tell no one what I tell you. And I'm saying this for your own good. Murders have occurred—'

'Then *you*—'

'Not *me*. I'm not a murderer. Eddie and I are detectives. We are in pursuit of murderers.'

'That thing is looking at me in a funny way.'

'It's the only way he knows.'

'Thanks very much,' said Eddie, and he shifted in his chair, which had Dorothy cowering.

'Please promise me,' said Jack, 'and I'll tell you everything.'

And Dorothy promised in a shaky voice and Jack then told her everything.

And when Jack was done there was silence.

Except for the background restaurant noise of large Californians chowing down on family chicken-burger meals.

'My head is spinning,' said Dorothy. 'But somehow I always knew it. I used to say to my little dog Toto, before he was sadly run over by a truck, somewhere over the rainbow . . .'

And Dorothy burst into song.

Which rather surprised the diners. And rather surprised Jack, too.

'Oh, sorry,' said Dorothy, bursting out of song. 'I'm rather prone to that.'

'It was very nice,' said Jack. 'I liked the bit about the bluebirds.'

'I didn't,' said Eddie. 'Ne'er a hint of a bear.'

'A land of toys,' said Dorothy.

'Well, a city,' said Jack. 'That was once Toy Town.'

'And the toys on the posters—'

'As I said,' said Jack, 'some of them are already dead and if we don't stop these doppelgängers of us, as you can see on the posters, many more folk in Toy City will die. Including Eddie here.'

'At least I seem to get star billing,' said the bear. 'I'm the last on the list.'

Dorothy smiled upon Eddie. 'He really *is* quite cute,' she said. 'Can I give him a cuddle?'

'You *cannot*,' said Eddie Bear. 'Most undignified.'

Dorothy smiled once more and shook her head. Her flame-red hair glittered in reflected sunlight. 'Let me help you,' Dorothy said. 'I'm sure I could do something to help.'

'I wouldn't hear of it,' said Jack, finishing his coffee. 'It's far too dangerous.'

'Because you're a girl,' said Eddie. 'No offence meant.'

'I think you did mean *some*,' said Dorothy.

'I think he probably meant plenty,' said Jack. 'But in a way he's right. Eddie and I are used to getting into danger. It's just about all we ever do. In fact, I can't imagine how we've managed to sit for so long in this restaurant without someone trying to shoot us, stab us, or blow us up.'

'It can't be danger *all* the time,' said Dorothy.

'Not *all*,' said Eddie. 'The danger is relieved periodically by bouts of extreme drunkenness and bad behaviour. So as you can see, it's no job for a girl. And Jack has a girlfriend anyway.'

Jack clipped Eddie lightly on the ear.

And then withdrew his fingers hastily to avoid having them bitten off.

'I *could* help you,' Dorothy said. 'You are strangers here and I know my way around LA. I could be very useful to you.'

'It's too dangerous,' said Jack. 'You could get hurt, badly.'

'I know how to handle myself.'

'Yes,' said Jack, 'of course you do.'

'Stand up,' said Dorothy. 'Try to attack me, see what happens.'

'Don't be silly,' said Jack.

'I'm serious. Try.'

'Some other time,' said Jack. 'Sit down.'

'Chicken,' said Dorothy.

'Hardly a well-chosen word, considering the circumstances.'

'You're still a chicken. Cluck! Cluck! Cluck!' And Dorothy made chicken sounds and did that elbow thing that people do when they impersonate chickens. As they so often do in passionate bedroom situations.

'You're making an exhibition of yourself,' said Jack. 'You'll get us thrown out.'

'She's a stone bonker, this one,' said Eddie. 'Give her a little smack, Jack, and make her sit down again.'

'I can't smack a woman.'

'Let me bite her, then.'

Dorothy began what is called in theatrical terms a 'dance

'improvisation'. Diners looked on briefly, then continued with their chowing down of chicken burgers. Because, after all, this *was* California.

'Just one little smack then,' said Jack, 'and we'll stop all this nonsense.'

Jack rose from his chair.

Dorothy ceased her dance improvisation, extended an arm and with her fingers beckoned Jack nearer.

Jack sighed, took a step forward and swung a gentle slap in Dorothy's direction.

And what happened next seemed to Eddie to happen in slow motion. Dorothy leapt into the air and somersaulted over Jack's head, turning as she did so to boot him right in the side of the gob.

It may have seemed like slow motion to Eddie.

It seemed very fast to Jack.

And as Jack hit the floor with a thunderous blow . . .

Dorothy landed several yards away, right on her feet, light as thistledown.

Eddie buried his face in his paws. 'That's going to hurt in the morning,' he said. 'And as this *is* morning, it will probably be hurting now.'

'Ow, my face.' And Jack did flounderings about. 'That wasn't fair . . . my face.'

'I'll get some ice,' said Dorothy.

'Eddie,' groaned Jack from his floor-bound repose, 'Eddie, bite her, please.'

'Not my battle,' said Eddie.

'But Eddie.'

'Sorry,' said Eddie. 'Count Otto kicked me over the big top. *That* really hurt. This woman could kick me all the way to England, wherever that is.'

Dorothy went and fetched some ice and then she helped Jack up.

'I can get up by myself.' Jack patted her away.

'I told you I could handle myself.'

'I wasn't ready,' said Jack.

'Well, if you're ready now you can take another shot. I'll close my eyes if you want.'

'Go on,' said Eddie. 'You might strike lucky.'

Jack sat down in a right old huff. Dorothy offered him ice in a serviette. Jack took this and held it to his jaw.

'It's call Dimac,' Dorothy explained. 'The deadliest martial art on Earth. My hands and feet are registered with the police as lethal weapons – I have to have a special licence for them.'

'Dimac?' said Jack.

'I sent away for a course. A dollar ninety-eight a lesson, from Count Dante – he's the Deadliest Man on Earth, obviously.'

'Obviously,' said Jack. And he clicked his jaw.

'So do I get the job?'

Jack sighed and almost shook his head.

'I know my way around,' said Dorothy. 'And I could come in very useful if anyone menaces you or Eddie.'

'Well,' said Jack. And then he said, 'Why? Why would you want to help us?'

'*Why?*' said Dorothy. 'Why? You have to be joking.'

'Jack's not very good on jokes,' said Eddie. 'Actually, as a comedy sidekick he's pretty useless. But it is a valid question. You want to be an actress, don't you? Why would you want to get involved with us?'

'How can *you* ask me that? You are a talking toy bear. Jack says that you and he came here from somewhere over the rainbow. I believe in fate. Our paths haven't crossed by accident – destiny led you to me.'

'Oh dear,' said Eddie, and if he had been able to roll his eyes he would have done so.

'And there's definitely a movie in this,' said Dorothy. 'I might eschew acting in favour of a role as producer.'

'Hm,' went Jack.

'Hm?' went Dorothy.

'Ignore him,' said Eddie. 'He's had woman trouble. The love of his life left him. I suspect that his "hm" represented something along the lines that your unexpected evolution from the wide-eyed innocent on Hollywood Boulevard to lean, mean killing machine with pretensions to movie moguldom within the space of a short half-hour is somewhat disconcerting for him.'

'You're a most articulate little bear,' said Dorothy.

'And most democratic,' said Eddie. 'I hold no prejudice. I bite man or woman alike if I consider that they are patronising me.'

'That flight of yours over the big top,' said Dorothy. Suggestively. 'I overheard that.'

'I'll get you when you're sleeping,' said Eddie.

'Stop it, please,' said Jack. 'All right, Dorothy, I *am* impressed. If you want to help us, it would be appreciated.'

'Not by *me*,' said Eddie. 'We're a team, Jack. A partnership, you and me, Jack and Eddie, bestest friends through thick and thin.'

'This won't affect our partnership.'

'Yes it will. It will lead to a romantic involvement and then there'll be all the drippy smoochy stuff and that will interfere with the action and the car chases.'

'Rubbish,' said Jack, although unconvincingly. The thought of indulging in some drippy smoochy stuff with Dorothy had indeed crossed his mind. As indeed had some of that get down, get naked and get dirty kind of stuff. 'She *can* help us, Eddie,' said Jack. 'And we need all the help we can get.'

'We were doing fine on our own. What happened to your inspired calculating stuff? It was you who calculated that the murderers would strike next at the Opera House, remember?'

'Ah,' said Jack, who in all the excitement and everything else had quite forgotten about Wallah the calculating pocket. 'About that.'

'We'll manage on our own,' said Eddie. 'Thank you for your offer, Dorothy, but you'll only get Jack all confused and he won't be able to keep his mind on the job.'

'Listen,' said Jack, wringing out his serviette ice pack into his empty coffee cup and shaking his fingers about, 'I'm up for you helping us, Dorothy, but I have to go to the toilet now. Eddie and I are a partnership, and it's a fifty-fifty partnership. If Eddie says no then I have to respect his decision, even if I don't agree with it. But I *am* going to the toilet, so please speak to him. I'm sure you can win him over.' And Jack winked at Dorothy.

It was an intimate kind of a wink and if Eddie had seen it he would have recognised it to be the kind of wink that meant, 'I would *love* you to help us and I'm certain that a beautiful, intelligent *woman* such as yourself can soon win over a stroppy toy bear.' And if Eddie *had* seen it and *had* recognised it, Jack would have received such a biting from Eddie that if Jack had owned a bicycle he would not have been able to ride it again for at least a week.

'I'll be back in a minute,' Jack said. 'Which way *is* the toilet?'

'Over there,' said Dorothy.

And Jack went off to the toilet.

And went into one of the stalls and locked the stall door behind him. And Jack withdrew Wallah from his trenchcoat and gave her a little stroke.

Wallah gave a little yawn and made a sensual purring sound.

'I'm sorry not to have spoken with you for a while,' said Jack. 'As you are probably aware, things have been a little hectic of late.'

'Naturally I am aware. That horrid woman hurt your face – it's all bruised. Hold me against it, I'll make it better.'

'Well,' said Jack.

'Please,' said Wallah.

And Jack held the pocket to his face. And it *did* feel rather nice.

'You don't need *her*,' whispered Wallah into Jack's ear. 'I calculate that although in the short term she might facilitate some success, in the long term disaster awaits.'

'You don't foresee a lasting relationship, then?'

'It looks unfavourable in percentage terms.'

'So I should dump her? Is that what you're saying? You're not being a little biased, are you?'

'Biased?' whispered Wallah. 'I don't know what you mean.'

'Yes you do,' said Jack, 'and *our* relationship, our *special* relationship will only continue if you are totally honest with me.'

'I am dedicated to your success,' said Wallah. 'In fact, our special relationship depends directly upon it.'

'Well, I'm asking for your help,' said Jack. 'I need all the help I can get. Which is not to say that I do not value yours above all others', of course.'

'I wonder,' said Wallah, 'whether a relationship actually exists anywhere that is based upon pure truth, rather than one partner telling the other partner what they think the other partner wants to hear, rather than the pure truth that that partner should hear from someone he or she trusts.'

With his free hand Jack scratched at his head. 'I'm not quite certain what all of that means,' he said, 'but I'm sure it's most profound. So, can you help me out here? Can you tell me what I should do next?'

'Not directly,' said Wallah. 'I can calculate odds. And I can tell you this: if you do not bring the malcontents to justice within one week, not a single soul in Toy City will remain alive.'

'One week?' said Jack.

'According to my calculations the evil is growing exponentially. It's working on a mathematical principle. You have one week at the most.'

'So what must I do?'

'Corporate enterprises such as this Golden Chicken organisation function upon a pyramidal principle. At the base you have the most folk, those in customer facilitation, the counter-service folk, the factory workers, et cetera. Next level up, lower management, supervisors – far fewer. Next level, middle management, then up and up, executive management, board of directors, chief executive officer. And he is not the pinnacle of the pyramid. Above him is a single figure. You must move up the chain of command, seek out this individual – they will be the brains behind it all.'

'That's rather obvious, surely,' said Jack.

'Obvious perhaps, but it's how you do it that counts. How you penetrate the chain of command, find your way to the top.'

'And how do I do *that*?' said Jack.

'I calculate your chances of doing so in your present situation as zero,' said Wallah. 'You will have to take employment with the Golden Chicken Consortium. Infiltrate, as it were.'

'Is there time for *that*?' Jack asked.

'Yes,' said Wallah. 'There is, just. I am susceptible to vibrations, Jack. I pick them up, assimilate them. You are now in a land that you do not understand, and I now *do* understand it. Within three days, if you work hard, persevere and keep your eyes and ears open, you will be able to rise up the pyramid sufficiently to discover who hides upon the pinnacle.'

'I'm hardly likely to get promoted up the management chain in three days,' said Jack.

'Oh yes you can,' said Wallah. 'You are now in a land called America where many things are possible. You will realise what is known as "The American Dream".'

'All right,' said Jack. 'I'll do my best.'

'You will have to do better than that.'

'My best is all I have. And I'll have you to help me, which I appreciate, believe me.'

'Sadly, that is not going to be the case. I calculate that I will only be able to help you for another twelve hours at the most.'

'Why?' asked Jack.

'Because I am dying,' said Wallah.

'What?' and Jack held Wallah out before him. 'What are you saying to me?'

'I'm saying that I'm dying. Me and my kind cannot survive here in this world. This world will kill us.'

'Why are you saying this? How do you know this?'

'Believe the evidence of your own eyes,' said Wallah. 'You were here no time at all before your wristwatch ceased to work, and less than eight hours after that so did your weapons.'

'Yes,' said Jack. 'I suspected that it was something like that when I tested the grenade in the alleyway.'

'I know,' said Wallah. 'The simple things die first, then the more complex. I have perhaps another day, maybe a little more. My calculations cannot be entirely precise.'

'Then I'll take you back right now,' said Jack, 'pop you through The Second Big O onto the other side.'

'And without my help you will fail and all Toy City will die.'

'But I can't let *you* die.'

'It's a percentage thing,' said Wallah. 'I will die so many will live.'

'No,' said Jack. 'I can't have that.'

'Then you will have to do more than your best.'

'Yes I will,' said Jack. 'I promise I will.' And then Jack said, 'Oh no!'

'I know what you're thinking,' said Wallah, 'and yes, it's true.'

'Eddie,' said Jack. 'You mean—'

'Three days at most,' said Wallah. 'I'm sorry.'

'Then I'm taking you both back.'

'And if you do you'll doom all of Toy City. You can't do this on your own, even with the help of Dorothy. You need us to succeed.'

'But I can't risk Eddie's life.'

'He wouldn't hear of you trying to save him at the expense of all the others. You know Eddie well enough – do you think that he would?'

'No,' said Jack. 'I do not. Eddie is—'

'Noble,' said Wallah, 'is the word you're looking for.'

'But I *must* tell him.'

'I think that's only fair. And by my calculations it is something that you should do now. And fast.'

'Fast?' said Jack.

'Very fast,' said Wallah. 'Trust me.'

'I do.'

And Jack slipped Wallah back inside his trenchcoat and then Jack left that toilet at the hurry-up.

And Jack returned to Dorothy and Eddie.

Or at least.

'Dorothy?' asked Jack. 'Where is Eddie?'

Dorothy looked up at Jack and said, 'Why are you asking me that?'

'Because I left him here with you,' said Jack, 'but he's not with you now.'

'No,' said Dorothy. 'That's not what you did. You went off to the toilet and then you returned. And I commented on how impressed I was that you had managed to clean up your trenchcoat in such a short time. Which rather confuses me now, as it is all dirty again. But then you said that you wanted a quiet word for a moment outside with Eddie and then the two of you left. And now you've come out of the toilet again – how did you do that?'

Jack's jaw did a terrible dropping, and then he gave vent to a terrible scream.

16

Jack left the Golden Chicken Diner at the hurry-up.

He sprinted through the open doors and out into the sunlit street beyond. The sunlit Californian street that was Hollywood Boulevard.

Jack was a very desperate lad. He sprinted here and sprinted there in desperation, up this way and down that way, but all to no avail. Passers-by did passings-by, but none paid Jack any heed.

Jack took now to shouting at and accosting passers-by.

'Have you seen him?' Jack shouted at a large man in a larger suit of orange plaid. 'Small bear, about this size? Being led along by me, but it wasn't me?' The large man thrust past Jack, continued on his way.

Jack started on another. Dorothy's hands caught Jack by the shoulders. 'Stop it, Jack,' said Dorothy. 'You'll get yourself arrested.'

'But I have to find him, time is running out.'

'He could be anywhere now – he was probably taken in a car.'

'A car?' and Jack made fists. 'I need a car. Do you have one?'

'Of course I don't have a car. Do I look like I could afford a car? And I'm too young to drive, anyway.'

'I've got to find him. How could you let this happen?' Jack turned bitter eyes upon Dorothy. 'I left him in your care.'

Dorothy's eyes weren't bitter, but they flashed an emerald fire. 'You did no such thing,' she said to Jack. 'You left him with me in the hope that I could win him over.'

'You're part of this.' Jack made fists and shook them all about. 'You're in on it. This is all a conspiracy.'

'Now you are being ridiculous. Come back inside and sit down with me and then we'll talk about this.'

'I've no time to talk. They've got Eddie and if I can't get to him quickly he'll die.'

'If they'd wanted to kill him,' said Dorothy, 'they could have done it there and then in the diner. Ripping a teddy bear apart would hardly have caused the customers much concern.'

Jack put his hands to his head and raked them through his hair. Knocked his hat off, stooped to pick it up, kicked it instead and watched as it rolled beneath the wheels of a passing car to be ground to an ugly flatness.

Dorothy stifled a smirk. This was no laughing matter.

'Let's go inside,' she said.

'I can't.' There was a tear in Jack's left eye. 'It's my fault, I shouldn't have left him. I should have protected him at all times. If any harm comes to him—'

'No harm will come to him.'

'That's a very foolish thing to say.'

'I've said that if they'd wanted to kill him they would have. They've taken him captive, probably as a hostage, probably to use to bargain with you.'

'With me?'

'To get you to stay out of their affairs.'

'That's not going to happen,' said Jack. 'I'll track this other me down and if he's harmed Eddie, I'll kill him. I'll probably have to kill him anyway, but if he's harmed Eddie, I'll kill him worse.'

Dorothy's green eyes fairly glittered. 'You really love that bear,' she said. 'You really, truly do.'

'Of course I do,' Jack said. 'He's my bestest friend. We've been through a lot together, Eddie and me. And he's saved my life more then once.'

'Come back inside, then, and we'll work out some plan together. We'll get him back somehow.'

Jack followed Dorothy back to the diner. 'I'm so sorry, Eddie,' he said.

Eddie Bear was rather sorry, too. Sorrowful was Eddie Bear, puzzled somewhat, scared a bit and quite uncomfortable also.

He was all in the darkness and all getting bumped about.

'How did I let this happen?' Eddie asked himself. 'How could I have been so stupid? I'm as stupid as. How didn't I know that it was the wrong Jack? Why didn't I smell a rat?'

But Eddie Bear had not smelled a rat and neither had he smelled that that Jack wasn't Jack. So to speak.

And this worried Eddie more than most things.

'I don't understand this.' Eddie sniffed at the air. Hot air, it was, and humid, too, as can be the way of it in the boot of a car on a hot and sunlit day. Eddie sniffed the air some more and then he growly grumbled. 'I've lost my sense of smell,' he growly grumbled. 'I can't smell anything. Why has this happened? Do I have a cold? This can't be right – my nose has never let me down before and OUCH!'

The car, in whose boot Eddie was presently domiciled, bumped over something, possibly a sleeping policeman, and Eddie was bounced about something wicked.

'I'll have things to say when I get out of here,' said Eddie Bear.

'And he'll die,' Jack told Dorothy over another coffee. 'He has three days left at the most. If I don't get him back to his own world before then, he'll die.'

'And how did you arrive at this revelation?' Dorothy asked.

'I have my sources,' said Jack. 'Let's leave it at that.'

'So we have to do something fast.'

'*You* don't have to do anything,' said Jack. 'I'll do this on my own.'

'We've been through all that. You need me, Jack. You won't last long here on your own. You'll get stopped by the police, they'll ask you for ID, you won't have any and they'll take you off to juvenile hall.'

Jack did grindings of the teeth. He felt utterly helpless. Utterly impotent. Neither of these were nice ways to feel. The second in particular didn't bear thinking about. So Jack did some heavy thinking about other things. And certain thoughts entered his head. Regarding his most recent conversation with Wallah the calculating pocket.

Wallah's advice to Jack, based upon her calculations, had been that he must take employment at a Golden Chicken Diner and penetrate the higher echelons by utilising the American Dream. Also that

Dorothy would prove to be a useful asset during the short term, if ultimately a disaster.

Jack leaned forwards, elbows on the table, and buried his face in his hands.

Dorothy said, 'Let's think about this, Jack. Work together, throw some ideas around.'

Jack groaned.

Dorothy continued, 'I think we have established that whoever is the brains behind the Golden Chicken Diner is the most likely candidate for being behind the murders in Toy City.'

'Yes,' said Jack. 'Of course.'

'Well, not necessarily "of course" – there could be other options to choose from. But he or she—'

'Or *it*,' said Jack.

'He, she or *it* is the most likely candidate. That entity is the one that you have to find and deal with.'

'And I will,' said Jack.

'So the question is, how?'

Jack nodded through his fingers.

'Well,' said Dorothy, 'the most logical thing to do, in my opinion, would be to gain employment at one of the Golden Chicken Diners, then work your way up into a position that would gain you access to this, er, entity.'

'Eh?' said Jack, and he looked up through his fingers.

'It's the most logical solution,' said Dorothy. 'By my calculations, it's the best chance you'd have.'

'By your *calculations*?'

'Yes. You see, it's an American thing – the belief that anyone in this country can do anything, if they just try hard enough. That they'll get a fair deal if they try. It's called pursuing the American Dream.'

'I know what it's called,' said Jack.

'You do?'

'I do. Do *you* really think it would work?'

'It might with my help.'

'Ah,' said Jack.

'You have no ID,' said Dorothy. 'You're, well, an illegal alien, really. You'd need a work visa. But there are ways. I could help.'

'I have no choice,' said Jack, and he threw up his hands, knocking over his coffee, which trickled into his lap. 'Oh damn,' went Jack. 'I think this trenchcoat is done for.'

Dorothy giggled, prettily.

Jack smiled wanly towards her. 'When I said I had no choice,' said he, 'I didn't mean it in a bad way towards you. I'm very grateful for your help. So how do we go about getting jobs?'

'Just leave that to me.'

Now it is a fact well known to those who know it well that in America, in accordance with the American Dream, you can always get a job in a diner. No matter your lack of qualifications, the fact that you cannot add up to ten, the fact that you have rather strange ways about you, a curious squint, buck teeth, answer to the name of Joe-Bob and hail from a backwoods community where your father is your brother and your aunty your uncle (although it has to be said that there *is* a more than average chance that you will be very good at playing the banjo), you can always get work in a diner.

In England (a small but beautifully formed kingdom somewhat to the east of America) it is the case that you can always get a job in a pub. Here, of course, you will not be expected to be able to count up to ten, as, if you are, like Jack, an illegal alien (probably from Australia, in the case of England), it will be expected that you will short-change the customers. Oh, and be an alcoholic, which is apparently a necessary qualification.

But this is neither here nor there, nor anywhere else at the present.

Twenty minutes passed in the Golden Chicken Diner and when these twenty minutes were done, certain things had occurred.

Dorothy now stood behind counter till number three, all dolled up in a golden outfit. And Jack stood somewhere else.

Jack stood in the kitchen washing dishes.

Jack had his arms in suds up to the elbows.

Jack had a right old grumpy look on his face.

'Back in the bloody kitchen again!' swore Jack, frightening

Joe-Bob, who was drying dishes. 'A couple of days ago I was washing dishes in a Nadine's Diner, and now I'm back at it again. Is this to be my lot in life? What is going on?'

'You ain't from around these parts, aintcha, mister?' asked Joe-Bob, spitting little corncob nibblets through his big buck teeth. 'You a wetback, aintcha?'

'I don't know what one of those is,' said Jack, 'but whatever it is, I'm not one.'

'You must be from England, then.'

'If this is some kind of running gag,' said Jack, really wishing that he'd rolled up his shirt sleeves before he began the washing up, 'then it stinks.'

'Not as bad as that trenchcoat of yours,' said Joe-Bob.

'No,' said Jack, 'but it's washing up nicely.' And he scrubbed at the trenchcoat's hem.

'I don't figure the manager'd like you washing your laundry in his kitchen sink,' said Joe-Bob. 'But I guess I'd keep my mouth shut and not tell him if you'd do a favour for me.'

'Listen,' said Jack, 'I can't lose this job. It's really important to me. But then so is a smart turn-out. I'll soon be done washing the trenchcoat. Then we can dry it in the chicken rotisserie.'

Joe-Bob shook his head and did that manic cackling laughter that backwoods fellows are so noted for. 'That's even worse,' said he. 'I'll want a *big* favour.'

Jack sighed deeply and wrung out his trenchcoat. 'You won't get it,' said Jack.

'Then I'll just mosey off and speak with the manager.'

'All right,' said Jack. And he sighed once more. 'Tell me what favour you want.'

'Well,' said Joe-Bob, 'you've got a real perty mouth and—'

Joe-Bob's head went into the washing-up water and then Joe-Bob, held by the scruff of the neck by Jack, was soundly thrashed and flung through the rear kitchen door into the alleyway beyond.

'And *don't* come back!' called Jack.

The head chef, who had been in the toilet doing whatever it is that head chefs do in the toilet – going to the toilet, probably, but neglecting to wash their hands afterwards – returned from the toilet. He was a big, fat, rosy-faced man who hailed from Oregon (where the vortex is)* and walked with a pronounced limp due to an encounter in Korea with a sleeping policeman.

'Where is Joe-Bob?' asked the head chef.

'He quit,' said Jack. 'Walked off the job. I tried to stop him.'

The head chef nodded thoughtfully. 'Tried to stop him, eh? Well, young fella, I like the way you think. You have the right stuff – you'll go far in this organisation.'

Jack did further trenchcoat wringings, but behind his back.

'I'm going to promote you,' said the head chef, 'to head dryer-up.'

'Well,' said Jack, 'thank you very much.'

'Not a bit of it,' said the head chef. 'Loyalty is always rewarded. It's the American Dream.'

By lunchtime Jack had gained the post of assistant to the head chef. He had risen rapidly through the ranks, from dishwasher to dryer-up to plate stacker to kitchen porter (general) to kitchen porter (specific) to head kitchen porter to rotisserie loader to supervising rotisserie loader to assistant to the head chef.

There had been some unpleasantness involved.

There had in fact been considerable unpleasantness involved and no small degree of violence, threats and menace. And a few knocks to himself. Jack sported a shiner in the right-eye department; the kitchen porter (general) was beginning a course of Dimac.

Jack's role as assistant to the head chef gave him a degree of authority over the lower orders of kitchen staff. Who were now a group of boisterous Puerto Ricans whom Jack had seen dealing in certain restricted substances outside the kitchen in the alleyway and asked in with the promise of cash in hand and free chicken for lunch.

Jack stood next to the head chef, decapitating chickens.

The chickens, all plucked and pink and all but ready, barring the decerebration, came out of a little hatch in the wall, plopped onto a

* Look it up. It's really weird.

conveyor belt and were delivered at regulated intervals to the chopping table for head-removal and skewering for the rotisserie.

Jack put a certain vigour into his work.

'You go at those chickens as one possessed,' the head chef observed after lunch (of chicken).

'What do you do with all the heads?' Jack asked as he tossed yet another into a swelling bin.

'They go back to the chicken factory,' said the head chef. 'They get ground up and fed to more chickens.'

'That's disgusting,' said Jack, parting another head from its scrawny neck.

'It's called recycling,' said the head chef. 'It's ecologically sound. I'd liken it to the nearest thing to perpetual motion that you can imagine.'

'Chickens fed on chicken heads,' said Jack, shaking *his*.

'Well, think about it,' said the head chef. 'If you want a chicken to taste really chickeny, then the best thing to feed that chicken on would have to be another chicken. It makes perfect sense, doesn't it?'

Jack looked up from his chopping and said, 'I can't argue with that.'

'Mind you,' said the head chef as he drizzled a little oil of chicken over a headless chicken and poked a rotisserie skewer up its backside, 'chickens are a bit of a mystery to me.'

'Really?' Jack nodded and chopped.

'I don't know where they all come from,' said the head chef.

'They come out of eggs,' said Jack. 'Of this I am reasonably sure.'

'Do they?' said the head chef. '*Of that* I'm not too sure.'

'I think it's an established fact,' said Jack.

'Oh really?' said the head chef. 'Well, then you explain this to me. Every day, in Los Angeles alone, in the Golden Chicken Diners, we sell about ten thousand chickens.'

'*Ten thousand?*' said Jack.

'Easily,' said the head chef. 'We'll do five hundred here every day and there's twenty Golden Chicken Diners in Los Angeles.'

Jack whistled.

'And well may you whistle,' said the head chef. 'That's ten

thousand, but that's only the tip of the chicken-berg. Every restaurant sells chicken, every supermarket sells chicken, every sandwich stall sells chicken, every hotel sells chicken. Do I need to continue?'

'Can you?' asked Jack.

'Very much so,' said the head chef. 'It's millions of chickens every day. And that's only in Los Angeles. Not the rest of the USA. Not the rest of the whole wide world.'

'That must add up to an awful lot of chickens,' said Jack, shuddering at the thought.

'I think it's beyond counting,' said the head chef. 'I don't think they have a name for such a number.'

'It's possibly a google,' said Jack.

The head chef looked at Jack and coughed. 'Possibly,' he said. 'But where do they all come from?'

'Out of eggs,' said Jack. 'That's where.'

'But the eggs are for sale,' said the head chef. 'We do eggs here. Again, at least five hundred a day. And that's just here, there's—'

'I see where you're heading,' said Jack. 'Googles of eggs everyday.'

'Exactly,' said the head chef.

'Well, the way I see it,' said Jack, 'or at least what I've always been led to believe, is that fertilised eggs, that is those that come from a chicken that has been shagged by a cockerel, become chickens. Unfertilised eggs, which won't hatch, are sold as eggs.'

'You are wise beyond your years,' said the head chef, 'but it won't work. The numbers don't tie up. Unfertilised eggs, fine – battery chickens will turn those out every day for years. Until they're too old to reproduce, then they get ground up and become chicken feed. But think about this – to produce the fertilised eggs you'd need an awful lot of randy roosters. Billions and googles of them, shagging away day and night, endlessly.'

'Nice work if you can get it,' said Jack.

'What, you'd like a job shagging chickens?'

'I would if I were a rooster. And it's probably the only job they can get.'

'Well, it doesn't pan out,' said the head chef. 'I've never heard of any chicken stud farms where millions of roosters shag billions of chickens every day. There's no such place.'

'There must be,' said Jack.

'Then tell me where.'

'I'm new to these parts.'

'Well, don't they have chickens where you come from?'

Jack remembered certain anal-probings. 'Well, they do . . .' he said.

'It doesn't work,' said the head chef, oiling up another chicken and giving it a little flick with his fat forefinger. 'Doesn't work. There's simply too many chickens being eaten every day. You'd need a stud farm the size of Kansas. It just doesn't work.'

'Well,' said Jack, 'I have to agree that you've given me food for thought.' And he laughed.

'Why are you laughing?' asked the head chef.

'Sorry,' said Jack. 'So what is your theory? I suspect that you do have a theory.'

'Actually I do,' said the head chef, 'but I'm not going to tell you because you wouldn't believe it. You'd laugh.'

'You'd be surprised at what I believe,' said Jack. 'And what I've seen. I've seen things you people wouldn't believe.' Which rang a bell somewhere.

'Well, you wouldn't believe *this*.'

'I'll just bet you I would. Trust me, I'm an assistant chef.'

'Well, fair enough,' said the head chef. 'After all, you are in the trade, and clearly destined for great things. But don't pass on what I say to those Puerto Rican wetbacks – they'll only go selling it to the *Weekly World News*.'

Jack raised his cleaver and prepared to bring it down.

'They are not of this world,' said the head chef.

Jack brought his cleaver down and only just missed taking his finger off.

'What?' said Jack. 'What are you saying?'

'Have you heard of Area Fifty-Two?' asked the head chef.

Jack shook his head.

'Well,' said the head chef, 'ten years ago, in nineteen forty-seven, a flying saucer crashed in Roswell, New Mexico. The Air Force covered it up, gave out this story that it was a secret military balloon experiment, or some such nonsense. But it wasn't. It was a UFO.'

'And a UFO is a flying saucer?'

'Of course it is. And they say that the occupants on board were still alive and the American government has done a deal with them – in exchange for advanced technology they let the aliens abduct a few Americans every year for experimentation, to cross-breed a new race.'

'Go on,' said Jack, his cleaver hovering.

'Half-man, half-chicken. Those aliens are chickens, sure as sure.'

Jack scratched his head with his cleaver and nearly took his left eye out.

'And I'll tell you how I figured it out,' said the head chef. 'Ten years ago there were no chicken diners, no fast-food restaurants. Chickens came from local farms. Shucks, where I grew up there were chicken farms, and they could supply just enough chickens and eggs to the local community. Like I said, the numbers are now impossible.'

'But hold on there,' said Jack. 'Are you saying that all these google billions of chickens are coming from Area Fifty-Two? What are you saying – that they're being imported by the billion from some chicken planet in outer space?'

'Not a bit of it,' said the head chef, oiling up another bird. 'Well, not the last bit. These chickens here are being produced at Area Fifty-Two. The alien chickens would hardly import millions of their own kind to be eaten by our kind every day, would they?'

Jack shook his head.

'When I say that they're being *produced*, that's what I mean. Look at these chickens – they're all the same. All the same size, all the same weight. Check them out in the supermarket. Rows of them, all the same size, all the same weight. They're all one chicken.'

Jack shook his head once more and made a face of puzzlement.

'They're artificial,' said the head chef. 'I'm not looking now, but I'll bet you that each of those chickens has a little brown freckle on the left side of its beak.'

Jack fished a couple of chicken heads from the bin and examined each in turn.

They both had identical freckles.

Jack flung the chicken heads down, dug into the swelling head bin, brought out a handful, gazed at them.

And said, 'Identical.'

'Sure enough,' said the head chef.

'This is incredible,' said Jack. 'But why hasn't anyone other than you noticed this?'

'It's only at the Golden Chicken chain that the chickens arrive with their heads on. They don't have their heads on in supermarkets.'

'Whoa!' said Jack. 'This is deep.'

'Do you believe what I'm telling you?'

'I do,' said Jack. 'I do.'

'Well, I'm glad that you do. You're the first assistant chef I've had who did. Mostly they just quit when I tell them. They panic and run. They think I'm mad.'

'Well, I don't,' said Jack. 'But what are you going to do about it?'

'Do?' asked the head chef. 'What do you mean?'

'I mean,' said Jack, 'that you know a terrible secret. You have exposed a dreadful conspiracy. It is your duty to pursue this to its source and expose the perpetrator. All of America should know the truth about this.'

'Well,' said the head chef, 'I'd never thought of it that way.'

'Well, think about it now. Surely as head chef you could follow this up the chain of command. Identify the single individual behind it.'

'Well, I suppose I could. We head chefs are being invited to head office tomorrow. I could make subtle enquiries there.'

'It is your duty as an American to do so.'

'My duty.' The head chef shook his head. It had a chef's hat on it. The chef's hat wobbled about. And now much of the head chef began to wobble about.

'Your duty,' Jack continued, 'even if it costs you your life.'

'My *life*?' The head chef's hands began to shake.

'Well, obviously they'll seek to kill you because of what you know. You are a threat to these alien chicken invaders. They'll probably want to kill you and grind you up and feed you to the artificial chickens that are coming off the production line.'

'Oh dear,' said the head chef. 'Oh my, oh my.'

'You'll need to disguise the shaking,' said Jack, 'when you're at the meeting tomorrow with all those agents of the chicken invaders. I've heard that chickens can smell fear. They'll certainly be able to smell yours.'

'Oh dear, oh my, oh my,' said the head chef once more, and now he shook from his hat to his shiny shoes.

'If you don't come back,' said Jack, 'I will continue with your cause. You will not have died, *horribly*, in vain.'

The head chef fled the kitchen of the Golden Chicken Diner upon wobbly shaking legs and Jack found himself promoted once again.

17

By the time Jack clocked off from his first day at the Golden Chicken Diner, it had to be said that he was a firm believer in the power of the American Dream.

'Head chef?' said Dorothy as she clocked off in a likewise manner.

'Hard work, ambition and faithfulness to the company's ethic,' said Jack, and almost without laughing.

Although Jack didn't feel much like laughing. Jack felt anxious and all knotted up inside. Jack worried for Eddie. Feared for his bestest friend.

Jack's bestest friend was more than a little afeared himself. He was afeared and he was hungry, too. Eddie had spent a most uncomfortable day travelling third class in the luggage compartment of a long black automobile.

There had been some stops for petrol, which Eddie had at first assumed were stops for winding of the key. Until he recalled that the cars of this world were not at all powered by clockwork. And there had been lots of hurlings to the left and the right, which Eddie correctly assumed were from the car turning corners. And there had been slowings down and speedings up and too many hours had passed for Eddie Bear. For as Eddie knew all too well, with each passing hour, indeed with each passing minute, the car was taking him further away, away from his bestest friend Jack.

'I can see that look on your face again,' said Dorothy to Jack. 'You are worrying about Eddie.'

'How can I do anything else?' Jack asked outside the diner as he slipped on his nice clean trenchcoat.

219

Dorothy shrugged and said, 'You're doing all you can. And my, that trenchcoat smells of chicken.'

Jack made that face yet again.

'I'll tell you what,' said Dorothy. 'I'll take you out tonight, to a club – how would you like that?'

'If it's a drinking club,' said Jack. Hopefully.

'I'll see what I can do.'

'Dorothy,' said Jack, and he looked into the green eyes of the beautiful woman. 'Dorothy, one thing. You only had enough money to pay for a couple of cups of coffee earlier. How come you can now afford to take me out to a club?'

'I stole money out of the cash register,' said Dorothy.

'Oh, that's all right then,' said Jack. 'I thought you might have done something dishonest.'

No further words were exchanged upon this matter and Jack and Dorothy walked arm in arm down Hollywood Boulevard.

Dorothy pointed out places of interest and Jack looked on in considerable awe, whilst wishing that Eddie was with him to see them.

'That's where the Academy Awards ceremony is held each year to honour the achievements of movie stars,' said Dorothy. 'One day I will go onto the stage there and receive my award for Best Actress.'

'I thought you were going into producing,' said Jack.

'Yes,' said Dorothy. 'Best Actress and Best Producer and I hope you'll be there, too. You'd look wonderful in a black tuxedo and dicky bow. Very dashing, very romantic.'

At length they reached the Hollywood Wax Museum.

'Would you like to see the movie stars?' asked Dorothy. 'They are here in effigy.'

Jack shrugged. 'About this drinking club. I've had a hard day and I do like to unwind over a dozen or so beers.'

'All in good time, come on.'

Now wax museums are very much like Marmite.

In that you either love 'em or hate 'em. There's no in between. No, 'I think I fancy a visit to the wax museum today, sort of.' It's either yes indeedy-do, or no siree.

At the door to the wax museum stood the effigy of a golden woman in a white dress, the skirt of which periodically rose through the medium of air-jets beneath to reveal her underwear.

'I like wax museums,' said Jack. 'Yes indeedy-do.'

'That's Marilyn Monroe,' said Dorothy as she purchased the tickets from a man in the ticket booth who looked like a cross between Bella Lugosi and Rin Tin Tin. 'She's the most famous actress in the world.'

'Does she have a nursery rhyme?' Jack asked.

'No, silly,' said Dorothy. 'Come on.'

And they entered the wax museum.

It was dark in there – well, they always are, it lends to the necessary ambience. And disguises, of course, the fact that wax museums are generally housed within crumbling buildings with really manky decor, faded damp-stained wallpaper and carpets that dare not speak their name.

But that's part of their charm.

Jack viewed The Legends of the Old West: William S. Hart, Audie Murphy, Jimmy Stewart, Gabby Hayes, Hopalong Cassidy, Clayton Moore, Roy Rogers and Trigger.

Jack then viewed The Mirthmakers: Buster Keaton, Charlie Chaplin, Laurel and Hardy, the Marx Brothers (whose hand prints Jack had viewed outside Mann's Chinese Theatre) and Abbott and Costello.

Then The Hollywood Horrors: Lon Chaney Senr., Bella Lugosi, Dwight Frye, Boris Karloff.

'Oh,' said Dorothy. 'They scare me.' And she nuzzled close to Jack.

And Jack took to this nuzzling and Jack turned up the face of Dorothy and kissed it, on the forehead and on the cheek and then on the beautiful mouth. And Dorothy kissed Jack and moved his hands from her shoulders down to her bottom.

And, as there was no one else around, and the lighting was so dim and everything, very soon some clothes were off and the two of them were having sex.

And somewhat sooner that Jack might have hoped, it was over, and somewhat soon after that the two of them were back in the evening sunlight of Hollywood Boulevard.

'Well, thanks for *that*,' said Jack.

But Dorothy put her fingers to his lips. 'It took your mind off Eddie for a while, didn't it?' she said.

'Damn,' said Jack. 'I wish you hadn't said *that*. Now I feel worse than ever.'

Eddie Bear felt worse than ever. He felt hot and he felt sick from all the bumping about and when the car finally stopped for good and all and the lid of his prison was lifted, Eddie Bear peered into the sunlight and felt almost exhilarated. Almost.

'Out,' said the voice of his bestest friend, which came not from that fellow.

'I'm wobbly,' said Eddie. 'You'll have to lift me out.'

'Out, or I'll kick you out.'

'Well, there's no need for *that*.' Eddie struggled up and over and down. To rest his paw pads on sand. 'If I ask you where I am, will you tell me?' he asked.

The other Jack shook his head grimly. 'Where you'll not be found,' said he. 'Come on, get a move on, that way.'

That way proved to be between the open steel-framed gateway of a tall and barbed-wire-fenced enclosure. Eddie looked to the left and the right of him. The fencing faded off in either direction. This was a large enclosure. There was a guard post by this gateway. A uniformed guard sat in it.

There was also a sign on an open gate. The sign read:

AREA FIFTY-TWO
UNAUTHORISED ACCESS FORBIDDEN

There were some rules and regulations printed beneath these words and these were of the military persuasion.

Eddie looked up bitterly at the other Jack. 'I'm hungry,' said Eddie. 'And thirsty, too. Is there a bar nearby?'

'There's plenty of bars where you're going,' said the evil twin of his bestest friend. 'All made of steel.' And he laughed, in that mad way that supervillains do.

'Most amusing,' said Eddie. 'But why have you brought me here?'

'Because you are *so* special,' said the anti-Jack. And he did more of the manic laughing.

Jack wasn't laughing. He now felt *very* guilty.

'Listen,' said Dorothy, 'you're doing everything you can. Didn't you tell me that as head chef of a Golden Chicken Diner you were invited to the head office tomorrow for a motivational training session?'

'I don't recall doing so,' said Jack, 'but that is what I'm doing.'

'So you'll probably be on the board of directors by lunchtime and in a position to find out where they've taken Eddie.'

'You really think so?' said Jack.

'Just follow the American Dream.'

'I am a little confused by the American Dream, as it happens,' said Jack as he and Dorothy walked on, passing the Hollywood Suit Company, which knocks out really natty suits at a price that one can afford. 'I mean,' Jack continued, 'if it is every American's born right to follow the American Dream and succeed in this following, how come most Americans aren't googlaires living in mansions?'

'It's their right to *try*,' said Dorothy.

And *that* was *that* for *that* conversation.

'Let's go on to a club,' said Dorothy.

Jack took to halting and gazing at her. 'Actually, let's not,' he said. 'As you might be aware, I have nowhere to sleep tonight.'

'You can sleep with me if you want.'

'I was hoping you'd say that. Why don't we give the club a miss, go to your place, have some more sex and get an early night? I have a hard day ahead.'

Dorothy looked up at Jack. 'All right,' she said. 'We should both have an early night. There's no telling what might happen to us tomorrow at the Golden Chicken headquarters.'

'Us?' said Jack. 'I will be going alone.'

'I think you'll find that all management staff have been invited. Restaurant management as well as kitchen management.'

'So that's why I'll be going alone.'

'And that's why you won't. I follow the American Dream, too, Jack. I manage *our* branch of the Golden Chicken now.'

'What?' said Jack.

'There was some unpleasantness with the previous manager,' said Dorothy. 'She didn't go quietly. I was forced to use my Dimac.'

'Early night it is, then,' said Jack.

The Californian sun rose once again. As it always does, unfailingly.

Its warmth and golden wonder did not fall on Eddie Bear, however, for he lay dismally in a barred cell, many floors beneath ground level in that Area known as Fifty-Two.

It touched upon the cheek of Jack, though, who lay in the arms of Dorothy in the single room she rented in a house in Blue Jay Way that would one day be rented in its entirety by George Harrison, who would write a rather pleasant song about it. But not yet.

Jack yawned, stretched, rose. Viewed his clothes, all washed, ironed and ready, hanging on a hanger. Looked down upon the sweet sleeping face of Dorothy and kissed her on the cheek.

Dorothy stirred and murmured, 'Not now, Brad.'

'*Brad?*' said Jack.

And Dorothy awoke.

'Brad,' said Jack. 'You said Brad.'

'Brad is the name of my dog,' said Dorothy.

'You said that your dog was named Toto.'

'Bradley Toto,' said Dorothy. 'He's a thoroughbred from England.'

Jack laughed loudly. 'Your first lie,' said he. 'We should celebrate it with some early-morning sex.'

'I'm not in the mood,' said Dorothy.

'Your second lie,' said Jack.

And when the early-morning sex was done and Jack was once more feeling really rotten about himself for having such a good time whilst Eddie was either in peril, or dead, they had their breakfast. Which Jack really hated himself for enjoying so much.

And then they got dressed and went out.

And that sun was still shining. Like it does.

And they caught a downtown train and it took them to downtown LA, where they alighted downtown.

And Jack looked up at GOLDEN CHICKEN TOWERS and Jack went, 'Wow, that's big! Especially the lettering.'

Golden Chicken Towers was located next to the Eastern Building, which remains to this day a triumph of Art Deco and is celebrated for the fact that *Predator 2* stood upon its roof and was not at all concerned when his retractable spear jobbie was struck by lightning.

The foyer, entrance hall, vestibule, lobby or whatever you might wish to call it of Golden Chicken Towers was nothing less than palatial.

It was sumptuous. It was golden. It was chickeny.

To either side of the expanse of golden floor tiles stood golden plinths, upon which rose statues of golden hens. These hens stood in noble attitudes. Some held tall upward-thrusting spears beneath their golden wings, spears capped with golden pennants, each emblazoned with the company logo. Some of these hens wore uniforms decked with golden medals. Others looked defiant, bearing golden guns.

'I don't know about you,' Jack whispered to Dorothy as they joined a queue to receive their official passes, 'but all this is *very* wrong.'

'It's like some temple dedicated to the God of All Chickens,' Dorothy observed. 'Those are very big statues.'

Jack craned his neck and peered along the queue. It was a long queue made up of eager-looking young Americans. They were all spick and span and as near to business-suited as they could afford. They had that scrubbed quality about them that is somehow unwholesome, although it's difficult to explain exactly why.

To Jack they all looked all of a sameness. And this, Jack felt, was odd. And then it occurred to Jack, perhaps for the first time, that they all *were* of a certain sameness. That everyone he had encountered since entering this world that was exclusively peopled by his own kind, even though they had certain superficial differences, they *were* all of a sameness.

They were all of a single race. The human one.

And suddenly Jack yearned to be back in Toy City. This was *not* his world, even if these *were somehow* his people. There was such diversity amongst the denizens of Toy City, the gollies and the dollies, and the teddies and the clockwork folk. Each with their own specific, particular outlook on life, their own ways of being. *They* were Jack's folk. Jack was one of them now. He had always been an outsider, always looking for something. But there was nothing *here* he wanted.

Jack looked towards Dorothy.

No, not even *her*, really.

Jack just wanted to be back with Eddie. Back in Toy City with all of this horror behind him.

'What are you thinking about?' asked Dorothy. 'Eddie, I bet.'

'More than Eddie,' said Jack. 'I was thinking about . . . well, no, it doesn't matter.'

But it did. It really did.

As they drew closer to the desk where they were to receive their passes, Dorothy said, 'Look at that, Jack. I bet you don't like that.'

Jack looked and Jack saw. Behind the desk was a tall glass cabinet. Very tall, very wide, glass-shelved. Upon these shelves were many little figures.

Jack peered and Jack saw and recognised these figures.

The clockwork clapping monkeys. The band from Old King Cole's. The orchestra from the Opera House. And oh so many more.

And right in the middle and larger than the rest sat a bear wearing a trenchcoat. And there was no mistaking *that* bear.

Jack made certain growling sounds and urged on the queue before him.

And presently it was his and Dorothy's turn to receive their passes.

'Name?' said a young tanned lovely, with a great beehive of golden hair.

'Dorothy,' said Dorothy. And then she added her surname. Dorothy received her pass.

'Next,' said the lovely to Jack.

'Jack,' said Jack to the lovely. 'Jack is my name. My name is Jack.'

'And Jack *what* would it be?'

'You have me on that one,' said Jack. '*What* would it be?'

'Your surname. You are Jack *what*?'

'I am Jack the head chef of the Golden Chicken Diner on Hollywood Boulevard.'

'I require your surname.'

'All right,' said Jack. 'I'm Sir Jack.'

'There's no *Sir* Jack on my list,' said the lovely. 'Please leave by the way you came in. Next, please.'

'No,' said Jack. 'Hold on there. I am the head chef.'

'Your name is not on the list.'

'I only started yesterday. I rose up through the ranks.'

'Ah,' said the lovely, batting preposterous eyelashes towards Jack. 'You are a migrant worker.'

'Exactly,' said Jack.

'No work visa, no ID, paid in cash and poorly, too.'

'That kind of thing,' said Jack.

'Then get out before I call security.'

'Now hold on—' said Jack.

'If *I* might explain,' said Dorothy. 'Jack is from England.'

'Oh,' said the lovely. 'England, is it? Where you all wear bowler hats and take tea with the Queen at three? Well, why didn't you say so?'

'Would it have made a difference?' Jack asked.

'Well, naturally it would. We Americans just *love* you English. Our politicians, in particular our President, are so keen to cultivate a special relationship with your Prime Minister. I have the gift of prophecy, you see, and I calculate that in some future time our President will be able to bully your Prime Minister into breaking the Nato Alliance and help him invade a Middle Eastern nation state.'

'Eh?' said Jack, accepting the pass he was now offered. 'What was that you said?'

'You want it *all* again? You see, I have the gift of prophecy. And I *calculate*—'

'That's enough,' said Jack. 'Can I use your toilet, please?'

'Well, you can't use mine, but you can use the men's room – it's over there.' And the lovely pointed with a lovely hand.

And Jack said, 'Excuse me, please,' and made for the door at the hurry-up.

And once inside the men's room, he locked himself into a stall and withdrew from his trenchcoat Wallah the calculating pocket.

'Oh,' whispered Wallah. 'Remembered my existence at last, have you, Jack?'

'I'm so sorry,' said Jack. 'All kinds of things have been happening.'

'Of that I am fully aware,' whispered Wallah. 'I have been plunged into dirty dishwater, then roasted in a rotisserie. Then washed and wrung out once again by your lady friend to get the smell of chicken out of me.'

'It's all been rather hectic,' said Jack.

'Well, all the sex you've been having certainly has.'

'It's just business,' said Jack. Which was a callous thing to say, more callous too because there was a more than even chance that he meant it.

'You are a very bad boy,' said Wallah.

'Eddie sometimes says that,' said Jack,

'And you behave very badly when that little bear isn't with you.'

'I behave *very* badly when he is,' said Jack. 'Often with his encouragement.'

'Time is growing short,' said Wallah, and her voice was faint. 'Eddie has less than forty-eight hours – you must move with haste.'

'I've got this far,' said Jack, 'thanks to you.'

'But I can take you no further. You forgot about me, Jack.'

'I didn't. Everything got hectic. I told you.'

'You forgot about me. But it doesn't matter. I thought I was special to you. But it doesn't matter. What matters is that you find Eddie and together you stop the fiend who would destroy Toy City.'

'I'm on the case,' said Jack. 'I'm trying.'

'I can do no more to help you but tell you this: I calculate trouble by teatime and I calculate that, given the choice, you should duck to the right.'

'Right,' said Jack in a puzzled tone.

'Right,' said Wallah. 'And so goodbye, Jack.'

'Goodbye.'

'Goodbye, Jack. I am fading fast. Time is up for me.'

'No,' said Jack, shaking Wallah about. 'You can't go now. You can't—'

'Die?' said Wallah. 'I'm dying, Jack. Would you do something for me?'

'Anything,' said Jack.

'Anything?' said Wallah. 'Anything I ask?'

'Anything,' said Jack. 'Anything at all.'

'Then kiss me, Jack,' said Wallah, 'and . . .'

Jack emerged from the men's room. He had a rather guilty look on his face. And it was a red and embarrassed face that this guilty look was upon.

'What have you been doing in there?' Dorothy asked Jack. 'You look as if you've been—'

'Don't be absurd,' said Jack. 'I've been in there by myself.'

'Then you were—'

'Stop, please,' said Jack. 'Let's get a move on with what we're supposed to be doing.'

'You *have* been,' said Dorothy. 'Every woman can recognise that look on a man's face, even though most women won't ever admit it to a man. You've been—'

'Stop!'

When all had been issued their passes, all were led by the lovely to a golden escalator, up this and into a great hall (all gold) with seating upholstered in a similar hue. The seating was set up in rows before a stage, which Jack found unsurprisingly to be all over golden panels. And at length blinds were drawn at golden-framed windows and a spotlight, remarkably white in its brilliance, shone on the golden stage illuminating a golden microphone held high by a golden stand.

And into this spotlight stepped a dramatic personage who wore a suit that was not of gold, but was beige.

'Howdy doody, golden people,' he bawled into the microphone.

The sitters mumbled some good mornings/howdy doodys.

The man at the mic shook his head.

Jack peered up at the man at the mic. There was no all-over

sameness about this fellow. He had *something*, something more. Just what was it? Jack wondered. A certain overconfidence? A certain *attitude*? He looked even more scrubbed than the sitters.

The man in beige had a big round head, with a big pink face and a kind of cylindrical body. His arms were long and so too were his hands, with very long fingers upon them.

His pink face surely shone.

'I said, "Howdy doody, golden people," ' he bawled.

The 'golden people' sitting replied, this time with a louder 'Howdy doody'.

'A very good howdy doody,' said the man on the stage, 'but not good enough for you golden people. One more time.'

And this time he got a veritable thunderstorm of howdy doodys hurled back in his direction.

With the notable exception of Jack and Dorothy. Although Dorothy did mumble *something*.

'Good enough,' said the man in beige. 'And welcome to Golden Chicken Towers. Welcome to you, the chosen ones. The special ones. The trusted ones. Your labours have brought you here. Your dedication to the company ethic. Your sense of duty. Your pride as young Americans.' And he raised a fist and shook it in a friendly fashion.

'Now who can tell me what *this* is?' he said. And he produced from his pocket . . . an egg.

Hands went up from the sitters.

Jack said, 'It's an egg.'

'It's an egg, well done.' The figure in beige smiled down upon Jack. 'It's an egg indeed. And what is your name, young man?'

'Sir Jack,' said Jack. 'I'm from England.'

'An Englander, is it? Well, up you come onto the stage.'

'And why would I want to do that?' Jack asked.

'Because I have chosen *you* to assist me with this presentation.'

'Well, aren't *I* the lucky one.'

'What did you say, young man?'

'I said, "Well, I *am* the lucky one." '

'As indeed you are. Up, up. Let's have a round of applause for Sir Jack.'

And a round of enthusiastic applause went up.

Jack shook his head and climbed onto the stage.

'Now, Sir Jack,' said the man in beige, putting a long beige arm about Jack's shoulders, 'what I'd like you to do is—'

'Work the slide projector?' Jack asked, as one was now being wheeled onto the stage by the lovely with the golden hair and the big dark batting lashes.

'Precisely.'

'And would I be right in assuming,' Jack asked, 'that the slides will display a sort of potted history of the company?'

'You are a most astute young man – I can see that career opportunities aplenty await you.'

'Splendid,' said Jack. 'And then I assume you will be giving us all a motivational speech.'

'Something of that nature, yes.' The man in beige gave Jack a certain look.

'Followed by a slap-up lunch,' said Jack.

'Why, yes.'

'Followed by more, how shall I put it, indoctrination?'

'Well,' said the man in beige. And he removed his arm from Jack's shoulders.

'Just so,' said Jack. 'But I think not.'

'I do not fully understand you.'

'Then perhaps you will understand *this*.' And Jack pulled from his trenchcoat pocket the cleaver that he had used the previous day for the decerebration of the chickens.

'Oh,' said the man in beige. 'What is *this*?'

'*This*,' said Jack, 'is a cleaver, And if you do not take me, *at once*, to your leader, I will use it to cut off your head.'

Now this caused some alarm, not only from the man in beige and the lovely on the stage, but also from the seated chosen ones, who now unseated themselves, preparing to flee.

'And sit down, you lot,' shouted Dorothy. Pulling, much to Jack's surprise, two pistols from her clothing. 'Anybody moves and you're dead.'

Jack looked at Dorothy.

Dorothy smiled. 'Well, get a move on,' she said.

18

There are moments.

Sometimes.

Special moments. Magic moments. Moments when everything becomes as clear as the air and you can see right through it, into eternity.

These moments are often reached via the medium of alcohol. In England, for example, where most folk wear bowler hats, take tea at three and know the Queen well, there are public drinking houses. And those who frequent these sociable establishments respect something that is known as the ten-o'clock watershed. It is understood that before this time, talk is generalised and covers many topics – the day's news, recent sporting events, trivial this and thats.

But beyond the ten-o'clock watershed, certain matters are deemed acceptable that would otherwise be considered taboo. Friendship is one of these and many is the time when two large masculine fellows will be seen putting their arms about one another and swearing to anyone who would care to hear, and many who might care not, that 'this is my bestest friend'. And 'I love this man'.

And although at nine fifty-five this would not be deemed the thing-to-do, beyond the ten-o'clock watershed it is A-okay.

This is but one example and the cynical reader might lean towards the opinion that it is in fact 'the alcohol speaking', rather than a moment. A special moment.

But who amongst us has not experienced a special moment? A moment of total clarity. A reality check. A revelation.

As Jack held his cleaver over the beige man's head, Jack experienced such a special moment.

For Jack it was not peace, or love, or a semi-religious revelation.

For Jack it was more a case of WHAT IN THE NAME OF ANY GOD THAT I MAY CARE TO BELIEVE IN **AM I DOING**?

It *was* a special moment. Jack saw the audience cowering beneath the guns of Dorothy. The beige man cowering, too, beneath Jack's cleaver. The great golden room with its Californian sunlight slanting through the slats of the window blinds.

The sudden terrible reality of it all.

And for one moment, and a special one at that, Jack thought of fleeing, dropping that cleaver and running away. This was real, these were people. What was all the rest of it? Chickens, spaceships, walking, talking toys? Eddie was gone and Jack was here and for one terrible, special moment Jack wondered whether all that stuff, all that mad unlikely stuff, really *was* real. Perhaps, Jack thought to himself, he, Jack, had gone insane, and perhaps now, at this moment, he had reawakened from the nightmare of insanity to this moment of absolute clarity.

Jack hesitated, all in confusion, for there is a problem with special moments: they play havoc with all your previous moments.

And Jack's hand loosened on his cleaver.

And Jack stared into the fearful face of the man in beige.

'I'm . . .' Jack was about to say 'sorry'.

'Hurry up, Jack,' shouted Dorothy. 'Pull yourself together. Eddie is in danger – don't forget that.'

Jack blinked and gazed towards Dorothy.

Had she known what he was thinking?

Jack didn't say, 'I'm sorry.'

Well, he did, but he didn't. He said. 'I'm sorry, Mister Man In Beige, but if you do not take me at once to your leader, I will chop off your ear.'

'No, please have mercy.' The man in beige sank down to his knees. 'Don't hurt me, please, I'm innocent.'

'No one is innocent,' called Dorothy. 'Get a move on, Jack.'

Jack hauled the beige man back to his feet. 'Your leader or your ear,' said he.

'No, please.' The lovely on the stage wrung her beautiful hands.

The manicured nails of the slender fingers twinkled in the spotlight. 'Please don't hurt him, please.'

'I'm sorry,' said Jack, 'but my best friend has been kidnapped by someone in this building. Someone in power. I demand to be taken to this someone. Now!'

'But we don't have the authority,' said the lovely. 'We don't know who you should speak to. Mister Tinto here—'

'What did you say?' asked Jack.

'Don't say anything, Amelie,' said the man in beige.

'Amelie?' said Jack. 'Mister Tinto? What is this?'

And then Jack saw it. Because perhaps *this* was the special moment. In fact, the other special moment, which had seemed like a special moment at the time, was, in fact, only a warm-up sort of special moment.

Jack stared hard at the man in beige.

And then Jack saw it.

And had a special moment.

The man in beige was Tinto. Well, he wasn't *the* Tinto, but he was, well, what was he? Yes, he was a human manifestation, a human counterpart – he was the *human* version of Tinto. And the lovely? The lovely? Yes! Jack glanced at her and his glance became a stare. She *was* Amelie. Amelie made flesh.

Jack fell back for a moment, gawping and shaking his cleaver about. It *was* them. Why hadn't he seen it immediately? He'd known there was something . . .

But . . .

'Jack!' shouted Dorothy, most loudly, too. 'Jack, get a grip on yourself.'

'But it's them.' And Jack did foolish pointings all around with his free hand. 'It's Amelie and Tinto. It's them. It's them if they were people. It is.'

Jack's confusion turned to anger. As is often the case.

'Elevator,' said Jack. 'Upstairs,' said Jack.

'Yes,' said Mr Tinto. 'Anything you say.'

'Dorothy?' called Jack.

'I'll follow,' said Dorothy. 'Once I've dealt with this lot.'

'You're not going to shoot them?'

Chefs and managers ducked and flinched.

'I'll just have a word with them.'

'You promise?' Jack had some doubts in his head.

'I promise,' said Dorothy. And as Jack led Amelie and Mr Tinto from the stage, one hand on the beige man's collar, the other holding the cleaver high, Dorothy addressed the shaking, trembling audience.

'Ladies and gentlemen,' she said, 'I am so sorry that this talk, which I'm sure you were all looking forward to, has been brought to a premature conclusion. I suggest now that you vacate the premises and do so in an orderly fashion. I would also strongly advise that you say *nothing* about what has occurred here. We have two hostages and should you inform the police, we will not hesitate to kill them. Do you understand?'

Heads nodded thoughtfully. Eyes strayed to the exit doors.

'Ah, just one more thing,' said Dorothy, 'before you leave. Which one of you is it?'

The crowd, as one, made a puzzled face.

'Come on,' said Dorothy. 'You know what I mean.'

The crowd, as one, shook its head.

'The hero,' said Dorothy. 'The one who will stay behind. The one who although working as a chef used to work for Special Ops, or something, but got sacked through no fault of his own, which led to the break-up with his wife, a bit of a drink problem. But who, rising to such a situation as this, will slip away from the departing crowd, crawl through air-conditioning ducts and bring my companion and me to justice. There's always *one*. We *all* know that.'

'Ah,' went the crowd, as one. Because, after all, *we all* know *that*.

'So come on, then,' said Dorothy. 'Which one of you is it?'

The crowd now took to a collective silence.

'All right,' said Dorothy. 'Then let me put it another way. I will count to ten, and if the hero has not identified himself before this time I will execute two people at random. Come on, now, I'm counting down.'

'Oh, all right,' came a voice from an air-conditioning duct. 'Don't shoot anyone, I'm coming out.'

Jack was making good progress along the corridor. If good progress can indeed be measured by progress along a corridor.

'We really can't help you,' said Amelie, wiggling in front.

Jack looked down at those long, long legs. They were just like re— Oh, they *were* real legs, weren't they?

Jack said, 'Get a move on.'

'Amelie's right,' said Mr Tinto. 'We can't help you. We don't know anything.'

'You know something,' said Jack. 'I've been following the American Dream, me, and I know how it works. You can lead me to the next person in the chain of command. That's how it works, I know it.'

They were approaching a lift. The doors of this were gold.

'That's not how it works,' said Mr Tinto. 'Well, I suppose it is in theory, but not in reality, no.'

'I have no time to debate issues with you,' said Jack, flashing the cleaver's blade before Mr Tinto's frightened eyes. 'I am a desperate man.'

'Well, clearly so, yes. But you are making a mistake.'

'They always say that,' said Jack.

'Who do?' asked the man in beige as Jack hauled him bodily onwards.

'Baddies,' said Jack. 'It's a threatening thing to say, "You are making a big mistake."'

'I don't mean it to be threatening,' the beige man protested. 'I'm just telling you the truth – you *are* making a big mistake.'

'We'll see,' said Jack. 'Get a move on, please.'

And on they went and they reached the lift. And at the lift Dorothy caught up with them.

'Is everything all right?' Jack asked her.

'Yes, it is *now*,' she replied.

'I don't like the sound of that.' And Jack reached out and pressed the 'up' button. 'What happened? You didn't kill anyone, did you?'

'No, I just knocked them on the head.'

'All of them?'

'No, just the one – the chef who'd stripped down to his vest and bare feet and hidden himself in the air-conditioning system.'

Jack shook his head. 'Do chefs often do that?' he asked.

'They do here in Hollywood,' said Dorothy. 'Going up.'

And the lift doors opened.

'Everyone inside,' said Jack.

'Do I really have to?' asked Mr Tinto.

'Yes,' said Jack. 'You do.'

'But you don't need two hostages. Why not just take Amelie here?'

All were now inside the lift and the lift doors closed upon them. Jack pressed the topmost button. The lift began to rise.

'What did you say?' asked Amelie.

'I'm only saying,' said Mr Tinto, 'that in hostage situations such as this, I'm the one most likely to get shot. They rarely shoot the pretty girl – she'll probably end up snogging the hostage-taker.'

'Snogging?' said Amelie.

'Well, shagging,' said Mr Tinto.

'What?' said Amelie, and she smacked Mr Tinto right in the face.

'Go girl,' said Dorothy.

'Not in the face,' cried Mr Tinto. And he burst into tears.

'She didn't hit you that hard,' said Jack. 'Don't be such a baby.'

'I'm not paid to get smacked,' said Mr Tinto. 'Taken hostage, yes, that was in my contract. But not smacked. I always demand a stunt double if there's any smacking involved. Or being thrown through windows.'

Jack rolled his eyes.

'Well, I've not been paid for any shagging,' said Amelie. 'That's work for a body double. I don't do *that* kind of work.'

'Oh, please,' said Mr Tinto. 'It's common knowledge that you've done stag films.'

'I've done no such thing. And we all know how *you* get work. Whose casting couch did you have to bend over to—'

'Would you please stop now,' said Jack. 'I'm in charge here. I have the cleaver.'

'Yes,' said Mr Tinto, 'and I've been meaning to talk to you about that. That is a *real* cleaver – you could have injured me with that. If I wasn't a professional I would have stopped you dead on the set and demanded a prop.'

'A *what*?' said Jack.

'A soft cleaver. A rubber one.'

'This is a real cleaver,' said Jack.

'Yes, I know, and you can stop threatening me with it now – we're no longer on camera.'

'We might be,' said Amelie. 'The director never called "cut".'

Jack looked towards Dorothy. 'Is it just me,' he asked, 'or is something not altogether right with these two hostages?'

'Oh, come off it, luvvie,' said Mr Tinto. 'Just because you're all Stanislavski method acting to disguise the fact that you can't remember your lines—'

'What?' went Jack.

'It's true,' said Amelie. 'You were far too rough with Sydney.'

'Thank you, Marilyn.'

'Sydney?' went Jack. 'Marilyn?'

'Oh please, sir,' said Sydney. 'As if you didn't recognise us.'

The lift went clunk and stopped. They had reached their destination.

'Now just *stop*!' shouted Jack. 'What is all this about? What are you saying? What is all this Marilyn and Sydney business?'

'You have to be jesting and your jest is in very poor taste,' said Sydney. 'Well, we're here now. Back in character everyone. And cue. Press the open-door button, please.'

Jack shook his head and pressed the 'open' button.

And the lift doors opened.

And Jack beheld.

And Dorothy also beheld. And so did Sydney and so did Marilyn.

And Sydney said, 'Typical, that.'

'Typical?' said Jack, and he stared. There was nothing. Nothing at all. The lift was at the top of its shaft, but there was no floor for them to step out onto. Just a big empty nothing. Four interior walls of the building. And these, it appeared, constructed from canvas and timber. Far, far below them there was to be seen the above parts of a ceiling below – the ceiling of the lecture room they had so recently left. And the above parts of another ceiling that followed the corridor that they had followed to enter the lift they now stood in. And stood in somewhat fearfully. Clinging onto one another now, for fear of falling the considerable distance to their doom below.

'Utterly typical,' said Sydney, pressing himself back from the open lift doors and flattening himself against the opposite wall.

Jack did more slack-jawed starings. Then he turned, shook Marilyn away from his arm and squared up large before Sydney. 'Speak to me,' Jack demanded. 'Explain what is going on here.'

'The set's not finished,' said Sydney. 'Utterly typical. Labour disputes with the union, I expect. I was on *Casablanca*, back in forty-two with Bogart, half the sets weren't finished. We had to double up the Blue Parrot Café with the airport lounge, although I don't think anyone noticed. They were too entranced by my acting.'

And Jack hit Sydney. Right in the face.

And Sydney broke down in tears.

'You beast,' howled Marilyn. 'How unprofessional. How dare you hit a Hollywood legend like that. He came out of retirement to play this part – you have no right to treat him in such a way.'

Jack turned upon her. 'You speak to me,' he said, 'or I'll throw you out of the lift and you can make your own way downstairs.'

'No, stop, please.'

'Then *speak*.'

And Marilyn spoke. 'We are actors,' she said. 'Surely you recognise us. This is Mister Sydney Greenstreet and I am Marilyn Monroe.'

'Marilyn Monroe?' asked Jack. 'But you can't be her. I saw her effigy at the wax museum, although—'

'It *is* her,' said Dorothy. 'But I didn't recognise you – how come?'

'Because when I play a role, I *am* that person.'

Jack looked *most* unconvinced.

'It is her,' said Dorothy. 'It really is. Could I have your autograph, Miss Monroe? I'm your greatest fan.'

'Now stop all this,' said Jack. 'It doesn't make any sense.'

'Of course it makes sense, man,' said Sydney. 'What is the matter with you? This isn't a real building. It's a set. It's part of a movie. But why am I telling you this? You're an actor. Although not a very good one, I might add. What have you been in before? Have I seen any of your work?'

'Actors?' went Jack. 'Set?' went Jack. 'What does this mean?' went Jack.

'It could mean,' said Dorothy, 'that we have fallen into a very large and elaborate trap.'

'No,' said Jack. And Jack shook his head. 'That's absurd. No one would go to all this trouble, set all this up, this building, the big foyer downstairs, all of this, simply to trap us.'

'Giving yourself airs and graces,' said Sydney, flinching as he said it. 'Who would want to trap *you*?'

Jack shook his head. 'But why?' he asked. 'Why all this? What is it for?'

'You know what it's for,' said Sydney. 'You read your contract, or your agent did. You signed the confidentiality clause.'

Jack was about to say 'What?' once more, but Dorothy, however, stopped him. 'Jack's from Arkansas,' she said. 'I'm sure you recognised his hokey accent.'

Jack said, 'What?' to this.

'Recognised it at once,' said Sydney. 'I can do almost any accent. But then I was classically trained. But then I'm from England, of course.'

'Well,' said Dorothy, 'Jack really *is* a method actor, trained at the New School's Dramatic Workshop with Brando, where he studied with Stella Adler and learned the revolutionary techniques of the Stanislavski System.'

'Overrated,' said Sydney. 'That Brando will never amount to anything.'

'What is this toot?' Jack asked. 'Where is this leading?'

'Just leave this to me,' said Dorothy to Jack. And to Mr Greenstreet she said, 'You see, Jack can't read or write. *I'm* his agent.'

Jack shook his head. He had given up on the 'What's'.

'A sort of actor-manager,' said Sydney. 'Like Henry Irving.'

'Henry Irving managed a theatre,' said Marilyn, knowledgeably. 'He wasn't an agent.'

'I do it all,' said Dorothy. 'And all my own stunts.'

'Might we close the lift doors?' asked Sydney. 'I have vertigo. Did a rooftop scene in the nineteen forty-nine remake of *Death is a Dame in a Doggy Bag*. A Lazlo Woodbine thriller. Brian Donlevy played Laz in that one and the final rooftop confrontation scene was shot on a real rooftop. *Cinéma-vérité* black and white. I nearly fell to my—'

Jack raised his hand.

Sydney said no more.

Dorothy said, 'I signed the confidentiality clause on behalf of Jack, but I didn't tell him about it. Sydney, please put Jack in the picture. We wouldn't want him blurting anything out – it would not help to advance any of our careers.'

'Oh, it's quite simple,' said Sydney, sighing as he said it. 'Your agent, Dorothy here, signed the confidentiality clause for you, which states that we actors, employed by Golden Chicken Productions, must not discuss the script or contents of the movie prior to its release. There's millions of dollars riding on this, what with the merchandising already being in place and everything. It's a revolutionary concept, the toys being given away free and no one knowing that the movie, with big Hollywood stars playing the parts of the toys, is already in production.'

'I'm very confused,' said Jack.

'No you're *not*,' said Dorothy. 'Think about it.'

Jack thought and thought hard. 'I'm *still* confused,' he said. 'If this is a movie, Tinto is a barman, *not* a—'

'Motivational speaker,' said Sydney. 'I know, I went up for the part of Tinto but I didn't get it. I'm only calling myself Mr Tinto because the "Motivational Speaker" doesn't even have a name. Do you know who got the Tinto part in the end?'

Jack shook his head. Strangely he had no idea at all.

'Gene Kelly,' said Sydney. 'Tinto the dancing barman, I ask you.'

'So let me just get this straight,' said Dorothy, 'for Jack's benefit, because he is from Arkansas. You two were hired for a single day's work on this movie, which is a Golden Chicken Production, a live-action movie based upon the toys that are presently being given away free in the Golden Chicken Diners.'

'There is something special about them, isn't there?' said Marilyn. 'I'm collecting them myself.'

'And the movie will star major Hollywood actors and go worldwide?'

'The talk at the studio,' said Sydney, sighing once more as he spoke, 'is that with the movie's release, the Golden Chicken Diners will also go global. It's a vast commercial enterprise – not one I would normally wish to associate myself with, but such exposure can only advance my career. And let's face it, dear, I came out of retirement for this and even if I never work again, the fact that I was in *this* movie will ensure that I can make money for the rest of my life doing signings at Sci-Fi conventions.'

'Sci-Fi conventions?' Jack asked.

'Well, this *is* a Sci-Fi movie. What with all the spaceships and stuff.'

'Spaceships?' Jack shouted, and his hands were once more on Sydney's lapels.

'Spaceships!' Sydney tried quite fiercely to shake off Jack's manic grip. 'It *is* based on *War of the Worlds*, isn't it? Although having chickens as the saviour of mankind is a bit far-fetched in my opinion. And this strap line – "Eating chicken makes you a winner, too". Gross, but business, I suppose.'

Jack was, as they say, 'losing it', although they probably wouldn't be saying it for at least another ten years, but then of course they wouldn't actually have chaps in vests crawling around inside air-conditioning ducts and bringing criminals to justice for perhaps another forty years, but this *was* and *is* Hollywood, where Dreams become Reality, so Jack 'held it together' and Jack now shouted, 'Show me the script of this movie.'

'I don't have it with me,' said Sydney. 'I learn my lines. I can't be having with improv.'

'Take me to your script,' roared Jack.

'It's all "take me to this" and "take me to that" with you,' replied Sydney, quite boldly, considering. 'Take, take, take, that's all you do.'

'Or it's out and make your own way down.'

'Easy, Jack,' said Dorothy. 'They're only actors.'

'*Only?*' said Sydney.

'Well, not *only*, of course,' said Dorothy. 'Anything but only.'

'I want to see the script,' said Jack. 'I need to see the script.'

'And so you shall, young man. Just calm yourself down.' Sydney freed himself from Jack's grip.

'Is this going to help?' Dorothy asked. 'Help to find Eddie, I mean.'

'What else do we have? All this is fake. There's nothing here.'

'All right, then. Let's go down.'

Jack pressed the ground-floor button. The lift doors closed.

'Thank you for that,' said Sydney.

'I'm sorry,' said Jack. 'I know now that none of this is anything to do with you. I'm sorry I was so rough.'

'I'm a professional,' said Sydney. 'But I wonder, are we supposed to do a second take downstairs? I'm no longer certain what my motivation is. Was I supposed to fight you off? It wasn't in my backstory. Do you have a rewrite?'

Sydney said no more. The lift descended.

Sydney *might* have said more. But he couldn't, for Jack had head-knocked him unconscious. Which wasn't really very sporting, as he *was* a Hollywood legend.

The lift descended.

At length it reached the first floor. Jack thumped at the ground-floor button, but the lift would go no further. It could go no further. There were lift doors on the ground floor, but they were only doors – there was nothing behind them.

'What about poor Sydney?' asked Marilyn as the lift doors opened on the first floor.

'I'm sorry,' said Jack. Who was sick of saying sorry, but felt that upon this occasion he really should say it. 'I lost my temper. He's a nice fellow. You have a copy of the script, I assume?'

'Don't hit me,' said Marilyn. 'I do.'

'Then we'll go and look at yours.'

'Whatever you say, all right?'

And Marilyn left the lift and Jack and Dorothy followed her and Jack gazed once more at Marilyn's legs and thought certain thoughts. And Dorothy, as if, once more, she was able to access Jack's thoughts, dealt Jack a hearty slap to the face.

The lecture theatre was deserted.

But for a fellow in a vest and bare feet who lay all prone upon the floor. Jack stepped over this fellow.

'It had to be done,' said Dorothy.

And Jack just shrugged, as he was beyond caring anyway.

They moved through the lecture theatre, then out onto the mezzanine floor, then down the great escalator into the greater entrance hall with its golden statues and reception desk.

No one sat behind this. Indeed, but for Jack and Dorothy and Marilyn, this great golden area was deserted.

'Gone for lunch?' Jack suggested.

'Let's just get this script,' said Dorothy.

And so they crossed the great golden entrance hallway, passed through the great golden doorway and into the great golden sunlight of Los Angeles.

And here they paused, all well lit in goldenness.

Before the Golden Chicken Towers were many police cars. Many black and white police cars. Which had conveyed many of Los Angeles' finest to . . .

The scene of the crime.

And a voice, coming through what is known as an electric bullhorn, called unto Jack.

And its call went thus ways. And so. And suchlike also.

'Drop your weapons and get down on the ground. You are surrounded,' it went.

Thus ways.

And so.

And suchlike.

Also.

19

LA Police Chief Samuel J. Maggott was having a rough one.

Such is the way with police chiefs, that they are generally having a rough one. Things conspire against them all the time. Things pile up. Often it is that they have just given up smoking, and drinking, and are going through a messy divorce. And that the 'powers that be' are coming down hard upon them, demanding results on cases that seem beyond all human comprehension.

Then there's the matter of their underlings. That feisty new police-woman who doesn't play by the rules but always gets results. And that troubled young detective who won't give up smoking or drinking and has never been married and gets all the girls and doesn't play by the rules, but also always gets the job done.

And then there's that coffee machine that never works properly and it's a really hot summer and the air conditioning's broken down and . . .

So on and so forth and suchlike.

And now there's *this* fellow.

LA Police Chief Samuel J. Maggott sat down heavily in his office chair, behind his office desk. The office that he sat down in was a proper police chief's office. There were little American flags sprouting from his inkwell. There were medals in small glass cases on the walls. Near the picture of the President. And the ones of Sam's family, which included the wife who was presently divorcing him. And there were other American flags here and there, because there always are. And there were framed citations won in the cause of police duty (above and beyond the call of it, generally). And there was a coffee machine and an air-conditioning unit, the latter making strange noises.

And there was *this* fellow.

This fellow sat in the visitors' chair, across the desk from Sam's. This fellow sat uneasily, uncomfortably. His hands were in his lap. His wrists were handcuffed together.

After he'd done with the heavy sitting down, Sam did some puffings. He'd been putting on weight recently. It was all the stress that he'd been under, which had caused him to put more food beneath his belt, which put him under even more pressure to lose some weight.

Sam sighed and inwardly cursed his lot. The things he had to put up with. And he hadn't even touched upon the racial politics, because Sam was, of course, a black man.

As are all American police chiefs.

Apparently.

Sam puffed and Sam sighed and Sam mopped sweat from his brow. He mopped it with an oversized red gingham handkerchief. It had belonged to his mother, who had died last week, and had only yesterday been put under.

And still there was *this* fellow.

This fellow sat, with his hands in his lap, naked in the visitors' chair.

Sam shook his head, which was thinning on top, and said a single word. 'Coffee?'

The naked fellow looked up at Sam. 'Did you say "coffee"?' he asked.

'I'm asking you, do you want coffee?'

'I'd rather have a pair of underpants.'

'Don't be foolish, boy,' said Sam. 'You cannot drink underpants. Unless, of course . . .' And Sam's mind returned to something he'd done recently at a club on the East Side, which he really shouldn't have been at, and wouldn't have been at if he hadn't been so depressed about his dog getting stolen and everything.

'Could I have my clothes back, please?' asked the naked fellow. He was a young naked fellow, rangy and tanned, spare of frame and wiry of limb.

'Are you cold?' asked Sam.

'No,' said the fellow, 'but it's pretty humiliating sitting here naked.'

'You've got nothing that I ain't seen before, fella,' said Sam, almost instantly regretting that he had. What *was* it his therapist kept telling him?

'Well, if men's genitalia are so commonplace to you,' said the fellow, 'I can't imagine what pleasure you will have viewing mine.'

'Pleasure don't come into this,' said Sam.

'I do so agree,' said the fellow.

'But anyway, your clothes are with forensics. We'll soon see what they have to tell us.'

The fellow, whose name was Jack, thought suddenly of Wallah. Suddenly and sadly too thought he.

'My clothes will have nothing to say to you,' said Jack.

'On the contrary.' Sam rose heavily from his chair to fetch coffee for himself. 'They've told us much already.'

'They have?' Jack asked as he watched the large black police chief worry at the coffee machine.

'Oh yes.' And Sam kicked the coffee machine. 'A great deal.' And Sam shook the coffee machine. 'A very great deal, in fact.' And Sam stooped heavily and peered into the little hatchway where one (such as he) who had pressed all the correct buttons above might reasonably expect to see a plastic cup full of coffee.

No such cup was to be found.

Sam peered deeper into the little hatch. 'A great deal of Aaaaagh!'

'A great deal of *what*?' asked Jack.

But Sam didn't hear him. Sam was wildly mopping boiling water from his face with his oversized red gingham handkerchief.

'Goddamn useless machine!' And Sam moved swiftly for a heavy man and dealt the machine many heavy blows.

The glass partition door opened and the attractive face of a feisty young policewoman smiled through the opening. 'Chief,' said she, 'I've just cracked the case that's had you baffled for months. I—'

'Get *out*!' shouted Sam, returning without coffee to his desk.

'Stressful job, is it?' Jack asked. 'The American Dream not working out?'

Sam, now once more in his chair, leaned forward over his desk.

Two little flags fell onto the floor along with an overfull ashtray. 'Now just listen here, fella,' said Sam, 'don't go giving me no lip. I don't like a wise guy, understand me?'

'Yes,' said Jack. 'About my clothes.'

'Ah yes, your clothes.' And Sam leaned back and Sam took up a folder. And having opened same, examined the contents therein. 'Fingerprints not on file,' said Sam. 'No ID. No record, it seems, that you even exist.'

'I'm from England,' said Jack, 'and I'm a friend of the Queen.'

'Is that so?' Sam nodded. 'And your name is Jack, no surname. Just Jack.'

'Just Jack,' said Jack.

'As in Jack the Ripper?' asked Sam. 'English psycho, said to be in league with the royal household?'

'I think we're going off on a bit of a tangent,' said Jack, uncomfortably shifting from one bottom cheek to the other. 'Could I please have my clothes back, please?'

'No,' said Sam. 'Those clothes of yours could well be my passport out of here.'

'I'm certain that if I listen long enough,' said Jack, 'I will be able to learn whatever language it is that you are speaking. But I do not have time. I must be off at once.'

'You're going nowhere, fella. Nowhere at all.'

'But I've done nothing. I'm innocent.'

'Innocent?' Sam laughed and loudly, too. And then he coughed, because laughing too much always brought on a touch of the malaria he'd contracted whilst fighting U-boats in the jungles of South-East Asia. 'Cough, cough, cough,' went Sam.

'If you'll unlock these cuffs,' said Jack, 'I'll gladly pat your back.'

'I'm fine.' Sam reached into a desk drawer, drew from it the bottle of bourbon that he'd promised his specialist he'd poured away down the sink, uncorked it and poured away much of its contents down his throat. 'I'm fine. Goddamnit.'

'Can I go, *please*?' Jack asked.

'No, fella, you cannot. You and your girlfriend held a crowd of managers and chefs at gunpoint, beat a chef called Bruce to within an inch of his life—'

'We never did,' said Jack.

'Took two hostages. Famous movie stars – Sydney Greenstreet and Marilyn Monroe.'

'Well . . .' said Jack.

'Beat poor Sydney nearly to dea—'

'Hold on.'

'Sexually harassed Marilyn—'

'I did *what*?'

'And we caught you with your chopper in your hand.'

'Cleaver, please,' said Jack. 'Let's not sink to that level.'

'Resisting arrest, et cetera, et cetera.' Sam closed the file. 'You're looking at twenty to life, if not the chair.'

'The chair?' said Jack, looking down at the chair. '*This* chair?'

'The electric chair, Old Sparky.' Sam mimed electricity buzzing through his own head and then death. And well he mimed it, too, considering that he'd no formal training in mime. Although there had been *that* incident that the department had hushed up, regarding that female mime artist, the raspberry jelly and the bicycle pump. *That* could always blow up in his face if he sought further advancement.

'I don't like the sound of that,' said Jack.

'You won't like the feel, either, or the smell as your brains boil in your head.'

'Listen,' said Jack, 'you don't understand. I've been trying to explain.'

'Explain to me about the clothes,' said Sam.

'Well,' said Jack, 'it's pretty basic stuff, really. The shirt is worn much in the way that you wear yours, although mine doesn't have those large sweat stains under the arms. The trousers, well, that's pretty basic also – you put your left leg in the left-leg hole and—'

Sam brought his fists down hard on his desk. Inkwells rattled, things fell to the floor. Jack was showered with paperclips. Jack ceased talking. And the glass partition door opened once again.

A young male detective stuck his head through the opening; he had a cigarette in his mouth. 'Any trouble, Chief?' he asked. 'Only I've just solved that other case that has had you baffled for months. I—'

'Get out!' bawled Sam. The young detective removed himself, slamming the door behind him.

'Now listen, fella, and listen good,' Sam said unto Jack. 'The clothes, your clothes, the ones with forensics – I have a preliminary report here. Let's deal with the labels first.'

'The labels?' And Jack shook his head.

'The Toy City Suit Company, Fifteen Dumpty Plaza. Explain that if you will.'

'It's the shop where the trenchcoat came from. It's not my trenchcoat.'

'So you stole it.'

'No, it belongs to someone who was murdered.'

'You took it from their corpse. Do you wish to make a confession?'

'I'd like to see a solicitor,' said Jack. 'I believe I am entitled to one.'

'Ah, yes,' said Sam. 'As I recall, your girlfriend shouted that at you when we had to have her carried down to the cells after she injured several of my officers.'

'I warned you not to try to cuff her,' said Jack. 'She knows Dimac.'

'That I know,' said Sam, sipping further bourbon. 'We located the official licence for her hands and feet. Registered here! But no matter. There is *no* Toy City Suit Company. No Dumpty Plaza.'

'It's in England,' said Jack.

'Which part?' asked Sam.

'The whole shop,' said Jack.

Sam didn't smile. But then who would?

'Which part of England is the shop in?'

Jack thought hard. 'The south part?' he suggested.

'The south part,' said Sam. And he said it thoughtfully.

'Next door to the Queen's palace,' said Jack.

'Right,' said Sam, and he plucked at his shirt collar. And, leaning back, he thumped at the air conditioner. Further strange noises issued from this and then it fell silent. Sam took to mopping his brow once more. 'There is no Dumpty Plaza in England,' said Sam.

'There is no Dumpty Plaza anywhere. And as for the fabric of this trenchcoat, there appears to be no such fabric.'

'Could I see a solicitor *now*?' Jack asked.

'Soon,' said Sam. 'When you have answered my questions to *my* satisfaction.'

'I don't think that's how it's supposed to work,' said Jack.

'Tell me again about this bear,' said Sam. 'This . . .' and he consulted the notes he had taken down (before his Biro ran out), 'this Eddie.'

'A valuable antique toy bear,' said Jack, as this was his present stratagem. 'Stolen from my client by an employee of the Golden Chicken Corporation. I tracked the bear to the headquarters of this corporation. I was interviewing two suspects.'

Sam did further big deep sighings. 'Ah, yes,' he said. 'Because you are a private eye, sent here from England to recover—'

'The Queen's teddy bear,' said Jack. 'Like I told you.'

'And the Golden Chicken Corporation stole the Queen's teddy bear?'

Jack made a certain face. It wasn't perhaps the *best* stratagem that he'd ever come up with, but he *was* committed to it now. 'Which is why I am here, undercover,' said Jack. 'With no identification.'

Sam did further shakings of the head. And further noddings, too. 'I wish,' said he, 'I just wish that for *one* day, *one* single day, everything would just be easy.'

'Listen,' said Jack, 'you're not going to believe me no matter what I tell you. If I were to tell you everything and the whole truth and nothing but the truth, you wouldn't believe me. You wouldn't believe a word.'

'But you *won't* tell me the truth.' Sam leaned back in his chair and all but fell from it. 'Because no one tells the truth. No one. Take my wife, for instance . . .' Sam swivelled round in his chair, rose and gazed through the window. Outside, LA shimmered in the midday sunlight, high-finned autos cruised along the broad expanse of thoroughfare, palms waved drowsily, birds circled high in the clear blue sky.

'My wife,' said Sam. 'I gave that woman everything. Treated her like the Queen of England, I did, me. She wanted dance classes, I got her dance classes. She wanted voice tuition, I got her voice tuition. She wanted singing lessons, I got her singing lessons. I paid for that woman to have plastic surgery, breast implants, nail extensions. And what does she do? Becomes a Goddamn movie star is what she does. Signs that contract and dumps yours truly. Is that fair? Is that just? Is that right? I ask you, fella, is that right?'

Sam turned to gauge Jack's opinion on the fairness and rightness of all this.

But Jack was nowhere to be seen.

The handcuffs he had been wearing lay on Sam Maggott's desk, their locks picked with a paperclip.

Now, it's never easy to escape from a police station. Especially during the hours of daylight. And especially when naked.

And Sam set off the alarm, which had police all running about. And Sam opened his office door and shouted at the feisty young policewoman and the troubled young detective who was smoking a fag and chatting her up. And all the other policemen and -women in the big outer office. And he berated them and ordered them to reapprehend the naked escapee *at once*, or heads would roll and future prospects be endangered. And police folk hurried thither and thus, but Jack was not to be found.

Jack eased his naked self along the air-conditioning duct. The one he'd climbed into from the police chief's desk, through its little hatch, which he had thoughtfully closed behind him. He was uncertain exactly which way he should be easing his naked self, but as far away from the office as possible seemed the right way to go.

'I don't bear the man a grudge,' said Jack to himself as he did further uncomfortable easings along. 'And I do think his wife treated him unfairly. But even though I am a youth, in the early bloom of my years, I am drawn to the conclusion that life is *not* fair and the sooner one realises this and acts accordingly, the less one will find oneself all stressed out in later years.

'I think that I will remain single and use women purely for . . . OUCH!' and Jack snagged a certain dangling part upon a bolted nut.

And as chance, or coincidence, or fate, or something more, or less, would have it, at that *very* moment, and many miles south of Jack, and many floors beneath the desert sand, Eddie Bear was having trouble with a nut.

'Nuts?' said Eddie, taking up a nut between his paws and peering at it distastefully. 'Nuts? Nuts? That is what you're offering me to eat?'

The other Jack grinned into Eddie's cage. 'That's what bears eat in the wild, isn't it? Nuts and berries.'

'I wouldn't know,' said Eddie. 'I never associate with such unsophisticated company. I'd like a fillet steak, medium rare, sautéed potatoes—'

The other Jack kicked at Eddie's cage. 'Eat up your nuts,' he said, 'like a good little bear. You're going to need all your strength.'

Eddie's stomach grumbled. And Eddie's stomach ached. Eddie didn't feel at all like himself. He wasn't feeling altogether the full shilling, was Eddie Bear. 'What do you want from me?' he asked. 'Why have you brought me here?'

'You have to pay for your crimes,' said the other Jack.

'I'm no criminal,' said Eddie.

'Oh yes you are. You and your companion shot down one of our spaceships. Murdered the crew—'

'Self-defence,' said Eddie. 'Your accusations won't hold up in court.'

'Would you care to rephrase that?'

'No court involved, then?' said Eddie.

'No court,' said the other Jack. 'No court and no hope for you.'

'What are you?' asked Eddie. 'What are you, really?'

'I'm Jack,' said the other Jack. 'I'm the Jack this side of The Second Big O. I'm the Jack in this world.'

'An identical Jack?' said Eddie. 'I don't think so.'

'Oh, we're all here, human counterparts, reflections of your world – or rather your world is a reflection of ours. We're all here, even you.'

'The murdering me,' said Eddie, peeping through the bars of his cage. 'The me who murdered the monkeys and the band and the orchestra?'

'And all the rest, soon. The contents of your world will be sucked into ours. For our use.'

'But for why?' asked Eddie Bear. 'To be produced as giveaways for promoting the sale of fried chicken? That's as mad as.'

'You eat up your nuts,' said the other Jack. 'I'll be back in a little while. Don't make me have to ram them down your throat.'

And with that the other Jack turned to take his leave.

'Oh, Jack,' said Eddie.

The other Jack turned.

'When my Jack gets here, as he will, he'll really kick your ass.'

And in his air-conditioning duct, Jack snagged his ass on a pointy something. And whispered, 'Ouch!' once again.

Jack could hear lots of sounds beneath him. The sounds of the alarm and the sounds of shouting and of running feet. And if his hearing had been a tad more acute he would have been able to discern the sound of gun cabinets being opened and pump-action shotguns being taken from these cabinets and loaded up with high-velocity cartridges. But there is only so much that you can hear from inside an air-conditioning duct.

Jack added to the easings along he had formerly done with more of the same, but more carefully. Where *exactly* was he now?

Light shone up through a grille ahead. Jack hastened with care towards it.

'Hm,' went Jack, peering down. 'Corridor, and by the look of it, deserted. Now the question is, how might I open this grille from the inside and lower myself carefully to the floor beneath?'

Good question.

Jack put his ear to the grille. Alarm, certainly . . . Ah, no, alarm switched off. Running feet? Shouting? Not in *this* corridor. Jack took a deep breath, then took to beating the grille. And then beating some more. Then rattling everything around. Then beating some more.

And then screaming, as quietly as he could, as the length of ducting containing himself detached itself from its fellow members and fell heavily the distance between the ceiling to which it had been attached and the floor beneath.

Which was uncarpeted.

Exactly how long Jack was unconscious, he had no way of telling. The police had confiscated Jack's watch. And it no longer worked anyway. Jack awoke in some confusion, crawled from his fallen length of aluminium ducting, climbed to his feet and rubbed at the bruised parts, which comprised the majority of his body. Wondered anew *exactly* where he was.

A sign on the wall spelled out the words:

POLICE CELLS: AUTHORISED ACCESS ONLY.

'I think *that's* fair,' said Jack. 'I deserve a little luck.'

And Jack made his way onwards upon naked feet.

And presently reached the cells.

Now, as we all know, and we *do*, police cells contain all kinds of individuals. And, curiously enough, all of them innocent.

It is a very odd one, that – that *all* police cells contain innocent, well, 'victims', for there is no other word. As do prisons. Prisons are full of folk who have never confessed to any crimes. In fact, *all* of them pleaded innocent at their trials. And even though the evidence piled against them might have appeared, on the face of it, compelling and condemning, nevertheless the 'victims' of 'circumstance' and 'injustice' protested their innocence and were unjustly convicted.

Odd that, isn't it?

Jack peered through another little grille, this one in the door of the first cell.

Here he espied, a-sitting upon a basic bunk, an overlarge fellow, naked to the waist, his chest and torso intricately decorated via the medium of tattoo.

'Wrong cell,' said Jack. Although perhaps too loudly. As his words caused the overlarge fellow to look up, observe Jack's peering face and rise from his basic bunk.

Cell two presented Jack with a small well-dressed gentleman who rocked to and fro on his basic bunk, muttering the words, 'God told me to do it,' over and over again.

'Definitely wrong,' said Jack.

And this fellow looked up also.

In the third cell Jack observed a number of Puerto Ricans. They sported bandannas and gang-affiliated patches. Jack recognised them to be the kitchen workforce he had employed the previous day.

'Hi, fellows,' called Jack.

The fellows looked up towards Jack.

And now Jack's attention was drawn back to the first and second cells. Their occupants were beating at the doors, crying out for Jack to return, shouting things about being the daddy and knowing a bitch when they saw one.

'Shush!' Jack shushed them.

But the cell-three Puerto Ricans now joined in the crying aloud.

'Damn,' went Jack. And Jack pressed on.

And finally found Dorothy.

'Dorothy,' called Jack. And the beautiful girl looked up from her basic bunk.

'Jack,' she said, and she hastened to the door to observe him through the grille. 'You are naked,' she continued.

'Well, yes,' said Jack. 'But—'

'Nothing,' said Dorothy. 'This is California. Please would you open my cell?'

'I certainly will.' And Jack spat out the *other* paperclip. The one he had kept in his mouth to perform this very function. Because he *did* think ahead, did Jack. Because he *was* a private detective.

And with this paperclip and to the growing cacophony of shouting victims of circumstance, Jack picked the lock on Dorothy's cell door and freed her from incarceration.

Good old Jack.

'Here,' said Dorothy, lifting her skirt and dropping her panties. 'Put these on, it will help,'

'Help?' Jack looked hard at the panties. Now in the palm of his hand.

'Unless you really want to run completely naked through the streets of LA.'

'But they're your . . .' Jack shook his head and put on the panties.

'It's an interesting look,' said Dorothy, 'and not one that would normally ring my bell, as it were, however—'

'Time to run,' said Jack.

And Jack was right in this. Because a door at the far end of the corridor, back beyond his fallen length of ducting, was now opening and heavily armed policemen and -women were making their urgent entrance.

'That way, I think,' said Dorothy, pointing towards a fire exit. 'That way at the hurry-up.'

And that was the way Jack took.

20

What they say about doors is well known.

As one door closes, another one opens, and all that kind of caper.

The door that Jack had opened he now closed behind himself and Dorothy and he dragged a dustbin in front of it and caught a little breath. And then he viewed his surroundings and said, 'This does not look at all hopeful.'

Dorothy shook her flame-haired head. 'At least the sun is shining,' she said, with rather more cheerfulness than their present situation merited. 'You'll get a bit more of a tan – it will suit you.'

'A bit more of a tan?' Jack put his back to the dustbin. which was now being rattled about by policemen and -women belabouring the door. 'We're in the police car park. This is not a good place to be.'

Dorothy glanced all around and about. There were many police cars, all those wonderful black and white jobbies with the big lights that flash on the top. All were parked and all were empty.

All but for the one a-driving in.

Two officers sat in this one, big officers both, one at the wheel and one in the passenger seat. They were just coming off shift, were these two officers. Officer Billy-Bob was at the wheel and beside him sat his brother officer, Officer Joe-Bob, brother of the other Joe-Bob, the one Jack had thrown out of the diner's kitchen the day before. (Small world.) They had had an unsuccessful day together in the big city fighting crime and were looking forward to clocking off and taking themselves away to a Golden Chicken Diner for some burgers.

These two officers peered through their windscreen at the young chap in the ladies' panties who was fighting with a trashcan and the flame-haired young woman, who appeared now to be waving frantically in their direction.

Officer Billy-Bob drew up the black-and-white, wound down the window and offered a gap-toothed grin to the flame-haired young woman. 'Any trouble, ma'am?' he enquired in a broad Arkansas accent.

'This maniac attacked me,' screamed Dorothy. 'He's taken my panties.'

'Taken your panties, ma'am?' Officer Billy-Bob took off his cap and gave his head a scratch. 'That's a four-sixteen.'

Officer Joe-Bob took off *his* hat. 'That's a four-twenty-three,' he said.

Jack continued his fight with the dustbin. 'Run,' he told Dorothy.

'Stay,' said Dorothy to Jack. 'I'll take care of this.'

'Take care of it? I'm not a maniac. What are you doing?'

Officer Billy-Bob climbed from the car. Officer Joe-Bob did likewise.

'Four-sixteen,' said Officer Billy-Bob. 'Cross-dressing in a car park.'

'A four-sixteen ain't that,' said Officer Joe-Bob. 'A four-sixteen is a Chinaman in a liquor store stealing liquorice with intent.'

'Intent to do what?' asked Officer Billy-Bob.

'Intent s'nuff,' said Officer Joe-Bob.

'Intense snuff? What you talkin' about?'

'I said, intent is enough. Like a four-thirty-eight, being tall with intent.'

'Being tall? What kind of gibberish you talkin', boy?'

'Excuse me, Officers,' said Dorothy, 'but I'd really appreciate it if you'd arrest this maniac.'

'All in good time, ma'am,' said Officer Billy-Bob. 'Law takes due process. If we run him in on a four-fifteen and it turns out to be a three-six-nine—'

'A three-six-nine is a goose drinking wine in a Presbyterian chapel,' said Officer Joe-Bob. 'You're thinking of a six-sixty-six.'

'Goddamnit, Joe-Bob,' said Officer Billy-Bob, 'six-sixty-six is the number of the Goddamn Beast of Revelation.'

'True enough, but you're thinking of it, you're always thinking of it.'

'True enough. But then I'm also always thinking of a thirty-six-twenty-two-thirty-six.'

'That's Marilyn Monroe.'

And both officers sighed.

And then Dorothy hit both officers. In rapid succession. Although there was some degree of that slow-motion spinning around in mid-air. As there always should be on such occasions.

Officer Billy-Bob hit the Tarmac.

Officer Joe-Bob joined him.

'To the car,' cried Dorothy.

And Jack ran to the car.

Dorothy jumped into the driving seat. Jack fell in beside her.

'I should drive,' said Jack. 'Climb into the back.'

'*I* will drive,' said Dorothy. And down went her foot. And Jack went into the back. Rather hard.

'Ow,' and, 'Ouch,' went Jack, in the back. And, 'Arrgh!' as the car went over a speed bump, which is sometimes known as a sleeping policeman. And, 'Oh!' went he as his head struck the roof. Then, 'Wah!' as Dorothy took a right and Jack fell onto the floor.

And now all manner of officers burst into the car park. The feisty female one with the unorthodox approach to case-solving. And the troubled young detective, with whom at times the very letter of the law was something of a grey area. A Chinese officer called Wong, who was in LA on a special attachment from Hong Kong and who spoke with a cod-Chinese accent but was great at martial arts. And there was a fat officer who got puffed easily if the chase was on foot. A gay officer, whose day was yet to dawn. And an angry, sweating black police chief by the name of Samuel J. Maggott.

'After them!' bawled Sam. 'Taking and driving away a squad car. Add that to the charge sheet.'

'And two officers down,' said the feisty young woman.

'And add that, too. Someone get me a car.'

'Come in mine, Chief,' said the troubled young detective. And as various officers leapt into various black-and-whites, the troubled young detective leapt into an open-topped red Ford Mustang (which he called Sally). It was an unorthodox kind of vehicle for police work, but the troubled young detective did have a reputation for getting the job done in it.

'No Goddamn way!' bawled Samuel J. Maggott.

'Then come in mine,' cried the feisty young female officer, leaping into an open-topped AC Cobra. Lime green, with a number twenty-three on the side.[*]

Samuel J. Maggott weighed up the pros and cons. The feisty young female officer did have a very short skirt. And he *was* going through a very messy divorce. 'I'll take my own Goddamn car,' declared Sam.

And he would have, too, had he not been run down by a very short-sighted officer with thick pebblelensed glasses, who was rather quick off the mark but not at all good at backing up.

'Did I just run over a sleeping policeman?' he asked.

And out into the streets of LA they went.

Dorothy with her foot down hard and Jack bouncing around in the back. The troubled young man in his Ford Mustang, Sally. The feisty young woman in the Cobra. And black-and-white after black-and-white and finally Sam Maggott, who was at last in a squad car.

Now it could be argued that the streets of San Francisco are far better than the streets of LA when it comes to a car chase. They have all those hills and the tramcars that get in the way. And the sea views are nice, too. And in the 1960s, Owlsley *would* produce the finest LSD that any generation had ever experienced, which although having nothing particularly to do with car chases (although you can have them on acid without actually leaving your armchair) ought to be taken into consideration when it comes to the matter of deciding whether to shoot the car chase for your movie in LA or San Francisco.

Although it could well be argued, in fact it is difficult to argue against, that the best car chase ever filmed was filmed in Paris.[†]

But this *was* Los Angeles and this was where *this* car chase was occurring. Now!

---

[*] Number twenty-three being *that* number which always turns up in American movies. On hotel room doors, on the sides of freight train carriages. Here, there, everywhere. Why? Well . . .

[†] *Ronin*. And what a great movie *that* is!

And at this point. Before things get very hairy. It might also be worth mentioning that anyone who has never visited LA knows what the headquarters of the Los Angeles Police Department really looks like. It *doesn't* look like that big building with the great columns and everything that you see in virtually every crime movie that's set in LA. That building is, believe it or not, the General Post Office.

The genuine headquarters of the Los Angeles Police Department is housed in an ivory palace that looks like the Taj Mahal, but with feathered wings and pink bubbles and . . . *

Dorothy swung a hard right.

'Speak to me, people, speak to me now,' demanded Sam from his squad car, which was being driven along at some speed by another officer. 'Speak to me, what's happening?'

'Escaped prisoners moving west on Wilshire Boulevard,' came a voice to Sam, the voice of the feisty young female officer. 'Am in pursuit. Hey, get back there.'

'Leave this to me,' came the voice of the troubled young detective.

Sam heard the sounds of a Mustang called Sally striking an AC Cobra.

Dorothy put her foot down and glanced into the rear-view mirror. 'They seem to be trying to drive each other off the road,' she told Jack, who had struggled up beside her. 'This is Koreatown, by the way.'

'Very nice,' said Jack. 'Look out!'

A police car travelling south on South Western Avenue crossed their path. Dorothy struck its rear end and sent it spinning around. The feisty young female officer crashed into this car, which put her out of the chase rather too quickly for her liking. The troubled young detective, however, kept on coming and behind him Officer Wong, the fat officer, the gay officer whose day was yet to dawn, but sadly not the short-sighted officer, who was now travelling south on South Broadway and heading for the beach.

Samuel Maggott was close upon the rear of the gay officer, though.

---

* Well, it would in the 1960s on Owlsley acid.

Which was something that he would have to discuss with his therapist at a later date.

Dorothy took another turn to the right, north onto Beverly Boulevard.

And what a nice neighbourhood that is.

Although.

A chap in a uniform jumped out in front of the speeding automobile, hand raised, face set in an expression of determination. Dorothy tried to swerve around him, but he jumped once more into her path. Dorothy slewed to a stop. The chap in the uniform with the determined expression on his face came around to the side of the car.

'Sorry, ma'am,' he said, 'but this is Beverly Hills. We don't allow car chases here, nor tourist buses. You'll have to go back the way you just came.'

Dorothy glanced once more into the rear-view mirror. The troubled young detective and all the other squad cars had halted at the Wilshire/Beverly intersection. They knew the rules. Some things were just *not* done.

'Sorry,' said Dorothy, backing up the car.

'What?' went Jack. Astounded.

'It's an American thing,' Dorothy explained.

'Speak to me, people. Oh, Goddamn!' Sam Maggott's car slammed into the rear end of the gay officer's.

And then Sam said, 'Goddamn,' once again as Dorothy shot past him, returning the way she had come. 'Will somebody shoot that woman?' cried Sam, and he drew out his gun and did it himself.

'Duck to the right,' cried Dorothy.

And Jack ducked to the right.

Bullets sang in through one side window and exited through the other.

'Duck to the right?' said Jack to himself. 'That's what Wallah said to me this morning. "Don't forget to duck to the right."' And Jack felt sad once more. And somewhat scared, of course.

Police cars were swinging around in further pursuit. Officers in passenger seats, who had mostly non-speaking parts and so needed no particular characterisation, were sliding cartridges into pump-action shotguns and looking forward to firing these.

'This is Chinatown,' said Dorothy to Jack as she took a left to head north on the 110.

Officer Wong overtook Sam Maggot's car. 'This job for me,' he said in his cod-Chinese accent. 'This call for much dangerous stunt work performed by me to much applause.' And he climbed out of the window of his speeding car and up onto its roof.

'What is that damn Chinee up to?' Sam asked his driver.

His driver just shrugged, for his was a non-speaking role.

'Whoa! Get down, Jack,' shouted Dorothy as Officer Wong's car drew level and Officer Wong leapt from the roof of his car and banged down onto theirs.

'That was impressive,' said Jack, 'although somewhat above and beyond the call of duty, I would have thought.'

'They'll give him a medal,' said Dorothy, slamming on the brakes.

Officer Wong flew forward, rolled over the bonnet and fell into the road. Dorothy drove carefully around him. 'And a neck brace, too,' she said.

Other police cars were now joining the chase. They do have a lot of police cars in LA. Mostly because during every police chase, they lose so many as they smash into one another and roll over and over into storefronts.

Dorothy swerved. Two police cars smashed into one another. One of them rolled over and over into a storefront.

'South Pasadena,' said Dorothy. 'Look – there's Eddie Park.'[*]

Eddie Park made Jack feel even sadder.

The big fat officer opened fire.

'Duck,' shouted Dorothy as shotgun shells blew out the rear window, causing Jack much distress and considerable ducking.

There was of course much to be enjoyed in all the excitement, in the screaming of tyres upon asphalt and pedestrians leaping out of the way and the motor cars of innocent motorists slamming into one another. And why shouldn't there be, eh? That's what car chases are

---

[*] And there is!

all about. And given their longevity, they probably *do* have the edge on explosions. Even really big ones.

'Ouch!' went Dorothy as the Mustang called Sally, being driven by the troubled young detective, shunted *her* rear end.

'Oi!' shouted Jack. 'That's *my* girlfriend's rear end you're shunting.'

And then Jack sort of vanished into the back of the car. Another impact crumpled up some of the boot, causing the rear seat to lift and Jack to roll into the boot.

Dorothy slammed on the brakes once more and the troubled young detective's Mustang Sally struck her rear end once more, then travelled onwards, travelled upwards, and . . .

In slow motion (praise the Lord).

Sailed forward.

And, as they had now reached a place known as the Santa Fe Dam Recreational Area, it sailed over the dam and down and down and down.

'Nasty,' said Dorothy. 'But I'm sure he leapt from the car in time.'

They were now, and praise the Lord for this also, travelling along Route 66. They were, they *really* were. Not that they were running from St Louis down to Missouri, taking in Oklahoma City, which everybody knows is oh so pretty. They were in fact passing Horse Thief Canyon Park, La Verne, Cable Airport and now Rancho Cucamonga, where a young Don Van Vliet, who would later change his name to Captain Beefheart and become a legend in his lifetime, would as a teenager try to sell a vacuum cleaner to Aldous Huxley.[*]

It's a really long straight road there, above San Bernardino. You can get up an unhealthy speed if you really put your foot down. Which was what the gay officer, whose day was yet to dawn, was doing. His police car overtook Sam's, much to Sam's disgust, because *his* police car had just overtaken *his*. The gay officer's police car now drew level with Dorothy's. The gay officer addressed Dorothy through his public-address system, which is located somewhere on

---

[*] Absolutely true.

police cars, although no one has ever been able to ascertain exactly where.

'Give yourselves up,' came his amplified voice through the special speaker in the radiator grille.[*] 'There's no need for all this kerfuffle. You don't really want to behave in this fashion. It's not your fault – you are a product of your upbringing, you are programmed to behave in this way. I have this self-help manual I could lend you—'

Dorothy swerved the car and drove the gay officer off the road. His car, once again in glorious slow motion, sailed from Route 66 and down onto the famous California Speedway, where numerous speeding motorbikes, with very nice leather-clad riders, the gay officer noted, before all things went black for him, came all a-mashing into his rear parts and everywhere else.

'Right,' said Sam. 'I'm angry now.' And he leaned out of his window and fired his gun once more.

And there at last it was.

Because we *have* been expecting its arrival for some time now, if only subconsciously. But there it was at last, that great big truck, with its great big dangerous cargo on the back. It was being driven towards them at considerable speed by a trucker called Joe-Bob, who was, coincidentally—

And who was also chatting on the CB to a fellow trucker called Joe-Bob, who was, coincidentally—

'Well, that's a big ten-four,' said driver Joe-Bob. 'Heading for the City of Angels on Route Sixty-Six. Pulling turkey with a shorthaired rabbit. Doing a manky dance rattle on my blue suede shoes.'[†]

'Come on?' said the driver called Joe-Bob at the message-receiving end.

'I said . . . Oh, Goddamn!'

And, 'Goddamn!' also went Police Chief Sam Maggott as Dorothy swerved around the on-rushing truck and Sam Maggott's car struck it dead on.

[*] Ah, that's where.
[†] (For there is much jargon involved in being a trucker in the USA and chatting on the old CB.)

Boom.

In slow motion.

Of course.

Some time later, Dorothy drew the raddled, bullet-pocked black-and-white to the side of the road, climbed from it and opened the boot.

Jack peered out. 'Are we still alive?' he asked.

'We're fine,' said Dorothy. 'We've shaken them off.'

Jack climbed out in a wibbly-wobbly way. 'How did you learn to drive like *that*?' he asked.

'My daddy won the Indianapolis Five Hundred,' said Dorothy. 'Oh, look, there's a police uniform in the trunk.'

'I know,' said Jack, dusting down his all-but-naked self. 'I've been fighting with it for several miles. It smells really bad.'

'Well, you'd best put it on. Then you can drive for a bit. We don't want to arouse suspicion.'

Jack's jaw dropped. 'Well, no,' said he. 'We wouldn't want to do *that*.'

And Dorothy smiled upon Jack and said, 'Well, hurry up now, come on.'

Jack dressed himself in the uniform, and but for its acrid qualities it did have to be said that he cut a rather dashing and romantic figure. He settled down into what was left of the driving seat.

Dorothy sat beside him. 'Mmm,' she said to Jack.

'Mmm?' Jack asked. 'What means "Mmm"?'

'As in, "Mmm, you look cute."'

'Cute?' said Jack. 'A teddy bear looks cute.'

'Not your one,' said Dorothy.

And Jack once more thought of Eddie. Not that Eddie had slipped Jack's mind, but what with all the excitement and everything . . .

Eddie Bear lacked for excitement. In his cage, many floors beneath the Nevada desert in Area Fifty-Two, Eddie Bear was having a bit of a snooze. And then things suddenly became exciting for Eddie, or perhaps 'alarming' was better the word.

Eddie awoke as hands were laid upon him. Rough were these hands, although not in texture. Rough as in violent and forceful.

'Ow!' went Eddie. 'That's as rude as. Get off me.'

But Eddie was hauled from his cage by the other Jack and flung to a concrete floor.

'There's no need for that!'

And then the other Jack kicked him.

'Oh!' went Eddie, climbing to his paw pads. 'You are *so* going to get yours when *my* Jack gets here.'

'No one is going to rescue you.' The other Jack took a big step forward. Eddie took several steps back. 'Along the corridor, hurry now.'

Eddie turned and plodded up the corridor. It was one of those all-over-concrete kind of jobbies with bulkhead lights at regular intervals. The number twenty-three[*] was painted on the walls at similarly regular intervals. Eddie assumed, correctly, that this meant that he was on the twenty-third level beneath the ground.

'Where are you taking me?' Eddie asked.

'To meet your maker,' said the other Jack.

'My maker was Mister Anders Anders,' said Eddie, 'the kindly, lovable white-haired old Toymaker.'

The other Jack laughed and his laugh all echoed around. 'He'll soon have his work cut out for him,' he said.

'And what does *that* mean?' Eddie asked.

'In twelve hours from now,' said the other Jack, 'Toy City will be wiped from the map. If there *is* a map with it on. My employer will suck it dry of all life. Lay it to waste. Oh yes.'

'Why?' Eddie asked. 'To what purpose?'

'Why?' asked the other Jack. 'Because we can. And to what purpose? To further our own ends.'

'Now, I'm only guessing here,' said Eddie, turning and peering up at the other Jack, 'but would these "own ends" be of the world-domination persuasion?'

---

[*] There it is again. Weird, isn't it?

'You'll know soon enough.' The other Jack nudged Eddie with his shoe. 'Now get a move on. To the elevator.'

'Where am I?' asked Eddie. 'Tell me where I am.'

'Where are we?' asked Jack. 'Exactly.'

He was making good progress, considering he had never driven a car with an internal combustion engine before. He'd almost got the hang of the gears.

Dorothy flinched as Jack changed from second to fourth.

'Exactly?' she said. 'We are travelling North on Interstate Fifteen. We just passed Las Vegas, which you would probably have liked, lots of lights and things like that. We are heading towards the Nevada desert.'

'And is that good?' Jack asked. 'Only I'm not sure what we should be doing next. The plan was to follow the American Dream. Find the top man. Beat the truth out of him.'

'Perhaps you were over-hasty bringing that meat-cleaver into play. But look on the bright side – at least we got to meet Marilyn Monroe and Sydney Greenstreet. I wish I'd got their autographs. And the names of their agents and—'

'Stop now,' said Jack. 'We'll have to go back to LA. We need the movie script. I'm sure a lot will be explained when we read it.'

'LA is no longer an option,' said Dorothy. 'And I don't know where this leaves my career. I know that it's expected of starlets to do disreputable things that will later come back to haunt them when they become famous, but I might just have stepped too far over the line this time.'

Jack sighed, changed from fourth to first, changed hastily back again and said, 'You do talk some toot at times.'

'Not a bit of it,' said Dorothy. 'The people who get to the top in this world do so because they are risk-takers. They thrive upon risk. Every woman or man at the top has a shady past. They've all done things that they wouldn't want their contemporaries to find out about. They wouldn't want these things to come out once they are famous, but they're not ashamed that they did these things. They did them because they got a thrill out of them. They did them because they are risk-takers.'

'So what are you saying?' Jack asked, as he performed another interesting gear change. 'That it's all right to do bad things?'

'It's never right to do bad things. Bad things hurt good people.'

'I don't mean to be bad,' said Jack.

'You're not bad,' said Dorothy.

'I am,' said Jack. 'I'm selfish. I put myself first.'

'*Everyone* does that.'

'Eddie doesn't,' said Jack. 'Eddie would risk anything to protect me, I know he would.'

'And you would do the same for him.'

'Of course I would,' said Jack. 'But time is running out for Eddie and if I don't find him soon and take him back to Toy City he will die.'

'You'll find him,' said Dorothy. 'Somehow.'

'Somehow,' thought Eddie, 'Jack will find me somehow.'

'Into the elevator,' said the other Jack. 'Go on now.'

Eddie entered the elevator. The other Jack joined him, pressed a button, the doors closed, the elevator rose. Eddie Bear fumed. Silently.

And then the doors took to opening and Eddie Bear gazed out.

And wondered at the view that lay before him.

It looked to be a big round room with shiny metal walls. There were all kinds of strange machines in this room. Strange machines with twinkling lights upon them, being attended to by men in white coats who all looked strangely alike.

'Where are we now?' asked Eddie.

'Central operations room,' said the other Jack. 'Go on now.'

'I do wish you'd stop saying that. It's as repetitive as.'

'Go on *now*.' And the other Jack kicked Eddie.

'But where shall we go *now*?' Jack asked.

'How about somewhere to eat?' asked Dorothy. 'Lunch would be nice.'

'I'm really not hungry.' But Jack's stomach rumbled.

'We do need a plan of some kind,' said Dorothy.

'Plan?' said Jack. 'What we need is a miracle.' Jack hunched over the wheel.

Presently they approached a route-side eatery. It was a Golden Chicken Diner. Jack drove hurriedly past it.

Somewhat later, with the police car making those alarming coughing sounds that cars will make when they are running out of fuel, they approached another eatery: Haley's Comet Lounge.

'This will do us fine,' said Dorothy.

The car clunked up to a petrol pump.*

A tall man with short hair smiled out from the shade of a veranda. He wore a drab grey mechanic's overall that accentuated his drab greyness and wiped his hands upon an oily rag, which implied an intimate knowledge of automobiles.

'Howdy, Officer,' said he as Jack wound down what was left of his window. 'Suu-ee, what the Hell happened here?'

'Nothing to concern yourself with,' said Jack.

Dorothy leaned over him. And Jack sniffed her hair. 'Fill her up,' said Dorothy, 'and check the oil, please, and the suspension.'

'Have to put her up on the ramp for that, ma'am.'

'Fine, please do it.'

Dorothy led Jack off to eat as the drab grey mechanic drove the stolen police car into the garage.†

'It's best out of sight,' said Dorothy to Jack as they entered the eatery.

'Do you have money?' Jack asked as he patted his uniform pockets. 'Because I don't.'

'Leave all the talking to me.'

The eatery was everything that it should have been. Everything in its right place. Long bar along the right-hand wall. Tables to the left with window views of Interstate 15. A great many framed

---

* This being one of those roadside diners that had a petrol pump in front. Which was quite convenient really.

† And a garage too. How convenient was *that*?

photographs upon the walls, mostly of men in sporting attire holding large fish.

There were some trophies on a shelf behind the bar, silver trophies topped by figures of men in sporting attire holding large fish.

Behind the bar counter stood a short man with tall hair. He wore sporting attire and held a large fish.

'Good afternoon, Officer, ma'am,' said he. 'Would you care to take a number?'

'A number?' said Jack. 'What do you mean?'

'So that I can seat you. In the right order.'

'But there's just the two of us.'

'In the right order to be served.'

'There's still just the two of us.'

'Take a number,' said Dorothy.

'Can I have *any* number?' Jack asked.

'You can have *this* number,' said the short man with tall hair. And he placed his fish upon the countertop, peeled a number from what looked to be a date-a-day calendar jobbie on the wall next to a framed picture of a man in sporting attire holding—

'Can we sit anywhere?' Jack asked. And he viewed the tables. All were empty.

'What number do you have?' asked the short man.

'Twenty-three,'[*] said Jack.

'Then you're in luck. Table over there, by the window.'

Dorothy and Jack sat down at this table.

'Was I supposed to understand any of that?' Jack asked.

'What's to understand?' asked Dorothy, and she took up a menu. It was a fish-shaped menu. Jack took up one similar.

'So,' said the short man, suddenly beside them, 'allow me to introduce myself. My name is Guy and I will be your waiter. Can I recommend to you today's specials?'

Jack looked up at the short man called Guy. 'Why don't you give it a go?'

'Right,' said the short man called Guy, and he drew a tall breath.

[*] Damn me, not *again!*

And sang a jolly song.

> We have carp from Arizona
> And perch from Buffalo,
> A great big trout
> With a shiny snout
> From the shores of Idaho.

> We've a pike called Spike
> And I'm sure you'd like
> A bowl of fries with him.
> There's a shark called Mark
> That I'll serve, for a lark,
> With salad to keep you slim.

> I've monkfish, swordfish, cramp fish, cuttlefish,
> Goby, goldfish, gudgeon.
> I've sperm whale, starfish, bottle-nose dolphin,
> I ain't no curmudgeon.

> If you like salmon, perch or bass,
> Mullet, hake, or flounder,
> Dory, plaice, or skate, or sole,
> Try Guy, he's a great all-rounder.

And there was plenty more of that, twenty-three verses more of that, all sung in the 'country' style.

'Well,' said Jack, clapping his hands together when the song was finally done, 'I quite enjoyed that.'

'Enjoyed *what*?' asked Guy.

'The song,' said Jack.

'What song was that?'

'The one about fish.'

'Oh, *that* song. I'm sorry, Officer, it's been a rough morning, what with all the toing and froing.'

'Yes,' said Jack. And added in as delicate a fashion as he could, 'Do you have anything other than fish on your menu?'

Guy looked puzzled. He *was* puzzled.

'Meat,' said Jack. 'Any meat?'

'A burger,' said Guy.

'A burger,' said Jack.

'Certainly, Officer. One mackerel burger coming up. And for your lovely daughter?'

'Daughter?' said Jack.

'So sorry, Officer, it's these new shoes, the insteps pinch.'

'I'll have the sardines,' said Dorothy, perusing the menu. 'Do they come with the quahog sauce?'

'Surely do, ma'am. And whiting mayo and chingree chitlins.'

'Mahser on the side?'

'With hilsa and beckti?'

'That's the way I love it.' And Dorothy smiled at Guy and he smiled back at her.

'And a mackerel burger for your uncle,' said Guy.

'Yes,' said Jack, 'With snodgrass and mong-waffle and pungdooey. Oh and add a little clabwangle to my little chikadee while you're about it.'

Guy bowed and departed.

'You made all that up,' said Dorothy.

'Well, so did you.'

'Here you go then,' said Guy, presenting his discerning patrons with an overloaded tray.

'That was fast!' said Jack.

'This *is* America,' said Guy, and he placed the tray upon the table and lifted food covers from two plates.

'That's not what I ordered,' said Jack.

'Nor me,' said Dorothy.

Guy burst into tears.

Dorothy reached out and patted his shoulder. 'There's no need to go upsetting yourself,' she said. 'I'm sure that whatever this is, it will be very nice.'

'What *is it*?' asked Jack, taking up a fork and prodding at the items that lay steaming up on his plate.

'It's chicken fish,' said the sobbing Guy. 'Locally caught and as fresh as the day is long.'

'It's chicken,' said Jack. 'There's no fish at all involved here.'

''Tis too,' said Guy.

''Tis not,' said Jack. 'It's chicken. That's a chicken leg.'

'It's a *fish* leg,' said Guy.

'Fish do not have legs,' Jack informed him.

'Chicken fish do.'

'I don't believe that there is such a thing as a chicken fish,' said Jack.

'There's one there on the counter,' said Guy. 'I was petting it when you came in.'

'It doesn't have any legs.'

'I de-legged it earlier. That's what's on the plates.'

'Fish don't have wings, either,' said Dorothy. 'There are wings on my plate.'

'Well, that's where you're wrong,' said Guy. 'Flying fish have wings, everybody knows that.'

'This is definitely chicken.' Jack sniffed at the chicken on his plate.

'Mine's definitely chicken, too,' said Dorothy.

'You're sure?' Guy dabbed at his running nose with an oversized red gingham handkerchief. 'You're absolutely sure?'

'Jack here *is* a police officer,' said Dorothy, 'so he knows these things.'

'I knew it!' Guy beat a right-hand fist into a left-hand hand-kerchief-carrying palm. 'I knew it. Chicken fish be damned. I've been cheated, officer. I wish to register a complaint.'

'Do you have *any* fish in this restaurant?' Jack asked.

Guy sniffed.

'That wasn't an answer,' said Jack.

Guy shrugged.

'Nor was that.'

'All right! All right!' Guy fell to his knees, although given his shortcomings in the tallness department the difference in height that this made was hardly perceptible. 'I'm so sorry,' he wailed, and he beat his chest with diminutive fists. 'Thirty years I've been in business here. Thirty years in these parts, winning every fishing competition, known in these parts as Guy Haley, Champion of Champions. I took an eighty-pound buckling up at the creek in forty-seven. Never been beaten. Never been beaten.'

'Where is this leading?' Jack asked. 'Only we *are* hungry. And we *are* in a hurry.'

'I'll leave you to your chicken fish, then.'

'No,' said Jack, 'you won't. I don't want chicken. I will eat anything that you have, but *not* chicken.'

'All right! All right!' Guy was back on his feet.

'Get up,' said Jack.

'I *am* up.'

'Then please, in as few words as possible, offer us an explanation.'

'For what?' asked Guy.

'Would you like me to hit him?' asked Dorothy.

Guy flinched.

'No,' said Jack. 'He's only little.'

'I'm not *that* little,' said Guy.

'True enough,' said Jack. 'I'll hit you myself.'

'No, please.'

'Then tell us. Everything.'

'Well, like I say, I've been fishing these parts for—'

Jack raised his fist.

'No, please, Officer, no.'

'Then tell us,' said Jack. 'Everything. And you know what I mean by that.'

'It's not my fault.' Guy wept. 'The chickens made me do it.'

'The chickens?' said Jack. '*The chickens?*'

'Out there.' Guy pointed with a short and trembly finger. 'Out there in the desert, twenty miles from here in Area Fifty-Two.'

21

'Area Fifty-Two?' went Jack, a-falling back in his seat. 'Chickens from Area Fifty-Two?'

'It's as true as I'm sitting here, although I'm actually standing up.'

'Chickens,' said Jack to Dorothy.

'Area Fifty-Two?' said Dorothy to Jack.

'Where the crashed flying saucer was taken. The head chef at the Golden Chicken Diner told me all about it.'

'It's a "chef thing",' said Guy. 'All chefs know about it.'

Jack looked very hard at Guy. '*What* did the chickens make you do?'

'Did I say *chickens*?' said Guy. 'I meant *chicken people*. The people who produce the chicken for the Golden Chicken Diners. It all comes from Area Fifty-Two, up the Interstate. The toxic waste from their factory out there in the desert polluted the creek, so I couldn't catch fish anymore. And I complained. I went out there. And their guys said that if I just kept my mouth shut they'd see to it that I had free supplies of chicken for life to sell as fish.'

'No one is ever going to be fooled by you passing off chicken as fish,' said Jack.

'No one's ever complained before,' said Guy.

'No one?' said Jack. 'How long have you been serving this chicken?'

Guy looked down at his wristlet watch. 'Since ten this morning,' he said. 'You're the first folk in the diner today.'

'Right,' said Jack, and he nodded. Thoughtfully.

'Listen, Officer,' said Guy, 'this is my livelihood. Could you not just eat the chicken and pretend it's fish? What harm could it do?'

'Mister Haley,' said Jack, 'I'm going to ask you a question and I'd like you to think very carefully before you answer it. Do you think you can do that?'

Guy Haley nodded also. Perhaps even a little more thoughtfully than Jack had.

'My question is this,' said Jack. 'Why don't you just sell chicken as chicken?'

'Sell it as chicken,' Guy said. Slowly.

Jack did further noddings.

'Ah,' said Guy. 'You mean *not* pretend it's fish?'

Jack made an encouraging face. And did a bit more nodding.

'If I might just stop you there,' said Dorothy, with no head noddings involved. 'I feel that this conversation has gone quite far enough. Which way is it to Area Fifty-Two, Mister Haley?'

'Not pretend it's fish,' said Mr Haley.

'Which way?' asked Dorothy.

'Say it's chicken,' said Mr Haley.

'Which way?' asked Dorothy once more.

'Now let me just get this straight,' said Mr Haley. 'What you're suggesting is—'

But suddenly he was up off his feet and dangling in the air. Dorothy held him at arm's length and then shook him about. 'Which way is it to Area Fifty-Two?' she demanded to be told.

'That way. That way.' Guy Haley pointed. 'Five miles up the Interstate there's a turn-off to the right, a dirt road. It goes all the way there.'

'Thank you,' said Dorothy, lowering Guy to the floor. 'We'll pass on the lunch, I think. Farewell.'

And she and Jack left Haley's Comet Lounge.

'Well,' said Jack as they stood in the sunlight, 'fancy that. What a coincidence, eh? Area Fifty-Two being just up the road. And it being the place where all the chickens for the Golden Chicken Diner are produced.'

'Yes,' said Dorothy. 'Fancy that.'

'If I believed in a God,' said Jack, 'I would believe that he, she or it was smiling right down on me now. That he, or she, or it, had provided me with the miracle that I'd hoped for earlier.'

'Would you?' said Dorothy. 'Would you really?'

'Yes,' said Jack. 'I would.'

'Hey, Officer,' the tall drab grey man with the short hair called out to Jack from the garage. 'Your auto's all done. Shall I bring it out?'

'Thanks,' said Jack. 'Please do.'

Sounds of engine revvings were to be heard and then the tall man drove the black-and-white from the garage.

Jack gawped somewhat at the black-and-white. It had been totally repaired. The bodywork was perfect, resprayed and waxed, too. The windows had been replaced. There was a shiny new back bumper.

The tall man climbed from the car and tossed the keys to Jack.

Jack was all but speechless.

'There's still a bit of rust inside the tailpipe,' said the tall mechanic. 'I hope you don't mind about that.'

Jack shook his head. 'You fixed it all up,' he said. 'That is incredible.'

'It's nothing,' said the mechanic, getting to work on his hands with an oily rag. 'After all, this *is* America.'

'Yes,' said Jack. 'Quite so. So, er, what do I owe you?'

The tall mechanic winked. 'Nothing at all,' he said. 'You scratch my back and I'll scratch yours, if you know what I mean.'

'Not exactly,' said Jack.

'Well,' said the tall mechanic, 'I have been guilty of one or two minor misdemeanours, and if you, as a police officer, could turn a blind eye to them, then we're all square. Is that okay with you?'

'Absolutely,' said Jack, settling himself back behind the steering wheel and taking a sniff at the Magic Tree that now hung from the rear-view mirror. 'This is America, after all. Consider yourself forgiven in the eyes of the law.'

'Why, thank you kindly, Officer.' The tall mechanic closed the driver's door upon Jack. Dorothy sat herself down on the passenger seat and patted at the refurbished upholstery.

'I mean, it's no big deal,' said the tall mechanic. 'And I only did twenty-three of them.'

'Twenty-three,' said Jack, sticking the key into the ignition and giving it a little twist. The engine purred beautifully.

'And they all had it coming, those daughters of Satan. High-school girls with their skirts all up to here,' and he gestured to where these skirts were all up to. 'Flaunting themselves. And those nuns, too.'

'Excuse me?' said Jack, looking up at the tall mechanic. All shadow-faced now, the sunlight behind him.

'Killed 'em quick and clean. Well, some not so clean, perhaps, but after all the torturing was done, they was begging for death anyway,' said the tall mechanic. 'And I only ate the good bits.'

'Right,' said Jack. 'Well, we have to be on our way now. Thank you for fixing the car.'

'No sweat!' The tall mechanic took a step back.

'Goodbye,' said Jack, and he drove away.

The tall mechanic sidled out onto the road, where he waved farewell with his oily rag.

'Twenty-three,' said Jack to Dorothy. 'Did he just say what I thought he just said?'

Dorothy said, 'Yes, he did.'

'That's what I thought.' Jack halted the car.

The tall mechanic stepped out into the middle of the road. 'Everything okay up there?' he called. 'No trouble with the engine?'

Jack looked at Dorothy.

And Dorothy looked at Jack.

And then Jack put the car into reverse, revved the engine, let out the clutch and reversed at considerable speed over the tall mechanic.

And then, to be sure, as you *have* to be sure, drove over the body once more.

Then backed up a couple more times to be *absolutely* sure.

And then proceeded on his way.

No words passed between Dorothy and Jack for a while.

And when words *did* pass between them once again, these words did not include any reference to the tall mechanic.

'Slow down a bit,' said Dorothy. 'We must be almost there.'

Jack slowed down a bit. 'There?' he asked. '*That* dirt road, do you think?'

That dirt road had a big signpost beside it. The signpost read:

DON'T EVEN THINK ABOUT DRIVING UP HERE.

'I think we should drive up there,' said Dorothy.

Jack steered the spotless police car onto the dusty dirt road.

'What are you planning to do,' asked Dorothy, 'when we get there?'

'Rescue Eddie,' said Jack.

'But we don't know for certain that he's there.'

'I do,' said Jack. 'He is.'

'But you can't know for certain.'

'Oh yes I can,' said Jack. 'I can feel him. In here.' And Jack tapped at his temple. 'The closer we get, the more I can feel him. I can feel him, and he's hurting.'

And Eddie Bear *was* hurting. He'd been kept waiting about in a concrete corridor outside a big steel rivet-studded door for quite some time now. The other Jack had passed this quite some time by kicking Eddie up and down the corridor. So Eddie was *really* hurting. And hurting more than just from the kickings.

Eddie felt decidedly odd. Slightly removed from himself, somehow, as if he didn't quite fit into his body any more. It was a decidedly odd and most disconcerting sensation. And it was not at all helped by the kickings.

The other Jack squared up for another boot. Bolts clunked and clanked and the big steel door slid open.

'Thanks for *that*,' said Eddie.

The other Jack kicked him through the opening.

Eddie came to rest upon a carpeted floor. It was most unpleasantly carpeted. With poo. Chicken poo.

'Urgh,' went Eddie, and he struggled up from the floor.

Eddie was now, it had to be said, a somewhat unsightly bear. He was thoroughly besmirched with sewage and cell dust and now chicken poo. Eddie was *not* a bear for cuddling, not a bear to be hugged.

'So,' said a voice, and Eddie searched for its source, 'So, Mister Bear, we meet at last.'

Eddie could make out a desk of considerable proportions and behind this a chair, with its back turned to him. Behind this chair and affixed to the wall were numerous television screens and upon these were displayed numerous scenes of American life. Most being played out via the medium of the television show.

The shows meant nothing to Eddie and so he did not recognise George Reeves as Superman, Lucille Ball in *I Love Lucy*, Phil Silvers as Sergeant Bilko or Roy Rogers on Trigger.

On one TV screen, Eddie viewed a newscast. It showed scenes of devastation, crashed police cars, a wrecked AC Cobra and a Ford Mustang called Sally. And a photograph was being displayed also. A mugshot of a wanted man. Eddie gawped at the mugshot: it was a mugshot of Jack.

The desk and the chair back and the TV screens, too, were all besmutted with poo. Chicken poo. Eddie Bear sniffed at the air of this room. It must have smelled pretty bad. But Eddie Bear couldn't smell it. Eddie Bear had no sense of smell left whatsoever.

'Who are you?' asked Eddie. 'Who is this?'

The chair behind the desk swung around and Eddie Bear viewed the sitter.

The sitter on the chair was no chicken.

The sitter was Eddie Bear.

'Whoa,' went Jack and he shuddered.

'Are you all right?' asked Dorothy.

'Yes,' said Jack. 'I suppose so. I went all cold there. Have you ever heard that expression about feeling as if someone just walked over your grave?'

'I've heard it, but I've never understood it.'

Jack peered out through the windscreen. He had the wipers on now – there was a lot of dust. 'Are we nearly there yet?' he asked.

Dorothy did peerings also. 'There's something up ahead,' she said. 'It looks like some big military installation with a big wire fence around it. What are you going to do?'

'Bluff it out,' said Jack. 'This is a police car. I'm a policeman. We'll get in there somehow.'

'Seems reasonable,' said Dorothy. 'Let's just hope that there's no real policemen around.'

'I don't think that's very likely out here,' said Jack.

'Out *where*?' asked Police Chief Samuel J. Maggott, shouting somewhat into the mouthpiece of his telephone. Sam was considerably bandaged, but back behind his desk. 'Speak up, boy, I can hardly hear you, what?'

Words came to him through the earpiece.

'You're saying what? You saw the midday newscast? The wanted maniac, Jack? That's right. Dressed as a police officer, at your lounge? Left without paying for his chicken-fish lunch? Drove over your mechanic? How many times? That many, eh? And he's gone on to where? I see.'

Samuel J. Maggott replaced the receiver.

And then picked it up again.

'Get me Special Ops,' he told the telephonist. 'Get me Special Ops, get me a chopper and put out an all-points bulletin.'

'You look put out,' said the Eddie in the chair. 'In fact you look all in. You look as wretched as a weevil with the wobbles.'

'What are you?' asked Eddie Bear. 'You're not me. What are you?'

'I'm the you of this world,' said the other Eddie.

'No you're not,' said the Real McCoy. 'Toys don't live in this world.' Eddie Bear paused. 'Or do they?'

The other Jack loomed over Eddie. 'Would you like me to knock him about a bit, boss?' he asked.

'That won't be necessary. Eddie and I are going to get along just fine, aren't we, Eddie? We are going to be as cosy as two little peas in a little green pod.'

Eddie looked down at his grubby old self.

'Yes, you're right,' said the other Eddie. 'You really are in disgusting condition. You're as foul as a fetid fur-ball. We'll have to get you all cleaned up. Jack, take Eddie to the cleaning facility, see that he gets all cleaned up.'

'Can I hold his head under the water? Or use the high-pressure hose?' asked the other Jack.

'No, Jack, I want Eddie in tip-top condition. He's very precious, is Eddie. After all, he'll soon be the last of his kind.'

'What?' asked Eddie. 'What do you mean?'

'Hurry,' said his other self. 'The countdown has already begun.'

The other Jack picked Eddie up and hurled him out into the corridor.

The *other* other Jack, the real Jack that was, drew the police car to a halt before a little guard post. A little guard issued from this post and made his way to the car.

Jack wound down the window.

The guard wore a rather stylish golden uniform with a Golden Chicken logo picked out in red upon the right sleeve. He took off his golden cap and mopped at his brow with an oversized red gingham handkerchief.

'Good day, Officer,' he said. 'It's a hot'n, ain't it?'

'Very hot,' said Jack. 'Would you open the gates, please?'

'Have to ask the nature of your visit, Officer.'

'Official business,' said Jack. 'I'd like to say more, but you know how it is.'

'Not precisely,' said the guard. 'Could you be a little more explicit?'

'Well, I could,' said Jack, 'but frankly I just don't have the time. Would you mind dealing with this, Dorothy?'

'Not at all.' Dorothy left the police car. Walked around to the guard's side. Dealt the guard a brutal blow to the skull and returned to the passenger seat.

'Thank you,' said Jack. 'Would you mind opening the gates now?'

'Why don't you just smash through them with the car?' asked Dorothy. 'It's so much more exciting, isn't it!'

'This is an exciting machine,' said the other Jack.

He and Eddie now stood in another room. One of an industrial

285

nature. There were conveyor belts in this room and big, ugly-looking machines into which they ran in and out again.

'Prototype, this,' said the other Jack. 'Chicken cleanser. Chickens go in this end,' and he pointed, 'through the cleansing machine, out again, along that belt there, then through the drier, then out of that, then through the de-featherer, then out again. Just like that.' And he ambled over to a big control panel, threw a couple of switches and pressed a few buttons. Great churnings of machinery occurred and conveyor belts began to judder into life. 'Never went into mass production though, this model. The chickens kept getting all caught up inside. Came out in shreds, some of them. Didn't half squawk, I can tell you.'

'Now just you see here,' said Eddie. 'I don't think that I—'

But Eddie was hauled once more from the floor.

And Jack in the car gave another terrible shudder.

'Through the gates it is, then,' said he, and he put his foot down hard.

'And put your foot down hard,' said Samuel J. Maggott to the pilot of the helicopter that now stood upon the rooftop of Police Headquarters, slicing the sunlit sky with its blades.

Horrible slicing, mashing sounds came from the chicken cleanser.
  And terrible cries from Eddie Bear.
  And then he was on the conveyor belt again.
  And into the drying machine.
  And great puffs of steam and smoke belched from this machine.
  And further cries came from Eddie.
  Cries of vast despair.
  And the other Jack clapped his hands together.
  And Eddie cried some more.

And the stolen police car smashed through the gates and Jack did further shudderings.

Ahead lay a long, low concrete bunker kind of jobbie. Jack swerved the police car to a halt before it.

'Looks rather formidable,' he said to Dorothy. 'I can only see one door, and it appears to be of sturdy metal. Should I try to smash the car through it, do you think?'

'No,' said Dorothy. 'Best not. We might well need to make a speedy getaway in this car. I'd use this, if I were you,' and she handed Jack a plastic doodad.

Jack examined same and said, 'What is it?'

'Security pass key card,' said Dorothy. 'I took it from the guard.'

Jack smiled warmly at Dorothy. 'Come on then,' he said.

'Come on then,' said the other Jack. 'Up and at it, Mister Bear. Oh dear.'

Eddie Bear looked somewhat out of sorts. He was certainly a clean bear now. Very clean. And dry, too. And sweetly smelling, although he wasn't personally aware of this. But there was something not quite right about Eddie. His head seemed very big and his body very small. And his arms were all sort of flapping sleeves, whereas his legs were thickly packed stumps.

And as for his ears.

'What have you done to me?' he asked, in a very strange voice.

'Your stuffing seems to have become somewhat redistributed,' said the other Jack. 'But no matter. I'll soon beat you back into the correct shape.'

And outside Jack gave another very large shudder.

And now up in the sky in the police helicopter, Samuel J. Maggott remembered that he had this pathological fear of flying, which his therapist had assured him stemmed back to a freak pogo-stick/low-bridge accident Sam had suffered as a child.

'Fly lower,' Sam told the pilot.

'Really?' said the pilot. 'Can I?'

'Of course you can – why not?'

'Because it's not allowed,' said the pilot. 'We're not allowed to fly at less than two hundred feet, unless we're landing or taking off, of course.'

'Why?' asked Sam.

'Helicopters have a tendency to crash into power lines if they fly low,' said the pilot.

'Fly low,' said Sam. 'And look out for power lines.'

'Can I fly above all the police cars and the military vehicles that are now speeding along Route Sixty-Six?' asked the pilot.

'That would be preferable,' said Sam.

'Splendid,' said the pilot. And he flung the joystick forward.

And Samuel J. Maggott was sick.

And so was Eddie Bear. He coughed up sawdust and nuts.

'Not on my floor,' said his other self. 'You'll soil my chicken droppings.'

'Sorry,' said Eddie, 'but this joker punched me all about.'

'But you look much better.'

Eddie patted at himself. 'I don't feel very well.'

'Then perhaps you'd like a drink?'

'If it's beer, I would,' said Eddie.

'Jack,' said the other Eddie, 'fetch Eddie here a beer, and one for me, too, and one for yourself.'

The other Jack looked down at Eddie Bear. 'I don't think I should leave you alone with him, boss,' said he. 'He might turn uglier.'

'He'll be fine. Eddie and I have much to discuss. Hurry along now.'

The other Jack saluted and then he left the room.

'He never makes me laugh,' said the other Eddie. 'Some comedy sidekick he is, eh?'

'Eh?' said Eddie. 'Eh?'

'Well, he's as funny as a fart in a lift.'

Eddie nodded and said, 'I suppose so.'

'Sit down,' said his other self.

'What, here, in the chicken poo?'

'Quite so – they are rather messy, aren't they? But they do call the shots, as it were, so who are we to complain?'

'I'll just stand then,' said Eddie.

'You do that, good fellow.'

And so Eddie stood. 'And while I'm standing,' he said, 'perhaps,' and now he shouted. Loudly. '*Perhaps you can tell me what in the name of any of the Gods is going on here?*'

'Quietly, *please*.' The other Eddie put his paws to his ears. 'It's a quite simple matter. And I am certain that an intelligent bear such as yourself, one skilled in the art of detection, has, as these Americans would say, figured it all out by now.'

'Are you in charge here?' Eddie asked. 'Are you the one in control?'

The other Eddie inclined his head. 'I'm in charge,' he said.

'And there's only the one of you? Not more than one, no other copies?'

'Just me,' said the other Eddie. 'Just me, just you.'

'And so *you* are the murderer,' said Eddie. 'The one who murdered the clockwork monkeys, and then the band at Old King Cole's, and then the orchestra at the Opera House. I saw you there.'

'And I saw you, and I applauded your enterprise, risking all to enter this world. Very brave. Very foolish, but very brave all the same.'

Eddie Bear made a puzzled face. 'Why did you do it?' he asked. 'Murder your own kind? To reproduce them as free giveaways to sell chicken? It doesn't make any sense.'

The other Eddie laughed. 'You call it murder,' he said, 'but here we call it franchising. Your kind are not my kind, Eddie. I am not of your world. Your world is very special. To those in this world it is a land of dreams, of make-believe, where toys live and have adventures. A world of fantasy.'

'It's real enough for me,' said Eddie Bear.

'But it's a mess. Every world is a mess, every world needs organisation.'

'This one certainly does.'

'Which is why *we* are organising it. Let's face it, you tried to organise yours, didn't you? When you were mayor of Toy City?'

'Ah,' said Eddie, 'that. Well, that didn't go quite as well as it might have.'

'But you tried your best and we observed your progress. You tried your best but it just didn't work. And so we decided that the best thing to do would be to wipe the slate clean, as it were. Out with the old and in with the new, as it were. Take the best bits out of the old, employ them in this world. Then do away with the worst.'

'I don't know what you're talking about,' said Eddie, 'but I know I don't like it, whatever it is.'

'I'll explain everything,' said the other Eddie. 'And then you can make your comments. Ah, here comes Jack with the beer.'

Jack entered bearing beers. He gave one to Eddie and Eddie took it between his paws and gave it a big swig.

'I spat in it,' said the other Jack.

And Eddie spat out his swig.

'That wasn't very nice,' said the other Eddie, accepting his beer.

'I know,' said the other Jack, 'but it made me laugh. Cheers!' and he raised his bottle.

'Cheers,' said the other Eddie. 'Oh and by the way, I saw a little light twinkling on my desk a while ago. It would seem that someone has penetrated the outer perimeter.'

'That's right,' said the other Jack. 'His friend,' and he cast a thumb in Eddie's direction.

'My Jack?' said Eddie.

'*Your* Jack,' said the other Jack, 'smashed through the gates in a stolen police car, in the company of some young woman, and entered the bunker using the guard's security pass key card.'

'Most enterprising,' said the other Eddie. 'And where are he and the young woman now?'

'In the elevator, on their way down.'

'Really?' said the other Eddie. 'Well, we can't have that, can we?'

And he reached out a paw and pressed it down on a button on his desk.

And in the elevator all the lights went out.

'Oh dear,' said Jack. 'I don't like this.'

And then the elevator juddered.

And then it began to fall.
And Jack in the darkness went, 'Oh dear me.'
And the elevator plunged.

22

Down went the elevator, down and down. Down and down in the dark. And up rushed the ground, it seemed, in the dark. Up and up and up.

And then there was a sickening sound that echoed all around and about.

Eddie heard something and felt something, too.

'What did you do?' he asked.

'Nothing to concern yourself with,' replied his other self, taking up his beer between his paws and draining much of it away. 'These paws are a real pain at times, aren't they? No opposable thumbs—'

'I had hands with those once,' said Eddie sadly. 'But tell me, *what* did you do?'

'Just switched off the elevator. Don't go getting yourself upset.'

Eddie rocked gently upon his paw pads. He felt upset, he felt unsettled, he felt altogether wrong.

'You look a little shaky,' said his other self. 'But never mind, it will pass. Everything will pass. But it is a great shame about the hands. They were very nice hands you had. I can't understand why everyone thought them so creepy.'

'What?' went Eddie, raising a now droopy head. 'How did *you* know about me having hands? I don't understand.'

'I know all about you,' said his other self. 'It is my job to know all about you. Learn every subtle nuance, as it were. *Be* you, in fact. I told you, we kept a careful eye on you when you were mayor.'

'I'll tell you what,' said Eddie Bear, 'I really hate sighing, you know. Sighing gets me down. I have a normally cheerful disposition, but once in a while I really feel the need for a sigh. And this is one of those times.' And so Eddie sighed. And a deep and heartfelt sigh it was, and it set the other Jack laughing.

'And so why sigh you, Eddie Bear?' asked his other self.

'Because,' said Eddie, 'I don't understand. I consider myself to be more than competent when it comes to the matter of private detective work. I pride myself upon my competence. But for the life that is in me, I do not understand what is going on around here. I don't understand why you've done what you've done, what you intend to do next, nor why you look just like me, and why this gormster—' Eddie gestured towards the other Jack '—looks like my best friend Jack.'

'And so you would like a full and thorough explanation, couched in terms readily understandable to even the simplest soul?'

Eddie sighed once more. 'Please feel free to be condescending,' he said. 'I've never been very good with subtle.'

'Nice touch of irony.' Eddie's other self finished his beer and set his bottle aside. 'All right, it is only fair. I will tell you all. Jack, you may leave us now.'

'Oh, I don't think so.'

'I think so, Jack. Take your leave at once.'

'But he'll go for you, sir – he's a vicious little bastard.'

'Language,' said Eddie's other self. 'Eddie needs to know and it is right that he should know. Bears have a code of honour, don't they, Eddie?'

'Noted for it,' said Eddie. 'Along with their sexual prowess. And their bravery, of course. Bears are as noble as. Everyone knows that.'

'And so if I ask you to swear upon all that means anything to you that you will make no attempt to harm me during the time that I am explaining everything to you, I can rely on you to honour this oath?'

'Absolutely,' said Eddie Bear.

'Because you see, Jack,' said the other Eddie, 'bears can't cross their fingers behind their backs, so when they swear they have to stick to what they've sworn.'

The other Jack made non-committal sounds.

'So clear off,' the other Eddie told him.

And, grumbling somewhat, that is what he did.

'Care to take a little trip?' asked Eddie's other self.

Eddie Bear did shruggings. 'Is my Jack all right?' he asked.

'Don't worry about your Jack. Would you care to take a little trip?'

'It depends where to.'

'I could just kill you,' said Eddie's other self.

'I'd love to take a little trip,' said Eddie. 'Teddy bears' picnic, is it?'

'In a manner of speaking. Step a little closer to the desk, that's it. Now, let me join you.' And Eddie and his other self now stood next to each other. 'And if I just press this.'

And then.

The horrible chicken-poo-carpeted floor fell away.

Eddie and his other self hovered in the air, borne by a silver disc that, it seemed, shunned the force of gravity.

And this disc, with these two standing upon it, slowly drifted downwards.

Eddie peered fearfully over the rim of the disc. 'What is happening here?' he asked in a rather shaky voice.

'Fear not, my friend, fear not. I am going to take you on a tour of this establishment. You will see how everything works and why it does. We shall chat along the way.'

'Hm,' went Eddie. And that was all.

And the slim disc drifted down.

'The technology that drives this,' explained the other Eddie, 'is years ahead, centuries ahead, of the technology that exists upon this particular world. And the denizens of this particular world will never catch up with such technology. That will not be allowed to happen.'

'The chickens from space,' said Eddie Bear.

'Well, hardly from space, but in a way you're right. There are many, many worlds, Eddie Bear, many, many inhabited worlds. But they are not out in space somewhere. They are all here, all next to each other, as the world of Toy City is next to the world of Holly-wood, separated by a curtain, as it were, that only those in the know are capable of penetrating.'

The flying disc dropped low now, over a vast industrial complex, great machines attended to by many, many workers.

'And what is this?' asked Eddie.

'Chicken production,' his other self explained. 'Humankind has this thing about eating chickens. But as logic would dictate to anyone who sat down and thought about it for five minutes, it is simply impossible to produce the vast quantity of chickens required for human consumption every day. It would require chicken-breeding farms covering approximately a quarter of this world's surface. So all the chickens that are eaten in the USA are produced here. They are artificial, Eddie, cloned from a single chicken. The pilot of a chicken scout ship that crashed here ten years ago. Soulless clones – they are not *real* chickens.'

'From space?'

'No, not from space. Do try to pay attention. Recall if you will the various religions that predominate in Toy City. You have The Church of Mechanology, followed by clockwork toys who believe that the universe is powered by a clockwork motor. The cult of Big Box Fella, He Come, a Jack-in-the-Box cult that believes that the universe is a big box containing numerous other boxes. There is more than a hint of truth to their beliefs. But what I am saying is this: all these religions have a tiny piece of the cosmic jigsaw puzzle. The chickens just happen to have a far larger piece.'

'Yes, well,' said Eddie, 'everyone is entitled to believe whatever they want to believe, in my opinion, as long as it causes no hurt to others. I happen to be an elder in an exclusive teddy bear sect, The Midnight Growlers.'

'You are its one and only member,' said the other Eddie as the flying disc flew on over the seemingly endless faux-chicken production plant. 'My point is this. All religions are correct in one or other respect. All religions possess a little part of the whole. The followers of Big Box Fella are about the closest. All life in the entire Universe exists right here, upon this planet. But this planet is not, as such, a planet. It is the centre of everything. The centre of production, as it were. There are countless worlds, all next to each other, each unaware of the existence of the world next door. Sometimes beings from one world become capable of penetrating to the world next door. And do you know what happens when they do?'

'Bad things,' said Eddie. 'That would be my guess.'

'Well, there have been *some* bad things, I grant you. But I will tell you what the beings from the world next door discover when they enter a new world. They discover that, but for a few subtle differences of belief and appearance, things are exactly the same. There are the many who toil and the privileged few who control their toiling and profit from their toil. This is a universal truth.'

'And so you and whoever or *whatever* you represent are going to do something about this injustice?' asked Eddie.

'You are seeking to be ironic, I suppose?'

'Very much so,' said Eddie.

'And not without good cause. It is not possible to change the status quo with anything less than force of arms. You tried, Eddie, when you were mayor. You tried to put your world to rights. And what came of your good intentions?'

'Bad things,' said Eddie, sadly. 'Hence the loss of my hands.'

'Exactly. You tried, but you failed. But it was the fact that you were trying that drew our attention to you. One of our craft penetrated the world Beyond The Second Big O. To your side of it. And we observed your efforts. And we thought to ourselves, things *could* work out in this world. Things could be better. And so *I* was created, to replace you, so that smoothly and without incident I could be substituted for you and run your world for our own ends.'

'You thorough-going swine,' said Eddie. 'And I mean that offensively, as some of my best friends are pigs.'

'But after all the effort of creating the perfect facsimile of you, what happened? As I was on the point of eliminating you in order to take your place, you made such a foul-up of being mayor, because in your naivety you thought that things could be changed in a nice way, that you were kicked out of office. Leaving *me* redundant.'

'Poor old you,' said Eddie.

'It was touch and go,' said his other self. 'They were all for melting me down, me and the Jack they'd created to substitute for your Jack. But I had a plan.'

'I often have a plan,' said Eddie, sadly.

'Of course you do, which is one of the things I like about you – we have so much in common.' And the other Eddie patted Eddie on the shoulder.

And Eddie considered just how easy it would be to push him right off the flying disc.

But then there just might be a problem getting off that disc himself.

And there was the matter of the bears' code of honour.

'So I came up with this plan,' said Eddie's other self. 'Why not clear out Toy City? It could become a decent environment, with a lick of paint and a bit of rebuilding. And what with the ever-expanding population of Chicken World—'

'Chicken World?' said Eddie. 'There really *is* a Chicken World?'

'Of course. And one with no natural predators. And you *would* be surprised at just how many chickens a single rooster can, how shall I put this, "get through" in a single day. The chickens are looking to expand – to your world, to this one. Once all the indigenous inhabitants have been, how shall I put this?'

'Murdered?' Eddie suggested.

'That's probably the word. Or at least subdued. So I took an overview of the denizens of Toy City. In this world, the young, and indeed the old, just love toys. Especially *special* toys. Collectables. They just love them. And so, I thought, why not have the toys of Toy City work for us, to aid us in our plans for expansion.'

'You sick, and how shall I put this? *Bastards!*' said Eddie.

'Tut, tut, tut. It's business – and survival, of course. Imagine, if you will, travelling to another world and discovering that its inhabitants feasted upon your kind. Bred them, slaughtered them and ate them. That is what the pilots of the first chicken craft, the one that crashed here in the desert near Roswell in nineteen forty-seven, discovered. One lone survivor was brought here to this establishment. Happily he was able to communicate, to make deals in order to ensure his survival. And when he offered an alternative to all the eating of his own kind that went on here, by demonstrating that it was possible, using advanced chicken technology, to mass-produce ersatz chickens and eggs at a fraction of the cost of real ones, the humans went for it. Fools that they are. And there you have it.'

'No,' said Eddie. 'That's not fair. I assume that you intend to have me killed. Am I correct in this assumption?'

The other Eddie shook his head.

'No?' said Eddie Bear.

'No,' said his other self. 'You will die – and shortly, too – but not at my hands. Your kind cannot survive in this world. There is a certain, how shall I put this, magic to your kind. We remain unable to discover just how the kindly, lovable white-haired old Toymaker imbues toys with life. But toys cannot live here. Surely you noticed when you arrived here – your companion's watch ceased to work, then his weaponry.'

'You *saw* that?'

'We see all. Remember, you and Jack were abducted and implanted with homing beacons up your bums. We've known where you were from the start. Jack's watch soon failed, then his weaponry and then that calculating pocket of his—'

'Wallah,' said Eddie. 'He nicked it from Tinto. I should have known. That's how he figured out about the Opera House.'

'Wallah is dead and you will soon die,' said the other Eddie. 'Sad but true. So I suppose it will do no harm to explain the rest. By channelling the very essence, the very soul-stuff of those toys, the monkeys, the band, the orchestra, and soon *all* of your kind, by drawing out their essence and funnelling it into free giveaways to promote the sale of our *special* chicken, we eliminate all competition. No real chickens will be eaten on this world again. And within one year, after the release of the movie, when the Golden Chicken chain goes global and every chicken that is eaten is one of our special chickens, this world will be ours.'

'I don't quite follow how,' said Eddie.

'Because,' said Eddie's other self, 'our special chicken has rather special qualities. It is, for one thing, highly addictive. The more you eat, the more you want to eat. The population of this world will grow fatter and fatter and they will also grow more and more aggressive as we up the dosages of certain hormones. By the turn of the next century this country, so well known for its love of democracy and justice, will begin to invade Middle Eastern states. And here, the religion of this world, well, at least one of them, which prophesies something called Armageddon, will prove correct in its prophecy. The world of men will wipe itself out. There will be no more men. And then the chicken population, having already expanded into *your* world, will take over this one as well. There's plenty of room here for a long time yet.'

'And when there isn't?' Eddie asked.

'Then the chickens will continue onwards.'

'Well, bravo to the chickens,' said Eddie Bear.

'What?' said Eddie's other self.

'I said, bravo. What else can I say? I suppose that whoever is at the top of, how shall *I* put this, the "food chain" wins the race for survival. And why would I expect chickens to respect my kind? Men do not respect my kind. The men of Toy City, the P.P.P.s, have no respect for toys. Bravo the chickens, I say.'

'You are taking this very well, considering.'

'Considering *what*? That I am soon to die? I'm resigned to it now, I suppose. How long do I have, by the way?'

'A few hours, perhaps.'

'I thought so,' said Eddie. 'I've been growing weirder ever since I got here. I'm not inside myself for much of the time. But then what can I say? I've had a good life, really, a long life, and I've done interesting things. Dying won't be so bad. I suppose.'

'I find that really quite moving,' said Eddie's other self.

'It comes to us all,' said Eddie. 'It will come to you too, eventually.'

Eddie's other self gave Eddie Bear another shoulder pat.

'Could I have a bit of a hug?' asked Eddie.

'Yes, indeed you can.' And Eddie's other self gave a big hug to Eddie.

'And could I ask you just one little favour?'

'Go on then, just ask.'

'Well,' said Eddie, 'I know that Jack shot down one of the chickens' flying saucers. But I personally didn't have any part in that, so I was wondering, do you think I could meet one of the chickens before I die? Just to say hello, just to try to understand. The King of all the chickens, perhaps.'

'It's the Queen, actually.'

'Then do you think I could meet her, perhaps? Is she here, in this complex?'

The other Eddie grinned from ear to furry ear.

'She *is*,' said Eddie. 'She *is* here, isn't she?'

The other Eddie nodded his grinning head. 'Oh yes she is,' he said.

'And do you think she might grant me an audience?'

'Well, she *might*. But I'm not quite certain why she would. You see, she's a little busy at the moment.'

'I wouldn't take up much of her time,' said Eddie. 'Because I don't have much time, do I?'

'No, that's true. But she *is* very busy, coordinating the final phase of the Toy City project.'

'The final phase?' asked Eddie.

'Tonight – well, within the hour – the task force will fly from here, through The Second Big O of the Hollywood sign, into your world and gather up the remaining denizens of Toy City. To be franchised.'

'All of them?' said Eddie.

'So you see, she *is* rather busy.'

'Well, it was just a thought.'

The other Eddie looked hard at Eddie Bear. 'You really *are* taking this *very* well,' he said.

And Eddie Bear shrugged.

And then a sound was to be heard. A terrible sound, as of sirens.

'What was *that*?' asked Eddie.

'A breach of security.'

'Jack?'

'*Not* Jack. I will have to take us aloft.'

'Do what you have to,' said Eddie.

And through some means that Eddie did not understand, but which evidently involved the application of advanced chicken technology, Eddie's other self took the flying disc aloft and soon they were back in the chicken-poo-splattered room.

And the other Eddie was back behind his desk and viewing TV screens.

'Most inconvenient,' he said. 'It would seem that we have a heavy police presence above.'

'Really?' said Eddie. 'Why?'

'Well, *that*,' and the other Eddie pointed to a screen that displayed the sweating face of a large and bandaged black man who was struggling from a grounded helicopter, 'is LA Police Chief Samuel J. Maggott. He arrested your chum Jack, who later escaped from police custody and found his way to the Haley's Comet Lounge. It was from there that your chum was directed to come here.'

'I don't quite understand *that*,' said Eddie. 'In fact, I don't understand it at all.'

'Mister Haley is in our employ. As are many others. However, it appears that Mister Haley overstepped the mark and reported your chum to the police. Mister Haley is what is known as a hick. He's as dumb as a dancing dingbat.'

'So what do you intend to do?' Eddie asked.

'I am not altogether sure.' The other Eddie pressed buttons on his desk. Other TV screens lit up to display many black and white police cars, all within the confines of the wire-fenced compound, and many armed officers climbing from these cars.

'Tricky,' said the other Eddie.

'Very,' said Eddie. 'And at such a difficult time for you. Do you think I might make a suggestion?'

'Well, you *might* – go on.'

'Well,' said Eddie, 'my end is near. I understand that and I *have* come to terms with it. Would I be correct in assuming that my Jack plunged to his death in that elevator?'

'Well . . .' said the other Eddie.

'I thought so,' said Eddie. 'But no hard feelings. You were doing what had to be done. I understand that.'

'You really *are* a most understanding little bear.'

'Most,' said Eddie. 'So, the police have come for Jack, haven't they? So why not give them what they've come for?'

'Give them his body. That's a good idea.'

'No,' said Eddie. 'That's a *bad* idea. That would attract much suspicion. Questions would be asked. Policemen would hang around the crime scene. Bad idea, don't do it.'

'No,' said the other Eddie. 'You're right. Then what?'

'I'll tell you *what*.' And Eddie Bear smiled. And it was a broad one. It was an ear-to-ear.

The other Eddie pressed another button. He had *so* many buttons on his poo-flecked desk. 'Jack,' he called into an intercom. 'Jack, are you there?'

'Yes,' said the voice of the other Jack. 'I'm here, boss – what do you want? Does that bear need further roughing-up?'

'No, Jack, no. But we have a bit of trouble upstairs. A lot of policemen have arrived. Would you mind going up to speak to them?'

'What do you want me to say to them, sir?'

'Well, you'll find a big sweaty black one puffing away next to a helicopter. Go up to him and say these words: "I give myself up." Do you think you can remember that?'

'Well, of course, sir, but I don't quite understand.'

'All will become clear. Just do it, please – it is a matter of the utmost importance. *And* a direct order. Do you understand *that*?'

The voice of Jack said, 'Yes, boss.'

The other Eddie switched off the intercom. 'I suppose you'd like to watch this on the TV screen,' he said to Eddie. Eddie Bear nodded. 'Could we watch it on *all* the screens?' he asked.

And Eddie Bear *did* enjoy the screenings. He enjoyed watching the other Jack shambling over to Police Chief Samuel J. Maggott. He enjoyed the look of surprise and shock on the face of the other Jack, which the other Eddie brought into close-up, when the other Jack found himself surrounded by *so* many armed policemen. And although he couldn't actually hear the remonstrations, he enjoyed the shouting faces. And then the truncheonings down and the police boots going in. Eddie did enjoy those boots going in.

Very much indeed.

'Now you see,' said the other Eddie, clearly enjoying it, too, '*that* makes me laugh. In fact, *that* is the first time that my comedy sidekick Jack *has* made me laugh.'

'I'm so pleased that I could be of assistance,' said Eddie, and he rocked somewhat as he said it.

'Oh,' said the other Eddie. 'You're all but gone, aren't you?'

'All but so,' said Eddie Bear.

'And do you know,' said the other Eddie, 'I *do* feel for you. Somehow. I *do*, really.'

'Thanks,' said Eddie Bear.

'And look.' The other Eddie pointed to the TV screens. 'They're leaving. All the police are leaving.'

'Glad to be of assistance. Like I said.'

'You're as genuine as a golden guinea,' said the other Eddie. 'I'll tell you what. As you haven't much time, I *will* let you meet Her Majesty. In fact, I will take you to her now. It's only fair – I owe you. Okay?'

'Okay,' said Eddie. 'Thanks.'

'Come on then,' said the other Eddie. 'Let's do it.'

And he pressed yet another button on his desk.

And they did.

23

The flying disc dropped down once more through the floor hole in the poo-splattered office. It drifted downwards and downwards and as it did so Eddie made enquiries regarding its motive power.

He received in reply a stream of technical data, which, even though he repeatedly smote his head in order to aid cogitation, passed over his head, due to its intricate nature.

'And these chickens created *you*?' asked Eddie as his knee parts wobbled uncertainly. 'How did they do *that*, exactly?'

'You weren't abducted only the once,' said his other self in reply. 'They took you off several times during your tenure as mayor. They grew me from bits of you as one might grow a plant from a seed. Although the technique used was considerably more complicated than that. Would you like me to explain it?'

'No,' said Eddie. 'I'm fine, thank you.'

'And of course, during your periods of abduction the chickens put a few ideas into your head regarding social reform in Toy City.'

'What?' went Eddie, in some alarm. 'You put ideas in my head? How?'

'It was somewhat easier than you might think – we just added our own special sawdust.'

Eddie now whacked at his furry head. 'I feel somehow . . . *dirty*,' he said.

'Dirty?' And the other Eddie laughed. 'If you think that us messing about with your head makes you feel somehow dirty, we won't broach the subject of the tracking device we stuck up your bum.'

'No,' said Eddie. 'I don't think we will. So where are we going now?'

'To the launch site, of course.'

'Well, of course, where else?'

'We'll be there in just a moment.'

The flying disc drifted downwards. Eddie viewed once more the massive engines and machinery of the ersatz-chicken production lines and shortly this was above them, as down they continued to the lowermost level of Area 52.

'Now let me ask you this,' said Eddie, 'as some bright spark might, if he, she or it were observing this – why would the "launch site" be on the lowermost level of Area Fifty-Two?'

'Good question,' said his other self. 'But then why some things are underneath other things has always been a mystery, hasn't it?'

'Has it?' asked Eddie.

'I watch a lot of TV,' said the other Eddie. 'They have these programmes on about archaeology, digging up ancient sites. But the ancient sites are always underground. Along with the ancient roads. How do you explain that, eh? Why are ancient walls always four feet deep in the ground? Where did all that earth come from that has to be dug away? Does it mean that this world is getting bigger every year? Growing and growing? Perhaps that explains why there are so many worlds all next door to each other. What do you think?'

'I think I'm not very well,' said Eddie, and his knee parts gave out.

'On your feet, soldier,' said the other Eddie. 'We're nearly there now, see?'

And Eddie saw and Eddie was impressed.

Afeared also was Eddie Bear, but very much impressed.

They were dropping down now into a massive underground compound, a vast concrete expanse lit by many high-overhead lights, a concrete expanse on which stood at least a dozen spacecraft.

These were of the variety that Eddie had seen before. Like unto the one that had pursued him up the hillside of Toy Town.

Fine-looking tin-plate craft were these, with many rivets, many portholes and those big dome jobbies on the top that proper flying saucers always have.

'The propulsion units are fascinating,' said the other Eddie. 'They employ a drive system powered by a cross-interflux, utilising the transperambulation of pseudo-cosmic anti-matter. Imagine *that*.'

And Eddie tried to. But did not succeed.

'You have to hand it to the chickens,' said the other Eddie, 'I think it must have been that eternal question that sparked them into advanced technology.'

'You mean, "What came first, the chicken or the egg?"'

'No,' said the other Eddie. '"Why did the chicken cross the road?" I feel that the answer must be that the chicken needed to know what was on the other side. *Really* needed to know. And now they know what's on the other side of so many roads and barriers between worlds and almost everything else. And one day there will be no life in the universe except chicken life and there's no telling what they'll do after that. Travel beyond death or beyond time, probably.'

'Well, bravo to those chickens,' said Eddie Bear once more. 'Are we nearly there yet, by the way?'

'Nearly there, and . . . yes, we're here.'

And Eddie had been watching as the disc came in to land. He had been watching all the activity around and about the flying saucers. All the comings and goings, all the liftings intos of stuff and fiddlings with all sorts of things. And Eddie had been viewing those who were all engaged in this industrious enterprise. For all and sundry engaged thus so were indeed of chicken-kind.

But somehow these were no ordinary chickens. No farmyard peckers, these. They were of a higher order of fowl. Clearly of superior intelligence, clad in uniforms and capable of using their wing-parts as a passable facsimile of hands.

Eddie viewed these dextrous appendages and wished like damn that his own hands had not been denied him.

As the flying disc settled onto the concrete floor, the other Eddie stepped nimbly from it and bid his wobbly counterpart to follow if he would.

Eddie stumbled onwards after his other self.

'Twelve spaceships,' the other Eddie told him as Eddie stumbled along, 'each equipped with a thousand jars to store the essences in. It was felt prudent to speed up operations. Take all in a single gathering. Which ironically enough will fulfil certain prophecies promulgated by the various religious factions in Toy City. So I suppose there must be something to religion, mustn't there?'

Eddie nodded slowly. There were no prophecies of doom to be found in the religious credo of The Midnight Growlers. There was love, there was laughter and indeed there was beer. But there was none of the grim stuff.

'The spaceships will fly out there,' said the other Eddie, pointing with a paw, 'up that tunnel, out and through The Second Big O.'

'Surely they will be seen,' said Eddie Bear.

'By humankind? Probably. But it doesn't matter. Those who believe in flying saucers are so vastly outnumbered by those who do not that their sworn testimonies are always laughed at. And as for those on the other side, they will never know what hit them. Fear not for them, Eddie. Their ends will be swift and painless. Their misery and enslavement will be over.'

'Will the chickens be hitting the meathead P.P.P.s?' asked Eddie, hopefully.

'Not yet. They'll crash a single saucer, as they did here. The "survivor" will wheel and deal with the P.P.P.s. Set up a production plant. Then they'll add a few ingredients to the ersatz chickens, something to make the P.P.P.s and all the humankind on that side of the barrier compliant. The chickens will need their services as a workforce to redecorate Toy City. After that they will be redundant. Then they will be disposed of.'

'It's all figured out,' said Eddie, 'isn't it?'

'Years and years of planning.'

'I am impressed,' said Eddie. 'Now can I meet Her Majesty?'

'All in good time.'

'But I don't have much in the way of good time left.'

'This is true,' said the other Eddie. 'This is true indeed.'

And back beyond The Second Big O and up the Yellow Brick Road, a clockwork barman called Tinto said, 'This is true indeed.'

'It is certainly true,' said Chief Inspector Wellington Bellis. 'But what do *you* know about it?'

'Not much,' said Tinto, polishing furiously at a glass that needed no polishing. 'I know Eddie's missing because he hasn't been in here for two days. And I think that's a bit poor. It's always me who helps him out on his cases *and* I wish to report the theft of my calculating pocket Wallah. Between you and me, I think that big boy Jack nicked her. Do you want me to fill out a form, or something? I have really nice handwriting.'

'That will not be necessary.' Wellington Bellis quaffed the beer that he wouldn't be paying for, because chief inspectors never have to, which is a tradition, or an old charter, or something, no matter where you might happen to be in the known, or indeed the unknown, Universe.

Along Tinto's bar counter, laughing policemen laughed amongst themselves, poked with their truncheons at things they shouldn't be poking at and laughed some more when these things fell to the floor and broke.

'And I'd really appreciate it if you'd stop them doing that,' said Tinto to Bellis.

'So you're telling me,' said Wellington Bellis, 'that you put a lot of ideas into the head of this wayward bear?'

'More than a lot,' said Tinto. 'Most.'

'You are the source of inspiration to him, as it were?'

'Yes, you might say that.'

'Same again,' said Wellington Bellis, offering up his empty glass.

Tinto hastened without haste to oblige.

'You see,' said Bellis as Tinto did so, 'we have a positive ID on the mass-murderer who did for the orchestra at the Opera House. The backstage doorman identified him.'

'Then you arrest the blighter,' said Tinto, 'and do so with my blessings. If you need them, which in my opinion you probably will, as I am lately informed by the vicar of the local Church of Mechanology that The End Times are imminent.'

'Yes,' said Bellis, 'word of such seems to be reaching me from all sides of late. But let us apply ourselves to the matter presently in hand.'

'The mass-murderer,' said Tinto.

'That very fellow. You see, it is my theory that he is not working alone. In fact I suspect he is an evil cat's-paw working on behalf of some supercriminal. A sinister mastermind behind his vile doings.'

Tinto nodded thoughtfully, though his painted face smiled on.

'A criminal mastermind who put ideas into the head of this monster. Who is the source of his inspiration, as it were. Do you understand what I'm saying?'

'Well,' said Tinto. 'Ah, excuse me, please, I have to serve this lady.'

The lady in question was Amelie, the long-legged dolly from Nadine's Diner. The dolly well known to Jack.

Bellis looked on approvingly and made a wistful face. Now *there* was a good-looking dolly, he thought. A dolly who could certainly bring a fellow such as himself a great deal of pleasure. And solace, too, of course, because Chief Inspector Bellis was, in his *special* way, a police chief. And so he was, as with all police chiefs, having a rough one today. What with all the pressure being put upon him from his superiors to get results. And his wife in the process of divorcing him and everything. And him trying to give up drinking, and everything. And his India rubber self now being so perished that bits and bobs of him kept regularly dropping off. And everything.

'Bring me something long and cold with plenty of alcohol in it,' said Amelie to Tinto.

'I don't think my wife's available,' said Tinto.[*]

'Just get me the drink, you clockwork clown.'

Tinto did as he was bid, chuckling as he did so.

Amelie turned to Chief Inspector Bellis. 'And have *you* done anything?' she asked.

'I've done all manner of things.'

'About my boyfriend. I reported him missing. The gormsters on your front desk just laughed and looked down the front of my frock.'

Bellis, doing likewise, ceased this doing. 'We're on the case, madam,' he said.

'Well, you'd better get a move on. I've just come from a chapter meeting and from what I've heard there's not going to be much time left to do anything.'

[*] The old ones really are the best.

Tinto placed Amelie's drink before her. It was short and warm, but it did have plenty of alcohol in it.

'Chapter meeting?' said Bellis to Amelie, averting his eyes from her breasts and straying them down to her legs.

'Chapter meeting, you dirty old pervert, I am a member of The Daughters of the Unseeable Upness.'

'Ah,' said Bellis, 'one of those.'

'And according to our Chapter Mother, tonight is the night of the Big Closing. After tonight there will be no more nights, ever.'

'Really?' said Bellis. 'And you personally hold to this belief?'

'I do,' said Amelie. 'Which is why I intend to get very, very drunk tonight and, if given the opportunity, fulfil my wildest fantasies.'

'Really?' said Bellis. 'And might these fantasies include having sex with a hero?'

'Women's fantasies generally do. When they don't include having sex with an absolute villain.'

'Interesting,' said Bellis. 'So would these fantasies include having sex with a police hero? One who brought to book the evil mastermind, the source of inspiration who puts ideas into the head of a mass-murderer?'

'Undoubtedly,' said Amelie, tipping her drink down her throat.

'Well . . .' said Wellington Bellis.

And, 'Well,' said the other Eddie to his failing counterpart. 'As time is now rapidly running out for you and the chickens are on a tight schedule, we'd better let you say hello to Her Madge, eh?'

'That would be nice,' said Eddie, tottering somewhat as he did so. 'Then I could wish her well and everything.'

'You are such a well-adjusted bear,' said Eddie's other self.

'I try my best,' said Eddie. 'Oh, and might I ask you something?'

'Indeed, my friend, you might.'

'Well, I was just wondering – what would happen if something were to happen to Her Majesty?'

'Happen?' said the other Eddie.

'Something bad,' said Eddie. 'Some accident or something.'

'That is *not* going to happen. Believe me, it is not.'

'No,' said Eddie, 'of course not. But say it did. Say the unthinkable occurred, something that you were unable to prevent. Some tragedy, resulting in Her Majesty's untimely demise.'

'Such is unthinkable, of course.'

'But imagine if you did think it. How would it affect the chickens' plans for inter-world domination?'

'Rather hugely, I imagine.' And the other Eddie laughed. 'You see, there is no royal line of succession in the chicken queendom. Too many princesses, you see. The chicken queendom is a matriarchy, democratically elected. But a queen will live for hundreds of years – chickens do if they're not interfered with. But it is the tradition that a new queen will overthrow and reverse all the policies made by a previous queen.'

'And why is that?' asked Eddie.

'It's a tradition,' said the other Eddie. 'It is, of course, the tradition everywhere amongst politicians. Here, for instance, in the USA, each new candidate for the presidency promises the people that should he gain the position of power, he will dump all his predecessor's policies and begin anew. And if the population believe him, they vote him in.'

'And so he does what he says?' said Eddie.

'No,' said the other one. 'He does nothing of the kind. Because he lied to the people. The problem with this world is that everyone lies to everyone else. Nobody tells the truth. Nobody. That's another reason why things are in such a mess. But chickens cannot lie. They always tell the truth. Should this Queen die, the new Queen would reverse everything. Not because she wanted to, but because it is tradition. Which is why it's a very good thing that chicken queens live for such a long time, or there would be no progress.'

'Interesting,' said Eddie Bear. 'So can I meet the Queen now, please?'

'Now, *I'm* saying please,' said Samuel J. Maggott, Police Chief of LAPD, 'because I'm such a nice man, and because I bear you no malice for the mayhem you wrought upon the personnel of this precinct.'

'Really?' said the other Jack. 'That's nice all round then, isn't it?'

They were in Sam's office, the other Jack handcuffed to the visitors' chair, a goodly number of knocked-about-looking officers standing around looking 'useful'. A troubled young detective smoking a cigarette. A feisty young female officer paring her fingernails with a bowie knife.

'All I want to know is *why*?' said Sam. 'Why the kidnappings at the Golden Chicken Headquarters? Why all the mayhem during your escape? And why flee to a secret military establishment, of all places? The mysterious Area Fifty-Two? What were you doing there?'

'I demand my phone call,' said the other Jack. 'I am entitled to my phone call.'

'And you'll get to make your phone call. As soon as you've answered my questions. Would you care for some coffee?'

'The coffee machine's still on the blink, Chief,' said the troubled young detective, putting his cigarette stub out on Sam's desk with a bandaged hand. 'We could send the feisty female officer here out to the diner to get some.'

'You could *try*,' said the feisty female officer, adjusting the arm that she had in a sling.

'And you'll do it if I tell you,' said Sam. 'So, young man, Mister Jack-no-surname, from wherever you come from – are you hungry, would you like something to eat?'

The other Jack said, 'Yes, I would, before I make my phone call.'

'Then pop out to the Golden Chicken Diner, would you, honey?'

' "Honey"?' said the feisty female officer, flipping Sam 'the bird'.

'Get us in coffees all round. And eats, too. We'll all have chicken burgers.'

'Chicken burgers?' The other Jack flinched. 'I don't want chicken burgers.'

'Don't want chicken burgers? Are you some kind of weirdo, buddy? No, don't answer that, I know you are. But don't want chicken burgers? What kind of madness is *that*? Everyone *wants* chicken burgers. Everyone *needs* chicken burgers. You'll *have* chicken burgers and you'll *love* chicken burgers. Just as everyone does.'

'Oh no I won't,' said the other Jack, struggling in the visitors' chair.

'I'm getting out of here. Let me go, you have the wrong man. You're making a big mistake.'

'Get the burgers, feisty lady,' said Police Chief Sam.

'No!' The other Jack fought fiercely.

'Don't go hurting yourself,' said Sam. 'Those cuffs are made of high-tensile steel. You'll not break out of them.'

'Oh really?' And the other Jack fought. And as Sam looked on and the officers looked on and a chap from the ACME Coffee Machine Company who had come to fix the machine in Sam's office looked on (through the glass of Sam's office door), the other Jack rose from the visitor's chair. The steel cuffs ripped down through his hands, ripped his hands most horribly from his wrists. The ankle cuffs restraining his feet fell down to the floor and the other Jack's feet fell, too.

Sam Maggott made a horrified face, which matched all others present. He fell back in considerable alarm as the handless, footless other Jack rose up before him. And then the officers fell upon this Jack and awful things occurred.

'Let us not speak of awful things,' said the other Eddie, leading the wobbly Real McCoy towards a flying saucer. 'Come aboard the mothership and you will meet Her Madge.'

'I think it had better be quick,' said Eddie, 'for I am all over the place.'

'You're doing fine. You're doing fine.'

'I'm not doing fine. I'm all in and out of my body.'

'Soon,' said the other Eddie, 'there will be peace for you. Peace for you and all your kind. Eternal peace. What better peace than that, eh?'

'None much better,' said Eddie. 'None much . . . better.'

'Come on then, up the gangway. This way, come. Come on now.'

And Eddie was led to the mothership.

And it had to be said that the interior of the mothership looked just the way that the interior of a mothership should look. Your basic pilot's seat, of course, in the cockpit area, with the steering wheel and the gear levers and the foot pedals. And the computer jobbies with the blinking lights. And the coffee machine.

'Whoa,' went Eddie. 'So this is what the inside of a spaceship looks like. What does *that* do?'

'You don't really have the time to concern yourself with *that*,' said the other Eddie.

'Does it matter?' Eddie asked. 'What does *that* do?'

'*That* does the steering. *That's* the steering wheel. Those are the foot pedals. Those are the weapons panels. That button there activates the, well, how shall I put this? Death ray, I suppose. It's as accurate as a time-clock at a Golden Chicken Diner. And they are really accurate, believe me.'

'Oh, I do,' said Eddie. 'All the controls look so simple.'

'Oh, they are. They really are. You can complicate things to death, but it's not necessary. The more advanced technology becomes, the more user-friendly it becomes. The more simple to use.'

'I'll bet I could have flown this,' said Eddie. Wistfully.

'I just bet you could have, too. But never mind.'

Eddie sank down heavily into the pilot's seat. 'I think I'd like to go to sleep now,' he said in a very drowsy, growly kind of a voice.

'Well, perhaps you should,' said the other Eddie.

'But I really would like to meet Her Majesty. Do you think I could have a glass of water, or something? Or better a glass of beer. My very last glass of beer. I'd like that very much.'

'Oh, I think that could be arranged.'

A chicken in a uniform clucked words into the other Eddie's ear.

'And at something of the hurry-up,' said the other Eddie. 'It's two minutes to take-off. Her Majesty is already on board and we must prepare for Operation Take Out Toy City.'

'Well done on the name,' said Eddie Bear.

'I'll just get you a glass of beer. You just sit and relax.'

And the other Eddie took his leave and Eddie sat and sighed.

And, 'Oh,' sighed Amelie also as Chief Inspector Wellington Bellis presented her with another short warm drink with plenty of alcohol in it.

*

And, 'Oh,' sighed Tinto, as he knew that Chief Inspector Wellington Bellis had no intention of paying for this or any other drink.

And, 'Oh-oh,' went laughing policemen as they knocked other things to the floor and laughed more as they broke.

And, 'Oh,' went the feisty female officer in Police Chief Sam Maggott's office as a blur of blood and guts enveloped her.

And, 'Oh,' went Eddie Bear as he sank lower and lower over the flying saucer's dashboard.

And oh it was to be hoped that there might have been some kind of something, some kind of solution to all this trouble and strife.

And then, 'Oh,' and, 'Holy Mother of God!' Sam Maggott drew his gun from his shoulder holster. And the feisty female officer and the troubled detective did their own particular forms of Oh-ing as a fierce metallic skull-type jobbie burst out through the top of the other Jack's head.

And another 'Oh' was heard, and this from the other Eddie. It was an 'Oh' of surprise, and one of alarm also. Because in the cockpit of the flying saucer, Eddie Bear had slammed his paw onto the ignition button and caused the engines to roar and the chicken crew to panic and flee.

And then all sorts of extraordinary things occurred.
    Which caused more Oh-ings all round.

24

'Oh no, no, no,' said the other Eddie, returning to the cabin with a beer. 'The last thing we need right now is for something extraordinary to occur – we are running to a tight schedule.' And he lifted Eddie's paw from the ignition button. And the powerful engines stuttered and died and all was at peace once more.

Much peace.

'You see,' said the other Eddie, and he grinned at Eddie Bear, 'it is this way and . . .' The other Eddie paused. Eddie Bear was slumped back in the pilot's seat. His button eyes were crossed and his mouth drooped oddly at the corners.

'Eddie?' went the other Eddie, shaking Eddie Bear. 'Eddie, wake up now. We can't have you dying on us just yet. We haven't kept you alive all this time, when we could simply have killed you, for no purpose. There are things we need to know from you. Eddie, wake up. Eddie?'

But Eddie Bear would not wake up.

Eddie Bear could not wake up.

His head rolled forward, his shoulders sank.

Eddie Bear was dead.

25

'That is most inconvenient.' The other Eddie called out to the chicken crew who had now returned to their duties tinkering with electronic doodads and ticking things off on clipboards. 'Toss him out of the hatchway, will you? No, on second thoughts, dump him in the hold. We'll deliver him home, toss him out when we make our first pass over Toy City.'

The chickens cackled with laughter, the way chickens will, and two of their number hauled the lifeless Eddie from the pilot's chair and carried him away to the hold.

'Right then,' said the other Eddie, seating himself in the pilot's chair and strapping himself in for good measure. Because you should never pilot a flying saucer without following all safety procedures, which include wearing your seat belt, putting your beer into the little holder on the arm of your chair, extinguishing your cigarette, of course, switching off your mobile phone and knowing where the exit doors are in case of a crash. Oh, and that business regarding the inflatable life jacket with the little whistle attachment, although no one ever really pays any attention to that because everyone knows full well that when whatever means of flying transportation you happen to be travelling in falls from the sky and hits either the ground or the sea, there really aren't going to be any survivors to inflate their life belts or blow their little whistles.

'Calling all craft,' said the other Eddie, slipping a pair of bear-style headphones over his ears. The ones with the little face-mic attachment. 'Calling all craft.'

Headphone speakers crackled, chicken voices cackled.

'Oh goody,' said the other, well, now the *remaining* Eddie. 'All present and correct, splendid. Well, ladies, you have all been briefed for this mission. It is of the utmost importance, in order to put overall plans for the domination of this world and our imminent expansion into the world of Toy City into action, that this mission goes without a hitch. I want this done by the numbers, ladies, smooth formation following my lead. Through The Second Big O of the Hollywood sign, full speed ahead to Toy City, then on with the evil soul-sucking death rays, hoover up the population. And then nuke Toy City.'

Rather surprised chicken cackles crackled through the remaining Eddie's headphones. There had been no previous briefings regarding any nukings.

'I know, ladies, I know. But let's face it – Toy City is something of a dump. The clean-sweep approach is probably for the best. Negotiating with the humans there will be such a long-winded process that I feel we should simply take the lot of them out in one fell swoop and have done with it. What say you?'

Chicken voices cackled in the affirmative.

'Splendid, splendid. My call sign will be Great Mother-Henship and this operation, as you know, is Operation Take Out Toy City. So, gangways up, hatchways sealed and then we'll run through the safety procedures. I want everyone to be certain that they know how to inflate their life jackets and use their little whistles. These things matter.'

Although it might appear to be a somewhat tenuous link, it did have to be said that certain *things* were at present really *mattering* to Samuel J. Maggott of the LAPD.

Staying alive in the face of a mad robot's onslaught being foremost amongst these.

Sam pumped bullets at the robot's head, but the thing was moving so swiftly about that he mostly missed and shot up the coffee machine.

'You've broken that for good this time,' said the engineer who had come to fix it. Ducking as he did so to avoid being struck by the troubled young detective as the robot Jack flung him through the glass of Sam's partition door.

Sam ducked down behind his desk as an officer flew over his head and left via a window, taking much of the faulty air-conditioning unit with him.

'Eat lead, you son of a bitch!' cried the feisty young female officer, bringing out her own special weapon, the one that was *not* police issue, and blasting away like a good'n.

The robot Jack, impervious even to such superior firepower due to the nature of his hyper-alloy combat chassis,[*] flung officers to every side, stormed straight through the partition door, causing much distress to the coffee-machine engineer, then stormed through the outer office and through the outer wall.

'After it!' bawled Sam to those who still remained conscious. 'Get that motherfu—'

But none seemed too keen to oblige.

Sam snatched up what was left of his telephone receiver and shouted words into it. 'Is my helicopter still on the roof?' he shouted. 'Right, then rev the son of a gun up,' he further shouted. 'And call every car, call everything – there's a robot on the loose.'

There was a moment's pause. As well there would be.

'Yeah, you heard me right!' shouted Sam. 'I said *robot*! *No*, I *didn't* say *Robert*. Yes, I *have* been taking my tablets. Get the . . . what? Oh, you can see it now, can you? It just burst out through the front of the building. Right. Then get everything you can get – we're going after it.'

'Generally speaking,' said Wellington Bellis to Amelie as he accepted two more free drinks from Tinto, a triple for Amelie, a diet swodge[†] for himself, 'on the surface, as it were, police work might seem mundane and everyday – petty theft, toys pulling bits off each other, that kind of thing. But once in a while something really big happens.

---

[*] It might well be asked why, if the other Jack was in fact an armoured robot, he didn't simply do away with the officers when they arrested him at Area 52. It might well be asked, but it's as sure as sure that it won't be answered. Surely he was ordered not to cause a commotion near the launch site, and at all until the launch time was up and he was sure that the operation was under way! It's possible, so let's stick with that.

[†] A soft drink popular amongst rubber toys.

And that is when I get personally involved. I'm a *special* policeman, you see. Supercriminals fear my name. Is that drink all right, my dear?'

Amelie hiccuped prettily. 'Do you have your own car and a *special* expense account?' she asked.

'Oh yes, I'm well taken care of. Don't be put off by all these perished bits, by the way. I've booked in for a makeover with the kindly, lovable white-haired old Toymaker.'

'I'll bet you're not perished *all* over,' purred Amelie.

'Excruciating,' said Tinto.

'Quiet, you,' ordered Bellis. 'I'm only postponing your arrest for crimes against toyanity until closing time because I am so enjoying my conversation with this fascinating young dolly here.'

'Fascinating?' purred Amelie. 'Jack never said that to me.' *And what of Jack*, Amelie wondered.

What of Jack, indeed.

The other Jack, or perhaps he should now be referred to as the *remaining* Jack, was making good progress through the streets of Los Angeles. He was doing all the things one might reasonably expect, in fact, unreasonably demand, of such a robot in such a situation. He was thrusting innocent passers-by aside, some, with inclinations to seek positions as Hollywood stuntmen, through plate-glass windows, and others of a frailer disposition into those piles of cardboard boxes that always seem to be there to conveniently cushion one's fall in such situations. Should such situations occur.

And then there was the lifting up and overturning of automobiles that got in his way. There's always a lot of mileage to be had from that kind of thing.

And then there was the kind of thing that we all really like. In fact, if it didn't come to pass, we'd all be bitterly disappointed.

And that is, of course, the climbing into the cab of a great big truck, flinging the driver out of the door, settling down behind the wheel and taking-and-driving-away.

Oh, and it needs to be a truck with a *significant* bit-on-the-end sort of jobbie, a great long canister on the 'bed' containing twenty tonnes of liquid oxygen, or highly volatile solvents, or toxic waste, or even nuclear nasties.

Or something.

Joe-Bob, the driver of the Sulphuric Acid Truck, made loud his protests as the robot Jack hurled him out through the windscreen and took the steering wheel.

Now in his helicopter, Police Chief Sam heard the call-in from the traffic cop who had witnessed the taking-and-driving-away. Witnessed it while parked on his bike beside a Golden Chicken Diner, munching upon a Golden Chicken burger family meal and admiring the little clockwork giveaway cymbal-playing monkey toy that he intended to take home for his daughter. There was something really special about that monkey.

'Westbound on Route Sixty-Six,' Sam told the pilot. 'I'll bet the S-O-B is heading back to Area Fifty-Two. After him.' And Sam thrust on headphones of his own with the little microphone attachment and shouted orders to all and sundry. Adding for good measure, 'And call up the Air Force, just to be sure.'

Call up the Air Force, just to be sure! Well, why not? You always have to call up the Air Force sooner or later. And there's always this troubled young pilot, who might well be black and want to be a space pilot, but keeps getting kicked back and is looking to prove himself and . . .

'Calling all craft,' went the remaining Eddie through his little fitted microphone. 'Follow my lead. Open outer launch doors.'

Up, up on the desert floor, great doors slid aside.

'And away we go!' And the remaining Eddie pawed the ignition, *brrmmed* the engines, put the saucer into gear and with a hum and a whiz and a whoosh and a swoosh, the saucer did its liftings off and dramatic sweepings away.

'Tally ho!' shouted the remaining Eddie. 'Onward, follow me.'

And up they went, those saucers all, off up the underground runway.

*

It was night-time now and the Californian sky was sprinkled over with stars. Were there worlds up there, one might wonder, with folk like us looking out at our sun and wondering, just wondering, were there folk like them down here? Well, perhaps, or then, perhaps not. Perhaps the Universe *is* nothing more than a great construction kit, given by God to his offspring and awaiting the day when his offspring will grow tired of it just sitting there and pack it up and put it back into its box.

Or is there really no Universe at all? Is it just an illusion, a dream, which, when the dreamer awakes, will cease to be?

Or perhaps the world *is* just an apple turning silently in space. Or a great big onion. Or a melting pot. Or perhaps, as has been mooted in many a public drinking house, some time after the ten-o'clock watershed, the real truth is that . . .

'Weeeeeee!' went the remaining Eddie as his lead craft shot up through the opening in the desert floor and into the star-speckled sky. 'Now *this is* a rush!'

And up came the other craft one by one, up into that sky.

'Full speed ahead,' cried the remaining Eddie. 'Make me proud of you, ladies.'

And aboard all the craft, the chicken crews did cluckings and cacklings and such.

'And such a night,' said Wellington Bellis, standing in the doorway of Tinto's and looking up at the dark and star-sprinkled sky. 'Hardly the night for an Apocalypse, I think you will agree, my dear.' And his perished rubber arm strayed about the waist of Amelie. And laughing policemen peering out from the bar counter nudged each other, did lewd winkings and made suggestive remarks.

'Now, I just want to make this clear,' said Tinto, 'in case any of you lot are thinking of truncheoning me senseless, I am *not* a super-criminal. I am a barman. And to prove this, I propose that I waive normal licensing hours on this occasion and continue to serve you fellows until all of you are too drunk to do any arresting at all. In fact, until you all agree that you are my bestest friends. What say you to this?'

The laughing policemen laughed some more and ordered further drinks.

'I don't suppose you have any drink in the glove compartment?' Police Chief Sam asked the helicopter pilot. 'Because, by God, I could use some.'

'Certainly not,' the pilot replied. 'That would be most unprofessional. We pilots *never* drink on the job. We do a bit of Charlie, of course, but who doesn't? Piloting a helicopter is a very stressful job, what with all those power lines you might crash into and everything. I always have a couple of lines before I go up.'

'Got any left?' Sam asked.

'In the glovey, help yourself.'

'Why, thank you . . . Oh my God, what is he doing *now*?'

He, the robot Jack, was doing what one would expect of him. He was bothering other road users. The great big truck with its highly dangerous cargo swerved from lane to lane on the highway, swiping cars to left and right.

'So,' said Sydney Greenstreet to Marilyn Monroe, whom he was driving home after the meal they'd just had together, 'my agent says that the producers are very pleased with my performance so far. They thought that the scene where we were taken hostage at the Golden Chicken Headquarters might well be the one that earns me an Academy Award for Best Supporting Actor.'

'Did he say anything about *me*?' asked Marilyn.

'He said you were okay.'

'Okay?'

'That's a compliment coming from him, dear. Oh, and they're changing the name of the movie now – did you hear that? They're calling it *The Toyminator*, whatever *that* means. And we're to do one last scene together. I have the revised script right here.'

Sydney handed Marilyn the revised script.

And she read it. ' "While driving home after a night out at the Golden Chicken Diner, where they enjoyed the Big Bird Munchie Special with extra fries on the side, the merits of which they are discussing whilst marveling at the special qualities of the giveaway clockwork pianist toy, they are run off the road by a speeding Sulphuric Acid Truck." '

'I said no to that bit,' said Sydney. 'That's work for a stunt double, I told my agent.'

Marilyn perused the script. 'There isn't any actual dialogue,' she said. 'It simply reads, "They scream." '

'I know – it's outrageous, isn't it?'

And then Sydney and Marilyn were run off the road by a speeding Sulphuric Acid Truck.

They screamed.

And out into the desert went that truck. And after it in hot pursuit came many a black-and-white. And overhead now came Sam Maggott's 'copter, all thrashing blades and bawling Sam.

And so on and suchlike.

And . . .

'Whoa!' went the helicopter pilot. 'Would you take a look at *that*?'

And Sam looked up and Sam looked out and Sam said, 'What *is* that?'

'*That* and *those*!' The pilot made a troubled face. 'They're coming towards us . . . They're flying saucers. Oh my God – and oh!'

And the fleet of saucers swept over the helicopter, spinning it all around. And on the desert highway below the robot Jack saw the saucers, slammed on the brakes of the big truck and swung *it* around.

'Going without me, eh?' he went. 'Well, that's not fair for a start.'

On-rushing police cars swerved and smote one another. The big truck ploughed through several of these, mashing them fiercely to this side and the other.

'Get back after him,' cried Sam. Hanging on for the dearest of life, as the helicopter clung to the air. 'Get after him and get after those flying saucers.'

'This really *is* a job for the Air Force now,' said the helicopter pilot.

'Although in all truth, I'm prepared to have a go at them myself. I've been applying to be a space pilot for years, but I keep getting kicked back. If I could take out a few flying saucers, I'll just bet that NASA will give me a chance.'

'You go for it,' said Sam. 'I've lost the plot good and proper now anyway. I didn't even notice you were black – I thought you were from Arkansas.'

'What *is* all this Arkansas business anyway?' asked the pilot as he steered the helicopter around in pursuit of the departing truck and similarly departing saucers. 'Some kind of lame running gag, do you think?'

'Like all that stuff that weirdo Jack told us about following the American Dream? Before he turned into a robot, of course.'

'Well, he did say he was from England. And as all we Americans know, the English have no sense of humour.'

'Well, I'm glad we've got all *that* out of the way,' said Sam. 'On with the chase, if you will, Mister Pilot.'

'Ten-four, Chief, ten-four.'

And on flew the flying saucers, low now over the outer suburbs of LA. The bits that tourists never see. Many gap-toothed fellows called Joe-Bob, who sat upon their verandas drinking from earthenware demijohns and smoking corncob pipes, viewed the saucers' passing. And many shook their dandruffed heads and said things to the effect that they were not in the least surprised, as they'd been abducted so many times, but could find none to believe them.

'Onward, onward!' cried the remaining Eddie. 'On through The Second Big O.'

And as there had been no apparent response from the Air Force, which was a shame because a really decent UFO/Air Force battle out-classes ground-based explosions, shoot-outs and car chases (no matter how extreme and prolonged) any old day of the week (with the obvious exclusion of Tuesdays), Sam's pilot said, 'Check this out!' and pressed certain buttons on his dashboard.

'What do you have there?' asked Sam.

'A special something,' said the pilot. 'Fitted it myself. State of the art. It's called an M134 General Electric Mini-gun. 7.62 mm. Full-clip capacity of 5,793 rounds per minute. 7.62 × 51 shells, 1.36 kg recoil adapters. Muzzle velocity of 869 m/s.'

'Nice,' said Sam. 'Then open fire on those alien sons of bitches.'

'Ten-four, Chief,' said the pilot, and he opened fire.

And down below and through the streets of Hollywood now roared that truck with the robot Jack at the wheel and all that dangerous acid on board. Along Hollywood Boulevard, past the Roosevelt Hotel, and Grauman's Chinese Theatre and the Hollywood Wax Museum.

And, 'Rat-at-tat-at-tat-at-tat-at-tat,' went the M134 General Electric Mini-gun. And Sam Maggott cheered as tracer bullets scoured the sky. And he bawled, 'You've hit one. You've hit one.'

And the pilot had.

A saucer wobbled, spiralled, span. The chicken pilot squawked.

And down and down the saucer went to strike the home of Sydney Greenstreet. Who was presently being loaded into an ambulance with many broken bones. Which really wasn't fair. But there you go.

'Well done,' cried Sam, patting the pilot. 'Oh no, one's turning around.'

And a single saucer was. The helicopter did nifty manoeuvrings. Hollywood residents looked up from their poolside soirées, rubbed at *their* rectal probings and said, 'I told you so.'

'Whoa!' went Sam, once more clinging on for the life of himself. 'Shoot that mother, will you?'

'Doing my best, Chief, doing my best.'

And down below the robot Jack drove onward in his stolen truck. Up now and towards the Hollywood hills in pursuit of the saucers. And police cars screamed after him, all flashing lights and wailing sirens. And cars swerved and passers-by took to their heels.

'Onward, ever onward,' cried the Eddie in the Mother-Henship, 'and engage the fiendishly clever miniaturisation units that will enable us to sweep through The Second Big O without touching the sides.' And his paw pressed the special button and in other craft wing tips did likewise.

'And did you see *that*?' shouted Sam. 'Did they just get smaller, or are they suddenly very far, far away?'

'Bit of both, I think, Chief.' The pilot rattled away with the M134 General Electric Mini-gun.

The robot Jack's truck bumped up the grasslands, but lost neither speed, nor size.

'Onward!' cried the remaining Eddie. 'Onward, ladies. Onward into the future pages of chicken world history. God of All Chickens, I love this job.'

And onward they swept towards the Hollywood sign.

And onwards too swept the robot Jack, his truck bouncing all about, but roaring ever onward.

And after him the black-and-whites, doing what black-and-whites always do in situations like these: crashing into one another, flying off cliffs in slow motion, having the occasional bit of comedy relief with blackened-faced officers staggering from wrecked police cars to the sound of incidental music going, 'Wah-waaaah.'

'They're going through, Chief,' cried the helicopter pilot. 'They're going through The Second Big O.'

'Then pull up. We'll get them on the other side.'

The pilot yanked back on the joystick. 'Oh my God!' he shouted. 'The controls are stuck. Oh my God! Oh my God!'

'Don't go without me, you rotters!' And the robot Jack put his foot down harder.

And then it all happened.

As it always does.

In slow motion, with some really great shots.

Picture it if you can.

The flying saucers moved from the horizontal into the vertical plane and swept one after another towards The Second Big O of the Hollywood sign.

The great big truck with its dangerous cargo did its own kind of sweeping up, which involved its wheels leaving the grasslands and the performance of a rather spectacular flying leap forward *into* the Hollywood sign.

To be joined there, at that very moment, by Sam Maggott's helicopter, big guns blazing and controls all gone to pot.

And then that explosion.

With the flatbed canister-load of sulphuric acid crumpling forwards, releasing its lethal load, swallowing up the robot Jack.

That *big* explosion. As of truck and sign and helicopter. And of a few surviving police cars, too.

And of the lone Air Force jet, which hadn't actually been scrambled but had been taken aloft by a young black pilot who was hoping for a job in the space programme with NASA.

And, by golly, at least a good half-dozen flying saucers that hadn't quite done the sweeping through The Second Big O thing.

And what a big explosion *that* was!

And all in slow motion, too.

And cut, and print, and that's a wrap.

Hooray for Hollywood.

26

'What was all *that*?' The Eddie at the controls of the Great Mother-Henship, which had now swelled back to its regular size, glanced into the rear-view mirror and called out in alarm. 'What happened back there? Speak to me, ladies.'

Chicken voices clucked into his headphones.

'How many ships lost? Six? No, seven! That's outrageous, impossible.'

Further chicken voices confirmed the sad news.

'Oh well, never mind,' said the remaining Eddie. 'There will never be a shortage of chickens. And they died nobly in a glorious cause. Their names will be forever remembered. Whatever they were. Does anyone remember?'

Further voices clucked.

'What, no one? Well, never mind. Onward, ladies, on to victory. You'll have to double up in all the soul-sucking-jar jobbies.Beam down those rays, suck up those souls and then we'll nuke the place.'

Chicken voices cackled in a merry kind of a way.

'And then you'll nuke the place?' asked a certain voice, which did not come through the headphones.

The remaining Eddie swung around in his chair. '*You?*' he went. 'How's this?'

'How's this?' said Eddie Bear. 'It's me, that's how it is.'

'But you're dead.' The other Eddie pawed the autopilot. 'You're as dead as a donkey dodo.'

'The rumours of my death have been greatly exaggerated,' said Eddie, padding his way to the centre of the cockpit.[*] 'As you can see, I am in remarkably fine fettle. And not too dead at all.'

[*] Or *hen*pit, possibly. Or possibly not.

'No!' And the other Eddie threw up his paws. 'This cannot be, it cannot.'

'Well, it can be and it is,' said Eddie, squaring up before his other self. 'And personally I think I deserve an award for my acting. I certainly had *you* fooled. And do you know what? Now that I'm back on my side of the barrier, back in my own world again, I feel fine. I'm as healthy as, and it's time to set matters straight.'

'Time for you to die properly,' said Eddie's other self.

'I think not,' said Eddie, making the fiercest of faces. 'Now land this craft or know my wrath – I'll bite your blinking head off.'

'Land this craft?' The other Eddie laughed.

'I really hate it when you laugh like that,' said Eddie Bear.

'Well, it is of no consequence to me. Guards, take this resurrected bear and throw him out of a porthole, or something.'

'Guards?' said Eddie. 'What guards?'

'The guards that I summonsed by pressing the special "guards" button next to the "autopilot" button. I pressed them both simultaneously, as it were, when you made your appearance.'

'You fiend,' said Eddie Bear.

'Yes, I can really be a stinker at times.' And the other Eddie laughed once again. And as he did so, chicken guards dressed in figure-hugging golden uniforms (which displayed their breasts to perfection), sleek golden helmets with beak-guards, high-heeled boots and the inevitable heavy weaponry jogged into the cockpit and surrounded Eddie.

'Ah,' said Eddie. '*These* guards.'

'Out of a porthole with him,' said the other Eddie. 'And if his fat belly gets stuck, shoot him up the bottom, that will do the trick.'

'I don't think that's a nice idea,' said another voice.

The guards and the other Eddie glanced towards the source of *this* voice. And Eddie Bear did glancings, too. And Eddie Bear said, 'Jack!'

'Nice to see you again, Eddie.' Jack brandished a large gun of his own. He aimed this at the other Eddie. 'Let Eddie go,' said he.

'Jack?' said the other Eddie. 'Now I'm damned sure that I killed you. You plunged to your death in the elevator.'

'Not quite so.' Jack brandished the large gun some more. Because in such situations as this you can never do too much brandishing of a big gun. He had acquired this particular big gun from a chicken guard at the launch site, whom Jack had taken by surprise and overcome through the employment of a handy spanner.

'I like the uniform,' said Eddie. 'Very dapper, it really suits you. Although it smells a bit.' And Eddie smiled as he said this, for his sense of smell had returned.

'Why, thank you,' said Jack. 'And you've had a wash and brush-up, I see.'

'I'd rather not think about *that*,' said Eddie.

'Now just stop this nonsense,' said the other Eddie Bear. 'You really should be dead!'

'I certainly would have been,' said Jack, 'if it hadn't been for Dorothy here.'

'Hi, Eddie,' called Dorothy.

'Hi, Dorothy,' called Eddie.

Chicken guards swung their weapons about, some aimed at Dorothy, some at Jack and some at Eddie Bear.

'Dorothy is not what she at first appears,' said Jack. 'Which I am a little sad about, but we won't go into that here. But she saved my life, pushed me out of the roof hatch in the lift, helped me cling to a dangling cable, that sort of thing. It was all very exciting.'

'Sounds so,' said Eddie. 'It's a shame I missed it. I spent the time being booted about by your doppelgänger.'

'I know,' said Jack. 'I felt your pain. I could feel what you were thinking.'

'And I could feel you too, Jack,' said Eddie. 'Something to do with my condition on the other side of The Second Big O.'

'Yes, yes, yes,' said the other Eddie, 'all *very* interesting, I'm sure. But how did you get aboard this craft?'

'We sneaked on while Eddie kept you talking,' said Jack. 'And now you must ask the guards to drop their guns or I will take great pleasure in shooting you dead.'

'Shoot *me* dead?' The other Eddie laughed some more.

'Oh, just shoot him, Jack,' said Eddie. 'I'm sick of all his laughing.'

'Tell the guards to drop their weapons and land the craft now,' said

Jack. 'Oh and order all the other ships to turn back, tell them that the mission is aborted.'

'You have no idea what you're dealing with,' said the other Eddie. 'I will *not* land the craft, *I* will *not* abort the mission. In fact.' And he swung about in his chair and disengaged the autopilot. And also swung the steering wheel, which caused the craft to swing.

And chicken guards went tumbling and so did Eddie and Jack.

And Dorothy went tumbling, too.

The other Eddie didn't tumble; he was strapped into his chair.

But he put the craft through a triple roll and the tumblers whirled all about.

'Kill them all!' shouted the other Eddie. 'Fly, you foolish guards. Fly and shoot them, toss them off the ship.'

And squawking guards went fluttering.

And unpleasantness occurred.

'Such a pleasant night,' said Wellington Bellis, his perished arm now tight about Amelie's waist. 'Such a night for romance.'

'Calling all cars. Calling all cars,' the radio crackled in Bellis's parked police car.

'Calling all cars?' said Wellington Bellis. 'Now what might this be, I wonder?' And he detached himself from Amelie and shuffled over to the car, reached in through the open window and took up the toy microphone that was attached by a length of string to the dashboard. 'What is all this commotion?' he said into it.

'Sir, sir – is that you, sir?'

'It's me, yes. Is that *you*, Officer Chuckles?'

'*Special* Officer Chuckles, yes sir. Calling all cars, I am.'

'And why are you calling all cars?'

'Because we are under attack, sir, from spaceships. They just blew up the remains of the old Toytownland sign. Half a dozen spaceships, sir, flying towards the city.'

'Have you been drinking, officer?'

'Of course I've been drinking, sir.'

'And where are you calling from?'

'From Tinto's Bar, sir – I'm looking out of the back windows. The saucers are coming. We're all gonna die. I'm converting to Mechanology. Out.'

'Out?' asked Bellis.

'Out,' said the voice of Tinto. 'This is my telephone and it's for use-of-barman only. Aaagh! Stop hitting me!'

'Flying saucers?' said Bellis.

And suddenly there they were.

Large as life in the Toy City sky. Great big saucers with blinking lights. The lead craft doing a sort of victory roll, the others flying steadily.

Bellis reached into his car and pressed buttons on his dashboard. 'Action stations. Fire at will. Operation Save Our City is *go!*' And then he replaced the microphone and smiled towards Amelie. 'Have no fear, my dear,' said Bellis. 'Everything is under control.'

'The End Times are upon us,' gasped Amelie. Huskily. Sexily.

'Not a bit of it,' said Bellis, re-establishing himself at her side and offering her a comforting hug. 'All will be attended to. I received a tip-off this morning from a clockwork spaceman. He told me an extraordinary tale, which I did not at first believe . . . Oh, duck, if you will.'

And Amelie ducked as a bolt of light swept down from above and carbonised Bellis's car.

'As I was saying,' said Bellis, 'an extraordinary tale. But I felt it prudent to take it at face value. So I put the Toy City Army on red alert. They'll soon shoot those aliens out of the sky.'

'My hero,' said Amelie.

And the words of Bellis were no idle words. Well, he hadn't risen to his present position of power through not being able to rise to the occasion. In fact, he intended to rise to the occasion with Amelie, quite shortly, when all the mayhem was over and done with.

'Excruciating,' said Tinto once more.

But then *he* had cause to duck.

A blinding light bore down into the bar.

Swept along the counter.

Crispy-crunchy husks of policemen toppled to the floor.

'Oi!' cried Tinto, rising from his duck and shaking a dextrous fist towards the ceiling. 'There was a slight chance that they *might* have paid for their drinks.'

The saucers now criss-crossed the sky, beaming down their rays. And to the great surprise of the chicken pilots and death-ray crews, fire was now being returned at them from below.

'Go to it, lads,' cried the Grand Old Duke of York, who may not have *actually* had ten thousand men, but had been given command of a legion of clockwork tanks.

Tank barrels spat their shells towards the sky.

And as this *was* Toy City, those toy shells carried force.

'I'm hit,' squawked a pilot, but in chicken tongue.

The other Eddie levelled his craft. 'Kill them all!' was the order he gave. 'Prepare the nukes and kill them all.'

Eddie and Jack and Dorothy rolled about on the floor. Chickens fluttered above them, but they still held onto their guns.

Somehow!

'And please shoot this troublesome trio,' ordered the other Eddie. 'And get it over and done with.'

And guns trained down on the troublesome trio.

And one of these leapt up.

She leapt up with a great degree of style, so stylish it could almost be called balletic.

And, as with all the best bits so far, it happened in good old-fashioned slow-mo – which, although it could be argued that there has been rather too much of it lately, it is exactly the way that this bit *should* and *did* happen.

Dorothy cartwheeled into the air and spun around, her left foot describing a wonderful circle, striking beak after beak-guarded beak, striking chickens from the air.

Eddie, in slow-mo, also leapt, towards his other self. He caught him a decent enough blow to the ear with the special tag and knocked him from his seat and seat belt. The two bears bowled across the cockpit. Things now became a bit tricky.

From beneath came vigorous gunfire. Toy cannons added to the tanks' assault. Toys of all varieties issued into the streets, many, in the more disreputable parts of town, toting illegal weaponry that they too discharged skywards.

A stricken saucer plummeted down and struck Toy City Town Hall.

Gunfire ripped into the undercarriage of the Great Mother-Henship.

The Great Mother-Henship, now pilotless, slewed hideously to port.

The Eddies bowled over and over, punching and biting and suchlike.

Dorothy dropped down nimbly into the pilot's seat.

'Do you know how to fly this?' asked Jack, swaying about in an alarming fashion.

'Now would be the time to learn.' And Dorothy yanked back the steering wheel.

The craft shot upwards, narrowly missing another craft that was rapidly on the descent.

This one struck police headquarters. Mercifully empty. Although Chief Inspector Bellis's entire collection of dolly porn went to ashes.

'Whoa!' went Jack, a-steadying himself.

The Eddies did further tumbling.

Separated.

Fell in different directions.

Dorothy took control of the craft, levelled it out and put it into a circular holding pattern.

Jack snatched up his weapon as the two Eddies prepared to engage in further battle.

Explosions burst all around the circling saucer.

Remaining saucers poured down fire.

Greater fire was returned.

'Stop it, you two,' Jack told the squaring-up Eddies. 'It's all over now – will you stop.'

The Eddies glared at one another. 'Shoot him, Jack,' said one.

'Don't shoot *me*,' said the other one. 'I'm the real Eddie. Shoot *that* one.'

Jack's big gun swung from side to side.

'I'm not shooting anyone,' said Jack. 'Land the craft, please, Dorothy.'

'That might be a problem,' said Dorothy. 'The controls appear to be jammed.'

'Let me have a go at them,' said an Eddie.

'No, let me.' And an Eddie snatched up a fallen big gun.

The other Eddie rapidly did likewise. 'Drop that gun,' he said. 'Drop your gun or I'll shoot you dead.'

'Shoot him, Jack,' said an Eddie.

'No, shoot *him*, before he kills us all.'

Jack's gun moved backwards and forwards and back.

Explosions rocked the craft.

Dorothy struggled at the controls. Said, 'I think we're going down.'

Eddies cocked their big guns both.

'Jack, shoot him,' said one. 'I'm your bestest friend. You know it's me. Shoot him, Jack.'

Guns were turning in all directions now. Upon both Eddies. Upon Jack. Even upon Dorothy.

Jack dithered, rightfully.

One Eddie said, 'Jack, after everything we've been through together, you must know *me*. I'm your bestest friend. The bestest friend you've ever had.'

'Jack, don't let this monster fool you. If you shoot me, he will shoot you, then both of us will be dead.'

'It's a dilemma,' said Jack. And he flinched as another explosion rocked the ailing ship.

'It's not a dilemma,' an Eddie said. 'Go with your feelings, Jack. Do the right thing. You've always done the right thing, really. You can do the right thing now – it's as simple as blinking.'

And there was another explosion.

And Jack's big gun went off.

And Eddie looked down at another Eddie. This one with a hole in his belly. It was a *big* hole. A lethal hole. Smoke rose from this hole. Which went right through to the other side.

'You did it, Jack,' said the vertical Eddie. Turning his gun upon Jack. 'Good boy.'

And . . .

Eddie dropped his gun. 'How did you know for sure?' he asked.

'Because I know *you*,' said Jack. 'He said, "As simple as blinking." You'd say, "As simple as."'

'Well, that *was* simple,' said Eddie. 'Well done.'

'Well done, nothing.' The perforated Eddie struggled to its feet and stood swaying on the swaying floor. 'It's not as simple as *that*,' said this Eddie. 'I don't die *that* easily.' And this Eddie put its paw to its head. And lifted it. Raised it from its shoulders, cast it aside.

Where it bounce-bounce-bounced across the cockpit floor.

And Jack looked on.

And Eddie looked on.

As the head of a chicken rose through the neck hole of the decerebrated bear. 'I cannot be killed so easily,' said this head, 'for I am Henrietta, Queen of all the hens.'

'Henrietta?' said Jack. 'Well, you're a dead duck now.'

And he squeezed the trigger.

But nothing came from the barrel.

'Sorry,' said Queen Henrietta, and wing tips sprouted through the Eddie paws, and these scooped up a fallen gun and levelled it at Jack. 'You have no idea what you've done,' said the Queen of all the chickens. 'Were I to die, all my policies would be reversed by my successor. That cannot be allowed to happen. This craft must return to Area Fifty-Two. We will return here tomorrow and destroy every inch of Toy City. But for now, you and this abominable bear must die. Right now.'

And the Queen of all the chickens squeezed the trigger.

And then gave a sudden shriek and fell in a jumbled heap.

'Dorothy,' said Jack. 'You—'

'Wrung its scrawny neck,' said Dorothy. 'Well, you'd have done the same for me. Wouldn't you?'

Jack was about to say, 'Yes.'

But he didn't.

Jack instead said, '*No!*'

Because fire from below rattled into the craft.

And the craft turned upside down.

And then the Great Mother-Henship, the sole surviving member of the chicken strikeforce, dropped from the sky.

And, 'No!' shouted Tinto. As it was coming his way.

And then there was another of those terrible explosions.

But no, not in slow motion.

Enough is enough is enough.

27

Chief Inspector Bellis looked all around and about himself.

A very great deal of Toy City appeared to be ablaze.

The bells of fire engines came to his ears.

The wreckage of his car once more to his eyes.

And the wreckage of the spaceship beyond.

'Well,' said Bellis, 'that would appear to be *that*. Job jobbed, but goodness, I dread the paperwork.'

Amelie looked through her fingers. 'Did we win?' she asked.

'Naturally, my dear. Most naturally.'

Amelie shook her beautiful head, beautiful, but drunk. 'I am *so* impressed,' she said. 'You saved Toy City. You are *so* a hero.'

'He wouldn't have done so if *I* hadn't tipped him off,' said a clockwork spaceman.

'Then *you* are *so* a hero.' And Amelie threw her arms around him.

'Oi!' said Bellis. 'Not so fast. He would never have tipped me off if he hadn't . . . How did you put it, spaceman?'

'Received a telepathic message,' said the spaceman. 'From the other side of The Second Big O. A bear spoke unto me. Told me what was to occur. Said he kept going in and out of his body, whatever *that* meant.'

'Well, let's not worry about *that*,' said Bellis. 'And get your spaceman's hands off my girlfriend.'

'Do you think there are any survivors?' asked Amelie, stroking the spaceman's tin-plate chest. 'And do spacemen have credit cards, by the way?'

'Big shiny gold ones,' said the spaceman.

'Survivors?' said Bellis, prising the hands of Amelie away from the spaceman's helmet. 'Aliens in need of shooting, now there's a thought.' And reached towards his car, then reached away, for it smouldered.

'Shoot 'em with *this*,' said Tinto, wheeling through the doorway and presenting Bellis with a shotgun that he, as indeed do *all* barmen, kept hidden beneath his bar counter.

Just in case.

Bellis took the shotgun and approached the craft.

It was pretty buckled up and smoking.

Some laughing policemen who had escaped annihilation through being in the toilet when the mayhem occurred backed up Bellis at a distance.

The fallen craft had flattened several shops. It lay half upon its side.

And as Bellis approached, and so too the policemen, the hatchway slowly opened.

'Hands up, you aliens,' cried the chief inspector.

And struggling down from the hatchway came a tattered trio.

Jack was helping Eddie Bear. And Dorothy helped Jack.

28

And Tinto served drinks on the house.

Jack toasted Eddie.

And Eddie, Jack.

And Bellis toasted himself.

'You did brilliantly, Jack,' said Eddie Bear, balancing upon his head on the barstool in order that he might really benefit from the beer. 'You are as brilliant as.'

'We both did okay,' said Jack. 'We're a team, you and me. We're the business.'

'And we should be back in business now.' Eddie struggled to pour further beer down his inverted throat. Jack gave him a little helping out. 'We can open for business big time now.'

'You think we've seen the last of the chickens?'

'I reckon so. The portal between the worlds is destroyed.' Eddie hiccuped. 'And from what we both know about the chicken matriarchy, the new Queen will reverse the policies of the old. Pretty daft system, I grant you, but they *are* chickens. And so I suppose that means that not only is our world saved, but the world of men also.'

'I didn't take much to *that* world,' said Jack, draining his glass and ordering several more. 'Things are problematic here, but out *there* . . . That place is mad.'

'I thought it held some appeal for you.' Eddie tried to remain on his head and did so with some style. 'What with that Dorothy. Where is she, by the way?'

'She's gone,' said Jack. 'She left.'

'Left?' said Eddie. 'Left for where and why?'

'She returned to the soil,' said Jack. 'I dug her in.'

'You did *what*?' And Eddie fell from the barstool.

Jack helped Eddie to his feet. 'She wasn't human,' he said. 'She was something else entirely. The last of her kind. She was, well, *is* a vegetable.'

'And you're kidding me, right?'

'No,' said Jack. 'I'm not. The chickens conquered her world a couple of years back. She escaped through another Big O, this one in a big sign that spelt out "SPROUTLAND". She escaped to Hollywood. She was waiting there for someone like me – well, someones like us, as it happens – to help her take her revenge against the chickens for wiping out her kind.'

'And you "dug her in"?'

'Into Tinto's garden. She'll take root. She'll bloom here. She's, er, been fertilised.'

'Excruciating,' said Tinto.

'That almost makes me want to cry,' said Eddie. 'But I'll fight the sensation and drink more beer instead.'

'I *really* liked her, you know,' said Jack, making a wistful face.

'A bit more than *liked*, I suspect,' said Eddie, climbing back onto his stool.

'Nothing of the sort,' said Jack. 'I'm as hard as nails, me. Women are just women.'

'Leave it out, Jack, you're as romantic as.'

'Yeah,' said Jack. 'I suppose I am. Now where is Amelie?'

'She went to the toilet,' said Eddie. 'To throw up, I suspect. Ah, here she comes now, wobbling somewhat. And, oh look, there's the Phantom of the Opera.'

Eddie waved towards the Phantom and the Phantom waved back.

And there indeed came Amelie. And she *was* wobbling somewhat. And she swayed up to Jack and gazed into his eyes.

And then she flung her arms about him.

And gave that Jack a snog.

And Jack for his part snogged her in return.

And Jack, as he would soon find out, was really, truly in love.

'And so all's well that ends well,' said Eddie, resuming his inverted position on the barstool and enjoying the sensation of all that alcohol draining back into his head.

'All's well indeed,' said Wellington Bellis, looking with distaste towards the snogging Jack and then with even greater distaste towards Eddie. 'And now I feel it is time to bring matters to a satisfactory conclusion. And make my arrest.'

'Your arrest?' asked Eddie.

'Bring the malcontent to justice,' said Bellis. 'To whit, arrest *you*, Eddie Bear, cat's-paw of the evil criminal mastermind, Tinto—'

'What?' went Tinto.

'Eddie Bear, mass-murderer, and clearly commander of the alien strikeforce, I arrest you in the name of the law. You do not have to say anything, but anything you do say will be twisted around and used against you as damning evidence. In order to condemn you to prison, or worse; and I can think up far worse.'

Eddie Bear said, 'Hold on there.'

And Bellis said, 'You're nicked.'

'No, hold on,' said Eddie, tumbling from his stool. 'It's not the way you think – I'm the good guy. I sent this telepathic message to the spaceman to warn you what was going to happen. You see, there were these chickens. You don't understand . . .'

Wellington Bellis laughed and laughed. 'Had you going there,' he said to Eddie. 'You're not really nicked, I was only joking.'

Eddie Bear looked up and huffed and puffed.

'Do you know what?' said Bellis. 'I feel you deserve some special reward for your services to Toy City. In fact I feel that you deserve some special position, or rank. I have the necessary clout to pull a few strings around here. How would you fancy taking on the job of mayor?'

'Well . . .' said Eddie Bear.

THE ORDER

OF THE

GOLDEN SPROUT

THE NEW OFFICIAL ROBERT RANKIN
FAN CLUB

12 Months Membership consists of . . .

Four Fantastic Full Colour Issues of the Club Magazine featuring:

Previously unpublished work by Robert Rankin
News
Reviews
Event details
Articles
And much more.

Club Events @ free or discounted rates

Access to members only website area

Membership is £16 worldwide and available through the club website:

www.thegoldensprout.com

The Order of The Golden Sprout exists thanks to the permission
and support of Robert Rankin and his publishers.